The Airshipmen Trilogy

Volume One

FROM ASHES

Praise for the Airshipmen Trilogy

The Airshipmen Trilogy is also available as one volume as *The Airshipmen*. The trilogy version carries a series of photographs for each segment of the epic saga.

*

A riveting story that plays out against the background of one of the most intriguing chapters in aviation history. David Dennington weaves a fascinating web of romance, courage, tragedy and shattered dreams and gives the reader a front row seat to eye-opening, high-stakes political battles on two continents. A real page turner with the constant feeling that something new and unexpected is about to unfold. ***David Wright, Daily Mirror Journalist.***

*

A very big novel in every way, unique, beautifully written and perfectly paced ... setting the scene so well ... the first of a true new genre ... weaving us around the events of the great *Airship R101* tragedy, the people and places we know well ... with wonderfully rich characters ... researched in immaculate detail. ***Alastair Lawson, Chairman, Airship Heritage Trust, Cardington.***

*

The whole future of the airship program in Great Britain rests on the famous flight of Cardington R101. Will politics play too large a role? Will Charlotte be able to handle the very real stress of being married to an airshipman? Will her psychopath stalker, Jessup, triumph? Will Princess Marthe say yes to Lord Thomson's proposal of marriage? Dennington deftly handles a blend of fascinating real people with the characters he has created. This story is written on an epic scale and a fine tribute to those who risked everything. *Jeffrey Keeten, Goodreads Top Reviewer.*

*

Hats off! A gripping story masterfully told, the book reverberates in the reader's mind long after it is over. ***Steven Bauer, Hollow Tree Press.***

*

This is a big story, layered and cinematic—one that I did not want to end. It's about a wonderful group of people that I came to love—full of secrets and surprises. I could not put this book down. ***Edith Schorah, Editor.***

*

An impressively crafted multilayered novel, ***The Airshipmen*** is a fully absorbing read from beginning to end and clearly showcases author David Dennington as a gifted storyteller of the first order. ***Midwest Book Review***

*

The Airshipmen is a very human story ... historical fiction based primarily in Britain in the 1920s and follows the sweeping passions and adventures of the airship industry... with beautifully flawed characters. ... an incredibly interesting fictionalized take on an important and experimental time in air travel history ... recommended for fans of history, air travel, and historical fiction with just a touch of fantasy. ***Portland Book Review***

*

An epic read ... a sure feast for those interested in ... pre-World War II aviation history. *Historical Novel Society.*

*

The Airshipmen is a love story wrapped around politics of the day, woven into a tale that reveals the rise and fall of the great airships of the 20th century. A truly gripping story. *Kathryn Johnson, Author of The Gentleman Poet.*

*

A marvelous book. I read it through in just a few days and was fascinated, moved and informed. *Peter Humphris, Goodreads Reviewer.*

*

I am a fan of author Nevil Shute and therefore knew of the R100/R101 adventure since Shute was deeply involved with ship constructed by Vickers. Fascinating subject matter, and well written. Perhaps the closest a person will ever get to the whole story. *James Reising, Goodreads Reviewer.*

*

I am sure you have been reading a book which you did not want to end: this was such a book for me. *Clifford Archer, Goodreads Reviewer.*

*

I loved this book. It was a very interesting era in Britain and of course, airships are fascinating. If found myself looking up events and characters on Google all the time. *Ruth Lee, Amazon Reviewer.*

*

A good book is when you must read it whenever you have a spare moment ... and you feel being in a vacuum having finished it. So was this book to me. Thanks for great research and fine writing. *Claus, Amazon Reviewer.*

*

Very interesting historical novel that weaves fiction and fact into an amazing story of love, ambition and politics. I found myself checking historical events as I read. The characters are full of life and through the tales told of them, you feel that you are experiencing and living in their period of history. I would love to see this story reach the 'big screen'. *Bob, Amazon Reviewer.*

*

An amazing debut novel! I got so involved with the plot and the intrigues surrounding the characters—never boring for a second. Plots were continually changing and the unexpected happening. It was a wonderful love story ... how you thought it was headed ... and then the final twist. I was sorry it ended, but it left me in a good place. *Cheryl R, Goodreads Reviewer.*

*

This epic is bursting with devastating, colourful images, great humour, lush storylines, tender love stories, exciting plot twists and a plethora of factual historical information. It is both fiction and non-fiction – 'faction' perhaps! *Lauren Dennington, Editor of The Airshipmen.*

*

An American wedding on St. John's Street, Howden, 1921.

THE AIRSHIPMEN TRILOGY

VOLUME ONE

FROM ASHES

BASED ON A TRUE STORY

LOVE, BETRAYAL & POLITICAL INTRIGUE.

DAVID DENNINGTON

THE FULL CAST OF CHARACTERS FOR THE TRILOGY
MAY BE FOUND AT THE BACK OF THE BOOK.

This is a work of fiction with both real, historical figures and fictional characters based on actual events surrounding the British Airship Program between 1920 and 1931. Some events, dates and locations have been changed for dramatic purposes and great artistic license has been taken throughout.

While *The Airshipmen Trilogy—Volume One—From Ashes* is based on real events, characters, characterizations, incidents, locations, and dialogue have been invented and fictionalized in order to dramatize the story and are products of the author's imagination. The fictionalization, or invention of events, or relocation of events is for dramatic purposes and not intended to reflect on actual historical characters, history, entities or organizations, past or present. This novel is not intended to right any wrongs or 'set the record straight' regarding past events or actions, but is intended to entertain. Readers are encouraged to research the vast array of books on this subject from which the author has drawn facts as well as the essence of events and characters. In all other respects, resemblance to persons living or dead must be construed as coincidental.

Printed by Amazon.

Available from Amazon.com and other retail outlets.

Also available on Kindle and other retail outlets through Amazon.

DESCRIPTION: This special edition of *The Airshipmen* is now published as a trilogy, (originally published as one volume).

TRILOGY IDENTIFIER: Paperback.

THE AIRSHIPMEN TRILOGY VOLUME ONE
FROM ASHES ISBN - 9798585384813

BY DAVID DENNINGTON

THE AIRSHIPMEN
(Now also available as a three-part series)

The Airshipmen Trilogy   Volume One   *From Ashes*
The Airshipmen Trilogy   Volume Two   *Lords of the Air*
The Airshipmen Trilogy   Volume Three   *To Ashes*

THE GHOST OF CAPTAIN HINCHLIFFE
Based on a true story

Airship R38/ZR-2 leaving her shed, June/August 1921.

Special thanks to Lauren, my daughter and consulting editor, without whose help and collaboration these books could not have been written.

For my mother and father.

TABLE OF CONTENTS

VOLUME 1

PART FIVE—CARDINGTON

BACK OF THE BOOK MATERIAL

"The brave pioneers who lost their lives shall not have died in vain. These mighty airships shall rise from ashes like the phoenix—bigger and stronger and safer—capable of flying enormous distances in any kind of weather. Airships are the wave of the future and they'll forge air routes around the world, binding our empire and improving the lives of millions. Mark my words, sir. Mark my words!"

Lord Thomson, House of Lords, July 4, 1929.

PROLOGUE

Arras, France. March 1918.

Midnight. The relentless German barrage continues ever closer, shaking the ground under her feet. She pulls back the tent flap and steps into hell. The dreary, foul-smelling casualty clearing station is packed with moaning soldiers. She lights her lamp and holds it out before her, illuminating her breath in the gloom; off duty after countless hours, back to give a sliver of comfort, to wipe a brow, offer water, loosen a dressing.

To one side, a priest administers last rites to a soldier, his leg, his arm, his life gone. She looks at the priest accusingly.

Where is your precious God? What use are your prayers in this miserable place where the devil roams free?

The priest continues his mumbling. "Yea, though I walk through the valley of the shadow of death, I fear no evil: for thou art with me; thy rod and thy staff they comfort me."

Stretcher bearers stand ready. The cot is needed. Dozens more are being brought in from no man's land by the hour. At the end of the tent, fifty yards off, a civilian wearing a black overcoat enters, hat in hand. He is accompanied by two officers in dress khakis. The young nurse frowns.

Another damned politician playing to the press, come to tell them this disgraceful crime is justified.

The man stops for a moment to witness a surgeon at work removing the remains of a young boy's leg. That area is well-lit and attended by orderlies and nurses holding the boy down. He cries out, but it's no use. The surgeon does not dally, proceeding with ruthless precision.

The civilian stands his ground a few more seconds, he can't just turn away. When he does, she sees his shoulders slump, the burden too heavy. As he passes, he glances at her with piercing blue eyes. In them, she sees tears of bewilderment and sorrow. He'd obviously meant to stop and offer words of encouragement to others. Instead, he moves wearily on and out through the entrance through which she had come. She glances at his back, now with respect. His escorts trail behind. They hear him retching outside in the darkness.

"Our future Prime Minister," one of them, a major, says.

"Preposterous!" his companion scoffs.

The nurse moves to sit beside a young soldier barely older than she, her look grave. The boy shakes uncontrollably, tears flowing from wild eyes. She unravels his dressings, caked in dried blood, and sighs.

If they don't get here soon, then God help us!

1918: American Troops enter the War.
Etching by Kerr Eby, Canadian military illustrator.

PART ONE

Maiden flight of *R38/ZR-2*, Cardington, June 23, 1921.

1

DEATH ON THE HUMBER

Wednesday August 24, 1921.

T he lighthouse keeper at Flamborough Head checked the time as
he peered at the airship cruising overhead. It was 4:40 p.m.
Aside from him, no one noticed except three carrion crows
intent on the carcass of a rabbit. They paused in their evisceration,
following the airship with blank eyes, as if it were a larger bird of prey
and then, after much scolding, returned to their meal, black beaks
tearing at the dead creature's flesh. The air was humid—a late summer
afternoon storm pending. Their instincts knew the day would end in
rain, and wind, and worse.

His Majesty's Airship *R38* swept across the Yorkshire sky at
twenty-five hundred feet. After this last training flight the ship would
become the property of the U.S. Navy. In the control car, crowded with
silent British and American officers and coxswains, Lou Remington,
newly promoted chief petty officer and former marine, anxiously
rechecked his watch. He glanced down at the lighthouse on the
headland surrounded by the North Sea, the salty air and cries of gulls,
drifting in an open window. They cruised smoothly at fifty-five knots
on six Cossack engines. The British commodore turned to Lou.

"Chief Coxswain, find out what Bateman's got to say about the
rudders and elevators. We need to start this last test if we're to land
before dark. Report back to me after the next watch change would you,
there's a good chap."

"Aye, aye, sir. I'll go and talk to him," Lou answered.Lou left the
control car and headed along the catwalk toward the crewmens' mess.
He needed to check on 'New York' Johnny before visiting Bateman
who'd been monitoring the control gear all afternoon in the stern
cockpit. These final tests could soon be over, perhaps within the hour,
depending on Bateman's report.

Maybe we can head home soon—God willing!

Lanky Josh Stone, a blond, Californian rigger, smiled pleasantly as Lou passed him on the catwalk. "Ready for some o' them good ol' American hamburgers, sir?"

"You betcha! And a cold one," Lou answered.

"I wish!"

Along the catwalks shouts and jeers in British and American accents echoed from all directions as riggers and engineers mustered for the watch change.

"I'll be glad to get away from you bloody Brits!"

"And your rotten, soggy fish and chips!"

"And yer lousy, warm Limey beer!"

"Tastes like cat's piss."

"*You* bin drinkin' it, ain'tcha!"

"It's better than what you gonna get over there, me old cock!"

Lou suddenly remembered Prohibition had started in the States the year before—a fact most of his crewmen had completely forgotten.

"California, here we come. Yeehaw!"

A Brit had the last word in this exchange, "Good luck to life wiv no beer, boys!"

Lord have mercy!

Lou knew he was going to miss this ragged bunch with their strange expressions and eccentric ways. Many of their foibles had rubbed off on the Americans. Goodness knows what their families would think when they got back to the U.S. These Brits were great guys and England was a manicured wonderland, but he longed to be home. He looked forward to sitting on his parents' porch in balmy Virginia air, playing his guitar, as he'd done as a kid. That all seemed a long time ago.

The atmosphere aboard *R38* was of both nervous tension and exuberance. The banter between the English and American crews had been building over the past few hours. Their elation was only natural —soon the ship would be officially re-designated USS *ZR-2*. Lou had listened to their merciless teasing all afternoon. At twenty-three, he was younger than many of the men under his command, including most of the British crewmen, whom he now outranked.

He rubbed the stubble on his chin while, like adolescents, they jeered and poked fun. They even danced and sang. Lou marched on, though their tempting Providence made him uncomfortable. There was no need to dampen their spirits—for now.

It's nervous bravado—they're damned scared, that's all.

When Lou entered the crewmen's mess, Al Jolson's latest hit, "My Mammy", was belting out from the gramophone and little Jerry Donegan, a lively soul from Kentucky, was doing a perfect mime on one knee, hat in hand, his face smeared with old engine oil.

On the final note, his small audience gave him a round of applause, while New York Johnny, a sandy-haired nineteen-year-old from Brooklyn, sat motionless, staring at the fabric wall. No one paid him any attention.

Lou leaned over him and whispered. "You gonna be okay to do your watch, Johnny?"

"Yes, sir," the boy answered weakly.

"You sure?"

"Yeah 'course."

"I'll come and get you just before five."

"Sir!"

Lou stepped out onto the catwalk and stopped for a moment. He worried about that kid.

This life's definitely not for him!

Lou would've stood him down, but he was a man short. Wiggy, an engineer from Cleveland, hadn't reported for duty at Howden before they took off. Something must have happened to him; he was usually reliable. Lou made his way toward the stern, studying the massive structure around him. He breathed in the odor of gasoline, grease, and dope, as if it were fresh-cut hay. Some days it was like being in church, on others, in the belly of a great whale: six hundred and ninety-nine feet of girders, beams of meccano-like steel, held together with rivets, cables, guy wires, nuts and bolts, shrouded by a silver-painted outer cover of finest linen canvas. Walking this labyrinth was exhilarating.

On completion of construction at Cardington and her launching eight weeks ago, the designers and British command had drawn up a comprehensive schedule of flight tests. After initial testing, *R38* was flown to Howden Air Station where another massive shed waited to house the dirigible. Due to time constraints, both the British and American governments insisted the tests were hastened. Lou had taken part under the command of British captain, Flight Lieutenant Wann; now it was time for the final round under the command of Air Commodore Maitland, Britain's most experienced airshipman.

Speed trials completed an hour ago had been satisfactory, although no testing had been done in inclement weather. To compensate, the Air Ministry decided that rough weather conditions could be simulated by stressful maneuvering at low altitude.

All that remained now was a series of these stress tests to prove her structural integrity, and at the same time, confirm that modifications to the rudder and elevator mechanisms had been carried out successfully.

At the end of September, the weather over the Atlantic would almost certainly deteriorate; another reason for rushing these tests. At first, the urgency wasn't so dire, since the fabulous new shed under construction in New Jersey had not been ready. But after the ship's own construction delays, completion had fallen behind and the shed at Lakehurst stood empty, waiting for its charge like a stable without its promised thoroughbred.

After additional training, they'd be on their way, leaving behind the moist, green hills of England and new friends they'd made—many girls—and heading for New Jersey. Although they looked forward to going home to their families, the upcoming passage brought a tinge of sadness and, for many, sheer terror at the thought of facing the Atlantic. Still, there'd been rumors of a ticker-tape welcome.

Why, soon we might all be famous!

Lou descended a long cat ladder to the keel and moved toward the stern, past brand new rolls of neatly-coiled rigger's ropes and spare bolts of linen, each with its own smell. Everything was 'ship shape.' Some crewmen sat in specially fitted machine gun nests studying the picturesque view of fields, villages and streams below. One held a message in a tube attached to a tiny parachute. It was common for crewmen to drop messages—sometimes miraculously received by the addressee.

"A love letter to your honey, Bobby?" Lou called.

"You know it, sir."

"She working today?"

"Yes, sir, she's a nurse in Hull."

"What's her name?"

"Elsie, sir ...Elsie Postlethwaite."

"That's quite a mouthful! Is it serious?"

"Absolutely, sir!"

"Maybe you should ship that babe home," Lou said.

"I'm gonna pop the question as soon as I see her. I want her to come to Baltimore ...after the baby's born, sir," Bobby said, holding up a ring box he'd fished out of his pocket.

"Oh ...okay. I see ...Right. Well, er, that's good. That's the message, is it?"

"Yes, sir."

"Perhaps you'll be able to ask her yourself tonight if we finish these last tests."

"That's what I'm hoping, sir."

"Good luck, Bobby!"

A Brit chimed in from another machine gun nest. "Hey, don't you bloody Yanks be stealing all our women!"

"You got a surplus of 'em, buddy!" Bobby yelled back.

"Yeah, and that's the way we like it, mate!"

Lou chuckled and walked on. He made several stops checking on his crewmen, giving words of encouragement, a pat on the shoulder, a smile. He passed rows of water ballast containers and newly fitted bomb racks, and extra banks of petrol storage tanks, installed at the request of the Navy. He made a point of observing the ship's structure, as trained, for signs of loosening fasteners or metal fatigue in the girders. He stared up with satisfaction.

Over the past twelve months he'd personally witnessed every part being hoisted and riveted into place at the Royal Airship Works at Cardington in Bedfordshire, monitoring construction for quality and keeping records and as-built drawings. Satisfied all was well, he climbed back up the ladder to the central level. From there, he made his way aft to get the answer to the commodore's question.

After four hundred feet, Lou reached the stern and opened the flap into a cockpit where Henry Bateman sat bundled in oilskins, pointing a camera at the huge tail structure. This tiny area was like a boat cuddy without a roof. From the ground, Bateman appeared as small as a freckle on a whale. Lou paused while Bateman snapped a picture. He shivered as the air enveloped him.

"It's freezing out here!" he shouted above the wind.

"Hello, Lou. It's bracing Yorkshire air, my boy—breathe it in!"

Lou glanced at the patchwork quilt of lush green fields and hedgerows below. Far beyond, across the flat Holderness Plain, he admired the North Sea. It was difficult to distinguish where the ocean merged with the hazy, azure-blue sky on the horizon.

"You're lucky. You've got a decent view," Lou said, moving into the cockpit. He sat down on the built-in wooden bench seat running around the perimeter. He peered up at the small, fluttering American flag attached to the tail fin and the *ZR-2* lettering stenciled on the rudder. Lou smiled broadly, exposing even white teeth.

Bateman laughed. "We're a little premature with the flag, aren't we, Lou? I don't think you've paid for the bloody thing yet."

"Don't know anything about that, pal. I'm only here to deliver the beast."

"You'll soon be on your way."

"How are the elevators and rudders?" Lou asked.

Bateman held up his clipboard. "Everything's working fine now. I've been noting course and altitude changes by the coxswains. Everything's on the money."

"Good."

"She's a fine ship," Bateman said. "Just drop a check into the Bank of England and you can drive her home."

"You sound like a damned car salesman!"

"Just pulling your leg, Lou. You know we like having you blokes around."

"I'll let the commodore know. They're gonna do another test in about half an hour. I've got to make a crew change. I'll check with you later," Lou said, getting up.

While *R38* glided majestically toward the city of Hull, the statuesque, twenty-two-year-old Charlotte Hamilton made her final rounds in the geriatric ward of Hull Infirmary. The cream-colored walls gleamed in the late afternoon sunshine, streaming in the windows overlooking the waterfront. The room was full of sick, elderly women propped up on pillows against ancient, white-railed bedsteads.

Charlotte and the other nurses moved from bed to bed, their black leather shoes squeaking on polished, linoleum floors that reeked of disinfectant. This shift would be over at 5 o'clock, but before they could leave, each patient's needs had to be met, beds straightened, bedpans emptied.

Charlotte went to the window and studied the scene on the busy waterfront and the river estuary beyond. Small ripples on the smooth surface indicated that the river was on the turn. Soon, it'd be a raging torrent rushing seaward. The sky overhead was partly clear, but dark cumulus clouds were building over the high ground in the west. Tiny waves, kicked up by the chilly breeze, slapped the wharf. A hundred yards off, Charlotte spotted her best friend's husband and son in a rowboat.

"Fanny, your Lenny's out there with young Billy," Charlotte said, as Fanny dashed by. "There's a storm brewing by the looks of it."

"Yes, I've seen them. They'd better be packing up and getting home. It's almost five," Fanny called over her shoulder.

On the side street opposite the hospital, five boys, about eight years old, were playing cricket. A lamppost served as a wicket. Two bored girls, around the same age, sat on their mother's front step, babysitting their infant brother. They watched a scruffy lad with close-cropped hair slam the ball down the road with an old cricket bat. The boy whooped. The others scowled, arguing about whose turn it was to go for it.

A safe distance from the boys, a group of girls was skipping, one end of their rope tied to a drainpipe, while one twirled. Two girls jumped in unison, chanting their verses in time with the rope as it kissed the ground.

One, two, buckle my shoe,
Three four, knock at the door,
Five, six, pickin' up sticks,
Seven, eight, they're at heaven's gate

Charlotte smiled as she turned from the window and went over to Mrs. Tilly, her favorite patient, who was engrossed in the girls' melody.

Up above the world so high,
Like a diamond in the sky ...

"Oh, I do love to hear their sweet voices," the old lady said.

"They make up their own rhymes as they go along, you know love. They see the airships coming over all the time from Howden. You have to laugh at them really—the girls, I mean. Is there anything you need before I go off duty, Mrs. T?" Charlotte asked.

If she dives, they all might die,
Oh, I wonder, why, why, why?

"Much as I love to hear 'em, I'm feeling a chill right down in my old bones."

Poor ol' Bobby, he's in the drink,
Should we pull him out—what do you fink?

Charlotte closed the steel casement window with a clunk. The chanting grew fainter.

Nine, ten ...

"Can I do anything else for you, love. You only have to ask."

"Don't go to a lot of trouble for me, dear," Mrs. Tilly protested.

"Come on, let me fix this bed for you."

She pulled the old lady gently up into a sitting position. Mrs. Tilly wheezed and coughed while Charlotte fluffed up her pillows and straightened the bedclothes. Charlotte read the birthday card on the side table next to a vase of flowers.

"I hope you've had a nice birthday, Mrs. Tilly."

"Eighty-one years I've been on this earth—it's long enough. I lost my 'usband last year. I'll be glad to join him and my sons in 'eaven."

"You've got a few more years to wait, I'm sure," Charlotte said.

Charlotte eased her frail patient down onto the pillows. The entrance doors to the ward rattled as a young nurse pushed in a tea trolley. Charlotte poured tea and brought it to Mrs. Tilly with a bite to eat.

"Here's a cuppa and a cucumber sandwich. This'll keep your strength up, love."

Mrs. Tilly's face brightened. "You're such a lovely girl."

The factory whistle blew—grating, but always a welcome sound on Prospect Street.

"It must be time for you to go and meet your young man," Mrs. Tilly said.

Charlotte grimaced. "Oh, no. Nothing like that."

"What! Why ever not?"

"Eligible men are scarce nowadays—most of them are buried in France."

"What about them Americans?"

"Oh, no, no. I can't be bothered."

"Why not?"

"I've heard too many stories. A lot of girls I know are in a right sorry state."

"Maybe you could find a nice one."

"No, I don't want to get mixed up in all that. Besides, I read they're all going back to America any day now."

The old lady seemed seriously concerned. "What a pity. Pretty girl like you should have a fella. You could have your pick, I reckon."

"Oh, go on with you!"

"With that marvelous black hair and beautiful figure you could be an actress."

"Bless your heart, Mrs. Tilly."

"You'll find someone special. I just know you will. And when you do, you grab 'im and 'old on to 'im and never let 'im go. I did. My 'usband was a lovely man and he gave me two wonderful sons. Oh, I do miss 'im so," she sobbed. Tears filled Mrs. Tilly's eyes and ran down her cheeks. "They're all gone now. Our first boy at Mons …the second at Ypres. All three of 'em. Make the most of this life, my dear. It's just a flicker of a candle. That's all it is …"

A dark cloud fell over Charlotte's face. She understood perfectly.

"I'm so sorry, Mrs. Tilly," she said.

The old lady stared up at the ceiling for a moment as though looking through a window to the past, or perhaps the future. After a few moments, she became calm and was at peace.

"I'll see you in the morning, love," Charlotte said.

"Don't forget what I said, my girl," Mrs. Tilly called after her. "Some of them Americans are really lovely!"

"Yes, I know they are, Mrs. Tilly," Charlotte whispered to herself.

After getting permission from Matron to leave, Charlotte went to the staff room where several nurses were washing their hands, combing their hair and freshening their makeup before leaving for the day. Others were getting ready to go on duty. Charlotte sensed desperation among some. One girl had been crying. She was starting to show and Charlotte wondered if her condition had escaped Matron's attention.

No chance of that!

Some were going on about their boyfriends. Charlotte frowned.

They're just so irritating!

"I hope they finish their testing today. I wanna be with my Bobby tonight," one said.

"Do you think they will, Elsie?"

"Bobby said they should and, all being well, they might fly over the city this afternoon."

"Oh, I do hope so."

"Bobby told me they're not expecting any problems, but I wish the test would fail so he could stay here for a few more months."

"But you know if they leave in October or November, it'll be everso much more dangerous for 'em, Elsie."

"Yes, you're right, but I love 'im so much. I don't want 'im to go, Minnie."

"I know. I love my Jimmy, too. I'm going over there, though. He's asked me to marry 'im. We're going to be wed next year."

"Oh, you're so lucky. I wish …"

"What love?'

"Oh, I got a feeling tonight Bobby's going to ask me …he did promise …"

The two girls looked up and saw Charlotte and glanced at one another.

"Oh hello, love. Why don't you get yourself a nice chap from the U.S. Navy? They're smashin', aren't they, Elsie? I could listen to my

Jimmy talk all night long. He's like a movie star. I've seen 'em in the talkies at the Odeon in Leeds," Minnie said.

"Not me. And if I were you, I'd make sure you get a ring on your finger before you do anything stupid, Minnie Brown," Charlotte snapped.

"It's a bit late for that, love," Elsie scoffed. At that, both girls doubled up, laughing uncontrollably. Charlotte scowled. Taking her make-up compact from her handbag, she peered into the mirror and puckered her full lips to apply a little plum-colored lipstick. Her vivid blue eyes stared back at her questioningly. She thought about what Mrs. Tilly had said.

Maybe a doctor? No, they're all old men around here, or ugly!

After applying a few dabs of her favorite perfume to her neck, she went to the wall mirror and untied her hair. She laid her head to one side and brushed her thick curls out with long strokes. She then flicked her head back, allowing it to cascade to her waist. The other nurses watched.

"Time you had that lot cut off, isn't it, Charlotte?" dumpy, little Minnie said, with a sly grin.

"No, I'm perfectly satisfied the way it is, thank you very much."

"You should go in for one of these, Charlotte. They're all the rage," the well-endowed Elsie said, running her fingers through her bob cut and thrusting out her bosom.

"You'd feel free as a bird," Minnie added.

"Like us!" Elsie exclaimed.

They rocked back and forth cackling again.

Jealous little cows!

"You're much too straight-laced, Charlotte," Elsie said.

"Aye, *straight-laced* is what I am! And *straight-laced* is what'll prevent me from landing myself in the right pickle you two are gonna be in," Charlotte snapped.

Charlotte ignored them further, taking off her white cotton apron. She put her foot on a chair and hoisted her light blue cotton uniform, pulled her black stockings up tight over her long shapely legs and refastened her garters. After smoothing down her skirt to the ankles, she re-tied her headscarf and put on her dark blue cape before making for the door. Elsie and Minnie stared after her, as if *she* were the foolish one.

Lou entered the crewmen's mess at the same time the factory whistle was sounding on Prospect Street (although he couldn't hear it). The lads still appeared to be in high spirits, except for New York Johnny whose mood hadn't changed. He sat in the corner staring at the wall, just as Lou had left him, elbows on the table, chin in his hands.

"Ready, Johnny?"

"Yes, sir," Johnny said.

He got slowly to his feet, without looking up. Lou led him along the catwalk to the opening above engine car No.1 and pulled back the canvas hatch to the exterior ladder. They were buffeted by the cold, noisy wind rushing over the ship's cover. The boy caught his breath.

"Right, Johnny?" Lou shouted.

Johnny nodded without speaking, staring at the fields below. A tiny goods train rushed along its tracks like a kid's toy train, a black smoke cloud billowing behind, while its whistle screamed a warning. Lou had watched the boy climb down this ladder dozens of times, but it got harder each time. Lou knew he'd developed a phobia. He'd seen it before.

This line of work's better suited to circus performers, or barnstormers. Climbing down ladders suspended from airships at two thousand feet isn't for the faint-hearted.

Lou understood phobias only too well. During the war, he'd developed one of his own—claustrophobia.

"Come on, Johnny, it's okay."

With terror in his eyes, the boy gripped the cold steel of the ship's ladder. Lou knew his heart must be beating like a sledgehammer. Clinging on tightly, Johnny gingerly began the twenty-foot descent to the engine car slung in mid-air beneath the ship.

Suddenly, Johnny froze and glared at the huge propeller whirring in a high-speed blur below him. He gasped for breath, his mouth wide open.

"Johnny, don't look down!" Lou yelled. "Look up at me, buddy!"

The boy remained stuck, screwing his eyelids tightly together to shut out the world.

"Look at me, Johnny! Look at me!"

Johnny tilted his head back and slowly opened his eyes. He peered up into Lou's confident blue eyes, assessing him. It was a face people trusted. Lou smiled and after a few moments the boy's terror subsided.

"Okay, Johnny, ease your way down, one step at a time."

The boy, now completely calm, moved one foot onto the next steel rung. Lou willed him down bit by bit, until he'd inched his way to the entrance of the tiny engine car. He slipped inside, as though returning to his mother's womb.

At six feet four inches and physically fit from his army days, Lou lowered himself down after the boy effortlessly. His close-cropped hair, square jaw, and finely shaped head accentuated his muscular physique. But now, Lou's own secret demons grabbed him by the throat. He took a deep breath, gritted his teeth, and wormed his way into the cramped engine gondola. He found it stifling and hard to breathe once inside.

The engine car was a tiny pod, housing one of the six ear-splitting Sunbeam Cossack III 350-horsepower engines. It was the engineer's little haven, smelling of oil, petrol, exhaust fumes, sweat, and sometimes urine. The massive engine generated suffocating heat and took up most of the eight-by-twelve foot space.

On two sides, small portholes allowed light in during the day. Overhead was a light for night-time use. The engineer sat on a small bench keeping vigil over the engine gauges, waiting for instructions from the control car—the telegraph bells would ring while the pointers moved from *IDLE* to *SLOW* to *MEDIUM* or to *FULL POWER,* depending on the captain's whim. Lou entered as Johnny was stuffing plasticine in his ears, the only protection for the eardrums against the deafening roar. Lou patted Johnny on the shoulder.

"Okay, Johnny, you'll be fine. I'll come and get you later," he shouted, knowing Johnny would have to lip-read. The boy gave a half-smile, mouthing a weak 'thanks.'

Lou and the engineer, whom Johnny had relieved, climbed back up the ladder into the hull to be greeted by Fluffy, the ship's long-haired tabby. She rubbed herself against Lou's leg. He picked her up and nuzzled her affectionately.

"Fluffy, you know you're my best girl, don't you?" he said.

He put her down and she ran to her own sheltered spot off the main walkway. On the subject of girls, he suddenly thought of Julia. He hadn't really thought much about her. He'd met plenty of girls in

England and been pursued by many, but none had taken his fancy. It'd be nice to see Julia again soon.

Charlotte stepped out onto the hospital entrance porch, pulling her cape around her shoulders. She gave the surrounding area a quick glance—something she did instinctively nowadays. The coast was clear. As she crossed the street toward the waterfront, she stared at the patchy blue sky overhead. It should remain pleasant for a while, though chilly. She eyed dark clouds in the distance which were moving closer.

Charlotte decided to go for a short stroll along the promenade, as she sometimes did on summer evenings. She had no reason to be in a hurry—nothing and no one to rush home to. Her calling was caring for the sick, which she did with dedication. A walk would do her good and help her relax after a hard day.

Workers from the Macey Brothers' factory, makers of fine furniture and mattresses, poured into the street through rusty iron gates, many on bicycles. She studied them. They appeared pathetic, with not many young men among them. Those she saw were disfigured, or had limbs missing. There were a few fourteen and fifteen-year-old boys. They wore cloth caps, jackets, and trousers in similar drab colors. Charlotte felt sorry for them. The bustling crowd was mixed with a higher percentage of women of all ages, their heads wrapped in headscarves tied like turbans.

These poor wretches are trying to get back to a normal life after that bloody awful war—that's if you call living without a son, a brother, a husband, or a father, 'normal'!

These thoughts made her tremble and her eyes moist with tears. She dare not let herself dwell on all that. It was like pulling off a scab. She preferred numbness. She tried to concentrate on the work done to the waterfront as part of a post-war beautification project: new paved walkways and small cherry trees planted with protective metal shields around them. She ambled along the docks toward Victoria Pier with hundreds of others, enjoying the last of the evening sunshine. There was much activity on the river, with work boats being moored at the quay alongside rusty freighters from Holland, Belgium, and as far away as Australia and New Zealand. Charlotte often saw dockers unloading wool, dairy goods, and frozen lamb.

She walked on, leisurely glancing at the tugboats lumbering toward the dock to be moored, their wakes shimmering behind them.

Men aboard vessels and on the docks, in grimy dungarees and rubber boots, tended mooring lines and checked everything was secure for the night. They took no notice of passers-by—until their eyes fell on Charlotte. Then their faces lit up and they called out to her.

"Hello, my lovely. You're looking beautiful this evening."

"She's a corker, all right!"

"Oh, to be thirty years younger!"

"What a little smasher!"

They were cheeky, older men, but she didn't mind their harmless flirting. She'd got to know many of them by sight and attended to some of them after accidents on the wharf. She stopped for a minute and peered out across the river at Fanny's husband and son in their rowboat. Lenny was telling the boy to pack up while Billy protested and sulked. Charlotte smiled when Lenny relented. He sat back and lit another one of his Woodbines, snapping his steel lighter shut. He took another drag and blew out the smoke, while Billy went on fishing.

Charlotte thought about the young men she'd known. Though she'd received many proposals, there'd been nothing serious—well, not really. There'd been the encounter with Robert of course; unforgettable, though fleeting. That was an era she'd erased from her mind, with memories too painful and difficult to share—though the brief meeting with Robert had been a pleasant one. That period had changed her life forever, but she couldn't bear to think about it or allow it to be mentioned. Did she regret it? No. She'd do it all again.

Her mind returned to the future and available men. The thought of one, made her wince. Jessup! He'd caused her, and her family, so much trouble—indeed the whole village. After reading up on the subject in medical journals, she realized now he was a psychopath. Her parents had tried to warn her, but she always tried to see the good in people, or to save the bad. She'd found out the hard way. He was obsessive and had a dreadful mean streak, especially after he'd been drinking. She'd gone out with him for only two weeks after her return to the village; that was all it took. Since then—for the last two years—he'd stalked her relentlessly.

God, how I hate him!

But she'd had worse things in life to deal with and she'd survive *him*. She needed to meet someone nice, but choice was practically non-existent. Charlotte knew Americans to be respectful and well-mannered, having been approached by many, but she'd steered clear to avoid complications.

Most of them are out for a good time. And who can blame them?

Charlotte thought if you met a sincere one, what good would that be? He'd soon be gone, back to Grand Rapids or Cincinnati, or some other place with an exotic-sounding name. No, they were not for her, as good-looking and manly as many of them were—and she had to admit, some looked gorgeous in uniform. But most of all, thinking back, she always remembered their sad, pleading eyes.

She'd leave the heartbreak and the muddles to the other girls in Howden and Hull with no common sense. There were girls who'd married after a whirlwind romance. Charlotte realized some might get lucky, but wondered what the chances were of those relationships lasting. They might hate America when they got there. Then what?

No, Charlotte Hamilton will not fall into that trap—better to be an old maid, dedicated to the sick, than endure the plight of those silly fools.

Lou set off down the catwalk behind Fluffy. He went through the officers' dining area and control room, and descended the polished mahogany steps into the control car where Flight Sergeant Walter Potter awaited him. Potter, a gentle soul, had spent a lot of time these past months mentoring the Americans, including Lou. He reminded Lou of Stan Laurel, the Englishman of the Laurel & Hardy duo who'd made dozens of hilarious short films. At times, his bland face made him appear dazed and befuddled, though he wasn't in the slightest. He made Lou laugh, especially when he played his accordion for the crew during lighter moments. He pumped the bellows, while his fingers glided over the buttons and keys, his face expressionless, except for those smiling eyes. They'd become fast friends.

The mood was somber, more so than before. As Lou entered, everyone briefly nodded in his direction. The American captain, Commander Maxfield, stood stiffly beside Commodore Maitland, the most senior man on the ship and in control of the tests. He appeared pretty relaxed.

That good ol' British stiff upper lip.

The commodore glanced at the clock—it was now 17:11 hours (5:11 p.m.).

Flt. Lt. Wann, the British captain, was positioned between two coxswains. The three officers stood silently, their eyes on the horizon. Lou sensed tension among them.

The windows wrapped around the control car, providing an excellent view. In the distance, ten miles off, Lou could see the City of Hull, a sprawling mass of factories, docklands, freight yards, offices, shops, and homes clustered along the river estuary toward the east.

The control car, about thirty feet long by twelve feet wide, had been finished in varnished mahogany similar to a ship's bridge. From the exterior, it looked like a tramcar on a city street.

The height coxswain stood at a console facing the starboard side. He controlled the altitude of the ship with a turn of the silver wheel in front of him. Lou checked the altimeter above the coxswain's head. It read: 2,500 feet. Everything appeared normal.

The helmsman stood at a similar wheel at the front, near the windows, facing forward. He controlled the rudders, which steered the ship. Both coxswains were American, dressed in white crew-neck sweaters, navy blue trousers, and white soft-soled shoes. A British coxswain stood beside each man, monitoring his activities and coaching him. They, in contrast, wore drab, blue boiler suits and grubby, black shoes.

A battery of telegraphs mounted on the port sidewall was for sending orders to the engine cars beneath the hull. From these, instructions were issued to the engineers controlling each of the six engines. Lou was always fascinated when he entered the control car. The behemoth was controlled from this room—'the bridge'—his favorite place. If the weather was clear, visibility was excellent for 360 degrees with the engine cars in full view in front and behind, their propellers a blur. Lou wondered if anyone in the control car had noticed the incident earlier with Johnny frozen on the ladder. The commodore turned and addressed Lou, surprising him. Lou had begun to think he and Potter had become invisible.

Typical of these Brit officers. Stuck up bunch!

"Chief Coxswain, do you have a report from Mr. Bateman?"

In U.S. parlance, Lou was called a chief petty officer, but the commodore used British terminology.

"Yes, sir. I spoke with Mr. Bateman fifteen minutes ago."

"And?"

"He said the elevator and the rudder cabling gear are working fine now, sir."

"Good," the commodore said, although he didn't appear the least bit happy.

The American captain, Cmdr. Maxfield, stood with his jaw clenched, his lips screwed tightly together.

"These tests have been woefully inadequate, but …" the commodore began.

"We have our orders, sir," Capt. Maxfield interjected.

"I'm not happy with this situation. I cannot condone shortening these tests—it's a grave mistake."

The American captain didn't reply. Lou was taking note.

Something's not right here.

"We'll start in fifteen minutes," the commodore said. They glanced at the clock on the wall. "That will be at 17:20. We'll come in over Hull on our present course and head out to the middle of the estuary where we'll turn sharply to the north. That will be your salute to the city."

"Yes, sir," Capt. Wann said. He'd been relaying the commodore's orders for the past few hours.

The commodore turned to Lou. "Chief Coxswain … I'm sorry, your name again?"

"Remington, sir."

"Ah yes, forgive me. Remington, go and quiet down the crew—*both crews*. Put *everybody* on high alert. Station men at fifty-foot intervals throughout the ship. Give them the task of watching for any structural deformity or weakness. Tell them to sound the alarm immediately if they spot the slightest abnormality or sign of failure. Tell them this is the last test and it will be more rigorous than the speed trials we've done."

"Yes sir."

"Report back when everyone's at their stations."

"Yes sir!"

Lou and Potter went straight to the mess. The men, still in a buoyant mood, fell silent as they entered. Everyone gathered around while Lou relayed the commodore's instructions. He did his best not to alarm them, but he needed them to be vigilant.

"Is all that clear, men?" They were unable to conceal their anxiety. "The good news is—this will be the last test." Lou glanced at the American faces. "After this, we get to go home!"

A weak cheer went up.

"All right!" Josh, the Californian, hollered.

"Thank the Lord for that!" a Brit shouted from the back.

Lou and Potter marched up the catwalk with the crewmen, positioning a man every fifty feet, with orders to 'hold on tight.' Along the way, the cat came out to greet Lou, hoping for more attention. Lou picked her up and thrust her into the arms of the sixteen-year-old cabin boy from Louisiana.

"Here, Gladstone, put her in the oil storage room out of the way." Gladstone usually took care of her.

Lou and Potter returned to the control car. "All crewmen are at their stations and on high alert, sir," Lou announced. The three uniformed officers remained grim-faced.

"Then let us proceed with the final test," the commodore said with cool detachment. "We'll make this a tough one. If she survives this, I promise you, she'll survive anything you'll meet over the Atlantic. I absolutely refuse to release an unproven ship into the hands of a green crew."

The American captain didn't respond and Lou wondered what he was thinking. All afternoon, he'd been haunted by the sensation that something was wrong.

Charlotte turned back from her walk along the waterfront and headed toward Victoria Pier. The droning airship in the distance caught her attention. She had an inherent dread of airships. German Zeppelins had bombed Hull during the war, striking terror into the local population. She pulled her cape tightly around her shoulders. The temperature was dropping.

Those horrible things give me the creeps!

When she'd reached her starting point, Charlotte noticed the children still playing cricket and jump rope in the hospital side street. An ominous black shadow swept down the road and over the kids. One girl screamed with delight when she looked up and spotted the airship. As it sped away over the river, Bobby's message tube floated down on its tiny parachute and fell at her feet. She scooped it up and began to run. A boy at the lamppost dropped his bat while the other girl bundled her infant brother into a battered pram. Together, they all dashed helter-skelter for the river, the baby bouncing and giggling along the way. Charlotte turned her attention toward the water when she heard Billy out in the rowboat, yelling to his father, who was laid back, smoking another Woodbine. Billy had leapt to his feet and was pointing at the sky, almost rocking them both into the water.

"Oh look, Dad, an airship!"

"Sit down! Sit down!" the boy's father shouted as he tried to steady the boat.

All around, city folk stood frozen, as though in a trance. Windows opened on upper stories and people stuck out their heads, hands shading their eyes, dazzled by the sun's last gleam. People emerged from shops and offices and raced for the waterfront. Charlotte got caught up in the excitement and found herself on the pier surrounded by the scruffy, breathless kids. Everyone watched the sky.

"Eee, loook at that! It's looovely in't it!" the girl with the pram exclaimed.

In the control car, the commodore calmly issued his first order.

"Full power all engines, Captain Wann."

"Full power all engines," the English captain repeated.

He leaned over and rang the telegraphs and moved six levers on the control panel to 'FULL POWER.' The trainee American engineers in the engine cars would be waiting for this signal, ready to move the throttle levers gently forward as Potter had trained them to do. Lou worried about New York Johnny, the kid who'd cracked earlier. He hoped he was coping all right down in engine car No.1. The engine notes changed to a full-throated roar. Anxiety showed in the officers' eyes. The British and American coxswains exchanged worried glances.

To the crowd, the change in engine note was like a signal. Something was about to happen; a bit of a show perhaps. People on Victoria Pier chattered excitedly above the airship's droning Cossacks. The five gossiping nurses from whom Charlotte had escaped twenty minutes earlier, now joined her. She gave them a dirty look.

Don't you dare embarrass me!

"It's here. It's here! Oh, it's so beautiful," Minnie yelled.

"My Bobby's in that airship," Elsie shouted proudly.

"And my Jimmy, too! We're getting married in America next year," Minnie announced. People turned and smiled, happy for her.

"Oh look, she's flying the American flag," Elsie said pointing to the tiny Stars and Stripes fluttering on the tail. Excitement was building.

"Look how she sparkles in the sunshine!"

"Like a diamond."

"Incredible!"

"Makes yer so proud, don' it!"

"My Bobby told me the airship might fly over this evening to say goodbye," Elsie told the crowd.

People began cheering and madly waving up at the ship. Shouts went from one to another along the waterfront like a recurring echo.

"She's come to say goodbye. She's come to say goodbye!"

Aboard the airship, the commodore issued his second order.

"Reduce altitude to fifteen hundred feet."

Capt. Wann instructed the height coxswain, "Reduce altitude: fifteen hundred feet."

The bow dipped dramatically and the ship gathered speed, aided by gravity. Lou focused on his American skipper, sensing the man's apprehension. His eyes were darting back and forth, from the scene outside, to the instruments, to the coxswains. Lou thought of Bateman, who he'd left minutes ago in the stern cockpit studying the movement of the gigantic elevators and rudders.

The ship flew directly over the city, Welsh slates on rooftops and brick chimneys in plain view. As they raced toward the river, Lou saw factory workers, shop people and office workers running in the streets. Some stopped in their tracks, staring up in wonder as the ship sped toward the estuary. When the commodore gave his third and final order, an uneasy frown passed over the American captain's face.

"Rudders—fifteen degrees to starboard."

"Additional fifteen degrees to starboard, sir."

Capt. Wann watched the rudder coxswain rotate his wheel to implement the radical turn. The compass needle moved rapidly. Alarm and disbelief registered in the American captain's face. The ship, traveling at considerable speed, began a sweeping turn over the estuary, followed by the eyes of thousands on the ground.

Charlotte turned to check on the children, who'd instinctively gathered around her. A small, black Austin came skidding to a halt at the curb and two men jumped out—one in naval uniform, built like a little bull, the other a rotund, lumbering man, about five feet ten. The fat one, unable to keep up with his companion, yelled after him.

Charlotte couldn't hear what he was saying above the crowd as they rushed onto the pier.

To the spectators, the airship was an extraordinary sight—a futuristic fantasy, but to these two men, the display clearly meant much more. Although his breathing was labored, the fat man's voice became audible as he stumbled closer.

"Hell, he's giving her a hammering!" he shouted in a broad Scottish accent.

They rushed up and stood close to Charlotte and the children.

"Nah! She can take it, Mac," replied the little bull.

"I don't like it, Scottie. It's bloody suicide! She's not built for this —you know she ain't."

Charlotte took her eyes off the airship and glared at both men. She didn't like that kind of language in front of children, but the desperate anxiety in the fat man's face struck her and she too, became alarmed.

High above them in the control car, the officers gripped handholds on the walls and ceiling. The coxswains clung to their wheels, but the commodore remained cool. Suddenly, a deep, vibrating boom reverberated throughout the ship, like the snapping of a great steel string on a giant bass instrument. Every man felt the awful jolt through their feet and hands.

"What the hell's that?" the American captain shouted.

The rudder coxswain spun his wheel without resistance, shrieking in panic, his face ashen. "Rudder's gone, sir!"

The ship was now in mortal danger. Terror showed in every face, including the commodore's. "Rudder cable's parted," he shouted. "Cut power to all engines!"

The American captain turned and screamed at Lou, "Remington— look to your crew!"

"Aye, aye, sir!" Lou replied over his shoulder as he and Potter raced up the stairs. When they reached the catwalk above the control car, crewmen clamored for answers.

"What happened, sir?" Josh, yelled.

"We've lost the rudders. Get your parachutes on, all of you."

On the pier, Charlotte and the children beside her gazed up at the airship, mesmerized. But then, almost in slow motion, a crease formed in its side, aft of the midsection, behind the control car. With a deep, sickening feeling in pit of her stomach, Charlotte realized she was about to witness something terrible.

"Oh, bloody hell!" Scottie groaned.

The crease grew into a diagonal crack at first, and then a gaping black hole, running from the top to well behind the control car. The five nurses screamed hysterically.

"Aaaaah no!"

"Bobby! My Bobby!"

'My Jimmy! My Jimmy!"

"It's breaking! It's breaking!" the children sobbed.

The crowd wailed as the two ends of the airship sagged downwards, the whole thing splitting open like a massive dinosaur egg. Suddenly, a huge explosion knocked the crowd to the ground. Flames and black smoke burst from the opening, and equipment, gas tanks, ballast tanks and men on fire tumbled from the envelope into the sky.

"Sweet Jesus save them!" yelled the fat man as he went down.

When the airship began to separate, Lou was standing twenty feet forward of the breaking point, close to one of the parachute racks. He grabbed the last parachute and held on to it. He'd put it on when he got a chance. Inside the ship everything was carnage and chaos. Struggling to keep his feet, he watched the writhing ship violently pulled apart by invisible forces—its cables and guy wires wrenched from their anchor points like sinews from a chicken's leg. They whipped around with lethal ferocity, decapitating Al Jolson, dismembering many, and lashing the faces and torsos of others—not a soul was left unscathed. Lou received a deep gash down the right side of his face. The dreadful creaking, moaning, and groaning of the steel girders sounded like a prehistoric creature in her death throes.

Wildly sparking electric cables were ripped from their sockets and pipes carrying fuel to the engines broke apart, dousing crewmen who rushed blindly like madmen in all directions. The gasoline erupted, followed by the first hydrogen gasbag. With an ear-splitting explosion, dozens of men enveloped in orange flame were blasted into the sky from the airship, now almost completely severed in two. Lou, Potter and Josh were in the blazing front section. The rear half hadn't yet caught fire, but Lou expected it would very soon.

With blood pouring from his wound, saturating his white jersey, Lou watched the cabin boy rush past him, trying to hold on to the terrified Fluffy. When the explosion came, the cat broke free, leapt the divide, and raced off toward the stern. The screaming cabin boy was blown off the catwalk, falling forty feet through the girders into the sky toward the raging river below.

The canvas cover—much of it on fire—made tearing and popping sounds as it was ripped off like paper. The rushing wind fanned the flames enveloping injured men. Now ablaze like flaming torches, crazy with fear and pain, they ran wildly up and down the catwalks, screaming. Inevitably, each one hurled himself out into the sky toward the icy water. Powerless to help, Lou watched his men perish all around him. Numb to his own physical pain, he felt as though his heart was being ripped from his chest.

As the gap widened between the two halves, something told Lou to make the leap to the other side. He did. Potter was right behind him. They heard a yell as Josh made a running leap. He barely made it before the gap widened and the front half broke away, leaving him clinging to a girder in space. Lou spotted Elsie's boyfriend, too frightened, and now too late, to make the jump. Lou threw his parachute to him.

"Put this on, Bobby!" he yelled.

Bobby caught it and struggled to put it on. Two more attempted the leap, but the gap had become too wide. They fell to their deaths. Josh, still clinging on, turned his head away in horror. Lou lay down and held on to the ship with his left hand and grabbed Josh's outreached hand with the other. Below them, he saw the control car, itself ablaze, separate from the plunging front section and veer off, cart-wheeling in the air. For a split second, Lou thought of the men inside, where he'd been only minutes ago. He noticed the engine pod on the port side— the engineer had managed to get out and was clinging to the struts.

Must be New York Johnny.

His chances looked slim. As Lou mustered the strength to pull Josh up, a girder collapsed, trapping and breaking his left arm. Adrenalin, or a miracle, allowed Lou to haul Josh up to a point where, with help from Potter, he was able to scramble onto the catwalk. Josh and Potter pulled up on the girder, releasing Lou's arm. Lou winced as they lifted him to his feet. Nausea and dizziness swept over him.

On the waterfront, spellbound spectators witnessed the disaster unfolding. Charlotte cried as she tried to comfort the distraught children beside her, while the five nurses clung to one another sobbing uncontrollably. The crowd had become as one in shock and sorrow. The fat man gasped in anguish and closed his eyes, at breaking point.

"Oh, dear God, what have they done?" he cried.

"My Bobby," Elsie whimpered, her face screwed up in anguish.

Another, more powerful detonation knocked the crowd to the ground for a second time. An eerie silence followed after the engines, starved of gasoline, sputtered and quit. All that could be heard now were heartbreaking cries of falling men, echoing over the water, crashing glass dropping from shattered windows across the city, and moaning, weeping people in the crowd.

The second explosion had also occurred in the front half of the ship—the rest of the gas bags exploding in a massive chain reaction. Lou, Potter, and Josh stood at the opening as the blazing front section fell away. Now without hydrogen buoyancy, the severed section fell like a rock with men in flames falling out or throwing themselves out, while the lucky ones, apparently unhurt, floated down in parachutes (one of them, Bobby). But luck is a fickle mistress; large swaths of the river were afire, blazing with gasoline spilled from ignited storage tanks. On Victoria Pier, people lay on the ground, as though dead.

Lou and his two crewmen made their way to check more parachute racks. They were all gone. Close by, an English crewman wearing a parachute was getting ready to jump. Two Americans watched with envy. The man hesitated, taking pity on them.

"Come on, you Yanks. Grab on to me," he hollered.

They rushed to him and wrapped their arms around him.

"Hold tight, boys!"

As they were about to jump, one panicked. "I can't swim! I can't swim!"

"Don't worry, I got you, mate," the Englishman shouted.

All three jumped into space. Lou was skeptical, not sure they'd made a wise decision. At least for now, this half of the airship hadn't caught fire. Lou and his two companions held on, watching the threesome descend. The chute suddenly burst open, breaking their freefall with a jerk, dislodging the non-swimmer. The screaming man fell and splashed into the black water.

Lou stepped back from the opening, wincing and clutching his arm. He looked up at the remaining part of the ship and flapping gas bags. For now, they had hydrogen and therefore, lift—too much lift! All around them, the wind howled. The remains of the outer fabric cover fluttered and loose parts of the structure chattered and vibrated.

"D'ya think she's gonna blow, Lou?" Potter asked, his face dead-pan as usual.

"No—but we're ascending," Lou said, pulling a switchblade from his pocket.

"Damn! You're right," Potter gasped, noticing they were coming up into higher cloud.

"Take this knife and slash the gas bags and open the valves—quickly!"

"I've got a knife," Potter said. Josh pulled out a similar one.

"Good, go help him, Josh," Lou said. "Meet me at the stern cockpit —there may be some parachutes there," Lou said, putting the knife back in his pocket.

Lou held his throbbing arm, and moved carefully along the catwalk, leaving a trail of blood. On the way, he found a thick rope, from which he cut a piece and fashioned a sling. When he got to the stern, Bateman had disappeared, but Fluffy stood on his seat snarling and spitting—eyes blazing, back arched in fury. There were no parachutes.

Lou heard someone yelling from outside the cockpit. He cautiously peered over the side where Bateman dangled precariously in space. Lou figured he'd thrown on his parachute in blind panic and hurled himself overboard, his lines hopelessly tangled with the hooks and ropes in the cockpit. Lou leaned over and, with his good arm, pulled the terrified man back on board. The badly shaken Bateman sank down onto the bench seat, shaking his head. They looked up at the rudder swinging freely from side to side.

"Oh, Lou, am I glad to see you, my friend."

"I told you I'd come back, didn't I?"

Lou's relief was mixed—their section of the ship was now *sinking* toward the flaming river. Below them, men with parachutes were descending into the inferno, their chances of survival poor. Lou thought he and the others would probably suffer the same fate.

Better we take our chances here than to be blown out over the North Sea.

On Victoria Pier, everyone struggled to their feet again. Charlotte helped Scottie pull Mac up from the ground. All eyes were glued to the front half of the ship, now a speeding fire ball, heading in their direction. *They* were the ones in danger now. The crowd stampeded toward the road.

One of the girls grabbed her infant brother from the pram and ran off with the other children and screaming nurses. Charlotte got knocked sideways into Scottie and Mac by the rushing mob and all three landed on the ground in a heap yet again. The flaming front half hit the water just short of the dock, spewing more bodies and gasoline into the river and sending a cascade of dirty water over the unfortunate ones still on the pier. The children managed to get clear and stood motionless in the middle of the road with the dazed, weeping nurses.

The river was blazing immediately in front of Charlotte and far out across the estuary. She stood dripping wet, while the parachutists, thought to be safe, dropped into the sea of flames. She watched her friend's husband and son as they clung to their upturned rowboat, not far from the fiery wreck. If they escaped being burned alive, they'd soon die of exposure in the icy river. Minutes later, she saw the rear half of the ship splash down in a flame-free area to the north, but it was soon caught in the clutches of the outward rushing tide. She wondered if anyone was inside.

Charlotte, Scottie, and Mac left the pier, which was strewn with the remnants of panic: shoes, clothing, newspapers, handbags, broken eyeglasses and the kid's pram on its side. They hurried along the wharf in the direction of the infirmary and boats tied up at the dock. They stopped for a moment, not quite knowing what to say. As is common at such times, a bond had developed between them. Storm clouds, accompanied by lightning flashes and rolling thunder had moved closer, adding to the misery. Smoke drifted across the river toward them and raindrops began to cut through the petrol-laden air mixed with burnt odors, which Charlotte pushed from her mind.

Mac spoke first. "What's your name, miss? I'm Fred McWade and this is Major Scott."

"Nurse Charlotte Hamilton."

"You're going to be busy, Nurse Hamilton," Scott said.

"Yes. I must get back to the infirmary."

"Come on, Mac, let's jump into one of these boats," Scott said, eyeing the boatmen along the wharf, already hurriedly untying their mooring lines. Scott called down to them.

"We're airshipmen. Can you take us out there?"

"Come on, guv, climb aboard," one replied.

Charlotte pointed toward the river. "Sir, please hurry and get to the boy and his father—look—clinging to their boat. They're my best friend's family."

Fanny came rushing up. "Oh, help me, help me, I beg you," she pleaded and then with a sob, "It's me 'usband, Lenny, and Billy, me little boy."

"All right, we'll get 'em," Scott said. He pulled out a silver hip flask and gulped down a couple of good mouthfuls before they rushed off down the quay. Charlotte sympathized—any man would need a drink to cope with scenes they were about to encounter. She put her arm around Fanny's frail shoulders as they watched the two men climb aboard an old rusty riverboat.

"Don't worry, love, they'll save them. Come on. Let's sort these kids out."

They went to the children who were standing in the road crying and soaking wet.

"Come on, let's get your pram. Your mum and dad will be worrying about you."

"We ain't got no dad, miss," one girl said, holding a message tube tightly to her chest.

"What's that you've got there, dear?" Charlotte asked.

"It cooome down from airship, miss. I picked it ooop 'ere int' street."

Charlotte recognized the name on the tube in large letters:

ELSIE POSTLETHWAITE C/O Hull Infirmary.

"You'd better give it to *me*, love," Charlotte said, gently removing it from the girl's grip. "Don't worry, I'll see she gets it. I promise."

After retrieving the old blue pram from the pier and sending the kids home, Charlotte and Fanny headed back to the infirmary.

Charlotte expected it'd be a long night and though she felt shocked and heartsick she'd steal herself to do her job. She'd seen worse.

Charlotte left Fanny with Matron and hurried to the staff room to dry off. There was no sign of Elsie. After that, she headed to the ward to get instructions. Once there, Charlotte, together with nurses and patients wrapped in blankets, gathered at the windows, watching the awful scene on the river—dozens of boats of all sizes had joined the search for survivors. She breathed a sigh of relief, seeing Scott and McWade had pulled Lenny and son, Billy, to safety. Their boat was now moving toward the middle of the estuary to assist in the search.

The rear half of the airship had landed on the water, raging and rushing toward the sea. At first, it was swept along, bobbing and rolling in the waves, but at the river bend it beached itself on a sandbar. Potter and Josh laid Lou on some blankets near the open severed end of the broken ship. He'd lost a lot of blood. They strapped up his broken arm with strips torn from bed sheets from the still-intact crew berths and gave him a wad to stave the bleeding from the gash to his face.

Josh, Bateman, and Potter, with the cat in his arms and his accordion slung over his back, stood next to Lou, surveying the hellish scene. Swirling red fires blazed on the surface and columns of black smoke rose from piles of twisted wreckage. Menacing clouds continued to close in and the smell of death permeated the air. The southwesterly winds carried the stench across the city.

A hundred yards away, the control car floated on its side, its fire extinguished. Lou presumed the occupants were trapped inside. A rescue boat had turned up to investigate and men were pulling someone out through a window. They couldn't see who it was. Lou and Potter exchanged grim looks. As soon as the man had been extracted, the control car rolled over and sank.

Lou looked across at Potter's accordion and spoke in nonsensical monotones. "Will you teach me to play that thing, Walt?"

Potter looked at him strangely. "Course I will, sir."

But it was a promise he'd never keep, and one Lou would soon forget, at least, for now.

"Look!" Josh exclaimed. A boat was heading in their direction. Within a few minutes, it maneuvered alongside and one of the crewmen threw them a line. Lou recognized Maj. Scott and Inspector McWade from his Cardington days. He'd spoken to McWade a few times—a gruff Scotsman. Scott was legendary. Bateman and Josh helped Lou into the boat, where they eased him into a sitting position.

"Any more men aboard?" the riverboat captain asked.

"Just us, I'm afraid," Bateman answered.

"You boys were bloody lucky!" Scott barked.

"Aye, that you were. Didn't even get your feet wet," McWade said.

The boy and his father from the rowboat were sitting down below, wrapped in blankets. Once on board, Fluffy wriggled from Potter's arms and ran below to the boy. The boat moved off and made for the wharf, checking for life among the floating bodies, some mutilated beyond recognition, many tangled in parachutes. Scott took another swig from his flask. Lou remembered how relieved he'd felt for his crewmen when the "lucky ones" had leapt from the dying ship in the last of the parachutes. Then he spotted Bobby. Like many others, he was burned and covered in oil, but one side of his face was clean and recognizable. He'd managed to get Lou's parachute on.

Fat lot of good it did him! And so much for his marriage proposal.

Lou recognized another victim: New York Johnny, not so badly damaged. He'd appeared so serene and peaceful when he'd last seen him on the ladder. He had the same look about him now. Near him, Gladstone, the cabin boy, lay on his back, his skin as black and shiny as the river. He, too, appeared strangely at peace.

The boat made its way to the wharf and they put Lou, barely conscious, on a stretcher and carried him across the road to the infirmary. The other three survivors along with the young fisherman and his dad, followed.

The six survivors rescued by Scott and McWade wound up on one of the wards cleared of patients ready to accept injured airshipmen. Charlotte had been assigned to the emergency operation by the matron. Her friend Fanny was truly thankful. Billy lay on a bed opposite Lou and kept looking across at him and then at his father on a bed beside him.

Lou, though weak and deathly white, was now fully conscious. His arm had been wrapped and temporary dressings applied to his face and naked torso. They'd each been given a thorough examination by a doctor and it was time for Lou to have the deep gash in his face stitched.

"Your name will be 'Lucky' from now on, sir," Josh said.

"We've *all* been lucky," Potter said.

Charlotte looked at Lou for the first time. She hadn't been paying attention. She glanced at the scars on Lou's upper arm and chest.

"What's all this?" she said.

He nodded to his right shoulder and then down at his chest.

"Belleau Wood … Saint-Mihiel," he answered.

Her face registered no expression, as if she hadn't heard. "Is *that* your name—Lucky?"

"No, it's Lou Remington."

"Lucky Lou!" Charlotte said.

"Those closest call me 'Remy'."

Lou's crewmen appreciated Charlotte's beautiful figure and the long legs that her prim nurse's uniform could not conceal. She leaned in closely to Lou's face, pulling the thread tight, drawing the wound together. When she spoke, Lou felt her warm, sweet breath on his face. He breathed in her lingering perfume.

That scent is heavenly. And my God, so is she!

The distraction helped dull the pain and fill the terrible void in his gut.

"Beautiful perfume," he mumbled, closing his eyes, then becoming immediately annoyed with himself.

"Je Reviens," she said softly.

"Je Reviens," he repeated.

"You're gonna look right manly, with this scar," Charlotte said, her voice husky.

Lou peered into her huge eyes, open wide while she concentrated on her handiwork. For a second, she glanced from the wound and met his eyes, before turning away. He felt a tremor course through his body. If it weren't for her striking blue irises, he would've taken her for Italian or French.

God, she's magnificent and she's totally unaware of me.

And she was. He was just another case.

"She does a beautiful job," Josh said. "How did you learn to stitch like that?"

"Practice," Charlotte replied.

"What's your name?" Lou asked.

She pointed to her name badge next to a Red Cross pin. "I suppose you people can read English, can't you?"

Lou squinted at the tiny print on her badge. "Charlotte," he said, nodding with a half smile to himself.

"What's so funny?"

"No—it's my favorite name."

She gave him a disbelieving stare.

"My grandmother's name is Charlotte Remington," Lou said. "You look Italian."

"Black Irish. On my mother's side," Charlotte said. "My grandfather came over to work in the mines."

Charlotte glanced across at Billy who'd been watching and listening to their every word. The boy seemed in awe of Lou. Two orderlies dressed in white arrived at Lou's bedside.

"They're taking you to get a cast put on your arm," Charlotte said.

The orderlies eased Lou into a wheelchair and pushed him out. After the door had swung closed, Potter spoke while Charlotte was gathering up the swabs and dressings.

"If I hadn't stuck with 'im, God knows where I'd be. I'd follow that man anywhere on this earth. God's truth!"

"We *all* owe him, I reckon," Josh said.

Bateman nodded in agreement. Charlotte remained silent. She left the ward sensing Josh watching her as she moved to the door. When she returned, she heard them discussing her behind the curtain. "My God. What a dream that girl is!" the American was saying.

"You might as well take yer eyes off 'er, me old cock. You're wasting your time."

It was Potter, the Englishman, with the rebuke.

"What are you talking about?" the American answered.

"You're looking at Charlotte Remington the Second there, mate."

Charlotte marched past the curtain and glared at them. They gave her a guilty, caught-out look and Josh sighed ruefully. She slid the curtain back roughly against the wall, leaving them no privacy. Charlotte saw Billy was listening intently.

His mother, Fanny, entered the ward. "You and Dad are staying here tonight. We're going to keep an eye on you," she said.

"Oh, that's good," Billy replied.

"Good? You're a funny boy! Snuggle down now. You've had too much excitement, son."

Fanny kissed him and turned to her husband, who was propped up, smoking a cigarette.

"I'm so glad you're all right, Lenny. I don't know what I'd have done if ..."

"Don't you be fretting, Fanny. We're safe and sound, thanks to that major and his Scottish friend."

"Charlotte sent them out to rescue you—God bless that girl!"

Around 2:00 a.m., Lou woke from his nightmare, finding it only too real. His dry mouth tasted of blood and his head throbbed. The cut on his face stung and his arm and shoulder ached. He tried to turn his body, but found it difficult. The smell of burning flesh wafting from the river, hung in the air, tangible and sickly.

In the room's half-light from the windows' glare, he could make out Potter, Bateman, and Josh asleep in their beds. The boy and his father were also dead to the world. The snores rumbled back and forth in unison. It would've been comical if the circumstances weren't so dire. Lenny snored loudly, his lips fluttering as air was expelled with guttural noises followed by long silences, and then spluttering. Answering snores came from down the ward like echoes.

Lou struggled out of bed and hobbled over to the window bumping into a chair, waking Billy. Although night, Lou could see clear across to the other side of the estuary, the river bright with floodlights vividly illuminating search vessels of all types. Some anchored, shone searchlight beams on the dark, fast-running water. Others moved slowly back and forth, scanning the surface. Stationary boats worked on tangled wreckage, trying to dislodge bodies held tightly in its grip. On a tugboat at the wharf, men were unloading covered stretchers, making Lou feel sick. He heard a sound behind him at the door and realized it was *her*. Charlotte came to him at the window. "You need to lie down and get some rest," she whispered. "You've lost a lot of blood."

Lou didn't move. He stood in silence looking toward the river.

"We must have our dead," he said finally. He slowly eased his way back to the bed where he slumped with his head in his hands. "I lost all my men," he said. "I should've done more."

"You did more than enough, I think. The men you saved think you walk on water. You'll feel much better when you get home to America."

"I'm not going home."

"Why ever not?

"I can't go home …not now."

Charlotte stood close to the bed and put her arms around him, holding his head against her breast. She felt his tears on the palm of her hand.

"Hush now. I'm sure you did everything you could. You got three of your mates out, didn't you?"

"Did they bring in any more survivors?"

"They've only found one, so far. The English captain."

"Captain Wann. My God!"

"They said it was amazing," Charlotte said.

"Where is he?"

"In intensive care. He's in a bad way."

"Is he gonna make it?"

She shook her head. "It's very doubtful."

Charlotte gave Lou two sleeping tablets with a glass of water and made him lie down.

She considered for a moment and then said, "One of the girls on the dock picked up a message from the airship. It had one of our nurse's names on it."

"Whose?"

"Elsie …Elsie Postlethwaite."

Lou sighed. "Did you read the message?"

"Yes, I felt I had to, for her sake…"

"What did it say?" But of course, he already knew.

"Marry me and come away. I promise to love you forever. Bobby."

"Did you give it to her?"

"No."

Lou laid his head back and closed his eyes, picturing Bobby holding up the ring box.

"God, it's strange how it goes," he said wearily. He lay still a few minutes, his eyes closed. Charlotte sat watching him. His eyes suddenly opened wide, startling her.

"What the hell's happened to Fluffy?"

"Who's Fluffy?

"The ship's cat. She came back on the boat with us."

"I'll find out what's happened to her. Don't worry," Charlotte said.

He nodded his head thankfully, closing his eyes again. Charlotte sat by the bed holding his hand until he fell asleep. She studied his hand—a strong, beautiful hand. Finally, she reluctantly let it go. She lifted her palm to her lips where his tears had been and kissed it. She stood up and carefully pulled the sheets around him and left the ward. As she left, she noticed Billy wide awake, watching her. He must've seen and heard everything. She put a finger to her lips. He rolled over and went back to sleep. The ward door swung closed behind her.

Damn that little rascal!

Charlotte had been asked to stay on the ward that night, a ward held open with twenty empty beds in case more survivors were brought in. There were none.

She slept on a cot in the nurses' room and two other nurses, one of them Fanny, did the same. In the morning, Charlotte checked on the survivors. They were all sleeping soundly. She then went straight to Mrs. Tilly's bed on her usual ward. Her bed was empty. Charlotte spun around scanning the room—Mrs. Tilly was gone. She knew the old lady had been on her last legs, but it came as a shock. She hurried to the nurses' room where she shed a few tears. Matron found her and sent her back to the ward.

"Get back to your patients. They need you. They all die someday, Charlotte," she said.

2

A COURT OF INQUIRY

May 15, 1922.

A court of inquiry was convened on a warm day the following spring at Howden's court, an old municipal building, far too small for such a gathering. The survivors of the accident attended, with the exception of Josh Stone, who'd been recalled for duty in the United States and Capt. Wann, who'd survived, but not recovered sufficiently to attend.

Lou's face had healed, but the mending of his broken arm had been slow. He sat with Potter and Bateman, also there to give testimony, in the front pew. Lou's companions appeared healthy enough, although they told him they suffered from painful memories and nightmares. It showed.

The stifling courtroom smelled of mildew tempered by cleaning fluid, reminding Lou of his schoolhouse days in Great Falls. It was jam-packed with high-ranking U.S. and British military, government officials, engineers and designers. The whispers and sobs of widows and girlfriends drifted down from the gallery. Maj. Scott sat stony-faced opposite the grieving families. Inspector McWade sat beside him, along with personnel from Cardington's Royal Airship Works, in attendance as expert witnesses. Amongst the hoard of pressmen, Lou recognized George Hunter in his scruffy raincoat. He gave him a nod.

The court rose to its feet as the president of the court, a man with priestly bearing, entered. He was impeccably dressed in a flowing black robe, open at the front revealing an elegant pin-striped suit. He strode to the mahogany desk on the platform and gazed around the room, exuding an aura of omnipotence. He put his hand to his mouth and gently coughed.

"Please be seated," he said.

Everyone obediently sat down. The president remained standing, his face stern, his voice rich—a Cambridge man.

"Good morning, ladies and gentlemen. It is my unpleasant duty to preside over this court of inquiry charged with ascertaining the cause of the tragic accident which occurred on August the twenty-fourth at thirty-seven minutes past five, when His Majesty's Airship *R38,* soon to be re-designated USS *ZR-2,* broke in two and crashed into the River Humber in the City of Hull. On behalf of the court, I wish to express sincere condolences to all those from both sides of the Atlantic who lost relatives and loved ones, colleagues and friends, in this unfortunate event."

The court remained silent, save for the sound of weeping wives and sweethearts who held handkerchiefs to their mouths, trying not to cause disruption. Lou found himself studying his feet. He'd been dreading these proceedings.

"The people of Great Britain are heartbroken over this tragedy which has caused loss of life, not only to our own, but also to our sister nation. This sad event has dealt a terrible blow to the morale and prestige of this country, its military and industry."

During the next four days, Lou listened to the testimony of two dozen expert witnesses, including designers and builders from Howden and Cardington. They discussed problems experienced with the airship during the first test flights. Lou learned much he hadn't known previously, but the questioning appeared to be orchestrated and truth became another casualty. By skilful interrogation, the solicitor general led the court through the events leading up to the accident without really getting to the heart of why the accident happened and how it could have been prevented.

This covered the purchase of the airship by the U.S. Navy for the sum of two million pounds; the design and construction at Cardington; and the arrival of a contingent of American naval airshipmen who were billeted in homes around Cardington and Hull to be trained to fly and maintain the airship, as well as monitor its construction. Lou had been part of that team.

They touched on the early flights only briefly, since the Americans hadn't been allowed to participate, causing a lot of irritation at the time. The subject of "rushing the tests" embarrassed all parties and wasn't dwelt on. Lou didn't have first-hand knowledge concerning this subject, but he and his crewmen realized the ship had not been sufficiently tested.

Lou was sure of one thing: Commodore Maitland hadn't been happy with the tests being cut short. The man had expressed his frustration in Lou's presence. Fierce and irresponsible pressure must have been exerted by both governments to hasten the process.

The three survivors testified at the end of the hearings, Lou being the last. He was to be questioned by the solicitor general, a short, aggressive Yorkshireman with steely, gray eyes and a bald head. Lou got up reluctantly, biting his lip as he buttoned the jacket of his dark blue suit. He marched stiffly across the hushed courtroom to the witness stand, his footsteps echoing on the oak boards. Today, he felt as nervous as New York Johnny. So many people had been waiting to hear Lou's testimony—especially the press—there'd been such a hullaballoo in the newspapers. He was sick and tired of it. Sweating profusely, he delved in his pocket for a handkerchief to wipe his brow, while coughing to loosen the tightness in his throat.

"Good morning, Mr. Remington."

"Morning, sir."

"*Mr*. Remington. Is that how I should address you? I notice you're not in uniform."

"Yes, sir, that'll do just fine."

"You were aboard the airship that afternoon?"

"Yes, sir."

"As an enlisted man?"

"A *senior* enlisted man."

"Not an officer?"

"No, sir."

"What role did you play on the airship?"

"I was chief petty officer, sir. That's similar to chief coxswain over here."

"It sounds like an important job. Were you in charge of a lot of crewmen?"

"That day, ten Americans and twelve British were under my command."

The solicitor general looked surprised. "British, too?"

"Yes, sir. I'd become senior in rank, although still mentored by the British."

Lou could tell by his dubious expression the solicitor general was thinking he'd been in way over his head. "How long had you been a chief petty officer?"

"I was promoted three months before the accident," Lou said.

He didn't much care for the man's tone.

"You're very young—too young, some might say. And I ask you these questions in order to prove your competence—you understand?"

"Perfectly, sir."

"So, prior to your promotion, had you experience in flying airships?"

Lou sensed everyone's eyes upon him, as if they thought he had something to do with the cause of the accident.

"I flew in blimps after the war, sir."

"You joined the Navy, or was it the Army—when?"

"The U.S. Marine Corps in 1914."

"At what age?"

Lou hesitated.

This is complicated.

"Sixteen, sir."

"Sixteen?"

"Yes, on my sixteenth birthday, sir."

The solicitor general frowned.

"What's the minimum age for acceptance into the U.S. Marines?"

"Eighteen, sir."

"How come they accepted you?"

"I lied on my application."

There were looks of surprise and a few raised eyebrows in the courtroom.

"They didn't kick you out?"

"No, they sent me to a special unit."

"They put you on ice, so to speak?"

"Yes, I trained for three and a half years in hand to hand combat and Japanese martial arts, observation and parachute training."

"You must have become a pretty dangerous fellow by that time?"

Lou had become lethal at karate and was on the verge of obtaining his black belt when they shipped him off to war.

"Yes, I became an instructor at Quantico."

Lou glanced up into the gallery and gave a half-smile. He figured someone up there would be paying careful attention.

"They made you a corporal, what the Americans refer to as an E4, before being sent to France in 1918?"

"Yes."

The solicitor general went to the table, poured water into a glass and swallowed a mouthful, pausing to think. He returned to Lou.

"Then after the war, with the rank of sergeant, an E5, you were discharged?"

"Yes."

"What did you do after the war?"

"I joined the Navy, based at Lakehurst, for training in blimps and airships."

"You seem to be a glutton for punishment! Why airships?"

"I thought they were going to be the next big thing, sir."

The solicitor general smirked. "*Cruise ships* in the sky?

Lou smiled faintly. "Yes, I suppose."

"And now?"

"I'm not sure."

The solicitor general peered around the court, searching for a reaction. There was none.

"You came to England when?"

"June, 1920."

"You were based at Cardington during the construction of *R38*?"

"Yes, sir, and then in Howden, after the launching."

"And you've left the Navy?"

"Yes."

"Discharged?"

"Honorably discharged, yes sir."

"Why?"

"I was about to sign on for five more years …"

"And then, this happened. …Are you married?"

"Yes, sir. I am."

"Good. I hope you found a nice, Yorkshire lass."

Lou couldn't help smiling. He peered up into the gallery again, scanning the faces for Charlotte.

"I did, sir."

He spotted her and grinned sheepishly. The solicitor general and everyone else in the court followed his gaze and saw Charlotte smiling down at Lou. Everyone looked happy for a moment.

"I want to say that all of us here in this court congratulate you, not only on your marriage to that lovely girl up there, but on your receiving the Navy Cross. …You did heroic things that day."

"I did *nothing*, sir."

"Mr. Remington, how many stitches did it take to sew up that gash in your face?"

"Seventy-eight."

"And that young lady stitched you up?"

"She did."

"Most people in court know what you did on that horrible day, but for the benefit of the few who don't, I'll elaborate." The solicitor general turned and addressed the court. "With a cut to your face requiring seventy-eight stitches, you threw your own parachute to one of your desperate crewmen. You led this man …" he said, pointing at Potter, "… to safety. You pulled Josh Stone, who was hanging on by his fingertips, back on board the airship, which was now torn in two, receiving a severely broken arm in the process. And you then heaved this man …" pointing to Bateman, "…whom you found dangling from the stern, back on board with your one good arm. No, sir, these actions could not be described as '*nothing*'! We're honored to have you living among us."

Lou wiped his forehead and glanced at the faces. They were all proud of him and one or two people actually shouted and clapped.

"Well done!"

"He's a hero!"

Lou sat shaking his head.

They're all wrong!

The solicitor general paused for the court to take a little pleasure from this moment. Then Lou saw his attitude change back to business. He could tell this lawyer was a skilled and artful interrogator. He'd probably been softening him up. He'd need to keep his guard up.

"Now, going back to the final tests, you and your crew were watching the structure of the ship for signs of weakness. Isn't that so?"

"Yes, sir."

"They told you to *expect* problems?"

"No, but we were instructed to stay alert—keep our eyes open."

Lou glanced around the courtroom. The attention of all was riveted on him. Suddenly, a baby cried out at the back of the court, breaking the stillness. They paused while the young mother in black, soothed the child. Lou glanced at her, and recognized Elsie as one of the nurses from the hospital.

That must be Bobby's child. Poor guy.

"How did you receive this order, Mr. Remington?"

"From the commodore, sir."

This surprised the solicitor general. He put his hand up to his head. Murmurs went up through the gallery. Scott and McWade glanced at one another.

"Really! How so?"

"I'd reported to the control car for instructions."

The solicitor general's eyes opened wide. "You were in the presence of the commodore himself?"

"Yes."

"Did you notice anything abnormal—among the officers, I mean?"

"No, sir. Everything appeared quite normal."

Lou's mind raced back. He remembered the expressions on the faces in the control car.

"Tell the court about the order you were given."

"The commodore said they were due to begin the final test, which would be a tough one. He instructed me to warn the crewmen to be alert and to keep a close eye on all parts of the structure."

"That sounds rather ominous. Did *you* find these tests especially dangerous?"

Lou glanced across at Maj. Scott. He remembered him coming to their rescue on the river estuary. Scott gave him an icy stare. Lou felt ill at ease with these questions. He was torn. He thought of Charlotte and all the English people who'd been good to him over these last months.

They treated me like a son, damn it!

"No. I wouldn't say that."

The solicitor general hesitated, staring out the window toward the quadrangle at the rear of the court. He appeared to be searching for the right words.

"Mr. Remington, there's been a lot of speculation and innuendo in the newspapers about the events of that day. This is a tough question, but one I must ask, I'm afraid. Did you get the impression anyone was trying to impress people gathered at the waterfront with some 'fancy flying'?"

The court fell silent, save for a buzzing sound. Lou gazed up at the clerestory window. A bumblebee was trapped, bumping against the glass. He sympathized with the creature. The droning filled his head, and his mind drifted. He found himself standing in the control car. The tension in the men's faces he'd seen before was now replaced with anguish and horror. Those expressions—now exaggerated and distorted by months of brooding—seriously disturbed him. He relived the commodore giving him the order and then going up to the crewmen who were waiting for him—waiting to do his bidding, to carry out his orders without question, like faithful dogs! Their trusting faces haunted him. Every damned *day,* they haunted him. Every damned *night* they haunted him. Could he have done more? Could he have done something, *anything*, to save them? His head became full of his own voice, yelling.

When the commodore gave me the order I should have screamed:"No! No! No! Don't! This damned thing's gonna fall apart!" Any imbecile would've known that—wouldn't they?

Lou remembered the uneasy tightness in his chest as he climbed those stairs.

I just didn't have the guts, damn it! I can never go home. I could never face their families. I know they'd want to meet me. They'd write and track me down. They'd want a first-hand account of how their sons died. They'd want to know how come I survived while their boys are dead. "What's so damned special about you?" they'd ask.

No longer conscious of anything in the courtroom, Lou heard the American captain shout. *"Remington, look to your crew!"*

Lou put his hand to his throbbing forehead. So many times he'd been woken in the night by the captain's voice out of the darkness. And so many nights Charlotte had consoled him. Lou found himself jarred back from the nightmare by the irritated voice of the solicitor general, his face no longer kindly.

"Mr. Remington. Mr. Remington! Was this about 'fancy flying'?"

Lou glanced up at the clerestory window. The bumblebee was gone.

No question the commodore had made a terrible miscalculation—foolish even, but he wasn't showing off.

"Not at all, sir. It was about a concerned man testing an airship."

The solicitor general's voice became silky—like a blade.

"To *destruction?*"

"As it happened, yes …to destruction," Lou said softly.

The solicitor general resumed his calm and became chatty. He leaned his elbow on the railing in front of Lou, confiding.

"Did anybody tell you this airship was a copy, an almost *exact* copy of a German Zeppelin 'height climber', not designed to carry out radical maneuvers at low altitude?" He then turned and addressed the U.S. naval officers sitting at the front. "*R38/ZR-2* was a copy of the German *L49* high altitude bomber shot down in France. Those airships were constructed with their weight and strength reduced to get out of the reach of our fighters. In other words, they were *pretty* fragile. So, gentlemen, if you're constructing any more airships, please keep that in mind," he said.

The Americans stared back with faces of stone. He turned back to Lou for a comment. Lou struggled to recover, feeling like he'd been slugged with a baseball bat. He knew they were constructing a sister ship in Lakehurst—*ZR-1*—*Shenandoah*—Josh's ship, another Zeppelin copy!

"Er, I didn't know anything about that, sir, no."

"But you do know now."

"Yes, I do now."

Later, Lou realized he'd been used as a pawn for publicity in British politics by the court and by the press. Although the British had done some calculations, the ship that had come apart had been based on a German Zeppelin not meant to be maneuvered at low altitude in the denser air of the earth's surface, where excessive stress would be put on the ship.

Lou knew her back had broken, pure and simple, due to too much rudder in a diving high-speed turn. He understood now why the officers in the control car had been so tense. But he couldn't bring himself to blame Commodore Maitland. Desperately worried about the testing not being adequate, he'd struggled with the responsibility of sending a 'green' crew off to face the Atlantic in an unproven airship. He'd taken drastic measures to prove the ship's airworthiness—fatal ones, as it turned out. Under the strain of full power and full rudder, it was impossible *not* to break the back of that airship. She'd jackknifed. Lou also knew that this charade, this well-choreographed show, had deflected blame from where it truly belonged and attempted to saddle the commodore with it, but Lou hadn't allowed that. He wondered about the solicitor general—wittingly or unwittingly he'd helped Lou make that possible

After three days of cross examination of eye witnesses, the court was adjourned. Before Lou left, he was surprised to find Scott standing beside him with McWade. They shook hands.

"Major Scott," Lou said.

"Just wanted to thank you for your testimony—and your honesty."

"No problem, sir."

"So, you're sticking around—not going home?"

"No, sir. This is home for me now."

Scott was all ears. "Really! What are you doing?"

Lou hesitated. "I'm working in a garage, pumping gas and fixing trucks."

Scott looked pained. "I see—"

The huge frame of the American commander appeared. Lou brightened on hearing his familiar voice. "Good testimony, Remington," he boomed. Commander Horace Dyer towered over them in dress uniform. He was the most senior officer in charge of the American contingent in Britain. They shook hands.

"Thank you, sir," Lou said.

"I just want to say, as far as the Navy's concerned, the door's always open."

"Kind of you to say, sir."

"We're all gonna be pushing off soon. You should think about coming with us. We'll find you another ship. Bring that beautiful bride with you."

"I'm grateful to you, sir. Maybe one day, but not right now."

Their attention was taken by two grief-stricken, nurses—Elsie and Minnie. Elsie, still rather large, was holding an infant, while Minnie looked ready to give birth at any moment. They waddled by, dabbing their eyes with handkerchiefs, sniffing. Lou pitied them.

"Looks like your boys've been busy," Scott said with a smirk.

"It's a damned shame," Lou said.

"If the silly little cows had kept their drawers on, they wouldn't be in this mess. Maybe you should take them back to the States with you, Commander," Scott said.

"Maybe we should," the commander replied. He turned to Lou and put his hand on his shoulder. "Stay in touch, Lieutenant." He gave a formal nod to Scott. "Major," he said and strode off.

Suddenly, there was a scream. Minnie stood by the door holding on to Elsie. Water poured down between her legs, pooling on the floor.

"Saints preserve us!" Scott muttered in disgust. A few people gathered around Minnie and helped her to a chair out in the reception hall. "Get that woman an ambulance!" Scott yelled.

Someone rushed off to find a phone.

Scott resumed as if nothing had happened. "Look, here's my card. I've heard good things about you. I don't like to see talent go to waste. If there's anything I can do, let me know. The airship industry will survive. Those men were all pioneers. They didn't die in vain. Remember that, son." Scott stuck out his hand again and abruptly marched off with the silent McWade. Lou nodded skeptically as they went.

That's the kind of crap people say at funerals.

Lou knew Charlotte would be waiting outside the courtroom and moved toward the doors. He spotted her from a distance and hesitated for a moment, relishing her beauty. He felt like the luckiest man in the world. He was ridiculously in love and it was mutual, but with the joy came gnawing guilt, which never left him. On seeing Lou, Charlotte's eyes lit up. She came and put her arms around him.

"How are you now, love?" she asked.

"It was all a waste of time."

"You were wonderful. I'm proud of you."

Lou didn't feel so impressed with himself.

"It's over. You can put it all behind you now," Charlotte said.

"That's the end of my Zep days, I guess," Lou said.

"Never mind. Who needs *them!* You've got *me* instead!" Charlotte put her hand to his face, gently tracing the scar with her slender fingers, from his right eye down to his chin. She kissed his mouth tenderly, her lips moist and delicious. While he embraced her, he ran his fingers through the mass of black hair cascading down her back.

"You look so handsome, darling. I told you, you would, didn't I?"

They moved through the reception hall, passing Scott and Cmdr. Dyer who kept glancing in their direction, while deep in conversation. Lou thought nothing of it at the time. Minnie now sat in an old leather chair moaning. Elsie stood beside her, holding her own baby. As Charlotte passed, holding Lou's hand, both women looked at Charlotte, bitterness and envy showing in their weary eyes. Charlotte's face registered a twinge of guilt. Bobby's message to Elsie was still in the drawer at her flat.

Damn! I was only trying to save you more pain, love!

Lou led Charlotte to the curb, where his shiny, black and red Rover motorbike was parked. He kick-started the engine and, after donning their goggles and gloves, they climbed on. Charlotte sat side-saddle hugging Lou tightly around the waist. They drove off hopefully into their shared future, but any contentment Charlotte may have felt was crushed by the sight of Jessup, standing some distance away. He dragged on his cigarette and shot smoke into the air from thick, rubbery lips. Mouthing curses, he glared at Lou and spat on the ground like a cobra spraying venom. He threw the dog-end down, grinding it into the dirt with the heel of his boot. God, she hated him! She wondered if Lou had seen him.

A silly question!

After this awful humiliation, it was vowed 'never again.' The British airship industry came to a complete standstill. Both the government and the public lacked the stomach for these monsters in the sky, unlike the Germans who were making a great success of their own program. And so, the enormous, sheds at Howden and Cardington fell silent and into a state of neglect, overgrown with weeds and ivy ... that is until Brigadier General Christopher Birdwood Thomson came bursting upon the scene.

PART TWO

The Flying Scotsman.

SCOTLAND

The young Major Thomson

3

THE BRIGADIER GENERAL & THE FLYING SCOTSMAN

New Year's Eve, December 31, 1923.

T homson bought a first-class return ticket to Aberdeen at King's Cross Station, costing one pound seven and six pence, money he could ill afford, but it wouldn't be seemly to be seen alighting from a second-class carriage with the future Prime Minister of Great Britain waiting to greet him.

He walked to Platform 10, where each day *The Flying Scotsman* left for Edinburgh at 10 o'clock sharp, stopping in York for a fifteen minute break. He had plenty of time. Dropping in at W.H. Smith, he bought peppermints and two newspapers: The left-leaning *Manchester Guardian* and the conservative *Daily Telegraph*. He liked to read both sides of a story, although he invariably agreed with the *Guardian*.

He strolled down the platform past the carriages—counting eight —until he reached the coal tender and the massive Super-Pacific engine. He looked up at the driver and fireman leaning over the rail in blue boiler suits. The two men stared down at him with sullen indifference.

They'll make disparaging remarks the minute I turn my back, I'm sure.

He lingered while the engine got up steam, admiring the magnificent machine in its traditional apple-green livery and crimson crash bars.

British engineering at its finest! No wonder small boys are fascinated with railway trains.

His mind briefly returned to his Boer War days as a young lieutenant tasked with keeping the railways open for the war effort in

South Africa and keeping Kitchener happy. His idle curiosity satisfied, he turned back along the platform and went to his carriage. He climbed into the empty compartment, hoping to remain its sole occupant. He found it torturous to sit for long journeys making polite small talk. Usually, by the end, fellow travelers knew far too much of one's business. Thomson had lots to contemplate, and needed to get his thoughts in order.

Best done in solitude.

After stowing his small suitcase on the overhead luggage rack, he removed his felt Homburg and put it on the seat next to the shabby, leather briefcase. He slipped off his woolen overcoat, folding it with care, though it'd seen better days, and placed it on the rack.

This last morning of December 1923 was damp and chilly, but the carriage was warm enough. It struck him how well appointed trains were nowadays, with corridors leading to the dining car, the bar and the lavatories and even through the coal tender, so crews could be changed without stopping. Transportation fascinated Thomson. This was the Golden Age, not only of fashion, but of luxurious travel by train, by ship, and soon, by air.

Such progress—and so much more to be made, by golly!

The journey to Edinburgh would take eight-and-a-half hours and another two-and-a-half to Aberdeen. He relished it. He'd read his newspapers, write a couple of letters and sit and reflect. He never minded his own company.

Marthe's company is infinitely preferable, of course.

He fished out a peppermint and popped it in his mouth and settled down to scan his newspapers. The price of butter was to be increased by ten percent. A loud blast on a whistle preceded slamming doors. The train lurched forward. No one had entered the compartment at the last moment.

Thank God for that!

He continued updating himself on current events. Both newspapers had run articles summing up the year's political highlights and the recent general election.

Baldwin's Blunder

The Manchester Guardian crowed.

The strategy of calling an election in order to increase the Tory majority had badly backfired. Prime Minister Baldwin already had a substantial majority and the move had been unnecessary.

Stupid fool!

The Conservatives were on the ropes and most likely going to fall. Thomson read the election results in the article, although he knew them by heart:

Tories   258

Labour   191

Liberals   158

If the Labour Party formed a coalition with the Liberals, they'd hold a majority. And with Labour winning more votes, they'd get to choose the leader—almost certainly Ramsay MacDonald—one of three men who'd recently created this new party. Would Labour come to power? That was the question on the nation's mind. Thomson and MacDonald believed their chances were excellent, but nothing in politics was certain. If the Tories collapsed, this would be the first Labour government; a momentous achievement for the radical left—revolution without violence.

The *Guardian* gleefully went on to speculate what Ramsay MacDonald would nationalize and what he might leave alone—the mines and railways being high on the list. Thomson had ideas of his own—the possibilities were infinite, with the sky, quite literally, the limit.

The train sped through St. Albans. Thomson looked up and grimaced. The very name made him squirm. He hated failure. Then, he brightened. If not for St. Albans, he wouldn't be on this train today. He went back to his newspaper. It wasn't long before he was chugging past Cardington toward Grantham through lashing rain. He looked up in time to spot the looming airship sheds in the distance.

To a stranger, at first glance, Christopher Thomson sitting alone next to the window might cut a rather striking figure. A closer look would reveal signs of a man who'd recently been going through hard times—not eating well, not looking after himself, pining for a lost love perhaps. Although his jacket was well pressed, the lapels were threadbare. His face was thin, his cheeks hollow and his close-set, deep blue eyes, which gave the impression of constant scrutiny, were sunken. He stood six feet five, and although slender, his shoulders were broad. His nose, broken by the vicious kick of a horse during a fall, had reshaped his previously symmetrical, angelic face, causing it to have a harsher, granite-like appearance. As a brigadier general, this had only served to enhance his overall demeanor. Under that impressive nose, he had a well-groomed, thick moustache, adding dignity. He could appear menacing when necessary, but congenial, even gentle at times.

Thomson pondered the circumstances bringing him to this point in his life. This was a pivotal moment. He felt certain he'd done the right thing giving up his commission in the Army. During the last twenty-five years he'd reached sufficient heights to satisfy his military ambitions and had played a significant role serving his country. At times, he wished he could do more to improve the lives of others—not a sentiment usually associated with a seasoned brigadier general.

The decision to resign had resulted from his attendance at the Treaty of Versailles as an aide to diplomats of the British delegation. He watched in dismay as European politicians fought over the scraps left after Germany's defeat, a country forced to its knees and made to accept peace terms he thought too harsh.

He decided the time had come to take a stand. He'd witnessed the suffering of people who didn't have the slightest control over their own miserable lives, let alone global events. This damned unnecessary war had been a prime example. 'Lambs led to the slaughter' is what they'd said and in his heart he believed it was a perfect description. He made the decision to enter politics and his journey had begun. The first two years had been a rough ride, in fact, a roller coaster of hellish humiliation.

Leaving the Army after twenty-five years service gave him a stipend of one hundred and fifteen pounds, which he put in his account at Barclays Bank. The grand sum of sixty-four pounds, sixteen shillings and five pence remained. He'd taken a low-priced bedsit in Stockwell, an easy walk to Westminster.

He had a few conservative friends, who thought highly enough of him to get him seated on a panel to advise the government on the wisdom of resuming the airship program. Dennistoun Burney, a director of Vickers Aircraft, had been rigorously promoting a plan for the company to construct six airships to be underwritten and operated by government. Thomson didn't care for Burney's type. A profiteer! The 'Burney Scheme' promoted a program whereby Vickers built *all* Britain's airships—an intolerable situation! Besides, 'state enterprise' would be the wave of the future in the new British Socialist State.

Burney's proposal had been accepted by the Conservative Government in principal, although not ratified.

I will certainly put a stop to that!

Thomson pulled out a file from his briefcase which had been passed on to him by Sir Sefton Brancker—a man always in the know, always with one ear to the ground and always ready to help—a bit of a dandy, but a loveable one. The file contained information concerning one Lieutenant Louis Remington, an American airshipman, who happened to be sitting around in Yorkshire doing nothing. "The man might come in useful," Brancker had said, "since we've lost so many of our own people." Thomson glanced at the man's war record. A marine …survived the war …bailed out twice from observation balloons (*that's amazing—I was in observation balloons, too!*) … survived being hit and buried alive for hours in a bunker with twenty-five others …joined the Navy to fly airships …posted to England … survived the *R38* disaster …displayed fine leadership qualities—gave excellent account of himself at the court of inquiry …discharged 1922. Thomson slipped the file back into his briefcase.

If things go well, I'll drop the Secretary of the Navy a line in Washington …or speak to him on the phone, perhaps. Sounds like a useful chap. That other American fellow—Zachary Landsdowne—they said <u>he</u> was a first class fellow when he worked here with us.

Thomson received no salary for serving on the airships panel, but it propelled him into the right circles. Now he needed to get himself elected to Parliament. It came as a surprise to his friends when he chose to join the Labour Party. Many became angry over the betrayal of his own class when he threw in with 'the radical Left.' The road might have been easier had he joined the Tories, but his idealistic notions prevented that.

In truth, Thomson had no real political doctrine or ideology clearly set in his mind. He'd met a few larger-than-life figures in his time, men he had reason to look up to. He begrudgingly admired visionary Cecil Rhodes, but had more in common with Socialists Lenin and Mussolini. Socialism had to be the answer to life's problems and inequalities. He found it seductive.

Thomson put himself up for a seat in Bristol Central. This hadn't been a pleasant experience and he began to question the wisdom of joining this new Labour Party. He went from one committee meeting to another at working men's clubs and women's organizations—all fiercely left wing. The reception he received from party supporters ranged from frigid to downright hostile. They regarded him as one of the enemy, a filthy capitalist, a toff, upper class, or worse, an aristocrat —the very people causing worldwide misery and keeping them down.

He said the words they needed to hear, but delivered in an irritating hoity-toity tone. Often he used words they didn't understand. They jeered and hooted at him, calling him a 'toffee-nosed git.' He couldn't do much about the way he spoke. His deep, gravelly voice made him sound gruff—perhaps too much like the officers who'd ordered men out of their rat-infested trenches into the German guns to die like vermin, to collapse in the mud and filth and left to rot on the endless dumpsite called 'No Man's Land', to later have their bleached bones tilled into the soil like fertilizer. All that, while the senior officers in their fancy uniforms and shiny boots remained in safety well behind the front lines. *They* weren't unwashed and plagued by lice, driven mad by trench foot, sickened by contaminated food and the stench of rotting bodies. That was the way they felt and at the mere mention of the war, they became infuriated and yelled abuse at him.

"Oh, yeah, where were you, then mate, eh? What were you doin' while our lot were dyin' up front?"

Thomson managed to increase Labour's vote count from the last election, although this hadn't been enough to win in that Conservative stronghold. He tried again the following year, putting himself up for a seat in St. Albans. He campaigned hard, said all the right things, but the result was the same. They called him an imposter and a spy. He became demoralized, not used to rejection.

Thomson had always scoffed at politicians, believing them to be a spineless, self-serving lot. Now, he found politics to be a rough business and his respect for its participants grew. Sometimes he questioned his own motives. Was all this really about improving the plight of the downtrodden, or was it more about *her*?

Thomson scratched his head and glanced at the gold watch given him by his mother. An hour had passed. He peered out the window, hoping for an answer in the sopping landscape. The sky had turned dark over what he guessed must be Grantham. In the gloom, his gaunt reflection stared back from the glass. Nagging guilt seized him. He was circumventing the system—not like him at all. He'd always earned his way—worked for everything he got.

After the crushing defeat in St. Albans, he'd received a letter bearing the Labour Party name with a return address in Lincoln's Inn Fields. It was a short handwritten note from Ramsay MacDonald, leader of the new party, asking him to meet at a tea room at Charing

Cross. Thomson knew of it as a place frequented by writers, artists, Fabian Society members and other left-leaning types. Thomson wasted no time writing back.

They met at the café in summer '23. When they shook hands, they took a liking to one another immediately. Everybody knew MacDonald, but here was a new face. Other patrons watched in silence, sensing an important moment. After two or three coffees, they walked along the Thames Embankment. MacDonald told Thomson not to dwell on his election defeats, though he didn't realize it now, his 'baptism of fire' was all to the good; he'd turn out to be a stronger politician.

MacDonald understood the obstacles Thomson had been facing, but there'd be a place for him in the party. He said being surrounded by hot-heads, he needed an ally and a confidante—someone capable of calm, rational thought. An election would be coming soon. MacDonald sensed it in his gut. He urged Thomson to sit tight.

During this time, Thomson served on the airship advisory panel and was befriended by Sir Sefton Brancker, Director of Civil Aviation. Brancker went out of his way to help him, sensing Thomson faced not just financial hardship, but perhaps ruin. He arranged for Thomson to go on a paid speaking tour in Canada, and Thomson gratefully accepted. Thus, another momentous friendship began.

MacDonald's instincts had been right. An election was held December 6, 1923 and the Tories didn't win a clear majority. MacDonald asked Thomson to forgo his visit to Canada and meet him instead at his home in Lossiemouth in the Highlands. Labour's time had come!

The train thundered through Sheffield, then Leeds and on to Doncaster through blinding rain, then toward brightening skies. At ten minutes past two, the train made its fifteen-minute stop in York. Thomson put on his overcoat and paced up and down the platform in the drizzle. He couldn't wait to get to Aberdeen.

Returning to his compartment he took out his fountain pen, and using his briefcase to rest on, made some notes in his bold hand.

Cardington

Airships

Employment

State Enterprise

Keep Capitalists (Burney) Under Control

Gov Funding

Links to Empire

Improvement and betterment of mankind

He crossed out the last line.

Too grandiose.

Underneath that, he wrote:

My Title?

The train rushed through the counties of Yorkshire and Durham toward the border, where it traveled the long viaduct and over the River Tweed into Scotland. After a brief stop in Edinburgh, it continued toward Aberdeen. Before crossing the Forth Bridge, the train slowed to half speed. At mid span, they were hit by a fierce squall, causing the carriages to shake and creak, rain beating against the windows like gravel. Thomson thought about the Tay Bridge, which had collapsed in a storm. He knew this bridge had been built to new designs by different engineers using steel instead of cast iron. He was unfazed, secure in the belief that British designers had learned their lessons from previous mistakes.

Let it blow all it likes! This bridge is as solid as the Rock of Gibraltar.

It was dark outside. The Flying Scotsman's rapid progress was now impeded by steep gradients and sharp curves of the Highlands. As it climbed, the wheels made a dogged, metallic 'clacking.' Lulled by the sound, Thomson's mind became filled with thoughts of Marthe. What would he do about her? What *could* he do about her? She was his most difficult, and by far, most important problem.

Problem? That's too harsh a term.

If he did call her a problem, she was certainly one he would not wish to be without. She caused him pain—exquisite pain that never went away, clawing at him constantly. He'd been so close in the past, but like a beautiful bird, she always remained just out of reach and ready to fly off.

I'm a man forever in pursuit—that's the mark of a true thoroughbred woman! Why am I—someone who has commanded thousands of men in the worst hells on earth—as docile and compliant as a new born lamb in this delightful creature's hands?

March 24th, 1915 had changed him forever. The Romanian King Ferdinand had hosted a soiree at Cotroceni Palace in Bucharest. There, British diplomats had told Thomson he'd be contacted by an official at the highest level. Thomson had stood in the lower hall of the reception area from which a grand staircase swept up to the galleries above, between cascading fountains and palm trees. While a five-piece orchestra played chamber music, he chatted with British embassy personnel about life in Romania—a mountainous country he found breathtakingly beautiful.

The walls flanking the staircase, lined with paintings of Romanian rulers and warriors from centuries past, reached up to the crystal dome a hundred feet above. He watched as Princess Marthe made her regal entry. Gliding down the stairs, she moved as though suspended in air. He took in every part of her: her beautifully shaped hands and fine fingers on the gleaming brass rail, her slender arms exposed from the three-quarter-length sleeves of a gown that did not hug her body, but hinted with subtlety at what lay beneath. Made of black and dark green satin overlaid with chiffon, the gown had a scooped neck, which perfectly set off a shimmering diamond necklace. He took note of her shapely ankles and delicate feet fitted into the latest-fashion shoes— stylish, black and dark green kid pumps with Louis heels, steel beaded and embroidered—perfectly complementing her dress. Her shining, dark brown hair, gathered and pulled back tightly to her head, accentuated her high cheekbones and fell in a coil at the neck. Her eyes were black and bituminous and her skin as smooth and white as porcelain. Her slightly open, full, red lips, revealed perfect, even, white teeth.

From the moment she put her foot on the top step, her eyes rested upon him, making him feel as though he were the only person in that crowded room. For months he'd been in miserable surroundings in France and Belgium, where the sight and stench of death were an unbearable weight he'd learned to live with. She awakened in him intense joy of living and of love, a sharp contrast after being dead so long in mind and body. Thomson stood and marveled, becoming deaf to all sound in the room—the orchestra and the chatter of people around him. He listened to the soft rustling of her dress as she approached. When she drew close, he realized her eyes were, in fact, dark green, not black. Staring into them for the first time, he saw both joy, and sadness, as well as the thing they most had in common—loneliness.

He was suddenly struck by the recognition that this had happened to him before. There had been a magnificent young creature in an open-topped white carriage on a summer's day in 1902 on Rue de Rivoli. She'd taken his breath away and he still carried the vision of that girl with him to this day. He often dreamed of her. How old would she have been? Fifteen—maybe younger! Surely, this couldn't be her, thirteen years older. He tried to calculate. His mind wouldn't function.

That was Paris. This is Bucharest. Silly romantic notions. Stop it!

His palms sweated. His throat became dry. He smiled at her, as though reuniting with a lost love. He reached out and took her hand and kissed it.

"Princess Marthe, I am—"

Her Parisian accent stunned and captivated him, once again setting off thoughts of the girl in the white carriage.

"My dear Colonel Thomson, I know exactly who you are and why you're here, and naturally, I'll be *completely* at your disposal," she said, fluttering her long, dark eyelashes. From that moment, Thomson was a lost soul. The evening was perfect, the attraction seemingly mutual. They conversed in English and French and even a little Italian and German. They didn't leave each other's side the entire evening. People assumed they were a couple.

Marthe became invaluable to him during his months in Romania, enabling him to accomplish the task that he'd been sent by Lord Kitchener to carry out—to bring Romania into the war—a mission he didn't believe in, since he knew that country was totally unprepared. Marthe had a complete grasp of Romanian politics and access to every politician who mattered—her father the Foreign Minister, the Prime Minister—even the King himself. They saw much of each other and Thomson's attachment grew into blind, unconditional love.

True, she'd been married into the aristocracy at fifteen. To Thomson, this didn't count as marriage, and besides, her husband was an absentee spouse, always in pursuit of fast cars, fast aeroplanes and loose women. Thomson was thankful and prayed the fool wouldn't learn the error of his ways. He soldiered on, hoping one day she'd be his. He couldn't bring himself to face the fact that Marthe, a devout Roman Catholic, would never divorce her negligent husband. But racing cars and aeroplanes were dangerous pastimes—who knew? Fate could intervene.

During that magnificent spring, their love grew with a magical intensity found only in romantic fairytales—'The Soldier and the Princess', this one might have been called. One night, at her home on the banks of the Colentina, thoughts of marriage must have been going through her head. She'd thoughtlessly left her diary open beside her bed:

Kit has been my guardian angel. Oh, to lift the veil to see what might be written in the stars! Tonight, he came to me with special roses and the promise of his eternal devotion.

Had it been thoughtlessness, or had she left it there purposely for him to read? Eight years later and he *still* couldn't fathom that. Thomson often thought about those words written in her beautiful hand, now etched into his brain. Had she been romancing? Or worse, leading him on? Did she believe, as he did, that her husband's activities were too dangerous for his survival? He must surely die in an air crash sometime. Or did she contemplate facing up to the Catholic Church? Most unlikely! At times, he put it down to a young woman's fantasy during a war-time romance brought on by the death of her beloved father. Impossible thoughts! His mind went round and round like a damned carousel and he began to curse the day he'd seen her diary. That careless or deliberate act had shaped his destiny and sealed his fate. Over the years, he tortured himself with longing, just as he was doing now on this dark night, alone in a railway carriage somewhere in the Scottish Highlands. He'd seen photographs of young, handsome men in ornate gold frames on Marthe's dressing table; one was George, her husband, two she said were beloved cousins, while another was 'a very dear friend'—Prince Charles-Louis, away at the Front.

After Thomson's negotiations with the government, Romania entered the war and in a matter of months Germany invaded and overwhelmed the country, just as he'd predicted. Before supervising the destruction of the country's oil wells (ironically, aided by Marthe's husband, George), Thomson helped Marthe escape to safety. Then he got posted to Palestine, where he spent the remainder of the conflict alone with his bitter sweet memories.

After the war, Thomson took part in the surrender of the Ottoman Empire aboard HMS *Agamemnon* at Moudros Harbor in the Greek Islands. After that, he worked on the Armistice in France until the end of 1919. Throughout the tumultuous years from their meeting to the present day, his romance with Marthe entailed endless separation, relieved by touching letters and all-too-rare meetings in London, Paris and, after the war, Bucharest. He always kept a few of her letters with him. He had some in his briefcase on the seat beside him tonight, along with one her shoes wrapped in white tissue. The letters were tied with one of her blue silk ribbons. He carefully took out one of the worn envelopes, and held it to his nose for traces of her divine scent. He clasped the sacred document, reading her words. He'd written to her constantly and she'd never failed to reply, albeit late sometimes, particularly as time went by. He suspected she must have been forming new attachments, or renewing old ones with 'dear friends' home from the Front.

His thoughts and actions constantly swirled around her. He was a man ensnared, but he'd have it no other way. He was blissfully happy in his unhappiness. If he managed to gain a post in His Majesty's Government, he believed his stock would rise, which might cause things to change dramatically in his favor. Where there was hope, there was life.

Thomson was jolted from his reminiscences as the train slowed and blew its whistle before entering Aberdeen. It eased its way into the quaint country station of damp, gray stone where Ramsay McDonald waited to greet him. Suddenly, he remembered it was New Year's Eve. His spirits rose.

Thomson stepped down from his carriage and the mustachioed McDonald came forward with two hands outstretched. He wasn't as tall as Thomson, but he exuded extraordinary charisma, making him larger than life. He had an earnest face and his blue eyes sparkled with both passion and with pain.

"My dear Thomson. Happy New Year to you!"

"Mr. MacDonald. Yes, I'm sure it's going to be a very special New Year for you and for us all! But you shouldn't have bothered coming to the station, sir."

"Nonsense! We've not a moment to lose, we've lots to talk about —and please call me Ramsay. Come, I'm in the local cab. One of the few cars we have in Lossie!"

The two men headed for the taxi, and once inside, McDonald pulled the privacy window closed. "Excuse us, Jock," MacDonald called to the driver.

The journey to Lossiemouth took almost two hours, during which time they made small talk. Although it was dark and he could see little, Thomson sensed he was in a desolate place.

"I hope you brought your walking shoes?" MacDonald asked.

"Yes, I remembered."

"We'll get some of this clean Scottish air down your lungs. We'll walk and talk whilst you're here, laddie," MacDonald said. "And we'll make plans."

"I look forward to that. I can't wait to see the beautiful countryside."

"This is God's own country. I promise you'll love it."

The taxi turned into a gravel drive and stopped outside a two-story house nestled between sycamore trees. The wind hissed in their swaying branches. Lights in the windows and on the porch were warm and welcoming. Before getting out of the car, MacDonald gestured toward the house.

"This is our home. Built this for my mother and children in 1909 and she lived here till she died two years later. She loved it and so do we, still. Nothing's changed since Mother's time—except we have electricity now. Ishbel, my daughter, keeps things running smoothly."

They climbed out of the taxi and Thomson attempted to pay the driver, but MacDonald told him to forget it. "I pay Jock for his services each week," he said.

A handsome young woman of about twenty opened the door with a gracious smile, the resemblance to her father clear.

"This is Ishbel. Looks like me, but lucky for her, she has her mother's common sense."

"Mr. Thomson, welcome to 'The Hillocks'. Please come in and make yourself comfortable," Ishbel said, in her distinctive Highland accent. "Come in and get warm. I'll get the tea mashing." She ushered the men into the parlor, where a fire crackled in a large fireplace with a black cast iron surround, incorporating a cooking stove. They stood for a moment warming themselves before removing their coats.

"My close friends call me Christopher, CB, or Kit. So, please, no more Mr. Thomson."

Ishbel smiled. "Very well, I shall call you Christopher," she said, taking the boiling kettle from the fireplace hob. She poured hot water into a brown earthenware teapot and put on the woolen tea cozy.

"And *I'll* call you CB!" MacDonald said.

Over the fireplace, on the two-tiered mantel among the knick-knacks, were family photos Thomson took to be of MacDonald's mother, wife and six children. Thomson listened to the loudly ticking clock at center as it began striking the eleventh hour. The day had been long.

One more hour. Who knows what the New Year will bring?

In a glance, Thomson realized his impression from the exterior had been correct; this was the coziest of places. He felt the presence of MacDonald's wife and mother looking over them, a position now fulfilled by Ishbel—a role she obviously took pleasure in. After several cups of tea and ham sandwiches, MacDonald announced a toast. He opened a bottle of local Scotch and poured out three glasses.

"We welcome you, my dear CB, to Lossiemouth and to our home. Here's to you. We wish you a most pleasant stay," MacDonald said.

"I'm honored to be here in this delightful place," Thomson said, "especially for Hogmanay—a time sacred for Scotsmen. I didn't bring you any coal and now I kick myself. Anyway, from this Indian-born Englishman, please accept sincere wishes to you both for a happy and progressive new year."

The three raised their glasses.

"Don't worry about the coal, CB. We'll soon have plenty, you'll see," MacDonald said.

MacDonald was right. As the clock on the mantel struck twelve, there was a commotion at the front door. Local people crowded into the house carrying lumps of coal and bottles of Scotch. Glasses were poured and toasts proposed. They wished MacDonald luck in his aspirations, though nobody mentioned the words 'Prime Minister.'

The small band of well-wishers was soon gone and Thomson, MacDonald and Ishbel were left alone in the parlor, uplifted, but exhausted. After clearing away the glasses and putting the pieces of coal in the hearth, Ishbel led Thomson upstairs to his bedroom, explaining that this was 'Mother's room' reserved for 'special guests.'

Thomson felt honored. The room was spacious, its slanting ceilings contoured to the roof with white painted beams and boards. White bed linens and curtains contrasted with the antique hardwood furniture and dark board flooring. At the center was an inviting single bed, with plenty of fluffed pillows and a matching eiderdown. Beside a small casement window was a chest with a bowl and water jug with neatly folded towels. Most welcoming of all: a fire in the grate, made him feel warm and secure.

Thomson thanked Ishbel as she left, closing the white, planked door behind her, the metal thumb latch clanking in its keep. This was luxury after his miserable bedsit in Stockwell. He wearily undressed and climbed into bed, the metal springs complaining until he was still. He was pleasantly surprised to find not just one hot water bottle in the bed, but two. He was asleep within seconds, dreaming.

It was Paris, the year 1902 on Rue de Rivoli. As a young lieutenant, he trudged behind a white horse-drawn carriage as it moved slowly up the dirt road, flanked by cloistered stone buildings. He could see the back of a young girl in the carriage. She wore a white dress and a matching wide-brimmed hat. He longed to catch a glimpse of her face, sensing he knew her. No matter how hard he tried, he couldn't keep up. He watched in dismay as the carriage gradually pulled away. The driver, dressed in black livery and a top hat, turned and looked over his shoulder at him with a mocking grin.

4

HIGHLAND WALKS

January 1, 1924.

Thomson didn't stir until Ishbel knocked gently and placed a tea tray on the floor beside the door. Thomson opened his eyes, squinting against the glorious morning sunlight that streamed through the small casement windows.

"It's seven thirty, Christopher. Breakfast will be served at eight," she called.

"Thank you, Ishbel."

"No trouble at all," she said.

Thomson listened to her footsteps receding down the stairs. He jumped out of bed and gazed out at the frosty fields and snowy hills in the distance. He felt marvelous.

Washed and dressed in brown corduroy trousers and a matching woolen sweater, Thomson went down to the parlor. MacDonald was already seated at the oak table drinking tea. He was slightly more formal, wearing a white shirt and a tie with a V-neck tartan jumper.

"Ah, there ye are, laddie. Did'ya sleep all right?" he asked. "Ready to face the day?"

There it was again. Thomson had never been called 'laddie', but took it as a term of endearment. "I've never slept so well in my life, Ramsay."

"After your journey, I expect you could've slept on a clothes line," MacDonald said.

"I actually enjoyed the train. Gave me time to think."

Ishbel put down plates of eggs, bacon and mushrooms in front of them. A young girl in a white apron stood holding a thick slice of bread to the fire on a brass toasting fork.

"Toast is coming. Martha is our helper," Ishbel said.

"Ah, Martha! My favorite name," Thomson said, making the girl smile shyly.

"I'm going to suggest you and I stretch our legs this morning. We have some wonderful walks in Lossie," MacDonald said.

"Splendid. I just peeked out of my window and the view is stunning."

"I like to walk. Clears my head. We can get to know each other."

After breakfast, they wrapped themselves up in warm coats and swallowed a tot of Glenfiddich. The air was cold, but it was sunny and the wind had dropped. Thomson found the calling of the seabirds overhead and the biting fresh air, exhilarating. They set off down the lane toward the little town center. After a few minutes, they stood outside a dilapidated, ridiculously small, stone cottage.

"I was born in this wee one-room house," MacDonald said.

Thomson was intrigued, realizing just how far this man had come. MacDonald led him along the street where people smiled and wished them a 'Happy New Year.' Others, though, crossed the road and passed by on the other side, refusing to look in their direction.

MacDonald chuckled. "You see, not everybody loves me," he said.

Thomson gave him a wry smile. "Apparently not."

After a few minutes they stopped again, this time in front of an ivy-clad house with an overgrown garden. This dwelling was much larger.

"This is where I grew up," MacDonald said.

Thomson was unable to tell if this was pride in MacDonald, or shame. The man was clearly showing him who he was and where he'd come from.

"Our childhoods couldn't have been more different. My earliest recollections are of India. I lived there until I was four," Thomson told him.

They walked to the Lossie River, which meandered lazily into the sea just a few hundred yards away. Crossing over a small wooden footbridge, they wandered down to the beach where the foamy surf at low tide made a soft hiss. Thomson sucked the sea air deep into his lungs. They strolled in silence for a while, wrapped up in their own thoughts. Thomson pondered the question of Marthe and whether he dare broach the subject. He took the plunge.

"Ramsay, there's something I need to mention from the onset."

MacDonald appeared mystified, perhaps a little worried, but waited patiently.

"I'm involved with a woman. Have been for the last eight years. She's married—a princess."

"My word, how splendid. A *princess* no less! My God, man, I thought you were going to tell me you'd committed robbery or murder."

Hugely relieved, Thomson smiled.

I'm a fool. This man already knows all about her. He's done his homework. Canny, old Scotsman!

"And you're in love with this woman?"

"I'm afraid so."

"Afraid so! Don't be afraid. I was in love with the most wonderful woman in the world, but I lost her."

"Yes. I'm sorry."

"My wife was the bravest person I've ever known. She fought for the working class all her short life, championing women's causes and encouraging them to unionize." Thomson knew that when his wife had died, MacDonald was sick with grief for years to the point of total collapse. "She was the sun in my universe. When she went, the world fell into pitch darkness—and it still is for much of the time."

"I hope you can take solace in the children she gave you," Thomson said.

"Yes, there's that to be thankful for." MacDonald turned his face away toward the sea. A squall was building on the horizon. Thomson bowed his head, sharing the man's sorrow. MacDonald suddenly looked up as though he'd received a shot of adrenaline.

"So you're in love, my boy. Wonderful! That's all that matters. Love is all!"

This pleased Thomson. Marthe's beautiful face filled his mind. He knew she'd be delighted to hear MacDonald's words, if only one day she could.

"I'm glad you don't disapprove, Ramsay."

"No, I *wholeheartedly* approve! Every man needs the love of a good woman. When love comes along, grasp it with both hands."

"You don't see this as being a possible hindrance or political embarrassment?"

"Och, no! Most of the people in Parliament have doxies on the side. Same with the Royals—the aristocracy are even worse!"

"And what about you? Do you see yourself marrying again?"

"No, no. Plenty of women show interest, especially now of course. But no one could fill Margaret's shoes. I could never fall in love with another woman. Real love comes only once in a lifetime. You know, there's nothing I wouldn't give to spend one more day with her. Just one day."

"But not your immortal soul?"

"Oh, no! I shall need that for when we're reunited, laddie." They continued along the beach in silence until the sand turned to shingle, then headed inland toward the river and followed the footpath along its bank.

"They said I was a bloody, godless, Commie bastard, you know," MacDonald said suddenly. Thomson showed slight surprise. He'd heard vicious things, but dismissed them."Wouldn't let me build our home on Prospect Terrace. 'No Red bastard will build up here,' they said. Oh well, I like it where we are. It turned out fine."

"It's a wonderful location," said Thomson.

"Well, they got it partly right. I am a bastard."

"Ramsay!" He'd heard this before and dismissed that, too.

"My mother was a seamstress, God bless her, and my father, a ploughman. She wouldn't marry him." MacDonald laughed, but it sounded hollow. Thomson found himself speechless. MacDonald pointed to the hills in the distance. "See the fairways over there? Moray Golf Club. They expelled me—for my stance on the war. I vehemently opposed it. Truth is, they got me out because I wasn't good enough—no pedigree."

"I'm sorry they treated you badly, Ramsay."

"Are you sure you want to get mixed up with me?" MacDonald asked earnestly.

"Ramsay, it'd be an honor."

The path led into a pine wood and, as they entered, MacDonald pulled out a hip flask and offered it to Thomson who took a swig, savoring the exquisite Scotch.

"Such a wonderful New Year's Day," Thomson said, wiping his mouth as the liquor warmed his belly.

"*This* is Macallan! Best Scotch in the world; distilled right here in Moray," MacDonald exclaimed.

"Mm, excellent!"

"When I opposed the war, they painted 'Traitor' on our front garden wall. Said I was a German sympathizer. I tell you this: I did oppose the bloody war and I'll oppose the next one, too—unless we're attacked, of course."

"I'm a soldier and I despise war myself. Most military men do."

"I may be a pacifist, but I went over to the trenches at the Front in Ypres to see our boys and they threw me out—had me arrested and shipped home," MacDonald said. Thomson was incredulous. "When I got back to England I went straight to Lord Kitchener and complained. He was furious."

"Kitchener was a good man," Thomson said.

"After that, he gave me free reign to go wherever I pleased on all fronts, which I did. Saw some action. It was dreadful—but I don't need to tell *you* that."

MacDonald offered Thomson the flask and he took another drink. MacDonald did the same. "CB, I may be a bastard, but I'm still a patriot—I'm not a bloody Commie. The carnage I saw on that battlefield and in those field hospitals was appalling—broke my heart, I can tell you. Convinced me more than ever: War is evil! I witnessed the slaughter and suffering of our men, driven mad by non-stop shelling, mustard gas, lice, sores, trench-foot, hunger and exhaustion. Just boys most of 'em, up to their thighs in water, filth and body parts. Blown to pieces—dead or maimed in mind and body. I was right to oppose it!"

"You *were* right, Ramsay. I was at Ypres, myself."

"Bless my soul! We may have rubbed shoulders in that hell hole."

They walked on in silence through the leafless woods until MacDonald stopped and took hold of his own coat lapels as if addressing a multitude.

"It was a crime against humanity, that's what it was!"

"Indeed it was."

"I love this little country and our great empire. My goal is to make sure the sun never sets upon it—and it never shall, as long as we honor

God and we're faithful to our convictions. Yes, yes, I know this all sounds odd coming from an old left-winger like me. Most Leftists, Progressives and Socialists are Atheists. I'm not one of 'em. I'm not *overly* religious, but I do believe in God. I really fear that if we turn our back on Him, *He* will turn away from us and say, 'Very well, if ye want Satan—then ye shall have him in *abundance*'."

Thomson nodded in agreement. He wasn't sure if MacDonald was quoting from the Bible. It sounded like it.

"You see, I'm not the radical they say I am. There's a vast difference between a Socialist and a Communist. I believe in fairness and opportunity for all people. Everyone deserves a doctor and a roof over their heads. I believe socialism is the best hope for the world."

MacDonald continued tugging his jacket lapels. He strutted around mesmerizing his audience of one. "Marx was right about many things; he said capitalism could never survive. I believe in freedom for all people. Socialism will provide that: freedom from poverty, freedom from hunger, freedom from suffering, freedom from fear and freedom from ruthless employers. The workhouse must be abolished forever! The working class deserves those freedoms. We must stand together behind the state, for state ownership and state enterprise. The wealth of the nation must be shared; it must be spread for the benefit of all. The pie is large and must be cut up into equal parts. I don't believe in revolution—not violent revolution—I'm not a revolutionary! But I *do* believe in change; change by persuasion, by appealing to people's intellect and their better nature. I'm not really an imperialist, or a colonizer, but I do believe, having *inherited* the situation, we have a golden opportunity and an obligation to improve the lot of others in all those far off places. Our goal will be: the betterment of mankind throughout the empire—and the world!"

"And we shall achieve that goal, Ramsay. I'm certain," Thomson assured him. "But when we've made the world into a perfect place, what need of us will they have then?"

"The poor will be always with us, CB. That's not something you need worry about—not in our lifetime."

Thomson listened in wonder, he'd much to learn. They came out of the wood onto a country road and walked to the Garmouth Hotel, a quaint stucco building with gabled roofs.

"You must be ready for lunch. I'm starving," MacDonald said.

The hotel manager greeted MacDonald warmly, obviously expecting them. He led them into a small dining room with low ceilings and a table set with fine linen and sparkling silver. First, they drank beer to quench their thirst. After a splendid lunch, they enjoyed brandy and cigars while they waited for Jock to come and take them back to 'Lossie'.

New Year's Day ended with a cosy evening at 'Hillocks' by the fire, exchanging stories. Ishbel sat crocheting silently in a corner. Thomson perceived Ishbel to be an intelligent young woman whose advice was often sought by her father. After an early nightcap and a cup of cocoa, Thomson excused himself and climbed the stairs to Mother's room.

Three more wonderful days passed, walking and talking and visiting various landmarks. On Thomson's last day during a walk in Quarry Wood, near Elgin, MacDonald stopped in his tracks, as if a thought had just occurred to him.

"What do you want?" he asked, his eyes piercing.

Thomson was taken by surprise. "What do I want?"

"What Ministry do you want? Foreign Ministry? War?"

Canny, old Scot! I like this man.

"Air, I think."

"Air! Why Air?"

"I thought you'd want to take the Foreign Ministry yourself. As for the War Ministry—I think it might ruffle a few feathers. Many of those people were my superiors."

"I suppose you're right. Might set off a few fireworks!"

"I've given this a lot of thought. I think I could do well with the Air Ministry, in view of my time on the airship advisory panel," Thomson said.

"Hmm. The Air Ministry?"

"There's so much potential. Air power will be one of the most important developments in the country's future—the empire's future. It has so much to offer regarding employment—absolutely vital to the success of your government," Thomson said.

"*Our* government!" MacDonald corrected him.

Later that morning, they were driven to the Elgin Hotel, one of the oldest and finest in Moray, where MacDonald had arranged luncheon. Once again, they were warmly welcomed by the manager who seated them at the window in a private Victorian dining room with splendid views of the countryside. Over bowls of mushroom soup, MacDonald raised the question of how Thomson was to be slipped into his government, should they take up the reins of power.

"To bring you in, it'll be necessary for me to raise you to the peerage, I'm afraid," MacDonald said, with an apologetic frown. Thomson had anxiously awaited this discussion. The future—especially where Marthe was concerned—rested on this. He was ready.

MacDonald continued. "So, you'll have to become 'Lord Thomson of something or other.' Any thoughts about that?"

"Of Cardington, I think." Thomson said without hesitation.

"*Cardington!* Where does that come from?"

"Cardington in Bedfordshire. The center of the airship industry, or it was. It will be from there, that we'll begin its revitalization. We'll create thousands of new jobs under this, the cornerstone, of our new state enterprise policy."

"You certainly *have* been giving this a lot of thought. Good. *Air* it is then. As long as you don't go buzzing around all over the place. I need a man with a wise head fixed reliably on his shoulders and his feet planted firmly on the ground."

"Thank you, Ramsay. I'm delighted."

"Airships, eh. I don't know. Aeroplanes are okay, but airships …"

"They've fascinated me since I got bombed by a Zeppelin in

Bucharest in 1914," Thomson told him.

"Sounds unpleasant. I hope you're not planning to drop bombs on anyone."

"No. The goal will be the building of a luxurious, mass air transportation system reaching around the globe. The Germans are well ahead in this field and we must catch up."

They sat through the next two courses discussing the nationalization of other industries, banking in particular. MacDonald spoke about the need to build vast tracts of 'state housing' for the working classes. Over dessert, Thomson laid out his ideas for setting up his 'New British Airship Program.'

"I'll propose that the whole scheme be set up as two entities, one being state enterprise, and the other 'private' or 'business—capitalist.' The head of Vickers, Dennistoun Burney, has ideas of private industry taking over the whole future airship industry—with profit being his sordid motive, of course. I plan to head Burney off and keep him contained. My intent is to show the country once and for all that we should look to government to do things properly—and fairly. Once we prove this point by building the best airships, the most luxurious and the safest in the world, the profiteers will never be able to compete, because government won't have the burden of profit built into the cost. They, on the other hand, will be shackled by the need to make money for greedy shareholders eager for their dividends. This will be a contest. A contest they can *never* win!"

"Most interesting and challenging! Well thought out. The world will be watching," MacDonald said. "We shall drink a brandy to your success."

"Burney knew I was on the airship panel. He must have known of my political leanings. He probably contributed money to the campaign funds of my opponents in my two election attempts," Thomson complained.

"He did nothing illegal. To capitalists, money is like mother's milk. Welcome to the cruel, rough-and-tumble world of politics, dear boy. But he didn't win did he? You're going to be the one in the driver's seat!"

"Yes, I'll defeat him and leave him in the dust. I plan to bury him along with capitalism."

"That's the spirit, CB!"

When Thomson inquired about a bill, it was brushed off. No bill was presented to the table—not that Thomson had much money to pay. He only had four pounds in his wallet.

"Your English money is no good here," MacDonald said.

"You're too kind, Ramsay," Thomson replied. "Now I must get ready for my journey home tomorrow."

MacDonald studied him kindly for a moment.

"I hope you'll forgive me for saying so, but I know you've been a little down at heel …living in that Stockwell bedsit …" MacDonald began. Thomson had seen him glance at his threadbare jacket lapels and felt ashamed. "…But all that's about to change. I know your pain. When I came to London before I was married, I was starving—no I mean, *literally* starving! My mother used to send me oatmeal by mail. My wife saved me in every sense. She was middle class and my life changed, and so will yours. I must also tell you I never had much respect for military men, but you have caused me to change my views. It's not fair that you should be hard up after all you've done for your country."

The next morning, MacDonald, always the gracious host, took Thomson in his taxi to Aberdeen Station. Two reporters and a photographer were waiting on the platform, presumably arranged by MacDonald. They asked a few questions and MacDonald answered them, though not in detail. After shaking hands—a moment caught on camera—Thomson climbed on board. After doffing his hat to a woman sitting with her young son, he sat next to the window and waved to MacDonald as his train pulled away. He sat back contentedly and gave his companions a beaming smile. The boy was dressed in his Sunday best—a grey jacket and short trousers with a matching flat cap.

"Is this your son?" he asked.

"Yes," said the Scottish woman proudly.

"What's your name, son?" he asked the boy.

The child looked at the floor not answering, but kept banging his foot against the paneling on the side of the carriage.

"His name's Stuart," the boy's mother said.

"And how old are you, Stuart?" Thomson asked.

"He's six. He's a little shy."

"Thomson pulled out the bag of peppermints still in his pocket from W H Smiths and held it out. "Here sonny, would you like a peppermint?"

"No."

"Stuart! Don't' be rude to the nice gentleman."

Thomson held the bag out to her. She took one to be polite.

"Do you like trains, son? Thomson asked.

"No, I hate 'em," the kid snapped, still looking at the floor as he swung his foot to and fro. The woman chimed in with an apologetic smile.

"I'm sorry. His grandfather was killed in the Tay Bridge Disaster. It's all he's ever heard about when it comes to trains."

"Oh dear, I *am* sorry," Thomson said.

There was an awkward silence. "Visiting Scotland are you? Business?" she asked finally.

"Oh, just a little holiday, visiting a dear friend."

Thomson looked at the boy again. "What about airships, son? Do you like airships?"

"No, I hate 'em. They're stupid and they always crash and burn," the kid sneered.

Two days later, most London newspapers carried the photograph of MacDonald and Thomson shaking hands at Aberdeen Station. They seemed to approve of Thomson being in the running for a cabinet post, if Labour should be victorious. Some conservative newspapers, not wishing to miss an opportunity, grumbled that he'd be getting in 'by the back door'—unable to get himself elected, as legitimate people are required to do. Over the photographs of the two men, they led with headlines:

THOMSON A POSSIBLE CABINET PICK?

And

ENTER LORD THOMSON OF CARDINGTON!

They reported if Labour came to power, Thomson would likely become Secretary of State for Air. The title bearing the name 'Cardington' had been leaked. This led to speculation about the resurrection of the airship industry—a good prospect for those in need of work—but for others, another inevitable disaster in the making.

PART THREE

St. Cuthbert's Church, Ackworth, Yorkshire.

THE RISE OF THE
PHOENIX TWINS

The Western Front.

5

LOU & CHARLOTTE

August - October 1921.

It was 10:50 a.m. November 11, 1918. Lou was moving forward with his platoon, his brothers-in-arms, his buddies. What had started as gleeful morning was ending disastrously; they'd first been ordered to stay in their trenches and keep their heads down. They'd survived the war and the slaughter would finally end at 11:00 a.m. But later, orders came down for them to attack. Incredulous and angry, the soldiers reluctantly climbed the ladders up and out on to the battlefield. They moved forward, keeping as low as they could. Lou couldn't see the enemy, but he heard the whine of the bullets slicing the air and hitting the bodies of men close to him—sop-sop-sop—sop-sop-sop.

The Germans were calling out. "Go back Yankee dogs, go home. It's over!"

He peered through the fog and smoke recognizing the uniforms of English and American crewmen from *R38*. Those in front and beside him, including Potter, Bateman and Josh were mowed down by machine guns or blown to pieces with deafening artillery shells. They fell writhing in pain into the mud, crying out for their mothers, guts hanging out, faces blown away, legs and arms blown off.

Some cried out to him, "Lou, help me. Help me, *please.*"

He moved on, miraculously unscathed and untouched. He stepped over the bodies of New York Johnnie, Bobby in his parachute, Gladstone, Al Jolson—not Jerry Donegan, the real Al Jolson in black-face—and then the dead German boy who lay staring up at him with cold, accusing eyes, babbling in German, "*Sie morder! Sie morder!* Murderer! Murderer!"

Lou turned to see Charlotte behind him, a shaft of sunlight falling upon her. She appeared pristine and beautiful in her perfect white apron and headscarf. She stood amongst the officers of *R38* in dress uniform, in the battered control car resting on the battlefield. Charlotte reached for him, imploring him not to go forward, but the others urged him on. Capt. Wann stood nearby, his face burnt and stony, his uniform saturated in blood.

"You could've warned us, Remington! March forward and die, you bastard!" the commodore shouted.

"He knew this would happen," Capt. Maxfield sneered.

"He knew all right. Let him die," Capt. Wann said coolly.

And lastly, off to one side, was Lou's father, about forty, hands on hips, hair receding, face angular. His penetrating eyes were mean and accusing, his lips drawn back in contempt. He said nothing. *He* didn't have to.

Lou woke, crying out, wretched and confused. He sat up and looked across the dark ward, not knowing where he was or when it was. Charlotte rushed into the ward and turned on a light beside his bed. She put her arms around him, putting her face close to his. "There, there, my dear. It's all right. Don't fret—you're safe," she said.

The dead men in Lou's mind were out of control. Lou's injuries were healing satisfactorily, but at night he had terrible nightmares, many of them about New York Johnny. He sometimes dreamed he was over the cat ladder coaxing the boy down to the engine car, below them the river estuary, its surface a sea of molten lava like a scene from Dante's Inferno.

"Come on, Johnnie! You can do it," Lou would yell.

"I don't want to. Please don't make me, sir. *Please!*"

Lou would wake up and lie there unable to go back to sleep. The doctors told him these dreams might get worse for a time. And they did. In another dream, he stood at the divide as the airship began to break in two, he on the flaming side, Charlotte on the other. No matter how hard he tried, he couldn't make the leap across the widening chasm. He watched Charlotte as he fell away from her, descending into the dark abyss.

Long before the inquiry, just after the crash of *R38*, Lou's decision to remain in Hull became firm. His dread of returning to the United States stayed with him, although he sorely missed his parents and his brother and sister. He wrote from the hospital, asking them to forgive him for not coming home just now; he needed to sort himself out. He also let them know about the matter of a certain nurse he'd become rather taken with. "Smitten" would've been more accurate.

He'd never encountered a creature so exquisite. It wasn't only her beauty; she had a wonderful intellect. She brought her favorite books in for him to read, and he became an ardent reader of British classics. If he returned to the U.S., Charlotte would have to be at his side. Lou stayed in hospital for three weeks where Charlotte nursed him. During this time, their affection grew to a level of intensity neither could have imagined. Old Mrs. Tilly would've been delighted.

Josh, Bateman and Potter left the hospital after a couple of days, their physical injuries only slight, but they visited Lou each day. They marveled at the relationship between Lou and Charlotte and boasted they'd seen it coming. Lou and Charlotte couldn't disagree, but Lou was filled with questions about life in general.

The 'Wiggy thing' got to him and would become a bizarre, recurring thing in his life. By a twist of fate, Wiggins, the engineer, who failed to report the day they took off, had escaped death. He visited Lou in hospital and apologized. His car had broken down and he'd arrived as the ship was lifting from the ground. Lou smiled, telling him he'd been miffed at the time, but glad for him now.

"Somebody up there likes you, Wiggins," Lou told him.

A week after the crash, a massive funeral procession for British victims passed by the hospital on its way to Western Cemetery. While church bells tolled across the city, patients and nurses crowded at the windows, watching in silence. Charlotte allowed Lou to get up and stood beside him. They saw Potter and Bateman marching solemnly in the procession, their heads bowed. After twenty minutes, Lou went back to bed. A few days after that, he was informed that the bodies of the dead American officers and crewmen were being sent to Davenport and then by sea to Brooklyn Naval Yard. Three, including the captain, would be buried in Arlington National Cemetery, overlooking Washington D.C.—a place Lou regarded as home.

Before August 24th, Lou had intended to extend his Navy enlistment when he got back to the States. After the crash, everything changed. The Navy told him to take as much time as he needed to recuperate. He'd served his country well, and whatever he decided, the Navy would respect his decision. All this was conveyed to Lou by Lt. Jensen, his immediate senior officer.

The lieutenant also told Lou that the newspapers wanted an interview and it might be a good idea, if he was well enough. Lou agreed and they sat and discussed an outline of what would be divulged. Only the human side of the tragedy could be talked about: the cause of the crash and events on board the airship were 'off limits.' The two men met with reporters next day, including the unshaven George Hunter, from the *Daily Express* who left him a business card.

Matron surprised Lou a couple of days later, announcing he'd be receiving visitors within the hour. 'Top brass' she said, from the U.S. Navy would be 'on deck' (as they put it), to pay him a visit. The nurses got Lou looking spiffy, sat him up, and wheeled his bed to an open area of the ward. Within the hour, a magnificent troupe of fifteen U.S. Navy men in dress uniform marched solemnly in step into the ward and stood at each side of Lou's bed. Among them were Cmdr. Horace Dyer, Maj. Scott, Walter Potter, Henry Bateman, Josh Stone, five reporters, and four photographers. The nurses and patients who were well enough gathered around Lou's bed. Charlotte stood beside Lou at the head. The voice of the imposing Cmdr. Dyer boomed down the ward.

"Chief Petty Officer Remington volunteered for the U.S. Marines in 1916 and served with distinction in the Belleau Wood and Saint-Mihiel offensives in France where he ended the fight in the Verdun sector until the last day of the war. After that, he joined the U.S. Navy and served with the Airships Division in Lakehurst before coming to England where he took a crucial role in the development of the U.S. Airship Program. It is an honor, Chief Petty Officer Remington, on behalf of the United States Navy, to award you the Navy Cross for bravery, exhibited at the time of the tragic accident that occurred to Airship *ZR-2* at 17:29 hours on August 24th of this year. This medal is awarded for heroic, unselfish action taken in saving lives of your crewmen, as well as the ship's cat Fluffy." There were titters and smiles at mention of the cat.

"You showed resolve and leadership and by your actions three men were saved, while 44 regrettably perished. You sir, by order of President Warren G. Harding, the Commander-in-Chief, are now promoted to the rank of lieutenant. On behalf of the United States

Navy and the Government of the United States, I now say, thank you and God bless you, Lieutenant Louis Remington!"

Cmdr. Dyer moved closer to Lou, and Lt. Jensen handed him the medal. He towered over Lou like a giant, pinning the cross to his chest over his pajamas. He stepped back and saluted Lou.

"Lieutenant!" he snapped.

Lou stared at the commander in astonishment. The cameras flashed, and everyone gathered around the bed and down the ward, cheered and clapped. Lou was unable to speak. Charlotte stood with tears flowing down her cheeks. After handshakes all round, the contingent marched out with the press ordered not to linger. However, George Hunter from the *Daily Express* did linger, and chatted with Lou for a few minutes. The following day, stories and photographs appeared in the British and American newspapers about Lou and he became an international hero. And Fluffy became famous.

After three weeks, Lou got discharged and returned to his digs on Castle Street. His face healed rapidly, but his arm was still in a cast, making it impossible to ride his motorbike. Frustratingly, there was little he could do but rest up at his flat and read novels, but at least he got to meet Charlotte at the end of her shift each day.

They usually walked along the waterfront for an hour, regardless of weather. Those walks were harrowing, with Lou staring out at the swirling black water. But Charlotte was determined they face their fears. Afterwards, they would go to Charlotte's flat where she prepared a meal while Lou fed Fluffy (whom Charlotte had managed to retrieve from the unhappy boat captain) and lit a coal fire in the tiny fireplace.

After their meal, Charlotte would light a candle and they'd snuggle down on the sofa—chaperoned by Fluffy, who supervised from the sofa arm. They often chatted well into the night, until the fire had become a flicker, and the room chilly. Charlotte asked about his family and he told her about growing up on his grandfather's farm in Great Falls. He spoke of his folks proudly, although she sensed there was friction between Lou and his father. Charlotte told him how she'd begun nursing and how she'd been sent to London for training—there, she'd seen her first airship, but she didn't elaborate. Lou noticed her cringe as she spoke of it.

They touched on their previous brushes with the opposite sex. Charlotte told him about meeting Robert on a bus and how they'd spent the day ambling around the city together stopping at various cafés and an art gallery. Robert was leaving for the Front the following day. He asked for her address and she gave it to him. She never heard from him again. She said besides Lou, he was the only decent boy she'd ever met. She told him there was no need to be jealous. Robert was most likely dead like all the rest. Just 'passing ships', she said. Lou sensed her loss, but understood.

All too soon, it came time for Lou to trudge back to his own flat through the misty night. Their kissing and cuddling often became intense and Lou wished he could stay over, but never suggested it. His respect for Charlotte never waned; that would've been unthinkable. But it got to the point where they could hardly bear to be out of one another's sight, or out of each other's arms. Charlotte made up her mind—she wanted his children one day—one day soon.

In October, Lou's sling came off and he took the motorbike for a spin around the city while Charlotte was at work. It felt good to be back in the saddle. The next day, he rode to Howden Air Station where his Navy friends came out to welcome him. They made a fuss, shaking hands and patting him on the back, genuinely proud of him. They told him they were cleaning the place up and removing all their stuff and going home at the end of the month. "Nothing to stick around here for," they said. Lou knew he'd be sorry when they went. The massive, double-bayed shed, covering more than seven acres, stood eerily quiet. It was completely empty, save for a toolbox and a few bits of scaffolding. Out front, a mountain of debris and scrap metal had been piled, ready to be hauled off.

After chatting for an hour, Lou rode off, feeling pretty damned low. When he met Charlotte later in the day, she sensed his mood and tried to buck him up, obviously worried he might up and leave, too. He put his arms around her and reassured her he'd never run out on her.

A couple of weeks later, Lou wore his new dress blues and went back to the Howden shed where three charabancs waited for Americans from the surrounding area. They were bound for Southampton to board a U.S. Navy destroyer. More than two hundred people were gathered, many of them young women come to say tearful goodbyes—a few temporary, most, forever.

Josh was in uniform like the rest, and he and Lou said their farewells.

"I just got my orders, sir," Josh said, as pleased as punch.

"Where are they sending you?" Lou asked.

"I've been assigned to the *Shenandoah* under construction at Lakehurst."

Lou looked apprehensive.

"Hey, don't worry about me, sir. It can't happen twice—not to *me*!"

"Be careful, Josh."

"I'm golden now—indestructible—and that ship's gonna be using helium—no danger of fire, sir."

"Just the same, don't take chances."

"Sir, do you think you might head back home soon? Maybe you'd be assigned to the *Shenandoah,* too."

"I'm not sure yet. I'm gonna rest up here for a while."

"I don't blame you for that, sir. You certainly are lucky …"

Lou knew he wasn't just alluding to their miraculous escape.

"I owe you my life, sir. I'll always be grateful."

"Don't be silly, Josh."

"I'll make sure and get down and see your folks in Virginia."

"I'd appreciate that. They'd love it if you did," Lou said.

"If there's anything I can do for you—let me know, sir."

"I will. Stay in touch."

"Good luck to you and Charlotte. She's very fine, sir."

Josh stepped back, stood stiffly to attention and saluted Lou, looking him squarely in the eye. A feeling of dread passed over Lou as he returned the salute.

"Remember what I said," Lou told him.

"Don't you worry, sir, I'll be fine."

Lou had a sinking feeling as he watched those little green buses drive away. He thought about his family in Virginia and felt like a deserter. And unbearably lonely.

6

LOW ACKWORTH VILLAGE

October 1921.

L
ater that month, Lou and Charlotte took a train to Charlotte's home in Low Ackworth, near Pontefract, fifty miles from Hull. "Where they make the liquorice sticks," Charlotte told him proudly. They tramped along Station Road in the sunshine over a carpet of gold and yellow rustling at their feet. Lou was taken by the beauty of the stone village set among the farms and streams and had a sense of déjà vu. Perhaps it was that exquisite painting of rural England he'd seen in the National Gallery in Washington when his parents took him as a kid. He remembered the cows, the river and tall oaks around lush green pastures. Even then, he knew he wanted to see this place. It must have been a Turner, a Constable, a Gainsborough—he wasn't up on that stuff.

After a twenty minute walk, they arrived at a terrace of four three-storey houses surrounded by giant oaks. Each dwelling had a Welsh slate roof, secure behind high walls of matching blackened stone. Radiantly happy, Charlotte opened the wooden gate and pointed to the window on the ground floor overlooking the front garden.

"That's where I was born, Lou," she said. "Right there in that front room!"

"Wow!"

Charlotte pointed to ropes hanging from the bow of one of the oaks. "And here's my swing!" she said, settling into its seat and swaying back and forth. The door burst open and Charlotte's excited parents rushed out with open arms and welcoming smiles. The resemblance between Charlotte and her mother was striking: same height, bone structure, hair color, though her mother's was a little faded.

A good-looking lady.

Father was tall, with graying hair and strong features.

And this man works in the mines.

Lou shook his large, rough hand. Both were finely dressed, as though going to church—Charlotte's mother in a blue, flowered dress, father in a neatly ironed white shirt, plain blue tie, tan jacket.

"Charlotte, you look so well, my darling. This must be Lou. Oh, he *is* handsome—just like you said," Mrs. Hamilton said. "We saw the pictures in the paper, your poor face covered in bandages and Charlotte standing beside you. We were so proud!"

"Welcome to Ackworth, Lou," Mr. Hamilton said. "I'm pleased to meet you, son."

Charlotte grabbed Lou's arm, anxious to show him the house and make sure nothing had changed. They entered a small vestibule and stepped into the spacious living room with beige carpeting, a flowery couch and comfortable matching armchairs. As soon as they went in, Lou smelled the glowing coal fire in the grate. Charlotte noticed his glance.

"When we're home, we keep the fire going every day, winter or summer," she said.

Lou's eyes swept the room. The heavy drapes at the Georgian windows also had a floral pattern, similar to the couches and wallpaper. An upright piano stood at one end, polished brass candlesticks on its front panel, several framed family photos on its top. One of Charlotte as a child caught Lou's eye. She knelt on a beach, her arms around a small, white dog. He picked up the frame for a closer look.

"That was Charlotte at the seaside at Scarborough with Snowy. She's seven in that photo," Mrs. Hamilton said. "Oh, how she loved that little dog!"

"I want another dog just like him, one day," Charlotte said.

Lou carefully replaced the picture frame. "A dog … what about one of these?" Lou said, running his hand along the top of the piano. "This is real nice."

"Charlotte plays. She's very good. She had lessons at the Quaker School since she was little. Perhaps you'll play for Lou," Charlotte's mother said.

"Oh Mum, I haven't played in ages. Don't embarrass me."

"I hope you'll knock out a tune for me, honey. I love the old Joanna," Lou said.

Charlotte opened the lid and ran her fingers over the keys, picking out "My Mammy."

"It's out of tune Mother," Charlotte said.

Lou grimaced, remembering little Jerry Donegan in blackface aboard *R38*.

Any song but that one!

The white mantel over the fireplace surround was loaded with knick-knacks and more photos. The armchairs were arranged on each side of the hearth, one obviously 'father's chair.' Lou made a mental note. Beside it, between the fire-breast and the wall, was a half-height built-in cabinet with a mahogany wireless on top.

I guess this is where Father sits and smokes, listening to the BBC evening news and then a play before bed.

"Sit down and make yourselves comfortable," Mrs. Hamilton said, rushing off to the kitchen. She returned within minutes with tea and sandwiches and set them down on the coffee table. Starving, Lou and Charlotte tucked in. There was a knock at the back door accompanied by, "Oowoooh, oowooh, it's only me, love."

This was a sort of a British bird call now familiar to Lou, meaning: 'Is anybody home?' Of course, one always knew exactly who 'me' was. Lou grinned.

"It's Madge from next door," Mrs. Hamilton explained. "They'll all be by, you'll see."

Lou soon realized entering by the front door was pretty unusual. A procession of neighbors, relatives and friends came to the back door on one pretext or another; the main reason to inspect Charlotte's young man. Each one entered smiling shyly, ready to be introduced. They took to him on sight. They'd read the newspaper articles about the American hero who'd saved some of his fellow airshipmen and been injured and then taken to Hull Infirmary to be nursed back to health by 'our very own Charlotte.' A fairy tale!

"Oooooh! 'ees loovly, 'int 'ee?" (Which Lou figured meant, "Oh! He's lovely, isn't he?") they said, one after another on entering the living room, where Charlotte sat proudly beside Lou on the couch. Lou drank endless cups of tea, something he'd never done before, but found palatable enough—a British ritual. He could live with that.

Mr. Hamilton didn't say much. He listened and smiled. Charlotte had talked a lot about him during their evenings together. "He is the gentlest of men," Charlotte told him and Lou could quite believe it. Lou remained the center of attention for the afternoon, by which time the room had filled with people: Mrs. Scargill, Auntie Betty, who had a face full of kindness, Auntie Jean and her five kids, Auntie Mary from the Brown Cow (a pub, they explained), Auntie Rose from the fish shop ont' corner, Auntie Ethel from the dairy and Mrs. Hendry from the farm across the road, and many more.

Soon, after their shift at Ackworth Colliery, a troop of miners filed in. Lou wasn't sure if they'd give him the same reception, but they did. Lou had one problem, however; when they talked fast, he couldn't understand a word. So, he sat nodding, feeling like a parrot.

They're not speaking French, but they might just as well be.

After most visitors had left, one of Charlotte's girlfriends, Angela, came in and the two girls hugged. She shook hands with Lou, but seemed unable to look him in the eye.

"A crowd of us are meeting at the Mason's Arms tomorrow night. Why don't you come?" Angela said. "The old gang will be there."

Charlotte turned to Lou.

"Sure thing, as long as your parents are going," he said.

More villagers to meet!

Exhausted by conversation and sated by a beautiful roast dinner, Lou fell asleep in the attic room as soon as his head hit the crisp, white pillow case.

The next day was cloudy and cool. Charlotte and Lou spent the day walking across the fields to the viaduct and down to the river. It was a magical place, reminding Lou again of his favorite childhood painting.

The Mason's Arms was a chilly mile's walk just off the main Ackworth road. With its low, beamed ceilings and wood floors, the pub was welcoming and cozy. The publican greeted them from behind the bar as they entered. Lou was led around by Charlotte and introduced to everyone, including her cousin Geoff, who hadn't shown up at the house the day before. He was a handsome young man, about twenty-four, with a pleasant smile and beautiful teeth. Lou received the same friendly reception as at the house and wasn't allowed to buy any drinks. The publican grinned when he tried to pay. "Yer money's no good 'ere, son," he said.

Many pints were drunk by the men while the women sipped gin, or some fizzy, champagne-like drink. Just before closing time, a disturbance erupted in the adjacent private bar, with much shouting and swearing. A man in his mid-twenties appeared at the doorway to a collective moan of disgust from the public bar. He was Lou's height and build with lank, greasy hair hanging down one side of his pockmarked face. Murderous brown eyes blazed and thick lips drawn back in a sneer, revealed large, uneven, wolf-like teeth.

"Oh no, it's Jessup," someone said.

The drunk tried to focus on the man who'd dared to speak. "You shut your bloody mouth, Alfred Braithwaite, or I'll shut it for yer!"

Lou stared at the fool, unimpressed.

"So where's our American hero?" the man snarled, staggering into the center of the room. The drinkers scattered, leaving Lou alone with Jessup. Charlotte stood horrified, off to one side with her mother and Angela. "What's *he* doing here?" she asked. And then to Angela, "Did *you* know your brother was coming?"

"No, er …" Angela stuttered.

"She knew alright! She told me you'd be 'ere, my lovely," Jessup shouted over his shoulder. "So this is your pretty boy Yank? Oh I'm *so* in love," he said, in falsetto and puckering his lips to Lou. "Ah, give me a kiss, pretty boy."

Lou didn't move, his face blank, eyes alert. Charlotte's father stood mortified while the publican seemed to have his feet nailed to the floor.

"Now look 'ere, fella, why don't you go on back in yer balloon to bumsnot New York or whatever rat-infested dump you crawled out of and stay there! This girl's mine. I 'ad her first—yes, that's what I said —*I 'ad her first*—and she'll always be mine! Got that, Yankee Doodle Dandy?"

In a matter of moments, Lou had become a stranger alone in a foreign land. He didn't lose eye contact with Jessup, enraging the drunk even more. He ran at Lou and punched him in the face twice, knocking him to the boards. Lou didn't raise a hand to defend himself. Jessup swung round and leaned over the bar-top to seize a brown beer bottle. He smashed it on the edge of the bar and turned back to Lou with the jagged weapon.

Before Jessup managed to reach Lou, cousin Geoff grabbed a long shard of broken glass from the floor and with a sweep of his hand, slashed the left side of Jessup's face, piercing the flesh through to his mouth and ripping his tongue. Jessup screamed and fell down, blood gushing from his cheek and babbling mouth. Belatedly, the publican leapt over the bar. He grabbed Jessup's feet and dragged him across the floor into the other bar, like a bleeding dead horse, leaving a thick trail of blood. Angela rushed in to her brother. Charlotte sank down to her knees over Lou and took his hand.

"Oh Lou, my poor love, are you all right?"

"I'm fine. Who the hell was that knucklehead?" he said, sitting up.

Charlotte was at a loss. Mr. Hamilton leaned over Lou.

"Come on, Lou, let's get you home, son," he said, taking his hand and pulling him to his feet. Everyone in the bar was shocked and sorry this had happened to a visitor to their village. Each of them came offering apologies.

Lou, Charlotte and her parents trudged home in silence. Once there, Mrs. Hamilton went to the kitchen with her husband, leaving Lou and Charlotte alone in the living room.

"Charlotte, tell me, what the hell was that all about?"

"Lou, I swear to you, he means nothing to me. I went out with him for a couple of weeks, that's all. That was two years ago."

"Sounds like the boy's pretty stuck on you."

"He seemed nice at first, but then he started to get fresh. And when he was drunk he got mean, like a rabid dog. He wouldn't leave me alone. He's tracked me ever since. I had to get out of the village. That's why I'm working in Hull. He's made my life hell."

"He seems to think he's got a claim on you."

"What he said is a filthy lie! And if you don't believe me, you can get out of this house right now!" Charlotte stormed as her father entered the room.

"Please don't argue. You've been so happy together and you've made us happy. Don't end a beautiful day like this. Go to bed and sleep on it and talk in the morning. Lou, Charlotte is a good girl. That boy's a real problem in this village. He's always been a bully, just like his father before him—he used to terrorize this whole area—and *he* died in the hangman's noose; killed the boy's mother. I've no doubt this one'll die a violent death, too."

"I'll say goodnight. Thank you for your hospitality," Lou said, making for the door.

Later, in the attic bedroom, Lou took his bag from the closet and was busy unzipping it as Charlotte entered.

"W-What ... are you doing, Remy?" she stammered.

"It's best I go. Perhaps we need time to think about all this."

"Lou, I'm sorry. I didn't mean it. Please don't go. I'd die if you left me. I love you so much."

He dropped the bag in the corner of the room.

"All right, we'll talk tomorrow. Leave now."

Charlotte went out, closing the door silently behind her.

7

ST. CUTHBERT'S

October 1921 – April 1924.

Lou lay on the bed without undressing, staring at the stars through the skylight for most of the night. He fell asleep as the sun was painting the leaves gold and the birds were bursting into song. The room took on an orange glow as the chickens on the farm next door started kicking up a fuss. But Lou was dead to the world.

He went down to the kitchen about ten thirty. Agitated and embarrassed, Charlotte's mother leaned over the coal-fired stove, cooking breakfast. "Lou, I don't know what to say …" she began.

"Mrs. Hamilton, please don't feel bad. Nothing that happened last night was your fault. The man is obviously deranged," Lou said, sitting down at the table.

"Evil is what 'ee is," Mr. Hamilton said.

"Against our wishes, he took Charlotte out a few times. We were horrified. She had no idea what a bad lot he was, but it didn't take long," Mrs. Hamilton explained. When Charlotte entered the room, Lou could tell she hadn't slept well either. He stood and she came to him and kissed his cheek. They sat down at the kitchen table and ate bacon and eggs—except Charlotte who had no appetite. Later, Lou and Charlotte sat in the living room.

"Lou, I'm so sorry for what happened," she said.

"You should've warned me—why did you keep it from me?"

"Lou, I had no idea this would happen. I know he keeps tabs on me. He comes to Hull and skulks around. He knows I won't even *look* at him—let alone speak to him."

"I wish you'd told me, that's all."

"Lou, why didn't you defend yourself?"

"A couple of blows to the head are the least of my problems. I guess I need to keep an eye over my shoulder from now on," he said with an edge of sarcasm.

"I don't know why you didn't stand up to him, Lou. It was like you were scared. That madman could have gouged your eye out."

Lou's eyes narrowed. "He's got more to fear from *me*, I assure you."

Charlotte looked skeptical. "Lou, at times I don't understand you."

"Don't worry about me, sweetheart."

"It was that Angela's fault—she obviously told her brother we'd be there. He never goes in that pub."

"Why d'you hang around with her? There was something I didn't like about her. She's got lyin' eyes."

"She seemed like a decent girl and wanted to be friends and I felt sorry for her—you know, because of her father."

"Sounds like she comes from a bad lot."

"You do believe what I said last night, don't you, love?" Charlotte asked.

"Of course I do. I have no doubts, Charlotte."

"Oh, Remy." Charlotte kissed him. He took a handful of her hair and ran it through his fingers—something he loved to do when they embraced.

"Will you please excuse me, honey? I need to speak to your dad," Lou said. Charlotte frowned. He left the room and went to the kitchen where Mr. Hamilton sat alone, listening to the wireless drinking tea. Lou stopped respectfully and listened while the BBC news continued.

'*It was announced today in the House of Commons that a proposal has been put forward to the Conservative Government by Mr. Dennistoun Burney, member of Parliament for Uxbridge and managing director of Vickers Aircraft Corporation's Airship Division, for the company to build six airships to be owned and operated by the government....*'

Mr. Hamilton turned off the radio. "They want to build more of them airships ..."

"Sir, I wonder if I could talk to you for a moment," Lou said.

"What is it, lad?" Mr. Hamilton's face fell. He obviously thought Lou wanted to talk about Jessup. "Let's go in the other room," he said, getting up. Charlotte had gone upstairs. It felt more formal in the living room.

"Mr. Hamilton, I know this is rather sudden, but I'd like permission to marry your daughter," Lou said. Mr. Hamilton's face lit up.

"We'd be honored to have you in the family. We've not seen our Charlotte looking so happy for such a long, long time." They shook hands and Mr. Hamilton reached up and took hold of Lou's shoulders. "You're a right good lad. She couldn't do better—and nor could you. I know I'm her dad, but it's true."

"Thank you, sir. I'll take good care of her, I promise."

"I know you will, son. This calls for a celebration drink," Mr. Hamilton said, making for the door to fetch some glasses. He opened the door to find Charlotte, her mother and Auntie Betty, listening. Everyone laughed.

"Come in, all of you," Mr. Hamilton said. "It's time for a toast."

There was another sound at the back door it was Auntie Jean and Auntie Mary. The faces of the women were filled with excitement. Mrs. Hamilton loaded a tray in the kitchen with gin, whisky, brown ale and tonic water, and marched in with the new arrivals.

"We've an announcement. Lou has asked permission to marry our Charlotte," Mr. Hamilton said.

"And what did you say, Harry?" the ladies all said at once, surging forward. Charlotte looked at her dad.

"I said we'd be delighted to have him as our son-in-law."

A cheer went up and some clapped. Lou stepped into the center of the room. He delved into his pocket and pulled out a small black box.

"Charlotte, I hope you like this," he said, opening and offering it.

Charlotte carefully removed the diamond ring from its red velvet cushion, her hand shaking a little. She held it out to him to slip on her finger. Every one cheered again, as he did so.

"It fits!" they said.

Charlotte held up her hand to show the small diamond for all to see, clearly ecstatic. Jessup's name wasn't mentioned again. The rest of the visit was joyful and Charlotte even played the piano for Lou. She was a bit rusty, but he was impressed. Maybe one day they'd have a dog *and* a piano.

Lou and Charlotte made a second visit to Ackworth over Christmas. On Christmas Eve they attended midnight mass with the family at St. Cuthbert's, located not far from the Hamilton home. The old Gothic church was covered in ivy and surrounded by gravestones, bearing the names of villagers from centuries past. After the service, they walked home as a powdery snow began to fall, turning the village and surrounding countryside into a silent wonderland.

On Christmas Day, the usual procession of neighbors, family and friends came by, each bearing a small Christmas gift—a cake or dish they'd made, a small bottle of brandy or whisky. Traditionally, this was a lazy day, with lots of eating. Lou left about eight thirty that evening to stay at Auntie Betty's home on the Wakefield road, where he'd been billeted this time.

Lou and Charlotte were married at St. Cuthbert's the following day, Boxing Day. It was cold but sunny, the fields laden with snow. Lou's family had sent a telegram wishing them the best for their future with 'great love.' They also said they hoped the couple would visit the U.S. before long. Potter, smartly dressed in a grey flannel suit, acted as usher, while Bateman, in naval uniform, performed duties of best man. (Lou and Potter were closer, but Lou knew Potter was too shy and wouldn't be comfortable.)

Lou wore his officer's dress blues with the rank of lieutenant. Charlotte suggested he wear his Navy Star, but he refused. She understood and didn't press it, although she longed to see it pinned on his chest. With or without it, he possessed the looks and charisma of an American movie star, making Charlotte remember poor, broken-hearted Minnie Brown.

Lou got to the church early, after Bateman and Potter picked him up in Bateman's Morris. They waited nervously in front of the altar rail. A couple of times Lou turned around and winked at Billy who sat with his father, Lenny. Lou made Bateman check three times to make sure he had the two rings in his pocket and each time the answer was same: "Oh my God, what did I do with them?"

Before Charlotte arrived, a commotion started at the church doors where a gang of twelve burly miners had gathered, a fact that had been kept from Lou. Lou found out later Mr. Hamilton had told his workmates from Ackworth Colliery about Lou's dust-up with Jessup at the Mason's Arms. Jessup arrived on the scene with two other unsavory characters, stinking of beer. They hadn't come to say prayers, or to leave offerings. Lou rushed to the church door as four miners frog-marched Jessup toward the steps at the foot of the graveyard. Jessup turned and saw Lou and flew into a rage.

"I've not finished with you—you bastard!" he screamed.

Lou watched the miners manhandle him to the top of the icy steps and throw him down. He slipped and landed in a heap at the bottom, bruised and bleeding, the deep wound to his slashed face, reopened. The men stood with their hands on their hips. Jessup's friends had already scarpered.

"Try it again, mate, and we'll break yer bloody neck—just like yer old man's!" One of the miners turned to Lou, "You can go back and wait for her now, son. Don't worry; we'll be at the door."

Lou returned to the altar rail amid anxious murmuring in the pews, relieved the miners were on guard, although Jessup didn't scare *him*. His only concern was for Charlotte. Her day wasn't to be spoiled. Presently, someone whispered that Charlotte had arrived. Lou turned and stood facing the back of the church in anticipation.

As she entered, a gasp went up from the packed pews. Charlotte was radiant, and when she saw Lou waiting, her face was joyous. She looked stunning in a full-length, high-necked, white lace over satin dress that fitted snugly at her narrow waist and around her shapely bosom. Fanny followed behind as maid of honor.

Charlotte carried a simple bouquet of red roses. Lou watched her make her entry and walk down the aisle on her father's arm. She was all he ever wanted in a bride. He only wished his family could be here. And then, for a brief moment, he thought of Julia.

After the service, in biting air, they hastily posed for pictures in the snowy church grounds, their new gold rings glinting in the winter sunshine. They drove to the Workingmen's Club in Pontefract in the shiny black Daimler that had carried Charlotte to the church. It was decked out with traditional, flowing, white silk ribbons.

At the wedding breakfast, Bateman read telegrams sent by well-wishers. One came from Maj. Scott, at the Cardington Royal Airship Works. This puzzled Lou; he wondered how Scott knew about their marriage, but thought it kind of him to take the trouble. No one told Charlotte about Jessup showing up at the church.

The wedding guests spent a long afternoon at Mrs. Scargill's quaint home next door to Charlotte's parents' house. In the evening, celebrations continued in the upstairs rooms of the Brown Cow, where Potter, with laughing eyes and a cigarette between his lips, delighted everyone by playing hit songs and polkas on his accordion. It created a fun, French atmosphere in the Yorkshire pub that night.

"You make that thing sound beautiful, Walt," Lou called across the room.

"If anything 'appens to me, it's yours, sir," Potter replied, out the side of his mouth.

Later that night, Bateman drove the newly-weds to Monk Fryston Hall, a stately manor house in the Vale of York, where they spent a blissfully happy four-day honeymoon. Charlotte was a shy virgin—about that, there was no doubt—but after a day or two, she became a tigress. The wait had been worth it. When not in their sumptuous room making passionate love or ravenously eating meals brought up to them, they wandered the thirteenth century building with its stone mullioned windows, inglenook fireplaces and ornate, paneled rooms. At other times, they strolled, arm-in-arm in the delightful gardens among stone lions and statues set in acres of frosty woodlands and frozen ponds.

The honeymoon was almost spoiled. Jessup showed up in Monk Fryston Village. He had another dressing on his face after his nasty fall in St. Cuthbert's graveyard. Lou spotted him lurking behind a tree as they left the hotel and then later, skulking around in the gardens, gazing up at the windows. He didn't tell Charlotte,

Once back in Hull, they consolidated themselves in Lou's ground floor one-bedroom flat, which was larger than Charlotte's bedsit. They took Fluffy with them. Lou, still on disability, decided it was time to notify the Navy he wouldn't be extending his service due to end in March. He found a job in a country garage where he worked as a mechanic and pumped petrol for customers. The people of Hull treated him like one of their own. His new employer appreciated him and they got on well. Lou was content doing this job—a welcome change, and therapeutic.

Around this time, Charlotte got word that her cousin Geoff, who'd slashed Jessup's face, had been rushed to hospital. He'd been set upon by four thugs wearing balaclavas who stole his wallet. He'd been stabbed and his face cut with a stiletto, his arm broken and all his front teeth knocked out. He couldn't identify his attackers. Lou and Charlotte visited Geoff in hospital. The identity of the 'robbers' wasn't hard to guess. Powerless, Lou filed the episode away for another day.

He still had bad dreams and thought about his dead crewmen much of the time. All this was entwined with his war experiences, which had previously subsided, but this latest catastrophic accident revived everything, giving old memories new life.

Lou often drove his motorbike to Howden Air Station, now an abandoned, lonely place. He sat outside the huge doors on an old chair he'd found in one of the scavenged, dilapidated offices. He'd sit searching for answers, wishing he could find peace. The crash of the *Roma* in his home state of Virginia that February caused him more distress. That airship, flying from Langley, near Great Falls, to Norfolk, hit overhead power lines and caught fire. Thirty-four men perished in the flames. He and Charlotte could not discuss it.

The air station became like hallowed ground. He went there often over the next three years, witnessing the ever-changing, rural landscape through the seasons—in rolling October mist from the river marshes, winter snow, April rain showers and summer sunshine. He sat outside the shed where he befriended the animals: squirrels, rabbits, deer, foxes, stoats, badgers and pheasant. Sometimes he brought them food and they became tame, scampering at his feet.

When he couldn't sleep, he slid out of bed without disturbing Charlotte. It wasn't until she heard his motorbike start up down the road and move away, that she woke up. She knew his destination and didn't worry, confident he'd get over it in time.

Lou liked to light a fire in an old oil drum and sit studying the stars over the old aerodrome, while owls and foxes and other nocturnal creatures made their eerie sounds. If the winds were howling across the desolate plain, he'd find a sheltered spot where he'd listen to the ghostly noise of the building's skin of loose corrugated sheeting chatter and whine, like a living thing, while the gigantic structure creaked and groaned like a ship at sea. He always returned home before dawn and crawled back into bed with Charlotte, who turned over sleepily, drawing him close. He felt safe entwined with her, and so did she.

No children came along, which made Lou thankful. They needed more time together and he wasn't earning enough to start a family. Charlotte was desperate for a child, but knew he was right. It was important they get established first.

8

CHEQUERS

January 1924.

A procession of Rolls-Royces, Bentleys, Daimlers, Mercedes and other luxury sedans made its way from Missenden along the winding lanes to the wrought iron entrance gates of Chequers, the Prime Minister's country residence.

Situated forty miles west of Ten Downing Street, Chequers sat below Beacon Hill, nestling inconspicuously in the Buckinghamshire countryside among the towns of Princes Risborough, Great Missenden and Wendover. From atop the hill, on a clear day, one could take in a sweeping panorama of the Berkshire Downs, the Cotswolds and Salisbury Plain, although there were no good views from the house itself. To the south, the ancient, well-trodden Ridgeway Trail crossed open parkland.

The ancient, russet brick Elizabethan manor with its multi-gabled roofs, leaded windows and tall chimneys was surrounded by high, stone-capped walls and boxwood hedges. The cars passed into the walled courtyard situated on the east side. They made their way on the gravel drive around the quatrefoil-shaped lawn at whose center stood the lead statue of Hygeia, the health goddess, who posed close to a giant tulip tree—said to be the finest in England.

At the imposing entrance, each vehicle disgorged a set of dignitaries, many enjoying a new-found status. They were led to the front door by servants holding umbrellas to protect them from the gently falling snow. This afternoon, the house looked especially magical, like a painting of a winter scene on a Christmas card. Light shone from the windows in the grey gloom, accentuating the Welsh slate roofs, lawns, surrounding hedges and trees, draped in snow.

In the December election, the Tories had failed to obtain a clear majority and after losing a confidence vote in January, Conservative

Prime Minister Stanley Baldwin had resigned. Labour joined with the Liberal Party and took up the reins of power and Ramsay MacDonald became Prime Minister. To celebrate this momentous occasion, MacDonald threw a party for Labour Party supporters and trade union bosses.

Thomson had arrived two days earlier and, at MacDonald's insistence, moved into the state bedroom. This room, with its ornate, Elizabethan four-poster bed, complete with carved, oak lions, was usually reserved for distinguished guests and heads of state. A coal fire burned in the grate under a marble mantel. The view from the windows faced south over Chequers Park and the driveway toward Missenden.

Thomson felt at home at once and found the historical residence had the same effect on other visitors. After his bedsit in Stockwell, his fortunes had taken an extraordinary turn for the better and he considered himself truly blessed. He and MacDonald had been going over matters of state for the past two days, and although they were still in the 'honeymoon period,' they appeared to make an excellent team— both were committed to improving the lives of ordinary people. MacDonald had already begun crafting the Housing Act, designed to set in motion the building of half a million homes for working-class families at affordable rents.

They had got off to a cracking start and now, this very afternoon, Thomson would lay the foundation stone of his brainchild. He liked to manage his time efficiently and today he'd do many things simultaneously: celebrate the success of the first Labour Party victory, hire a genius to head up the program, make friends with people who couldn't relate to him, and lastly, drive the first nail into the coffin of Dennistoun Burney and the rest of those money-grubbing profiteers.

In order to get the airship industry back on its feet, the negative image would first have to be overcome. To do this, he'd move in a new direction, starting with hiring some new people—the best people. Changes would be made in the way things were managed. The process of selling the program to the public would need to be carefully controlled.

The celebration was held in the Great Hall, an imposing room, thirty feet high, with a gallery on the east side adjacent to a huge stone and brick fireplace, alive with blazing logs. An impressive brass chandelier hung at center, casting its glow over a pale green carpet, overlaid with exquisite Persian rugs. Original art covered the walls, and coats of arms, ranging from Lord Lee back to William Hawtrey, adorned all corners of the room.

Thomson stood chatting with MacDonald under a painting of *The Mathematician* (thought to be a Rembrandt) opposite the galleried end of the room, close to the entrance. Thomson oozed confidence, every inch a polished politician, debonair in a borrowed black tuxedo, stylish wing-tipped collar and silver tie. He was at his most seductive. He'd *need* to be.

Ishbel, at MacDonald's right, acted as 'hostess' while Thomson stood at his left. The three of them greeted guests as they arrived: first MacDonald, then Ishbel, then Thomson. This gave Thomson immediate status, or so it was hoped. He saw the pleasure of being at last, close to the center of power written on the faces of all who entered—that is, until their eyes fell on *him*. They gave him inquiring glances, and he sensed their burning resentment. He read their minds.

Who is this man who has leapfrogged into the inner circle? What has he done to get MacDonald elected? Nothing! We're the ones who've worked hard all these years to build this party. Now, from nowhere, here comes this interloper—this upper class fraud!

Thomson gritted his teeth and smiled as he greeted them, but they turned away, openly hostile. Thomson knew he had mountains to climb. He'd need to be patient. He listened to barbed comments— meant for his ears.

"I 'eard 'ee killed a lot of Germans in France, Bulgaria *and* Romania."

"*I* 'eard 'ee's having an affair with some 'ot blooded, gypsy woman over there."

"Bloody disgusting!"

"The movement can do without the likes of *'im!* "

"We need to cleanse the party."

"We can't have our people 'obnobbing with the upper-classes."

"We must be vigilant!"

Thomson had made sure Barnes Wallis's name was included on the guest list and had briefed MacDonald. He was keeping an eye on the door.

If only Marthe were here. I could confide in her. She understands the common people so well. She has those peasants in her village eating out of her hand. She'd love this place and my goodness, what a hit she'd be—even with this surly bunch!

He put Marthe out of his mind as a man stepped into the Stone Hall just inside the entrance vestibule.

This could be him.

The man took off his black overcoat and handed it to one of the servants, who brushed snow from its shoulders, before taking it to the cloakroom. Dressed in a grey suit and a somber blue tie, he walked into the room, as though stepping into a minefield. His name was boldly announced. "Mr. Barnes Wallis of the Vickers Aircraft Company, Prime Minister!" All eyes fell on Wallis as if he were Satan, himself. Wallis showed no reaction.

"Ah, yes, we've been expecting you, sir. I know Lord Thomson here has been looking forward to your visit," MacDonald said, glancing at Thomson who studied Wallis intently. He was thirty-seven, average height and build, possessed a stony face and expressionless, steely blue eyes; eyes that revealed nothing, but which seemed to take in everything in one sweep with camera-like precision, to file away. His stern demeanor and full head of prematurely graying hair, made Wallis appear older than his years and formidable.

A man easily under-estimated. A good poker player, no doubt.

"Thank you, Prime Minister, and congratulations to you," Wallis said, with calm assurance. His grey suit was a metaphor for his personality—blending in without calling attention—but it *did* call attention, since every man in the room was dressed in black.

Maybe he's making a statement—not one to run with the herd!

Thomson stepped forward, hand outstretched. Wallis's hand was more delicate than his own—more like that of a violinist—but his handshake was firm enough. "I'm honored to meet you, Wallis. We've heard so much about you. Come let me introduce you to everybody, then I'd like to show you the house."

After presenting Wallis to Ishbel, Thomson led him around the room, introducing him. For a rag-tag bunch of rabble rousers, the guests were well turned out, Thomson thought. Not in every case, but generally he was impressed. Women were adorned in the latest fashions of delicate silks and colorful fabrics, loose fitting at the waist, some short at the knee, others to the ankle. The men wore tuxedoes or lounge suits.

These people have gone into debt to be here today.

Thomson knew how that went. The group included government civil servants, party members, party workers and hangers-on, along with several balding trade union bosses from the docks, mines and transportation industries, wearing steel rimmed spectacles. Thomson called them 'Lenin-look-alikes.'

Thomson cast his eye across the room. He'd done his homework memorizing the names of everyone on the guest list, positions held, names of their wives, children and girlfriends. Through research he'd learned of their ambitions and hobbies. After spending a polite and reasonable amount of time on pleasantries, Thomson led Wallis up the staircase to the gallery overlooking the Great Hall.

"This building is a special place," he began. "Only two other Prime Ministers have resided here—usually at weekends—Baldwin, and before him, Lloyd George, of course. And now here *we* are."

Thomson perceived Wallis's eyebrows raise slightly as he injected the '*we*'.

"That's nice," Wallis uttered coolly.

Thomson leaned on the railing and stared grandly up at the ornate ceiling with its octagonal glazed cupola and then down at the gathering below. He waved to MacDonald.

"Seven years ago, Lord Lee of Fareham bequeathed his stately home to the nation for use of future Prime Ministers, for rest and relaxation, to confer with heads of state and distinguished guests."

"That was awfully generous of him," said Wallis.

"You know there's history attached to the name, too. It's thought to have been the home of the King's Minister of the Exchequer during the twelfth century."

"Interesting."

Suddenly, a blast of bagpipes took everyone by surprise—much to MacDonald's evident delight. A small band of Scots Guardsmen, in full dress of the Black Watch, filed into the Great Hall and gathered at the center of the room. They were followed by four dancers carrying swords. Thomson glanced down at them, shouting above the din.

"Come, let me show you the library. We must endeavor to preserve our eardrums." Thomson led the way down the steps. They moved along a corridor to an ornate wooden door, opening onto what Thomson called 'The Long Gallery', a room running the length of the west side of the house. The place smelled of smoke and damp logs. On one side, seven-foot-high mahogany bookcases were stacked with ancient, leather-bound books, many of them first editions. The bookcase was interrupted at the center by a carved stone fireplace where another log fire blazed. Soft, comfortable chairs and occasional tables had been positioned for cosy chats, a well-stocked bar within easy reach. Then Thomson had a thought.

"Ah, I know—this'll interest you," he said, again leading Wallis away. Wallis obediently followed. Thomson went to the bookcase and opened a section, complete with dummy books. Behind, was another door.

Thomson pushed it open with a flourish. "Voilà!"

"My goodness!"

"Isn't that fun?" Thomson said. "This is the Cromwell Passage. I should warn you, they say this place is haunted. At least, Lloyd George's dog thought so. He used to bark like mad in the Long Gallery. Do let me know if you spot any ghosts!"

Wallis stared at him blandly, as if he were mad. Thomson pointed to the paintings hung along one side of the corridor.

"Here's Cromwell as a child. He's two years old in this one. Cute little fellow, isn't he! Here he is again at the Battle of Marsden Moor. Now, that was a strong man—and altogether quite unpleasant!"

Wallis studied the painting intently. Cromwell sat on a black horse with a sword in one hand, his other arm in a sling. They proceeded along the corridor and Thomson showed him more portraits of Cromwell and his family. Wallis seemed mildly interested, but exhibited no sign of being in awe, as others might. But his eyes missed nothing.

"Ah, and look here, Cromwell's death mask," Thomson said, pointing to a cast lying on a side table. Wallis peered down at it, without comment. At the end of the corridor, Thomson stopped and slowly turned. "I expect you can guess why I invited you here, Wallis?"

Thomson had thoroughly reviewed Wallis's background. Wallis had the reputation for being the finest and most experienced airship designer in the country. The only thing was—what were his political leanings? If he leaned left, it should be easy, but if he was a dyed in the wool Dennistoun Burney disciple, things might prove difficult—or impossible.

If he's just a regular Conservative, I expect we can seduce him— they're all for sale. All they think about is money. But this man's hard to read.

Unusual for Thomson.

"My guess is—something to do with engineering?" Wallis answered.

Thomson chuckled. "Let's go back to the library, shall we?" he said, leading the way to the warm hearth. The sun's last rays were shining through the stained glass windows at the end of the room. Thomson went to the bar and poured two large glasses of twelve-year-old Macallan. He handed one to Wallis.

"I'm glad you came, Wallis," he said, holding up his own glass.

"My pleasure, sir. Thank you for the tour." Wallis held up his Scotch, but did not drink. Thomson wasn't sure what to make of him.

Is he being sarcastic? Perhaps he doesn't drink.

"I must congratulate you, on your government's victory and your appointment as Air Minister," Wallis said.

Ah, that's more encouraging.

"Thank you, Wallis. That's why you're here. We're hoping to do great things. We must get started on a grand new global transportation scheme." They sat facing each other over the coffee table.

"Sounds exciting," Wallis said. This pleased Thomson. Finally, a sign of interest.

"It's a matter of national security for us to revitalize the airship industry without delay. The Germans have got too far ahead of us," Thomson said.

"Indeed they have."

"We must seize the initiative, Wallis."

"I must agree, sir."

"I attended the Treaty of Versailles and I can tell you quite bluntly, we were too hard on Germany. I said it then, and I say today: This peace will not hold!" Thomson said.

"That would be most unfortunate."

"If there is another war, which I think is likely, we must be prepared, Wallis!"

"I hope not, but you're right, of course—war might be inevitable. It's more likely though, that it'd be because we weren't *hard enough* on Germany."

Thomson was surprised Wallis had the temerity to contradict him.

"That's your considered opinion, is it, Wallis?" he said.

"One general warned we'd have to 'do it over' if we allowed them to walk away from the battlefield with their army intact and Germany left totally unscathed."

Thomson frowned. "Who said that?"

"General Pershing."

"Old 'Black Jack' said that, did he?   He would!" Thomson snorted.

What the hell do you know, Wallis? You weren't there!

There was a long pause and then at last, Thomson spoke again.

"I want someone to head up the New Imperial Airship Program. The industry shall rise again like the proverbial phoenix," Thomson said, getting away from the subject of war.

"Yes, you'll need the right man."

"This is where you come in. I believe *you're* that man."

"You understand my position with Vickers Aircraft, Lord Thomson?" Wallis said, with slight discomfort.

"Yes, I do, Wallis, but this is all much too important. It's my belief Vickers's intention is to monopolize the airship industry, and we certainly can't allow that. This has got to be more about the good of the country—not just about profit. There are people out there ..." Thomson jerked his thumb toward the sound of the bagpipes, "...hell-bent on nationalizing Vickers and just about every other company in the land. To them, 'profit' is a *very dirty* word. Private business has its usefulness, but it must be held in check for the 'common good'. You do understand, don't you, Wallis?"

Wallis showed no sign of what he was thinking. "I think I understand perfectly, sir, yes."

"Government took the lead in the production of airships until the unfortunate accident, but it's time to put all that behind us and restart the program. Vickers will have its role to play—an important role. Our new government will not only undertake the design and construction of airships of its own, but will oversee airships built by Vickers under contract to us. And this is where you come in, Wallis."

"What are you saying *exactly*, sir?"

"I want you to oversee the entire program, as Secretary of the Airship Committee."

Wallis showed emotion for the first time. He was aghast.

"You're planning to build airships by committee?"

"Yes, why not?"

"Well, I, I ..."

"You *are* the best man we've got after all—or so I've been led to believe." Thomson paused. "Now your country needs you, Wallis."

Wallis sat and stared down at his shiny, black lace-up shoes. Thomson waited, while the fire crackled in the grate. "I take it I'd be at liberty to pick and choose my own teams on both government and private sector projects?"

Thomson hadn't seen this coming. He stared away at a painting of Charles I, searching for the right words. This was a loaded question.

This man is his own master. He'd certainly be strong enough for the job.

"Yes, to some extent, but naturally, I'd require you to take over the team at the Royal Airship Works at Cardington," Thomson answered.

"The same people who built *R38*?"

Thomson tried to slough that off. "Well, yes."

"The same team that built the airship that plunged into the Humber three years ago?"

The man's tone is becoming irritating.

"As I said, they'd be working under your direction, yes."

"I cannot believe you'd actually contemplate keeping those people employed—they're totally incompetent. If I were in the position to, I'd sack the lot tomorrow. Some of them should've gone to prison. They shouldn't be rewarded with another airship to build. That'd put more peoples' lives in danger. It'd be a serious mistake indeed, sir!" Wallis said.

Stunned, Thomson stared down into his whisky and then slowly raised his head, his eyes boring into Wallis's. "I take that, sir, as a refusal of your government's offer?"

"I refuse to be part of another major airship disaster," Wallis answered.

"I was rather hoping you would *prevent* one," Thomson said with finality.

There was a long awkward silence. Wallis put down his untouched glass of whisky and both men got up and moved toward the door. A footman stood in the corridor waiting for instructions.

"Kindly fetch Mr. Wallis's coat from the Stone Hall cloakroom and show him out through the west door to his car. Mr. Wallis, please wait here. I bid you good day, sir." Wallis showed no emotion whatever as they parted without shaking hands. Thomson went up the main staircase to his room. He needed to unwind. This had been a disaster.

An unmitigated damned disaster!

He went to the sink and splashed his face with water. He trembled as if he'd been punched in the stomach. He hadn't anticipated this reaction from Wallis and felt he'd misjudged him—mishandled the whole thing. He was furious, mostly with himself—his first important task and he'd failed miserably. It left him questioning the way the program was to be set up. Wallis's sarcastic jibe kept running through his mind.

You're planning to build airships by committee?

Thomson gradually calmed down and went to the window in time to see Wallis trudging to his car. He watched him climb in and white puffs shot from the exhaust. The car moved off unsurely in the snow toward the sun disappearing below the tree line. Thomson sat down in an armchair, staring at the fireplace until he felt composed. He thought about what Wallis had said about the Cardington people. The truth was, the design people who'd been responsible for *R38* had perished with the airship. He concluded Wallis must have been ranting about government enterprise—his sacred cow!

Later, he went down to the Great Hall where the Scottish Guards and the dancers were finishing their performance. He slipped into the room as the servants were turning on table lamps and wall sconces. He moved to where MacDonald stood with a group around him.

Sensing Thomson's disappointment, MacDonald's glance showed he instinctively knew the interview had been a failure. As the guardsmen and dancers wrapped up, MacDonald started the applause and everyone joined in. He eased his way over to Thomson and they went under the galleried arches into the White Parlor.

"Why so glum, CB?"

"It didn't go well with Wallis. He seemed quite receptive at first. But then he said his first task would be to fire all the staff at the Royal Airship Works."

"My goodness!"

"The nerve of the fellow," Thomson said.

"We're supposed to be creating jobs, not laying everybody off!"

"He may be the greatest engineer in the world, but we can't have someone like that going around laying down the law, telling us what's what!"

"You don't really know if he *is* the best engineer available. There must be others, surely?" MacDonald said.

"Time will tell, Ramsay."

"Well, old chap, don't let this little hiccup spoil this wonderful party. Let's go in there and tell them about all our plans," MacDonald said.

They reentered the Great Hall and Thomson picked out one of the Lenin look-a-likes and went to work.

"George Casewell, isn't it? I'm Christopher Thomson," he said, thrusting out his hand. "You're with the Yorkshire Miners Union. The future is looking bright indeed. We have plans afoot to nationalize the coal mines and introduce more safety regulations, you know."

The rough-and-ready Casewell peered at Thomson as if assessing him for the first time, obviously surprised to hear such sweet words coming from someone of his sort. Thomson sensed the man melt. His manner changed before Thomson's eyes—yes, he was being reappraised.

Progress indeed!

9

OUT OF THE BLUE

January 1922 - April 1924.

Lou enjoyed working at the garage. John Bull, the owner, was a gentle man with hands that tremored and words that faltered. He stood six feet tall, with sad blue eyes and a full head of grey hair and a matching, close-cropped beard. His disarming smile, though rarely seen, hinted at his inner goodness. Lou sensed he possessed a strong business acumen, but clearly his heart wasn't in it; perhaps once it had been, but not anymore. Lou didn't ask questions. It wasn't hard to figure. If Mr. Bull wanted him to know, he'd tell him in his own time.

Lou guessed John had read about him in the newspapers from a few things he'd said. One day while Lou was working on a truck in the shop, John brought in two mugs of steaming tea and leaned on the bench.

"My son was in France, too," he said.

Lou shook his head, sadly.

"Died at Passchendaele with hundreds of thousands of other young boys," John said, staring at the ground, the memory raw and unbearable.

"Awful," Lou said, remembering that indescribable horror.

"Blown to bits, I suppose, or drowned in the mud. They said he was 'missing.' No body, no funeral. No *nothing!*"

Lou screwed up his face, recalling the macabre faces of the dead. He'd encountered many gruesome skeletons in rags wearing helmets, propped against barbed wire, grinning—their faces eaten away by rats.

"When we got the news, it was the most miserable day of our lives."

"I'm so very, very sorry, sir," Lou said.

"So many of our young boys are gone—*thousands and thousands* of them from around here—gone forever. It just wasn't right!"

"It was all a waste, Mr. Bull. A terrible waste."

"Please call me John. No more sirs, or Mr. Bull, eh lad?"

"All right then …John."

John went silent for a few moments as though deciding whether to ask—not sure if he really wanted to know. In the end he spoke.

"Tell me, what was it like for you? Where were you?"

"I was in Belleau Wood and then Saint-Mihiel with the Marines. I started out in observation balloons until they were shot down by enemy planes."

"What happened to you?"

"I bailed out twice, but I was okay."

"You were bloody lucky!"

"That's what they called me, especially later," Lou said.

"Why what happened?"

"Once the balloons were down they sent me to the trenches. I got blown up by German artillery in a deep bunker with twenty-five others and buried."

John was horrified at the thought. "How long were you buried?"

Lou grimaced. "Six hours."

"Six hours! Oh no! Were you okay?"

"Yeah, I was a bit banged up. They sent me to the field hospital for a few days."

"You're okay now though?"

"Well, it stayed with me. I can't bear being shut in—gives me the horrors."

"What about the other men?"

"All dead."

"Oh, dear God. What happened to you then, son? Did they send you back to the trenches?"

"I requested to be sent back with my Army buddies. But that wasn't the worst of it."

John looked at Lou with compassion. "Tell me what happened to you, I want to know."

"On eleven, eleven …"

"The last day of the war?"

"Yeah. After first standing us down, we were ordered to attack. We climbed the ladders out of the trenches into No Man's Land. There were waves of us. It was pretty quiet for a long time—the Germans were holding their fire."

John was mortified. "What time was this?"

"We got to the German line about ten minutes to eleven."

"Dear God! Then what?"

"The Germans kept shouting: 'Go back, Yanks. Go home!'"

"But you advanced?"

"Yes. They fired over our heads at first. They wanted no part of it."

"And then?"

"Finally, they understood we meant business and were coming to kill them."

"And you would've?"

"Yes. We were under orders to kill them to the last second. They started firing at us. I saw my buddies to my left going down and then they all went down."

"What about you?"

Lou paused for a long time, unable to answer.

"I went down, too," he said finally.

"You were hit?"

Lou hesitated. "I guess I blacked out."

John was reliving this with Lou who'd turned white. "What happened then?"

"I came to, lying beside my friends." Lou wrapped his hands around his head trying to banish the memory.

"They were all dead?"

"Yes."

Lou saw the look of thankfulness on John's face. "But you were alive!"

Lou nodded, ashamed.

"Then I heard bugles sounding, claxtons going off and cheering."

"What was the commotion?"

"It was the cease fire signal. The war was over. I walked back to camp.

"You must've been happy."

"It was the saddest day of my life," Lou said.

Lou noticed a slight change in John over the coming weeks. He was a little brighter and his hands shook less. John had taken to Lou. He could never take the place of his son, but having Lou around seemed to help ease the pain. For Lou, he had someone to talk to. He confided in John about his own demons from the war and the *R38* debacle.

A couple of weeks later, John asked Lou to take a ride with him in his car. "I've got something to show you," he said.

They drove in silence to the village of Peacehaven, about seven miles away. Stopping outside an old but very beautiful stone cottage, they climbed out and John opened the squeaky wooden gate. The sign beside the front door, its paint peeling, read: 'Candlestick Cottage'.

"I wanted you to see the cottage we bought for our son before he went off to war." John reverently opened the front door and they entered the musty-smelling living room. Lou glanced around. The room was cosy with black beamed ceilings and a quaint, stone fireplace. "He loved this place. He only came here once. In his letters he promised he'd come back and live here," John said bitterly. "I thought if we bought it, somehow he'd return. He *would* survive—he'd *have to survive*! ...All I did was put a *jinx* on him."

"Your son would've been happy here," Lou said.

"We want you and Charlotte to live here. You can have it for whatever rent you are paying now."

Lou hesitated, not sure what to say.

"Hell, you can live here for nothing," John said, his voice faltering, his eyes filling with tears.

Lou put his hand on John's shoulder. "John, we couldn't possibly. This place is too important to you and Mary."

"Yes, that's the point. Lou, I want you to talk to your wife. In fact, I'd like to speak to her myself. We'll bring Charlotte over here tomorrow and see what she thinks."

Charlotte fell in love with the cottage immediately. She particularly liked the box room next to the bedroom—perfect for a baby's crib. Perhaps it was a sign! But she had reservations.

"We'd be taking advantage of these lovely people," she whispered.

John would have none of it.

"I have to tell you honestly. Mary and I'd be thrilled if you lived here—it'd give us peace of mind," he said. "And it needs to be lived in … it needs life!"

Charlotte relented on the understanding they'd pay a fair rent. Lou and Charlotte moved into Candlestick Cottage a week later, where they settled into a dreamy contentment and as newlyweds, they were blissfully happy. It was a dream come true. John and Lou got to work repainting the place and fixing things. They sanded and refinished the wood floors. Lou touched up the peeling sign at the door. Charlotte worked hard with Mary to make it comfortable with colorful curtains and soft chairs bought from Friedman's Second Hand Furniture & Removals in Hull.

Charlotte's parents had their piano delivered ('on loan') to the cottage by the same company for Charlotte. Delighted, she rushed out and picked up the sheet music for Irving Berlin's "What'll I Do?" It was all the rage. She practiced playing and singing the mournful song every day until she was perfect. Money was short, but that didn't spoil their happiness. Charlotte made the twenty-minute ride to the hospital in Hull each morning on a little green bus and Lou continued at the garage.

A few weeks later, Charlotte took Lou with her to the music shop in Hull to buy a couple more songs. Lou noticed a second-hand guitar in the window and asked to see it. It was a Martin guitar, more than twenty years old, made in Nazareth, Pennsylvania. The back and sides were of Brazilian rosewood, the front, white spruce. Lou really knew a thing or two about guitars and was taken with the inlaid ivory rosette, bridge pins and knobs. He adjusted the gut strings and tuned it. Suddenly, the shop was filled with beautiful, melodious sound. Charlotte was amazed.

This was a talent she never realized he possessed—he'd never mentioned it. Lou asked the shopkeeper the price. It was five pounds. Lou knew it was well worth it, but reluctantly handed it back. Charlotte resolved that somehow that guitar would be his. The next day, she put down half-a- crown to hold it. Over the next two months she worked extra shifts and paid down more. In the end, the shopkeeper told her to take it home and continue making weekly payments. Charlotte gleefully hid it under the bed in its black, coffin-like case until Lou's birthday that June, when she presented it to him wrapped in brown paper. He was thrilled. Charlotte was delighted when he sung country songs—cowboy music! Sometimes, he accompanied her when she played the piano, and he began writing his own songs.

That spring, Charlotte started a vegetable garden, which she tended at weekends. She proved to have a green thumb. Soon, colorful flowers and vines were blooming around the cottage in beds, rockeries, trellises, and hanging baskets. John often came by, cheered by the new life in this little home. His demeanor improved and he and his wife began to think of them as more than friends. Lou was content, especially now the court of inquiry was behind him. He missed his family in Virginia, but at least they exchanged letters every week.

Life moved along pleasantly until April of 1924. One bright Saturday morning, Charlotte, in headscarf, long apron and rubber boots was preparing a patch in the garden to plant carrots and potatoes, while Fluffy sat on the stone wall, watching.

"Mrs. Remington?" a man's voice called over the front gate.

Charlotte stood up, shielding her eyes from the sun. He wore British Airshipmen's blues, resembling a naval uniform.

"Oh hello, Major ...er," Charlotte said.

"Scott," he said. "I wasn't sure if that was you in the wellies."

"Ah, yes, Major *Scott*. How are you?" she asked, puzzled.

"I was in Hull on official business and thought I'd drop by. I hope you don't mind."

"No, but how did you find us?"

"You stop the first person you meet and ask for 'the American.'"

Charlotte laughed. "I suppose that's true."

Scott peered over her shoulder. "Is he about?"

"He's at work—should be home in half an hour."

"All right, I can come back, if that's all right?"

"Why don't you come in and wait. I'll make you a cup of tea, if you like."

"Wonderful! I could murder a nice cuppa."

Charlotte led Scott through the planked front door into the living room with Fluffy following. A coal fire glowed in the fireplace. She was pleased when Scott glanced around appreciating their work: painted black beams, a colorful rug over highly polished wood flooring, throw-covers and the dozens of cushions of all colors and sizes strewn haphazardly about.

"My, what a lovely room," Scott exclaimed. "Hey, I recognize that cat!"

"That's Fluffy. I had a fight with the boat captain. He wanted to keep her."

"Ah yes, the famous Fluffy!"

Scott's eyes fell on the bottle of sherry on the sideboard and then on Charlotte—perhaps lingering a little too long. She could overlook that. He'd done a lot for all of them that day—she'd never forget *that*. His face was red and she caught a whiff of alcohol. She remembered him taking a swig from his flask before rushing off to the boat.

Must've had a heavy session in Hull last night!

Charlotte gestured toward one of the soft armchairs.

"Make yourself comfortable, Major."

Before disappearing into the kitchen, Charlotte picked up her knitting and bent over the couch and put it in a basket out of sight. She sensed him watching her.

She soon reappeared with a tea tray, which she placed on the low table in front of the couch. Scott looked up pleased. "Good. We can chat before Lou comes in. How is he—in himself, I mean?"

"He's much better," Charlotte said as she poured the tea. "He's getting over the accident pretty well."

"Is he happy?"

"Yes, *very* happy."

"Working?"

"He works in a garage."

"Oh, yes I remember. He told me at the inquiry."

Charlotte got up to poke the fire and add a few shovels of coal from a brass scuttle. They sat and chatted for half an hour. Scott was interested to know about all aspects of their lives, including Charlotte's folks in Ackworth and their own plans to start a family. In the end, he came to the point.

"I have a proposal for Lou and in some ways it's good I talk to you first, because if you're not in favor, it wouldn't work. 'Behind every good man ...'—you know the old saying. He'd be able to put his valuable knowledge and experience to good use," Scott said.

Suspicion showed in Charlotte's face. "What sort of proposal?"

"I expect you've heard. The British Airship Industry is about to be revitalized and Lou could play an important role."

Charlotte and Lou had, in fact, heard things on their new wireless and read glowing reports in the *Daily Mirror*. They'd listened to a speech given by the new Minister of State for Air, a rather pompous-sounding Lord something-or-other with a voice like a gravel pit.

Charlotte screwed up her face and shook her head. "Oh, I don't know."

"You want him to be happy, don't you?"

Charlotte sipped her tea and thought for a moment, staring out the window into the garden.

Damn! Why did he have to show up here?

"Yes, of course I do—but those contraptions are too dangerous."

"They won't be," Scott said.

"Another one went down in America. Killed 34 men. All of them burned to death. That was in Virginia—Lou's home state."

"You're talking about the *Roma*. That thing was just an Italian sausage balloon—stone-age technology. *That* can't happen again."

"I'd be too worried."

"No need to worry. Government is drawing up massive new safety regulations."

"I don't like them."

"Airships will be as safe as houses. Huge new industry—thing of the future."

Charlotte shook her head, unconvinced.

"The pay will be substantial for officers in the fleet—a good living indeed!"

"I'll talk to my husband," Charlotte said.

"Yes, yes, of course. He'd be working only down the road from here at Howden. You wouldn't need to move—not for three or four years anyway. I think you'd both be very happy."

They heard the front door opening and Lou walked in, looking surprised. "Major Scott! What brings you here, sir? I wondered whose car it was outside."

Lou kissed Charlotte and Scott jumped up to shake hands.

"I had business in Hull, Lieutenant. Just thought I'd drop by."

They sat down around the low table. Charlotte poured tea for Lou.

"More tea, Major?"

Scott hesitated and glanced at the sherry bottle. "I tell you what. A glass of your sherry would be nice."

"Of course." Lou went to the sideboard, poured out a glass and handed it to Scott.

Scott raised the glass. "Here's to both of you." He took a polite sip and leaned forward in his chair, stroking Fluffy purring at his feet.

"Were you happy in the Navy, Lou?"

"I loved the Navy, sir."

"How would you like to be back in?"

Lou glanced at Charlotte. "I don't understand how that could be possible, sir."

"I was telling your wife, things are opening back up at Howden. I don't suppose you want to work in a country garage for the rest of your life?"

Lou hesitated. "Er, well I suppose not."

"If you want back in, it can be arranged. In fact, it's *already* arranged. If you're both interested—just say the word," Scott said, swallowing the rest of his sherry.

Charlotte shot Scott a look of surprise. He hadn't told her that earlier.

"I can't believe this," Lou said.

"The Minister has spoken with the Secretary of the Navy in Washington. You'd be seconded by the Air Ministry to work on the New British Airship Program."

"Where?"

"You'd be based here in Howden as part of the Royal Airship Works team, which is totally responsible for the ship Vickers Aircraft Company will construct. You'd monitor the construction and report to us at the R.A.W. I know you did the same job when you were based in Cardington—I remember you very well.

"Sounds interesting," Lou said, refilling Scott's glass.

"You'd be here full time until this ship is completed. Then you'd move to Cardington—a beautiful little village, by the way," Scott added, giving Charlotte a reassuring glance.

"Wouldn't all this be unusual, me being in the U.S. Navy and ..."

"Not as unusual as you might think. Allies often second members of the each other's military for training and assistance. Commander Zachary Lansdowne was trained here and worked with us. He flew with me as American observer when I made the first return flight to the United States. He was awarded the Navy Cross and I received the Royal Air Force Cross. ..." Then he added wryly, "Others got knighted for less."

"I served under Commander Landsdowne for a short time," Lou said.

"Yes, so I understand. He's just taken over command of the *Shenandoah*," Scott said.

"We know someone else on that ship—one of Lou's crewmen," Charlotte said, without enthusiasm.

"These are exciting times. It's up to you," Scott said.

Lou sat stunned at this opportunity out of the blue. "I don't know what to say, sir."

"Don't say anything yet. You and Charlotte need to talk things over and think about your future and your new family." Charlotte saw Scott's eyes go in the direction of her knitting basket behind the couch and he nodded. She dropped her eyes—he'd noticed her hide her knitting. "Bedford will become one of the biggest travel centers in Britain, with regularly scheduled flights to the United States, Canada, India, Australia and New Zealand—it'll be known as 'Airship City.'"

"Sounds like they've got big plans," Lou said.

"Your first job would be to manage the re-commissioning of Howden Air Station, including repairs to the shed. That'll take a couple of years and should be interesting," Scott said.

Lou pondered that. He'd been sorry to see that place fall into ruin.

"Sounds great, sir."

"Howden used to be the biggest airship base in the country. Oh, and another thing. You'd be working with one of the finest airship engineers in the country—fella by the name of Wallis, Barnes Wallis."

While he stroked Fluffy, Scott talked generally about the airship industry and Lou's future prospects. Finally, he stood up and took out his wallet.

"Here's my card. Give me a call next week. If you decide against it, that's fine. I'll totally understand. You're under no obligation. I must be going—and thanks for the sherry—and the tea."

Scott shook hands with them and they watched him drive off in his little, black Ford. They closed the door after he'd gone and Charlotte cleared away the tea things in silence. The prospects were exciting—though much less for her.

"I guess there's not much to think about, is there?" Lou said.

Charlotte couldn't stop him. It'd make him happy and might be therapeutic. There'd be benefits, too: a better standard of living, a house of their own, they could seriously think of starting a family—maybe even get a little dog named Snowy!

"It's too good to turn down," Lou said

Charlotte reluctantly agreed, forcing herself to put negative emotions aside. It'd be years before any of these airships would be ready to fly. She could always talk him out of it later.

On Monday morning Lou had the unpleasant task of breaking the news to John Bull.

"John, something has come up, completely out of the blue," Lou told him. There was disappointment in John's eyes.

"What is it, Lou?"

One of the Air Ministry guys came by the cottage Saturday ..."

"And offered you a job?"

"Yes."

"Airships?" John tried to hide his dread.

"Yeah. They're gonna be building one at the Howden shed."

"That would be so handy for you, son."

"Long term it looks good and they've already squared things with the U.S. Navy. They're talking about me becoming a ship's officer—maybe even a captain, one day."

"My goodness! They must really want you."

"They asked me to manage fixing up the air station—that'll take a couple of years."

"I'm really excited for you, Lou. Sounds like a wonderful opportunity."

"Yes, but I'd hate to leave. I love working here with you, John."

"Lou, you must do what you must. You've got your whole life ahead of you. Mary and I want the best for you. You can't stay here all your life, can you?"

"I don't know, John …Charlotte and I have been very happy."

"No harm in trying things out. We'll still be close by. You're like a son to us."

Tears formed in John's eyes, making Lou feel wretched.

"And if things don't work out there'll always be a job here if you need one—and perhaps a lot more …" John said, taking Lou's hand between his own.

"The cottage …" Lou began.

"The cottage is yours as long as you want, my son, you know that."

Lou went home to Charlotte, his mind in turmoil.

The following week, Lou called Scott with their decision. He'd take the job. Scott told him to 'sit tight.' Two weeks later, Lou received a letter from Scott saying the offer had been approved; Lou would be hearing from the U.S. Navy and he'd be seconded by the Air Ministry, as discussed. A week later, Lou received a wire from the Navy confirming he'd been reinstated and would receive the rate of pay for a U.S. lieutenant based overseas, with travel and housing allowances. He was to take orders from Maj. Scott and Wing Cmdr. Colmore at the Royal Airship Works at Cardington under control of the British Air Ministry. He would observe British military ranks.

Scott was in Hull again two weeks later and he and Lou visited the Howden shed to make an inspection. Scott was interested to view the condition of the property since money would need to be allotted for renovations and additional equipment to turn the place back into a habitable working facility.

While the skylarks sang in surrounding fields, they drove around the thousand acres of low-lying ground, stopping at various dilapidated buildings. Their movements were watched by a herd of grazing cows, and scattered sheep bleating in the distance.

"The first thing you'll need to do is to reclaim this place from all these bloody animals!" Scott declared.

In the main shed, Lou showed Scott a vixen's den under the concrete slab in the hydrogen pipe ducts where she lived with her cubs. The shed floor was covered with chicken's feathers. They had a good laugh about that before driving off to The Railway Station pub in Howden where they ordered ham sandwiches and pints of Tetley's Best Bitter. Amused, Lou watched the barman pull up their beers with the bar pump handle. It frothed and overflowed, running down the glasses and over the bar.

I reckon these people would take a bath in this stuff if they could.

"I think you're going to do well here, Lou," Scott said, after taking a long swallow, half emptying his glass. He licked his lips. "Ah, that's much better."

"I'm looking forward to it, sir."

"You'll become a ship's officer in no time if you study hard."

They tucked into their sandwiches and Scott ordered more beers. Lou hadn't finished his first. "No, no more for me, sir."

"Come on, man, have another. It'll put hair on your chest," Scott said, and to the barman, "Give him another." Scott drained his first pint and went on. "You'll need to come down to Cardington next month to discuss your duties here and your relationship with Vickers."

"Okay, sir. When?"

"I'll let you know. Lord Thomson, the new Secretary of State, will be holding a press conference and making a public announcement about the program. They'll be broadcasting his speech on the wireless."

"You don't say!"

"I want you to attend. I'll introduce you to him."

"Great," Lou said with both awe and apprehension.

"I'll check and give you the exact date. You'd better arrange to get the telephones reconnected at the shed and get one installed at your cottage. We'll need to be in touch constantly. Oh, there's someone I must warn you about."

Lou was intrigued.

"Fella by the name of Dennistoun Burney. He's the man who heads up Vickers airship division. He's a royal pain in the arse. So, when you meet him, be polite, but don't take orders from him. Just say, you'll discuss the matter with your superiors."

"Right. Thanks for the warning, sir," Lou said.

"The others are okay. Barnes Wallis is a good man. Norway I've never met. He's with deHaviland Aircraft, but I understand he'll be joining their team as chief calculator this year. I don't think he knows anything about airships."

"I look forward to meeting everyone," Lou said.

Scott sank his second pint, while Lou struggled with his.

"Well, I must be going," Scott said, jumping up. "Come on, I'll drop you off."

10

BACK IN BEDFORD

May 1924.

During the first week of May, Lou traveled to Bedford. He was familiar with the area from his days working on *R38* in 1920 and '21. Lou felt the optimism in the air as soon as he got off the train. He sensed it on the familiar, old, green bus on the way to the Cardington gate. Though it was good to be back, he felt pangs of grief and as well as nostalgia. Passengers noticed his uniform and his American insignias. They smiled sympathetically.

The bus conductor remembered him. "Hello, sir. Lovely to have you back," he said. Lou forced a grin and looked out the window. They were passing Rowe's Tobacconist Shop, also known as the 'corner store,' where his buddies used to buy cigarettes and newspapers.

"We were all so choked up about what happened to you and your shipmates," the conductor said. Lou said nothing. He watched the people hurrying along the high street. The sun blazed and new leaves shone fresh and green. There was no evidence of his compatriots ever living or working here. Life had moved on. He looked out and saw a good-looking girl. Oh, those girls! They used to go mad for him and his buddies. It used to make the Bedford boys so angry. The haunting lyrics of Irving Berlin's "What'll I Do?" came into his mind. Charlotte had been playing that damned song all week. Desolation washed over him.

"I've been following you in the papers, sir. You didn't go home with the others, then?" the bus conductor said.

"This is home," Lou answered.

He thought about Charlotte and realized how much better he'd been since he got married. Lou held out a shilling for his fare. The conductor refused his money and winked. "Welcome home, son," he said, walking to the other end of the bus. Lou looked out the window again. His thoughts were disturbed by a plaintive voice behind him.

"Excuse me, sir."

Lou turned around to find a young man about twenty-six, skinny and angular with a fine nose and earnest, small, blue eyes. He removed his cap and held it in his hands, prayer-like.

"I couldn't help overhearing you're going up to Cardington, sir."

"Yes, why?" Lou noticed his right eye and cheek. He had a nervous twitch.

"I'm interested to find work, sir, and wondered if you might be able to help me in that regard."

"I'm not sure I can. This is my first day here, and I'm really only a visitor. What d'you do?" Lou asked.

"I'd like to work on the construction and I'm very good with engines. I'm a very 'ard worker, sir, 'an I'm very, very faithful."

"What's your name?"

"Joseph H. Binks, sir, but everybody calls me Joe."

Lou took out a small notepad and wrote down his name. "I'll see what I can do. Can't promise anything. Here, write down your address."

"I understand, sir. Work's scarce, you know, and I've got two young'uns at 'ome. Since I came out the Navy fings 'av been very 'ard," Binks said.

The bus came up to the gate and Lou got off with Binks behind him.

"Well, thank you, sir," Binks said, thrusting out his hand and bowing at the same time. "Lovely to have met you, sir."

"And you, too, Mr. Binks," Lou said, shaking his hand.

"God bless you, sir," Binks called after him, still holding his cap and bowing. Lou looked back, smiling. Binks trudged off and joined a long queue of men who, Lou presumed, were waiting for day work. As he walked toward the gate, he spotted Walter Potter standing by the gatehouse. Lou grinned, happy to see his old shipmate.

"Walter!"

"Sir! They said you was coming down. I couldn't wait to see you," Potter said, grasping Lou's hand. "I thought I'd wait and say hello."

"That's nice of you, Walter. How've you been? Are you working?"

"No. There's not much to do around here yet." Potter gestured to the line of men looking for work.

"Haven't you had enough of airships for one lifetime, Walter?"

Potter threw his head back and snorted. "Yeah, I have, but it's all I know. It's work. And a job is what I desperately need right now. Can you help me, sir?"

"You know I will, if I can. You live close by?"

Potter indicated with a sideways nod. "Shortstown. Just up the road."

Lou got out his pad again. "Write down your address. I'll see what I can do. I'm sure they'll find you something," Lou said. They chatted for a few minutes. Lou checked his watch. "I'd better go. They're waiting for me up there."

"Okay, sir, I hope we'll meet again soon."

"I'll be down every month. We'll have a pint. I'll see what I can do for you, don't worry." Lou gave him an assuring wink as they parted.

The guardhouse had been painted and the flower beds at the gate freshly planted with daffodils, making the place look spic-and-span. The gatekeeper greeted him warmly.

"Lieutenant Remington! How are you, sir? They told me to expect you," he said. "I'll get you a lift. Wait a mo.'" He held his hand up to a car coming through the gate. "Hey, Harry can you drop off our old friend the Lieutenant at the Admin?"

"Sure," the driver said, peering at Lou with a spark of recognition.

Lou climbed in and they traveled up the driveway lined with flowering cherry trees. "I remember you, sir. My name's Harry, Harry Leech. I'm one of the engineering foremen."

"Your face is familiar. You're the engine wizard," Lou said. "Looks like this place is coming back to life."

"You bet! This bloke Thomson might be our savior," Leech said.

"Never can tell," said Lou.

The enormous sheds dominated the skyline and the surrounding area with all their ancillary buildings—housing machine shops, a gasbag factory, a hydrogen plant, electricity generators and warehouses. The area bustled with activity. Contractors' vehicles passed by—builders, painters, plumbers, electricians and landscapers, while others delivered scaffolding, planks, lumber, and assorted building materials.

In the distance, at the sheds, men stood on ladders fixing lighting while others painted the areas around the entrance doors. The weeds and brush, which had taken over, were being cleared and loaded onto a lorry.

"Good to see the ol' place resurrected," Leech said. "I'll be glad to get back to work." Lou nodded, realizing the enormity of his own task at Howden—that property being older and far more run down. He also had twenty derelict homes to renovate on the base for use by staff and their families. Cardington was years ahead in getting their facilities back in commission. Vickers' Howden team would be at a disadvantage from day one.

They traveled up the gravel road to Cardington House, an imposing stately home, previously owned by a wealthy industrialist and philanthropist. He'd made the property a gift to the government for the sake of airship research and development. The classical stucco great-house, set in magnificent gardens, now served as the headquarters for the Royal Airship Works (the R.A.W.). The building stood in a sea of daffodils with a backdrop of flowering tulip trees, magnolia trees, azaleas and rhododendrons. The place was a bird sanctuary with magpies, swallows, robins, pigeons and sparrows flying busily from tree to tree. Fragrances from this colorful paradise were overpowering. Lou paused to take it all in, not noticing the three black crows cawing and blinking slyly at him from their low branch.

Scott met Lou in the entrance hall of Cardington House and took him to meet Wing Cmdr. Colmore, Deputy Director of Airship Development in his ground floor office which looked out across the airfield. Lou had only been in the building a few times in the past, usually to deliver a communication or memo from the U.S. Navy to the R.A.W. brass.

Colmore, a charming man of forty-five, had graying hair, very short at the back and sides. He put Lou at ease immediately and confirmed Lou would begin restoration work at Howden as soon as possible, so Vickers could get started. The money had been budgeted and was available immediately. After the air station was up and running, Lou would continue to be based at Howden, assisting Vickers with the airship's construction and keeping records of progress as one of the general overseers—'not as a watchdog, but as a pair of eyes for the R.A.W. and there to assist Vickers in any way necessary.' He would not betray confidences from either side.

This relieved Lou. He didn't want the Vickers staff to think of him as a spy in the camp. Lou would visit Cardington once a month to report on progress and relay anything Vickers needed. Lou got a further boost when Colmore told him he'd be his 'special assistant'—a liaison officer. He winked at Lou and told him there'd be an increase in his salary paid by the Air Ministry. To Lou's amusement, Colmore reiterated the warning about Dennistoun Burney, who Colmore said was a bit of a 'bloody nuisance.'

After lunch in the dining room with Colmore and Scott, the building came alive. The heavy, white paneled office doors opened and closed constantly and people dashed in and out of the marble reception hall where Thomson's press conference was scheduled to take place. Broadcasting equipment and microphones were being set up and tested. Thomson would be on the air in two hours.

Suddenly, there was a great fuss at the entrance—Thomson's limousine had arrived. Lou went out with Scott and Colmore and other R.A.W. staff to greet him. Thomson got out and climbed the steps, his military bearing evident, though he appeared pale and gaunt. He came across initially as a forceful, energetic man. Word had traveled fast—the new Minister of State from Whitehall was on base. Everyone was anxious to catch a glimpse.

Inside the majestic reception hall, Thomson peered around at the seating, nodding with pleasure at the preparations. He was led to the conference room by Colmore and Scott, and the door closed behind them. Lou went and sat in the reception hall. Thirty minutes later, Lou was sent for and taken to the conference room to meet 'the man'. He entered in time to see the chief steward receiving generous praise for the 'delicious cucumber sandwiches' he'd served Thomson with his tea.

Thomson, long-necked and vulture-like, stood with his slender hand extended. His sagging, weary eyes and hollow cheeks made his nose prominent and beak-like. His shoulders were stooped and his threadbare, black coat ill-fitting and loose around the collar. Lou assessed him as a man who'd seen rough times. Though Thomson was courteous, Lou couldn't help feeling intimidated, but at the same time sympathetic. At times like this, he remembered what his grandmother once told him: 'Remember, son, inside every man there's a small boy'. Her words floated down from the ether at this moment.

"Lieutenant Remington! I'm pleased to meet you," Thomson said, shaking Lou's hand, the grip of his long, delicate fingers firm, but not overly so.

"Likewise, sir."

"I've had conversations about you with your people in Washington. Are you happy with the set up?"

"Yes, sir, I'm very pleased."

"We're honored to have you with us. You're highly thought of, both here and at home. I think this arrangement will be beneficial to both countries," Thomson said.

"Thank you, sir."

Thomson seemed about to end the conversation, but had an afterthought.

"You were at the Front?"

"Yes, sir—Belleau Wood and Saint-Mihiel."

"And thank God you were, Lieutenant. I was at Ypres. I read your war record. You were buried alive with twenty-five other men, weren't you?"

"Yes, sir."

"Awful business. Any ill effects?"

"No, sir. I'm fine," Lou lied.

"What about the others?"

"All dead, sir."

Thomson nodded sadly. "Well, welcome aboard. We'll be changing the world together. These new airships will be the next big thing," Thomson said, looking from Lou to Colmore and Scott.

After more small talk, Lou left the conference room to find the reception hall filling up. Those gathering appeared to be the well-to-do from the local area: businessmen, bankers, solicitors, doctors, accountants—mostly professionals. Others included Whitehall civil servants, members of Parliament and military personnel in uniform. Two dozen reporters and about twenty photographers were also present. Lou took a seat off to one side. Some reporters recognized him. A nerdy-looking young man in a Harris Tweed jacket, sitting nearby, also seemed to be taking quite an interest in him.

11

THE DIE IS CAST

May 1924.

At ten minutes to three, Thomson marched in and mounted the low podium where he was joined by Colmore, Scott and another R.A.W. man Lou hadn't seen before. Thomson took a sip from a glass of water. After testing the microphones, a BBC technician wearing headphones told Thomson he'd be on in four minutes. As the time came up, the man held up his fingers, counting down seconds. Thomson cleared his throat and began in his gravelly, baritone voice.

"Good afternoon, ladies and gentlemen and listeners. It gives me great pleasure to speak to you from the Royal Airship Works at Cardington, in Bedfordshire—home of the British airship industry for more than ten years."

The two hundred people in the audience listened with rapt attention. "It is with pride that I announce today the beginning of the New British Imperial Airship Program and I'm here to describe my vision of a future fleet of luxurious airships that will compete globally with ocean liners."

Thomson smiled benevolently into the flashing cameras while reporters scribbled. "The proposal I put to the Cabinet was approved by the Prime Minister, who put it to the House of Commons where it was overwhelmingly approved. I presented this proposal to the House of Lords, explaining how this program will be the most ambitious airship building program ever undertaken. Once again, the program received enthusiastic support."

Thomson paused to make sure he had everyone's attention.

"After careful deliberation, I've decided the government will underwrite the construction of two airships at a cost of one million, four hundred thousand pounds. Each will have the capacity of five million cubic feet of hydrogen, giving a lifting capacity of one hundred and fifty tons." Thomson paused again for reporters to write the numbers down.

"Weight shall not exceed ninety tons—leaving sixty tons of lift for passengers, fuel, stores and ballast. The top speed will not exceed seventy miles per hour—four times the speed of a passenger liner! High fuel loads and high speeds will give these airships the range and power necessary to reach all corners of the globe.

"The first ship, designated *Howden R100*, will be constructed for the government by Vickers Aircraft at Howden in Yorkshire under a fixed-price contract. Those in charge of constructing *Howden R100* will report directly to, and be administered by, the Royal Airship Works Staff."

Thomson paused, remembering his meeting with Wallis as he gestured grandly to the three men standing with him at the podium. They smiled serenely while a series of camera flashes started again.

"The second ship, designated *Cardington R101*, will be built by the government team here at the Royal Airship Works."

Murmurs of excitement were building.

"This ship will be one of a new class in design. Now, before introducing the Royal Airship Works team, I will say this: The acceptance of the New British Airship Program is a rejection of the 'Burney Scheme,' which proposed Vickers build six airships costing tax payers a whopping four million eight hundred thousand pounds. A proposal far too grandiose, and meaning Vickers would have a complete monopoly—an unacceptable state of affairs, if I may say so."

Thomson seemed to have the approval of most, but not all.

"In the early stages, it will be my intention to enlist the help of private enterprise—not in competition, but in a spirit of cooperation—each assisting and improving the performance of the other."

He paused and looked down for a moment. "I may take a risk when I say I don't believe even the most aggressive businessmen will be wholly inspired by sordid motives—in other words, by greed—when they assist the government in the conquest of the air! The earlier pioneers in aviation made sacrifices at first, but in the end, they made money—lots of money. In order to make a success of this venture, sacrifices will have to be made by private enterprise—for the *Common Good.*"

There were a few shouts of "Hear, hear" and weak applause.

"Under the Burney Scheme, if the first ship crashed, all would be lost. Under our plan, if we lose one of the ships, we will still have the other ship plus the experts, the designers and the engineers. We would still have our air routes, our infrastructure and the will and determination to carry on with this project to see it through."

There were frowns on some faces. Some found his line of reasoning hard to follow, but they'd go along—jobs were all that mattered.

"At the end of the day, we'll learn that state enterprise in industry, business, finance, transportation and communication will be enormously more efficient than private enterprise. This program will be a learning experience. State enterprise will be the cornerstone of our socialist policies. I will now introduce you to the team."

Thomson gestured grandly toward the three men standing behind him. "Wing Commander Reginald Colmore as Deputy Director of Airship Development and will be overall administrator of the Airship Program. Colmore has had fifteen years experience in this industry. During the war, he developed an effective anti-submarine patrol strategy using airships in conjunction with surface ships and aeroplanes to hunt down the enemy. So effective was his brainchild that the system was set up around the entire coast of Britain. Wing Commander Colmore has been involved from the inception of this program and assisted in writing the specifications. He has a proven track record as a fine leader."

Colmore stepped forward and bowed his head slightly while receiving gentle applause. Thomson had assessed him to be a rather humble, well-bred man of grace and charm. They said Colmore didn't possess a mean bone in his body. Thomson had reservations—perhaps he wasn't forceful enough. Furthermore, although Colmore thoroughly understood airships, he'd made it known he believed they had their limitations.

Can he give me one hundred percent?

"Now I introduce Major Herbert Scott. Most of you know this man and why he is such a valuable asset." Thomson smiled and so did Scott, who took a pace forward. Thomson thought of him as hard driving when the going got tough, but he had a reputation for recklessness. Thomson was well aware of past instances of this. He'd been in command of the Parseval PL-18 when she crashed into her shed in Barrow in 1915. That was in fog—ages ago. He'd also been in command of R36 when she was badly damaged during mooring operations at Pulham in 1921.

Despite all that, he's a man who'll inject momentum into this team. He'll need holding in check. Men like this—prepared to take risks— built the Empire.

"This man is a true pioneer in British aviation and a man to whom we owe a debt of gratitude. He was the *first* man to fly the Atlantic, as the captain of *Airship R34*, making the return journey between Scotland and the United States in 1919. Major Scott will be in charge of testing and flying the aircraft and training personnel. He'll make sure we have the best men in our fleet."

Thomson looked across briefly at Lou who showed no reaction. The applause this time was loud, with a few cheers, delighting Scott who waved to the audience.

"Last, but not least, I want to introduce Colonel Vincent Richmond, who will head up management of the design team. The design of *Cardington R101* will be in this man's hands."

Richmond, average height, slightly rounded, with a head of dark, shiny, Brylcreemed hair, stepped forward to give the audience a curt nod and a begrudging, crooked smile from thin lips. Thomson also had reservations about Richmond. He sensed the man was confident, perhaps overconfident. His colleagues considered him pompous. Thomson knew he was ambitious, which made him glad. He really didn't care about his other traits.

He has a high opinion of himself, no doubt. We'll see what he's made of. What good would these people be, if they weren't confident and ambitious? Competence and leadership are what we need.

This position would carry not only immense responsibility and pressure, but the stigma of failures by previous government designers. None of this seemed to phase Richmond. This was a man who sensed his time had come and was ready for the challenge. Richmond received meager applause. Thomson went on, squinting over his pince-nez spectacles, smiling at reporters.

"As soon as construction and testing are complete, each ship will be required to make an intercontinental flight—*Howden R100* to Canada, *Cardington R101* to India."

This caused a buzz of excitement. Thomson beamed with pleasure.

At this point, the BBC technician signaled that the broadcast segment was coming to an end. Thomson paused while the radio announcer wrapped things up with a few words to the radio audience after which, Thomson continued with his press conference.

"If you have any questions, gentlemen, I'd be pleased to answer them."

An eager reporter leapt to his feet. "Tom Brewer, *Daily Telegraph*. Lord Thomson, the feeling in this country, after so many crashes and loss of life, is that airships are totally unsafe."

Thomson held up his right hand as though directing traffic and lifted his chin defiantly, staring over the reporter's head. The man had become invisible.

"Good, good. A wise, thoughtful question, indeed, sir—one this government will take seriously. One thing I stress above *all else*: 'Safety First' is the unbreakable rule!" Thomson put on a determined frown and shook his finger at the ceiling. "*And 'Safety Second' as well, by Jove!*"

An overweight reporter in a khaki raincoat stood up next.

"Bill Hagan, *Daily Mail*. Lord Thomson, there were reports that Barnes Wallis was going to head up this program. What happened? He *is* the best airship engineer in the country, is he not?"

Thomson's memory of his encounter with Wallis at Chequers tasted like acid reflux in his throat. He covered his mouth and coughed, carefully formulating an answer. He hadn't realized that meeting had got out.

"We considered a lot of people for the position and discussed all possibilities at length. We have a wonderful team of experienced men and I know the two teams will work well together toward a successful outcome." Thomson hoped no one sensed any lack of conviction.

A thin, well-dressed reporter in a Savile Row suit was next.

"William Haines, *The Times*. My question is directed to Colonel Richmond," he said, turning the pages of his notepad. "What do you think about having jurisdiction over Vickers? Are you confident in overseeing Barnes Wallis?"

Ouch!

Richmond glanced at Thomson as though for help. Thomson ignored him. "I don't think this will be an issue. Mr. Wallis will not need *supervision* from me, or this team. As you say, he's a superb engineer and we can all expect wonderful things from him."

This answer seemed to satisfy everybody. Richmond had been magnanimous. Thomson noticed him biting his lip and screwing up his eyes as he stepped away from the podium. Another reporter raised his hand. He had a Yorkshire accent.

"You say Vickers is building their ship for a contract sum. Do you know 'ow much your airship will cost and will you be able to build it for the same money?"

Thomson answered. "We don't know exactly, no. The airship has not even been designed, but the Cardington ship will certainly cost less —since it's being built at cost with no *profit* involved." He spat out 'profit,' grimacing. He pointed at the next reporter. A short, rotund Londoner stood up.

"Edmund Jones, *Daily Mirror*. Colonel Richmond, the last airship broke in half, killing forty-four people. How do you know your airship won't do the same?"

Richmond stepped forward. "I've spent a great deal of time studying the *R38* mishap. It's possible that sacrifices were made for lightness. I assure you, the strength of this airship will be our *top priority*. We'll go back to basics. Through strength we shall achieve safety—and, I should add, absolutely no expense will be spared in that regard."

A tall reporter wearing a scruffy raincoat and a five o'clock shadow had been pacing around impatiently at the back of the hall. It was George Hunter. Thomson pointed to him.

"George Hunter, *Daily Express*. Lord Thomson, you say you don't care much for the idea of Vickers getting a monopoly on the airship business. The way you've set all this up means *government* will have the monopoly. Is there *really* any difference?"

Thomson tried to hide his irritation. "Certainly. Government is entirely different. We represent the people and the *Common Good*— that's Common with a capital C and Good with a capital G."

George Hunter followed up. "But if a private company messes up, they go out of business, or are not hired again—ever! Things don't work that way with government, do they? Government just carries on as if nothing happened."

This infuriated Thomson.

Who is this man? Must be one of Burney's people!

"I'm not sure if I should dignify your statement with a rebuttal, sir."

The team on the podium appeared distinctly uncomfortable, nervously shuffling their feet. Tension became palpable. The angry reporter wouldn't let it go. He stalked down the center aisle to the foot of the podium, raising his arms and yelling up at Thomson.

"Do any of you people remember the horror of *R38*—any of you?"

Thomson recovered and did a commendable job of composing himself, his expression heartsick. "Yes, sir. All of us do. In fact we have someone in this room who remembers that awful day only too well."

Many of the reporters had already turned to gauge Lou's reaction. Thomson's gaze was followed by the rest of the people in the room, including Inspector Fred McWade, whom Lou noticed for the first time at the front. The man in the Harris Tweed jacket stared intensely at Lou. Their eyes met.

Who the hell is this guy?

"I want to present Lieutenant Louis Remington of the United States Navy, who has graciously agreed to be here today and who will be assisting us with these projects. Would you be kind enough to stand up, Lieutenant?"

Thomson didn't mention Lou's connection with *R38*. It wasn't necessary. Lou got out of his chair, standing as though for inspection. He didn't smile and hadn't been expecting this. Thomson continued. "We take this whole matter very seriously indeed, especially concerning safety. As I said, safety in the design of these airships will be our main concern. I don't think the lieutenant would be working with us if he didn't believe that to be true. Thank you, Lieutenant Remington."

Lou sat down.

"Now, one final thing I wish to say: If I thought the ships being constructed under this program were unsafe, I wouldn't fly in them myself. It's my intention to be on board *Cardington R101* for her maiden voyage to India. You can put that in your diaries gentlemen. And you can take it to the bank!"

A boffin-like reporter in a striped shirt and tussled frizzy hair stood up and referred to notes through gold wire glasses. "Sir—John Jacobs, *Aeroplane Magazine*. What did you say the useful lift will be?"

"Sixty tons," Thomson answered.

"*Sixty tons?*"

"Yes," Thomson said.

"*Sixty tons*," the reporter repeated, scribbling the number down. "When you spoke of the government's *Cardington R101*, I got the impression you were saying this ship would be the more advanced ship

—hence the higher designation number—with more innovation—a different class to *Howden R100*. Is that the case?"

"Oh no, I didn't mean to imply that at all, no, no. I'm sure the Howden ship will be as strong and as safe," Thomson replied. The *Aeroplane Magazine* reporter didn't seem entirely satisfied with the answer, skepticism registering in his face as he began to sit down. But he had another thought and stood up again, referring to his notes. "You said, 'In the early stages you'd enlist the help of private enterprise.' What will you do after that—*nationalize them?*"

This was irritating. "No, no. That's all too far off to contemplate," Thomson said with a wave of his hand. The reporter scratched his head and sat down again. A few less serious questions were asked and Thomson answered with patience and humility until all topics were exhausted. He began a series of closing statements, but before he'd finished, photographers were packing up their equipment and reporters were snapping their notepads shut, ready to head for the telephones to file their reports.

"Thank you for coming, gentlemen," Thomson shouted over their noisy departure. He smiled happily, watching them rush off, not irritated by their rude exit. He knew there'd be a big spread in the papers the next morning. And that was really all that mattered.

After the conference, Colmore introduced Lou to Col. Richmond whom Lou found aloof and cold. Lou wasn't sure of the reason. Perhaps it was Lou's connection with *R38*, which they didn't discuss, or maybe it was because he was based in Howden with 'the enemy.' Later, he put it down to the man's nature combined with the superior attitude of design engineers. While Lou was talking with Richmond, he noticed the Harris Tweed guy hovering near the door, looking his way. He seemed to have something on his mind. The next time Lou looked, the man had disappeared.

After that, Lou spent an hour with Scott going over the Howden renovations. He'd draw up a preliminary schedule of items to submit within two weeks for review. It'd be necessary to meet with Vickers to introduce Lou and to discuss these improvements. After that, estimates would be submitted. Lou pulled out his notepad and tore off the top sheet.

"Major, here are two names and addresses. One is Walter Potter who flew with me on *R38*. The other is a fella named Binks—I like the looks of him. They both need jobs."

"Potter, I remember him. Sure we'll fit him in somewhere."

"What about Binks?"

"Yes, all right, give it to me. I'll take care of them both," Scott said gruffly, taking the sheet of paper.

Although irritated at being used by Thomson as a prop, Lou left Cardington in good spirits. These were heady days, but he knew the euphoria couldn't last. In the meantime, he'd make the most of it. Close to the cottage, he could even pop home for lunch and make love to Charlotte! The coming months would pass without much pressure. This was going to be fun.

While Lou was riding the bus to Bedford Station to catch his train home, Charlotte was on her way to Ackworth Station from her parents' house. She'd listened to Thomson's speech on the wireless with her mother. The sky was threatening. As she walked along Station Road, she recognized the figure approaching, shoulders hunched, hands in his pockets. From a distance, except for his posture, he had an uncanny resemblance to her husband. Her heart thumping, she doubted this encounter was an accident. As he drew close, he stopped and leered, his eyes bulging and bloodshot.

"Hello, my lovely."

"Get away from me, Jessup!"

"No baby yet, then? Been a long time now, hasn't it?"

"Shut up and go away."

"I heard you've been tryin'. They bin talkin' about you in the village. My sister's been tellin' me all about it."

That little bitch Angela. I'll strangle her!

"Now I'd like to help you out, my love. I guess he just ain't doin' you right."

"Leave me alone! You evil bast—"

"Uh-uh-uh! Mummy wouldn't like you using that kind of language. Come on, sweet pea, give me a kiss. You know you find me irresistible. Try me. I'll have you knocked up in a week."

Jessup took her by the upper arm and leaned in to kiss her. Charlotte, repulsed by his beery breath and body odor, wrenched herself away, breaking her heel. With the broken shoe in one hand, she ran awkwardly toward the station. Jessup roared with laughter as she fled.

"I'll get you, don't you worry. You high and mighty little cow!" he screamed after her.

12

OH, SHENANDOAH!

May 1924 – October 1924.

As soon as Lou got back to Howden things moved rapidly. He arranged for a caravan to be delivered as a temporary office and for telephones to be installed in accordance with Scott's instructions. A couple of weeks later, Barnes Wallis showed up unannounced. Lou liked him. He appeared quiet and unassuming. Lou had the feeling he was a man easily misjudged on first impression. Wallis and Lou went around the aerodrome as he'd done with Scott, but more thoroughly. Wallis took in every detail. They examined the buildings and utilities in need of refurbishment or replacement, including the sewage plant, water treatment plant, water storage tower and electrical generating shop. Wallis surveyed a brick building he'd use to manufacture helical tubing for framing the ship. They inspected the hydrogen plant located next to the shed. That needed work.

Lou coordinated between Cardington, Vickers at Westminster (where Wallis was presently based), Yorkshire County and many contractors. A crew of twenty men came up from London to make the shed watertight; thousands of sheets of corrugated iron cladding had rusted or become loose and in need of replacement. Lou also organized local contractors to complete the renovation of the brick-built offices located inside, down one side of the shed. He put these same companies to work restoring the twenty bungalows situated along the boundary of the aerodrome. These would be home to design and engineering staff, including Wallis and Burney and their families.

For Lou and Charlotte, this was the happiest period of their lives. Sometimes, if Charlotte wasn't working, Lou dropped by the cottage for lunch, or Charlotte came by the caravan on the bus. The work crews were pleasant and everyone was on familiar terms.

One time, Charlotte came by the caravan with Lou's lunch and it turned into a passionate exchange. The caravan shook and rocked, squeaking on its chassis and Charlotte cried out. Afterwards, they lay in the bunk exhausted. Some time passed before they registered the knocking. Lou scrambled to make himself respectable and went to the door, red-faced and embarrassed. A delivery truck driver stood outside. He took off his cap and gave Lou a knowing smile.

"I was just taking a nap," Lou said.

"Sorry to disturb you, gov.' I 'spect you was 'avin a bad dream," the driver said.

"Er, well …"

"Got a load of timber 'ere. Where d'yer want it?"

Lou came out of the caravan and pointed to the shed doors.

"Drive inside the shed and find a dry spot."

The driver hesitated a moment. "Er, you might like to know, sir, there was a bloke 'ere, right 'ere, looking in the window of your caravan. When he saw me, he scarpered right quick."

"What'd he look like?"

"A lot like you, actually. Same height, same build, 'cept he was an ugly, mean-looking sod with thick greasy 'air and a scar on his face like you—blimey you could be twins!"

"Where'd he go?"

"In them woods over yonder. He must've been on a motorbike. I heard it start up and drive off down the trail."

"Thanks, I'll be on the lookout."

Lou went back inside the caravan, but said nothing to Charlotte about the 'peeping Tom.' Later, he asked the workmen if they'd seen anyone lurking around. They told him they'd noticed a man at the edge of the wood staring at the caravan once or twice, but thought he might be someone looking for work.

In July, trouble was brewing in London for Thomson and the Labour Government, but he failed to appreciate its seriousness. Since Labour didn't have a majority, it was difficult for the more radical social issues to be moved forward, but MacDonald's bill promoting the construction of 'council housing' passed through the House without fuss.

With Thomson acting as his confidante and council, MacDonald put much energy into international affairs in his role as Foreign Secretary in addition to being Prime Minister. He did his best to repair damage done by the Treaty of Versailles, tackling reparations issues and shaping agreeable terms with Germany concerning the French occupation of the Rhur—actions some saw as appeasement. The 'London Settlement' was signed and an Anglo-German Commercial Treaty put into effect. MacDonald's main goal was the disarmament of Europe and though noble, it was not one Germany would later share.

As soon as he'd assumed office, MacDonald set about normalizing relations with the Russian revolutionaries. On February 1st, The government recognized the Soviet Union and negotiated a treaty guaranteeing loans to the Bolsheviks. Large segments of the public, previously willing to give MacDonald the benefit of the doubt, became suspicious, believing him to be a communist after all. These treaties were unpopular, not only with Conservatives, but with Liberals who shored up his hold on power.

Another nail in the coffin came in July when J.R. Campbell, the communist editor of the *Worker's Weekly,* wrote a highly inflammatory article. Thomson went to No. 10 Downing Street to discuss the matter with MacDonald. He'd heard about the article, but paid little attention to it. These were people out on the fringe—every country had them. Thomson entered the Prime Minister's study overlooking the gardens. A small, mahogany desk and a couple of chairs had been placed in the room, which was otherwise bare; there were no photographs of MacDonald's family on the walls, no pictures. MacDonald looked up from his desk while Thomson stared at the boxes stacked around the walls.

"Good morning, Ramsay."

"Don't bother looking at all that, CB. It's hardly worth unpacking."

"Why not?"

"I expect you've read this rubbish?" MacDonald said, pointing at a copy of *Worker's Weekly* on the desk.

"No, but I heard the rumpus."

Thomson picked up the paper and scanned it quickly, reading aloud.

" '*Open letter to our Fighting Forces. Comrades:* '"

Thomson looked up at MacDonald. "That's a good start!"

" '*You never joined the army because you were in love with war ... In most cases you were compelled by poverty or misery of unemployment ... when war is declared you are expected to kill the enemy. The enemy are working people just like you, living in slavery ...*

*So, I say soldiers, sailors, airmen, flesh of our flesh, bone of our bone
—The Communist Party calls on you to let it be known, in war, be it
class war or military war, you will not turn your guns on your fellow
workers, but will instead, line up with your comrades and attack the
exploiters and capitalists. Refuse to fight for profits! Turn your
weapons on your oppressors!'"*

Thomson's jaw dropped. "He's telling them to shoot their officers!"

"The Attorney General has announced that this editor and some of
his cronies are to be prosecuted under the *Incitement to Mutiny Act of
1797.* We're under tremendous pressure from our backbenchers to put
a stop to legal action against these fools. What's your opinion?"
MacDonald asked.

"If you let the prosecution go ahead, we'll have rebellion in the
party. Me personally, I think these people should go to prison, or be
shot. This is treason, no question. If you quash this, there'll be hell to
pay from Conservatives and Liberals. We'll be finished," Thomson
replied. He suddenly thought of Marthe and his hopes for the future.
He put his hand to his head.

Damn! Things had started off so well.

"Point is, CB, these are just a bunch of silly fools no one's
listening to. The more fuss we make, the more we empower them."

"You and I know that, Ramsay, but some people are up in arms. I'd
hate to see them get away with this. If they'd been in my regiment,
they would've been executed."

"But they're *not* in your regiment, CB."

"More's the pity," Thomson sniffed.

"There was a time when you would've had to shoot me, too!"

"I suppose so," Thomson begrudgingly agreed.

"The people pressuring me are the ones who have supported me
from the beginning. I cannot desert them now."

Thomson got up to leave. "You must do as your conscience
dictates, Ramsay. Whatever you decide, naturally, I'll support you
without reservation."

"I'll need time to think," MacDonald said. "Come back tomorrow
morning."

Thomson descended the imposing staircase troubled and
disappointed.

Life knocks you down—just when things couldn't be better.

Re-commissioning progressed well at Howden. Another crew was sent from the south to refurbish the hydrogen plant and would finish next spring. Inside the shed, contractors rewired the offices and made general repairs while others worked on the bungalows.

Lou started making his monthly visits to Cardington as required. He reported on expenditures and submitted budgets for renovations. Fifty thousand pounds was a lot of money and the Air Ministry was anxious the budget wasn't exceeded. While in Cardington, Lou saw no progress at all and was told that team was working furiously on revolutionary 'state of the art' designs. The Air Ministry gave the press the same story. Articles were published regularly in glowing terms, describing what the public could expect to see rolling out from the Cardington shed in the future—marvels designed by geniuses. By comparison, *Howden R100* was rarely mentioned. That suited Wallis.

Thomson returned to No.10 Downing Street the following morning. MacDonald looked grave and got to the point as Thomson sat down.

"I've decided to drop the prosecution of the editor."

"I see," Thomson said, trying his damnedest to hide his disappointment.

"With our friendly attitude toward the Soviets on trade and now this, we'll be up against severe criticism. They're saying the party is under the control of the radical Left," MacDonald said.

"Yes, they are."

"In any case, I'm not going to allow these people to be put on trial."

Thomson appeared skeptical. "They're talking about a motion of no confidence."

"Yes, I know—but I think we can weather the storm. I believe the British people know we're their best hope. I'll announce my decision in the House next week."

Surely, a baby must come soon!

That would make everything perfect. Charlotte continued making baby clothes and wrapping and folding them neatly in the chest of drawers in the bedroom. She daren't think about the airship and its completion.

That's years down the road.

Charlotte's friend Fanny had become a frequent visitor to the cottage. When off duty, she came during the week while Billy was at school and Lenny was at the saw-mill in Hull. Some Sundays, Fanny's family, the Bunyans, came over for tea and the boy made a big fuss of Fluffy. Billy, now thirteen, idolized Lou and they often played football in the garden, while Lenny leaned on the damp, stone wall smoking Woodbines. Fanny knew Charlotte was mad for a child and constantly gave her advice.

"God will make you pregnant when He's good and ready. Don't be in such a rush, love," Fanny would say. And then laughing, "Meanwhile, enjoy all that good lovin'!" But this didn't satisfy Charlotte's obsessive longing.

In August, the Prime Minister announced charges against the editor of the communist *Worker's Weekly* would be dropped. A storm of outrage, both in the House and in the press, erupted immediately. The Conservatives entered a censure motion while Liberals entered an amendment of their own. These motions were put to a vote of "no confidence" which carried, and Parliament was dissolved. A general election was set for October 29.

In September, while Charlotte was doing housework, Fanny arrived at the cottage, rapping furiously on the front door. Charlotte answered, carrying her dusting pan and brush. Fanny rushed in, in great distress.

"Oh, Charlotte. Have you heard?"

"What's happened, Fanny?" Charlotte asked with growing panic.

"The *Shenandoah's* gone down in America. The BBC announced it."

"Oh, no." Charlotte's eyes filled with tears. "Josh is on that ship."

"Yes, I know, love. That's why I came straight here."

Charlotte threw the dusting pan and brush at the wall. "Damn, damn, damn! I hate bloody airships!"

Charlotte and Fanny spent the rest of the afternoon sobbing in between cups of tea—the English cure-all—until Fanny had to leave.

When Lou arrived, he'd obviously heard the news.

"Was Josh on the ship?"

"Yes."

"He's dead, isn't he?"

"Yes."

Charlotte screwed up her eyes and her tears flowed again. Lou slumped down onto the couch, his head in his hands. "I knew three of the others, too. Fourteen were killed. I called the Washington Navy Yard and got the full story. They were on their way from Lakehurst to Ohio. The ship broke up in a storm."

"Oh Lou, I'm so sorry. I know they were your mates, love."

"Josh said he was golden," Lou said, bitterly.

"He was such a lovely fella."

Lou didn't speak for some time. "It's amazing—twenty nine actually survived. I served under Landsdowne for a short time. He died, too."

"Major Scott will be upset," Charlotte said. "He'll be drowning his sorrows I expect."

Charlotte spoke no more about it, but all her fears had been re-awakened with a vengeance. It was a sleepless night.

They all die someday, Charlotte.

A cloud of grief hung over the Howden shed. They were all brothers, these airshipmen. Lou knew this had come as a severe blow to Charlotte, jarring her out of the vacuum. But there were no more explosions or hysteria, just a tacit agreement never to mention the *Shenandoah* again.

The election campaign was spirited and MacDonald believed Labour would pull it off. However, another issue reared up, complicating matters further. Thomson was summoned to Chequers. And so, on a damp autumnal morning in October, while mist rolled across the Berkshire Downs, Thomson was driven up the gravel drive. He entered the Prime Minister's study, a comfortable room lined with leather-bound books and ticking clocks. MacDonald sat looking out the window into the mist. He turned on hearing Thomson enter.

"Ah, CB, thank you for coming. More problems, I'm afraid. The foreign office received a letter addressed to the Central Committee of the British Communist Party purported to have been sent by a Mr. Zinoviev."

"Who the hell's he?"

"A Bolshevik revolutionary in the Communist Party in Moscow. He's calling for agitation in Britain."

"You mean revolution?"

"Yes. In concert with the Bolsheviks, promoting Leninism in England and the colonies."

"Damn these people!"

"It's probably a forgery perpetrated by the Tories, or the White Russian intelligence, or both."

"This couldn't have come at a worse time," Thomson said.

"This is no accident," MacDonald said.

"When was it written?"

"It's dated September 15th. Received by the Foreign Office October 10th."

"If this gets out …"

"Oh, it *will* get out. I'm sure the newspapers already have a copy of this letter."

"Surely they won't publish it, if it's a forgery?"

"CB—don't be naïve! Of course they'll publish it! I've sent a letter of protest to the government in Moscow. I intend to beat the conservative newspapers to the punch and make an announcement to the House and the press exposing the matter, with a copy of my letter. With luck, this'll blow up in their faces and help us in next week's elections."

Thomson puffed up his cheeks and blew the pent up air from his lungs. It'd be close. "When are you going to do this, Ramsay?"

"Ten o'clock tomorrow morning."

Thomson returned to Ashley Gardens.

The next morning he sat at his dining table while Gwen served him scrambled eggs on toast. She brought the newspapers to the table. By her expression, she'd already caught the *Daily Mail* headline. Thomson held it up, hardly believing his eyes.

LETTER FROM RUSSIAN COMMUNIST PARTY PRESIDENT ENCOURAGES BOLSHEVIC REVOLUTION IN BRITAIN & COLONIES

A letter has come into this newspaper's hands which is purported to have been written by the president of the Russian Communist International, Mr. Grigory Zinoviev, a radical Bolshevik revolutionary ...

Thomson scanned the article, laid down the paper and put his hands to his head.

Damn! It's all over!

He called to the housekeeper, who'd made herself scarce.

"Gwen, I'm leaving. I'll be at No.10."

"What about your breakfast, sir? You've hardly eaten anything!"

"No time," Thomson said, dashing out the door.

And I don't have any appetite now!

At No.10 there was an atmosphere of panic. An usher waved

Thomson to go up. He bounded up the stairs and knocked on the Prime Minister's door.

"Come in," MacDonald's dull voice replied from within.

"Ramsay ..."

"Yes, yes, yes. They beat us to it."

"Now what do we do?"

"Our chances are slim to none. We'll make the case it's a forgery and a conspiracy, but with four days to go, it's unlikely we'll convince anyone. The Foreign Office thinks the damned thing's genuine."

"Who leaked it?"

"It really doesn't matter, CB."

The day after the elections Thomson went to Chequers to help MacDonald collect his belongings and enjoy the place for a couple of hours before Baldwin's people arrived. They took coffee in the Great Hall and sat analyzing the election results. The Conservatives had won a stunning victory, gaining 155 seats, giving them a total of 413. The liberals had been crushed, with the number of seats held slashed from

158 to 40. MacDonald thought, overall, Labour hadn't done badly, losing 40 seats, holding on to 151.

"I'd hoped we'd hang on, but it wasn't to be, laddie."

"What will you do now?" Thomson asked.

"I'm going to fly up to Lossie and do a lot of walking, golfing, fishing, thinking and writing. I'm gonna be planning our future! Why don't you come?"

"Good idea."

"We'll fly with my new pilot—chap named Hinchliffe."

"Where did you find him?"

"Sefton Brancker recommended him."

"Good old Sefton."

"He'll put us down in the field near the house. I'll pick you up tomorrow at nine."

"Right."

"After a spell at Lossie, I suggest you go and see your lady-love in Romania."

"Perhaps I shall."

"Main thing is—don't give up. We'll be back. Count on it!"

"I *am*," Thomson said.

"Write a book or something whilst we bide our time."

"I've been planning to do that. I've already chosen the title."

"Well, what is it?"

"Smaranda," Thomson said.

"Sounds like a fascinating story about a Romanian Princess."

While Thomson and MacDonald were clearing out their possessions from Chequers, a small ceremony was taking place at Howden Air Station celebrating the formation of Vickers's Airship Guarantee Company to handle design and construction of *Howden R100*. The contract had just been ratified. A little 'sign planting' party was arranged to commemorate the occasion.

Those gathered in the drizzle at the entrance under umbrellas included, Wing Cmdr. Colmore, Maj. Scott, Dennistoun Burney, Barnes Wallis, newcomer Nevil Shute Norway and Lt. Lou Remington. George Hunter, the *Daily Express* reporter and angry journalist at the Cardington press conference, had traveled up from London. The local Hull newspaper sent a reporter and a photographer. Norway, Lou remembered as being the guy in the Harris Tweed jacket who'd taken such an interest in him. When they were introduced, neither acknowledged prior contact.

Two holes had been dug for the posts on one side of the driveway at a location chosen by Lou. While the group waited for the truck to arrive with the sign, Burney fussed around and decided the location was all wrong. Two new holes were dug and another thirty minutes of standing in the rain was endured until the sign was duly erected. It read:

Airship Guarantee Company

A Subsidiary of Vickers Aircraft Corp.

A meager round of applause went up from the party of bored souls. Lou opened a couple of bottles of champagne and poured it into fancy glasses on a small, wet table. Hurried toasts were drunk and a few words said. No one wanted to be there, but it was a ceremony which seemed necessary at the time. It contrasted strongly in Lou's mind with the kick-off meeting conducted by Thomson at Cardington in May, and he said as much to Wallis and Norway.

Wallis smiled. "Let them have their pomp and circumstance. We have no need of it here," he said.

PART FOUR

An Airship Under Construction.

13

A SLEEPLESS NIGHT

April 1929.

Lou stared at the ceiling, listening to the clock's 'tick, tick, tick', beside him, while the wind whistled through the tall elms outside. He rolled over and checked the time. It was 2.30 a.m. He could tell by her restlessness Charlotte was awake, too. Neither spoke. This'd be their last night at the cottage. Lou had been posted to Cardington and they'd travel to Bedford on the train in the morning. A deal had been struck with the devil and payment was due. Was he being unfair to Charlotte? He felt selfish to the core, but confident they were doing the right thing. He thought of his dead *R38* buddies. It always came back to that, as if he were tied to them for eternity.

The price of being a survivor.

This was his second chance, a way of redeeming himself. Or was he being overly dramatic? Then there was John Bull. He felt miserable about leaving him—and disloyal. Everything went around in his head. He lay in the gloom considering the events of the past three years…

14

THE WALLISES

Summer 1926 - Spring 1929.

By summer of 1926, the air station had been restored to a functioning facility—not as modern as Cardington, but good enough for the Howden people, who were always at a disadvantage; like relatives from the wrong side of the tracks. Renovations of the twenty bungalows were complete and freshly painted. Design staff and senior personnel, including Barnes Wallis, his new bride, Molly, and their three-month-old son moved in. Burney and his wife took one, though absent most of the time. Burney was busy much of the time with his duties as a Conservative Member of Parliament. He also traveled abroad extensively.

The offices were also ready and Lou furnished them with second-hand furniture from Hull, much of it the worse for wear, but 'perfectly adequate', as Wallis put it. A week after everyone had settled in, Wallis called a meeting with his staff. Lou was first to arrive and Wallis expressed satisfaction with his office, which smelled of new, white distemper and an almost-new piece of brown carpet.

Ten team members sat at the old, chipped conference table and the remaining seventeen squeezed in around the walls. The group was mixed, with male and female staff from the drawing offices and workshops, including shop foremen, engineers, engineering draftsmen, Norway's calculators, and lastly, Philip Teed, the chemist, and his assistants, who looked after gas management and purity. Wallis stood at the head of the table dressed in a dark blue suit. He smiled at the enthusiastic faces—rare for him.

"I called this meeting to welcome you to Howden and to let you know what I expect—to lay down ground rules and give you my opinions about certain matters. I'm calling this a 'meeting of mutual understanding.'

Wallis raised his hand toward Lou.

"First, I know by now you've all met this man, but I want to introduce you officially to Lt. Louis Remington of the United States Navy. I'd personally like to thank the lieutenant for his work in getting this old, broken-down aerodrome into working order. He's done a great job. Thank you, Lieutenant."

There was a spontaneous round of applause.

"He has considerable experience in airship construction and in flying them—you all know his history. He's familiar with this air station and with Cardington. Please understand I have absolute trust in the lieutenant. He's a man of the highest integrity. We shall keep no secrets from him and treat him as one of our own. Besides assisting our team, he's also here on behalf of the Air Ministry and the oversight group in Cardington."

There were a few questioning glances in Lou's direction.

"Cardington is overseeing this operation. That was the mandate and it's something we have to live with. Personally, I'd *rather* have oversight, as long as it is thoughtful and intelligent. Lieutenant Remington will use his discretion as to what information he will pass on to Cardington. Technical data, much of which will become patented, I'm sure he will not divulge until we're ready to release it. As well as assisting us here in monitoring the work, Lieutenant Remington will make monthly visits to Cardington where he'll give the Deputy Director of Airship Development a report covering our progress for the month, a schedule for the upcoming month and detailed costs of work to date."

Lou was relieved Wallis had got this out of the way. He and Wallis understood one another perfectly.

"Now, what are we all doing here in the backwoods of Yorkshire? Ladies and gentlemen, this is our mission: We have the task of delivering an airship built to concise specifications, for a stipulated contract sum, by a certain date, ready for an intercontinental voyage. No more. No less."

Wallis paused. His eyes swept the room.

"This airship will be the best we can design and build. We will not pay attention to what others are doing, or saying. What they do is *their* business. We shall stay focused right here in this shed and not be sidetracked or upset by politicians and news hounds."

Everyone nodded their heads in agreement.

"We must always remember our awesome responsibility. Peoples' lives are at stake. It's not just about our survival as a company, not about looking good and trying hard—that won't be good enough. This is true of all things in life. Just showing you're trying to do a good job won't enable you to survive an Atlantic crossing. Nice appointments, nice berths, nice showers, nice tables and nice white table cloths with glistening silverware are things which look good in the shed—but none of that stuff will get us to Montreal. In a matter of only a few years, we're attempting to build ocean liners in the sky—vessels that took hundreds of years to develop. We must *not* forget these aircraft are experimental!"

Wallis stopped and rubbed his chin thoughtfully.

"I must inform you of my opinions on certain matters—and this is confidential. Only one team will survive this ridiculous competition. I believe that's always been the intention of the Air Minister. I know he's gone, but everything in politics is temporary. I'm sure he'll be back. His intent is to show how much better government can do things. The ultimate goal is our demise. Both teams are essentially supposed to be building the same airship, at least if you read the specification requirements you might think so. For two reasons, they won't be the same; our two philosophies are different, and they have unlimited money—but *that* could be their undoing. Although we're the underdog, we shall win this competition. We came here to win, and win it we shall!"

There was an enthusiastic round of applause and cheers. The meeting made a big impression on Lou.

Wallis began holding weekly progress meetings with key members of his team. Attendees included Lou, Norway and Teed. Burney attended rarely. At the first meeting, Lou learned what the team had been doing in the south for the past eighteen months while he'd been managing the re-commissioning of Howden. Wallis had the concept of the airship developing in his head during the summer of '24 and by Christmas, had the engineering details worked out down to the smallest details.

Wallis decided to get away from the Zeppelin design, which he considered fatally flawed, and began from first principles. Much of what Wallis said went over Lou's head. He spoke of longitudinal shear, bending moments, aerodynamic forces, point loads, geodetic design, changes in buoyancy and lift behavior due to atmospheric changes.

Lou did, however, fully understand the meaning of 'catastrophic failure.'

Wallis mysteriously seemed to be able to feel every force within the airship while working on design, which he now had down on the drawing boards. He had an uncanny instinct, enabling him to pinpoint forces in girders, transverse frames, guy wires, fabric meshing and gas bag supports, as well as in every rivet, nut and bolt! He sensed these forces as if they were in his own body—forces that would be forever changing due to effects of weather, gravity, aerodynamics and cataclysmic events.

Lou had no clue what 'geodetic design' meant, but after patient explanation by Wallis, he understood that when one part of the structure became overstressed, or broken, its load would be taken up by another part. These principles were also applied to the gas bag harnessing system. Wallis lived and breathed internal structural forces. The man was a genius.

Wallis seemed to be able to go to that place where great composers or distinguished writers go for inspiration and answers—*the wellspring*. Many times, Wallis came into the shed early in the morning with a bright smile, announcing he'd dreamed of the answer to some inscrutable riddle he'd been wrestling with for weeks. He'd be as excited as a schoolboy, charging into his office to write it all down and make sketches. When this happened, Lou shared his euphoria.

Wallis was hard to get to know. His puritanical nature was softened by a willingness to have fun, especially with his wife, Molly, now pregnant with their second child. One day in the autumn of 1926, at sunset, when the shed cast its giant shadow across the field, Lou approached after hearing strange sounds coming from inside. He went to the door and found Wallis zooming Molly around wildly in a workmen's wheelbarrow, while they both childishly shrieked and howled like wolves. Every so often, they stopped and listened to echoes receding down the shed, counting to fifteen each time, until the vast space descended into silence. Lou watched for a few minutes until they became aware of him. They were embarrassed at first, and then they all burst out laughing.

Wallis, the outdoor type, taught Molly how to skate and play golf. Often, they went out camping in all kinds of weather with only a side and top to their tent—Wallis's way of toughening them up; learning to live with and understand the elements.

In the autumn of that year, the Wallises knocked on the cottage door during a terrible rainstorm. Wallis and Molly liked to go on long hikes visiting neighbors and friends. They'd travel five miles by road and five miles across country 'as the crow flies', using a compass to guide them. They came inside like drowned rats, staying until they'd dried out by the fire and had been served (despite their protestations) a meal of sausages, baked beans and coffee.

During their surprise visit, Lou and Charlotte learned Wallis and Molly were cousins-in-law, having been married the previous year after an agonizing courtship. Their marriage had been strongly opposed by Molly's father due to their sixteen-year age difference. When they'd met, Wallis had loved her on sight and stayed close by, coaching her in mathematics, usually by mail. Now, all appeared to be well. They'd been left alone to enjoy their lives together in this desolate place in Yorkshire.

The Wallises, like Lou and Charlotte, seemed blissfully happy, except that *they* had a baby and another on the way. The only blight on their happiness was the managing director of the company, Dennistoun Burney. Lou and Charlotte learned much from the Wallises about various people and their relationships that rainy afternoon.

Burney owned everybody who worked for him and they were not allowed to forget it. Any successful task they performed became *his* doing. During his visits to Howden, Burney made everyone's life miserable by his sheer arrogance. The greater the distance from Westminster out of the public eye, the more obnoxious he became.

At the end of the day or at weekends when in residence, Burney liked to call on the Wallises to discuss work without regard to convenience. His wife, just as annoying, showed up on Molly's doorstep at all hours to make camp. Wallis couldn't stand the woman's powdery smell, and whatever she put on her hair made him sneeze.

Scott also offended Wallis's puritanical sensibilities, but at least his visits were infrequent. When he came up by train, Lou fetched him from the station in the works truck and he'd stay overnight at the Railway Station Pub or the Grand Hotel in Hull. Wallis had a high regard for Scott's flying skills, but abhorred his drinking and hell raising.

If Scott showed up at the cottage, he usually demanded gin, and when Wallis requested a 'drink' allowance from Burney for these unwelcome visits, the request was denied. When Burney and Scott were both in town, the drinking got out of hand, much to Wallis's annoyance—especially when they drank in his home and *he* was footing the bill.

That summer of '26, Wallis's factory began producing duralumin tubing. By Christmas, they'd built one of the central transverse frames and hung it from the roof decked in Christmas lights. To complete the festive ambience, a pine tree from the nearby forest was installed in the shed with decorations and a nativity scene.

That first Christmas had been a happy occasion. Lou and Charlotte went to the Wallises' bungalow on Christmas morning and Wallis poured them Bristol Cream Sherry. Charlotte took a baby's white, knitted sleepsuit she'd made for her own longed-for child. When she handed Molly the present wrapped in tissue, Molly embraced Charlotte after seeing tears in her eyes.

Lou's role at Howden had changed. With the renovations finished, his task now was to monitor activities and make daily reports. These were typed and filed by a young secretary named Monica. He also kept a deficiency log after reading and filing the inspectors' reports. These records were kept current and discussed at Wallis's weekly meetings.

Howden Airship Station became a happy place, not unlike a British holiday camp, and to Lou, it remained special. The management personnel worked hard and played hard together, forming life-long friendships. Lou and Charlotte spent countless hours socializing with them. People understood their time in Howden to be temporary. They were far from home in pleasant, country surroundings. Most had grown up as city folk and this was an adventure. In this 'unreal' atmosphere, inevitably, one or two affairs got started.

They enjoyed being close to the animals, too. Molly told Charlotte she liked to watch the rabbits hopping around their garden and see cows poking their heads through their windows, except when they chewed her flowers on the windowsill and broke her vases. This community was a separate place, divorced from the outside world. They played soccer and rugby on the airfield, keeping it mowed and rolled. Wallis had a tennis court set up with a low perimeter fence where he and Molly practiced. In summer, they had Sunday tea parties and the wives brought homemade pies, cakes, jellies and blancmanges, while their men played cricket. The 'shed people' never attended these get-togethers, not being invited. On rare occasions, shop foremen received a special invitation.

The atmosphere was always pleasant, as long as Burney and his wife weren't in attendance; they would bust their way into every conversation and lord it over all, talking non-stop shop. Burney had the gift of being able to turn his employees against each other. Lou thought this must be caused by some survival instinct people have when in the company of individuals with power over them. If the Burneys showed up on these Sunday afternoons, most people drifted away early, whereas the games and socializing normally carried on until dark.

Burney was never impolite or bombastic toward Lou or Charlotte. Perhaps he saw Lou rising in the Naval hierarchy in Washington where he'd become a useful contact for his airship business. During the times Burney was in residence, a nasty cloud hung over the place and the backbiting became unpleasant. On his departure, the sun came out and a state of tranquility descended across the plain, peace restored. Lou heard him referred to as a little prick, a nuisance, a hemorrhoid, a pillock, and an arsehole, though he never made comments about the man himself. But Charlotte did.

15

'MR. SHUTE' & FRIENDS

Autumn 1926 and onwards.

One day in autumn of '26, Lou and Charlotte invited Norway to Candlestick Cottage for dinner. It was customary for families to eat a roast late in the afternoon on Sundays. Lou had come to enjoy these feasts, especially in the dreary months of late autumn and winter. A log fire crackling in the grate and a glass or two of frothy Yorkshire ale always made it special and the cottage extra cozy.

Norway, an Oxford graduate, had been hired by Wallis as chief calculator to head the team of mathematicians who would sit for years calculating the stresses and sizes of each girder for manufacture in the metal shop. Norway had left de Havilands to join Vickers. He'd worked down in Kent at an office in Crayford until Howden was ready. Although well versed in aeronautical engineering, he had no airship experience whatsoever and made no bones about it. He loved to fly aeroplanes.

At ten minutes to three, they perceived a gentle knock. Charlotte opened the front door to find Norway every inch the intellectual, comically boffin-like, and hating herself for thinking this—no beauty. He was of average height and build and, though a year younger than Lou, seemed older. He wore a green and brown Harris Tweed jacket with leather elbow patches, which they'd learn he wore in all weathers for all activities. He carried with him the smell of aromatic pipe tobacco, which Charlotte found quite pleasing.

Norway's beady, blue eyes peered out from under bushy eyebrows. When working on his endless calculations or poring over drawings, his hooked nose supported thick, horn-rimmed glasses. Capping everything, Norway had a stutter—a real doozy. Lou and Charlotte wanted to help him by finishing his sentences, but forced themselves to resist. Lou noticed the more they got to know each other, the less Norway stuttered. At times, it disappeared altogether.

He stood stiffly to attention on the step under the porch roof, clutching a bottle of wine.

"Hello! You must be Mr. Norway," Charlotte said, putting out her hand.

Norway became flustered, overcome by her beauty. She wore a stunning red dress and her favorite perfume. He thrust the bottle into her outstretched hand.

"Er, p-p-please c-call me N-Nevil," he said.

"Right then, Nevil! Oh, you shouldn't have done that," she said, examining the bottle. "Oh, it's red. My favorite! Thank you so much. Come in and make yourself comfortable."

Norway peered around the room, at the crackling fire and the round table, beautifully laid for dinner, overlooking the damp, autumnal garden. Norway breathed in the smell of roast lamb, mint sauce and scorched Yorkshire puddings.

"S-smells w-wonderful and what a l-lovely c-cottage …And I m-must say I do like your p-perfume."

"*Je Reviens!*" Lou shouted from the kitchen. He then appeared. Norway looked visibly relieved to see him.

"It means, 'I w-will r-return.'"

"Charlotte told me the name of it when we met. I never thought about what it meant. I wish we could speak French," Lou said.

"Glad you could come, Nevil. I've cooked a roast. Hope you like lamb?" Charlotte said.

"Oh, yes, I d-do. M-marvelous. Yes, thank you."

Charlotte picked up the bottle and squinted at the label. "Nevil's brought us a bottle of wine. It's called Chateau er, neuf du P-P- er …er …"

"Pape!" Norway blurted out. They all roared with laughter, Norway revealing all his large, crooked teeth, reminding Charlotte of a horse. She felt dreadful again.

"Looks so expensive. We'll have this with dinner," Charlotte said.

"I got a crate of pale ale from the pub. Would you like one before dinner, Nevil?" Lou said, giving Norway a wink.

"Oh, yes s-splendid."

Lou and Nevil drank their beers and chatted while Charlotte put the finishing touches to the meal.

"D-Dinner smells t-t-temptingly d-delicious and one f-f-feels so at home here," Norway said, his eyelids fluttering under the strain of trying his best not to stutter.

"Charlotte grows all our vegetables. I'm real proud of her," Lou said.

After a couple of beers Norway settled down and talked about himself. He obviously felt comfortable and, as a young man away from home, appreciative of their hospitality. Norway told them he didn't want to live on the aerodrome close to work and his bosses and had therefore taken rooms over a pub in Howden with two colleagues. He'd settled down to life in Yorkshire and joined a flying club in Sherburn-in-Elmet.

Over an excellent meal, washed down by Norway's fine wine, they learned that joyriding in aeroplanes wasn't all Norway did for fun. After packing his pipe with Balkan Sobranie and filling the room with sweet-smelling clouds of smoke, Norway told them that, for his own amusement, he'd written a novel in his spare time. And, to his amazement, a draft had been accepted by a London publisher. Since Norway thought his employers might think he wasn't taking his day job seriously, he'd had the book published under his middle name, 'Shute.' He was now working on a second novel in the evenings. This intrigued Lou and Charlotte. They'd never met a writer before.

Norway was interested in Lou's experience and his survival of the *R38* crash. He told Lou he'd attended Thomson's press conference in Cardington, incognito. He said he'd badly wanted to talk to Lou about that ship, but in the end decided not to intrude. Lou nodded and smiled, telling him he *had* wondered—Norway didn't look like a reporter. Norway said, before moving to Howden, he'd made a study of *R38* and was horrified to learn it was basically a copy of a Zeppelin without fresh calculations. He said he believed her factor of safety had been less than 1. He explained that it should have been at least 1.5, that is to say, designed for one and a half times the stress it was likely to encounter. From this, Lou realized neither *R38* nor *Shenandoah* had stood an earthly chance of survival.

During the months that followed, usually over dinner, they had many conversations about *R38*. This wasn't a subject Charlotte enjoyed talking about, and even though the first piece of structure hadn't been erected, *Howden R100* was becoming a reality. The airship would soon encroach upon their lives. The subject of *Shenandoah* never came up—Lou had warned Norway not to speak of it. Despite all the talk of airships, Charlotte came to adore Norway, pleased to have a writer for a friend, especially when he asked them both to critique his second book. Charlotte liked the title: '*So Disdained.*' They laughed when Norway was coming over to talk about his writing, referring to him as 'Mr. Shute.' It was their little secret.

One weekend, Charlotte and Fanny had a heart-to-heart talk while they sat at the dining room table watching Lou and Billy playing soccer in the garden. Billy and Lou scrambled and dribbled, while Lenny leaned on the stone wall coughing and wheezing as he tried to light another Woodbine.

"Your boy's growing fast, Fanny."

"Yes, he is. He idolizes your husband, you know."

"You're right, he does," Charlotte said.

"I tell him, 'You should try and be like your Dad,' and d'you know what he says?"

"What, love?"

"He says, 'I want to be like Lou.' It really upsets me. His dad's been through so much. They gassed him in the trenches at the Somme, you know."

Charlotte winced. She felt Lenny's agony.

Fanny began to cry. "He got TB after the war and now look at 'im, poor love. He's having trouble smoking a fag. He suffers with his nerves and melancholia and oh, 'ee loves that boy *so* much."

Charlotte was overcome by sadness.

"You mustn't talk about that bloody awful war to the boy, Fanny," she said bitterly.

"No, I don't want to upset him with all that horror." Fanny changed the subject and perked up. "Anyway Charlotte, no news yet?" she said, dabbing her eyes and then patting Charlotte's tummy.

"I don't think it's ever going to happen."

"Be patient. When the Good Lord's ready, it'll happen, you'll see," Fanny said, forcing a smile.

"I've been to the doctor and he said it's not me. *He* won't go. I'm sure it's his fault," Charlotte said, looking in Lou's direction.

"Charlotte, you don't know that!"

"Then what's wrong with us?"

"Things have to be right. Don't get so desperate."

"Desperate! We've been married five years now. He's more interested in that bloody airship."

"You mustn't nag him about it—entice him," Fanny said. Charlotte sighed and stared out the window at Lou, she watched him for a while. She'd thought he was gorgeous when she first saw him on that ward— and he was still gorgeous. After a moment, she turned back to Fanny.

"I guess I fell in love with Lou the moment I laid eyes on him, you know, Fanny."

"Yes, I know you did, love. We *all* knew."

Over the following months, the stream of visitors to the cottage at weekends increased. Sometimes everyone showed up at once: John and his wife, Mary, Fanny, Lenny and Billy, Norway, and sometimes the Wallises and Charlotte's parents. Everyone in this diverse group got on well and these get-togethers usually ended with a sing-song. Charlotte sat at the piano playing all the latest hits: "Tea for Two," "Yes Sir, That's My Baby," and "What'll I Do? " She was banned from playing "Mammy." Sometimes, Lou accompanied her on the guitar and played a few country songs from the Deep South which delighted Billy. Charlotte always encouraged Molly to bring the children, though it made her both happy and sad. She and Molly became close over the next four years.

16

CARDINGTON VISITS

December 1926 and onwards.

L ou visited Cardington each month. It was usually a day trip. He showed Colmore and Scott drawings and photographs of the work executed during the last month and work projected for the next. He also submitted a schedule of costs to date. Lou found most of the R.A.W. staff polite, but sensed underlying hostility—not toward him, but Howden.

Lou got to know Col. Richmond over the three-year period of construction and his arrogant manner confirmed Lou's earlier impression. Around Christmas that first year, Lou arrived at Cardington House only to be informed Colmore and Scott were away and Col. Richmond would be available in half an hour or so. Lou waited in the reception area for ninety minutes before being sent to Richmond's office on the second floor. Lou knocked on the door and entered. Richmond rose from behind a fine mahogany desk, well-dressed in a blue serge suit and red tie.

"Ah, Lieutenant Remington, thank you for coming," Richmond said. After slight hesitation, they shook hands and sat down. Richmond stared at Lou for some moments without speaking.

"So, what's happening in that mud hole up north?"

Lou opened his briefcase and pulled out drawings of *Howden R100* with photographs of the metal fabrication shop. Richmond held up his hands.

"I don't need to look at all that stuff, just tell me what's going on."

"The ship's pretty well engineered. They're using a geodetic design. They're still working on the tail, the elevators and rudder configurations."

Richmond appeared uninterested, but Lou continued, his demeanor pleasant.

"The metal factory is set up and is producing components. The central frames are being fabbed and …"

"Fabbed! What is this word 'fabbed'?"

"Prefabricated, sir."

"Ah, it's one of your Americanisms. You people love to shorten everything, don't you."

"The first of the central frames is set in place. I can show you …" Lou said, opening a drawing of the ship's frame.

Richmond waved it off, wrinkling his nose.

"I don't need the details. What about gas bag harnesses?"

"Gas bag harnesses? Oh yes, they're designed. Mr. Wallis seems happy with them."

"*Is* he indeed?" Richmond grimaced. "And gas valves?"

"Yes, they're designed, too."

"Really?"

"Yes, in Germany."

"What you mean is: They're using the ones the Germans have been using for donkey's years."

"Well, yes. Mr. Shute …er Mr. Norway said they're tried and tested."

"Tried and tested!" Richmond guffawed. "Who is this Mr. Shute?"

"He's nobody, sir. I misspoke. I'm sorry. I meant Norway."

"The gas valves are coming from Norway?"

"No, sir, I meant *Mr.* Norway. Not Mr. Shute."

"Ah, I see. And who is this Norway person?"

"Howden's chief calculator, sir."

"How much airship experience does *he* have?"

"None, sir."

"None! And where did they drag *him* up from?"

"He came from de Havilands. I understand he's an aeronautical engineer, sir."

"But with no airship experience?"

"None whatsoever, no."

"What are they doing about gas bags?"

"They're being ordered from Germany, too."

"Yes, of course. They don't have facilities to make their own, do they?" Richmond sneered.

"No sir, they are not as fortunate."

"What else are the Germans doing for our Howden friends?"

"I believe that's about it, sir."

"Perhaps Wallis should have the Germans build the whole ship for him. They would've stood a better chance, I should've thought."

Lou played dumb. "I'm sorry, sir, I don't follow."

"Well, I don't suppose you do, Lieutenant."

Lou sat and waited for Richmond, who rested his chin in his hand pouting at the wall. "This whole thing's all a bit of a farce, Remington, let's face it."

"How do you mean, sir, exactly?"

"Vickers's people are all up there scratching around in that broken-down old shed. To be honest, I feel *sorry* for them. They're not going to be able to compete with us. We've got a state of the art facility, unlimited funds, Bolton and Paul's engineering department with their steel works just down the street—not to mention the resources of the entire British Government—all at our disposal!"

"That's a real nice position to be in, Colonel."

"And d'you know what's best of all, Remington? Time is on our side—time to get it right. They're stuck with a schedule and an impossible set of conditions they can't possibly hope to fulfill. No, they're up a creek without a paddle, I'm afraid."

Lou said nothing. Richmond got fidgety. "What do *you* think, Remington—honestly?"

"Oh, me, sir, I'm not qualified to give an opinion, not being an engineer."

Richmond paused and looked away, mulling it over.

"No. Bit unfair of me to ask, really. Well, our goal here is to construct the finest airship ever built, *anywhere*. Better than anything the Germans have produced and certainly better than anything the Howden people could conceive of. *Cardington R101* will be cutting edge—as comfortable and as smooth as any luxury liner that ever put to sea—and the *safest*, of course."

"That will be a wonderful thing, sir."

"Yes, and no doubt you'll be aboard her as an officer, one day."

"I look forward to that."

"And so you should, Lieutenant. And so you should!"

Lou left the building turning their conversation over in his mind.

If these people have all the advantages, why the hell is he so uptight?

In the coming months, Lou had more contact with Richmond. He was even invited to his home office where he met Richmond's wife, Florence, or 'Florry', as he called her. Lou found her to be a classy lady and they seemed devoted. In those surroundings and in Colmore's absence, Richmond became more amenable. He clearly hoped to get a feel for how *he, Richmond*, was doing compared to Wallis. Lou sometimes thought Richmond was torturing himself. Naturally, despite what Richmond said previously, Lou was there to be pumped for information about *Howden R100*.

Lou couldn't help comparing the two men leading the teams. They were complete opposites. Richmond seemed to be more of a manager, whereas Wallis was himself the hands-on engineer and designer. He was a perfectionist, and like all perfectionists, kept absolute control over all things. In Cardington, it was a project being managed by a committee. Lou hoped the airship wouldn't turn out like the proverbial camel. He realized the Cardington team's goals couldn't be more different than Wallis's. It seemed to be more about being the best for the sake of it.

The other motivation for Cardington was to not repeat the old mistakes—a sensible goal. The attitude was: No matter how long it takes, and at whatever cost, *Cardington R101* will be built not just state of the art, but to the state of perfection. They weren't under the same restrictions and operated with virtually no oversight—they were their own judge and jury. This made the government types—be they military men, government bureaucrats, or airship works employees— arrogant and condescending toward Howden.

In the early part of 1927, Richmond took Lou into the shed before construction had started and proudly showed him a mock-up of a forty-foot section of the airship, complete with a gasbag. This sample had been fabricated by Bolton and Paul to prove their structural theories. After study and inspection, it was demolished. This experiment, Richmond proudly told him, had cost the British taxpayers forty thousand pounds. Lou thought it was a good idea but knew Howden couldn't afford such experiments to prove Wallis's theories or Norway's calculations.

Later that year, Richmond shared their designs for gas bag harnesses, gas valves and servo mechanisms (to assist in steering the airship), designed by his assistant, Squadron Leader Rope. Richmond also showed him pictures of the Beardmore diesel engines on order from Scotland, due for delivery next spring.

Lou couldn't tell whether all this was an attempt to demoralize Howden, thinking Lou would divulge these details and they'd be overcome by their brilliance. Or, maybe, Richmond was looking for Lou's reactions, which were always congenial and reassuring— perhaps even a tad patronizing. Richmond, like most English people, was unable to appreciate the subtle nuances of American polite conversation. It wouldn't have occurred to him such a thing existed in American culture—after all, Americans could hardly speak the language.

Richmond asked Lou not to mention these things at Howden and he didn't. He knew Wallis wouldn't be the slightest bit interested anyway. Lou felt the petty jealousy and rivalry increasing between the teams, but refused to pick sides or let himself be drawn in. He and Charlotte had their own growing personal problem to contend with— *Jessup!*

17

'BURNEY'S MEETING'

Spring 1927.

By spring of '27, work in the Howden shed was in full swing. The noise struck visitors first—the crash of steel against steel, banging, shouting and often, laughter and singing. Half the transverse frames, up to 130 feet in diameter, had been hung from the ceiling beams from center toward bow and stern. The place was alive with men everywhere like ants—on dangling bosun's chairs, swings, webs of scaffold and swaying firemen's ladders.

While working at Howden and visiting Cardington, Lou sensed this mounting tension between the two teams. He saw increasing strain in other quarters, too—within Howden itself. During a visit to Howden, Burney attended one of Wallis's meetings after enjoying one of his liquid lunches at The Railway Station pub. He made a point of sitting at the head of the table, in Wallis's chair. Wallis sat at the opposite end with Lou, Norway and Teed. Burney, the purple veins in his cheeks pronounced, sat hunched forward over the table like a greyhound. The room soon smelled of Burney's beer and whisky breath.

"I called this meeting to discuss where we stand on all components of the airship. I'm concerned we're falling behind," Burney announced.

Wallis said nothing. This was one of Wallis's regularly scheduled meetings held in his office every Monday afternoon. Burney hadn't called it—he'd merely shown up.

"Let's start with gas bag harnesses, gas bags and valves. Where are we on those items?" Burney asked, looking around the table.

"The harnesses are designed. I'm satisfied with them. As for the gas bags and gas valves, we'll get them from Zeppelin. We don't have the means to manufacture gas bags here, and I suggest we don't try to get them from Cardington," Wallis said.

"Absolutely not," Burney agreed. "They'd string us out 'til kingdom come."

"The German gas valves can't be improved on and the price is reasonable," Teed said.

"No point in reinventing the wheel," Wallis said.

"Quite. What about weight? Where do we stand?" Burney glanced sharply at Wallis. "This is critical."

"We're on target," Wallis answered.

"And what about factor of safety? What are we working to?"

"Around 4.5. Which means we have plenty of margin of safety," Wallis answered.

"I don't need *you* to tell me what it means." Burney snapped. "What about the servo assistance for the elevators and rudders? A little bird told me Cardington has designed elaborate systems for their ship. I'm disturbed to hear we haven't done so. Why not?"

Norway leaned forward. "I s-studied this for m-months. M-my c-calculations sh-show we don't n-n-need them."

"Are you *absolutely* sure?"

"Y-y-yes."

"Come on, spit it out, man!"

"Y-y-yes."

"I want you to go through all your calculations again and when you've done *that,* check them again. After that, have them checked by Professors Bairstow and Pippard," Burney demanded. Wallis often consulted the two professors with the Airworthiness Panel on various structural issues. Wallis grimaced and his face began to flush.

"Now I want to talk about procedure," Burney said, looking accusingly at Wallis. "I want you to make a habit of visiting the engineers on a daily basis at the same time of day. I'm seeing too much rework in the machine shop which could've been avoided if you'd caught these mistakes on the drawing board."

"I don't need *you* to come here telling me how to manage operations. I'm the design engineer and I'll run things the way I see fit!" Wallis said, his face beet red.

Burney was unfazed. "The deficiency lists are too long. The rework in the shops is costing me a fortune. This is stuff you should've caught before shop drawings were issued."

There was an angry silence. Burney leaned back in his chair with his hands behind his head. "I see it's necessary for me to teach you people the facts of life. Money is what makes the world go round. This ship will be a financial loss to this company. We're fighting a war of attrition here, but you seem not to understand. We knew it'd be a loss before we started, but it's an investment in our future. We want to build a successful airship, not a bloody pie in the sky like those silly arses at Cardington."

Burney leaned forward again, elbows on the table. "So gentlemen, this is why I'm intent on guarding against waste—wasted man hours, wasted research, costing money we don't have. Let's talk about the engines: Where are we with them?" Burney looked from one to the other.

"We looked into d-developing a k-kerosene-hydrogen engine—"

"And?"

"That's years away in development and I've dropped the idea," Wallis said.

"*That's what I'm talking about.* Don't just drop ideas without talking to me first," Burney fumed. "Working on ideas costs me money!"

"I-I've been doing research on the B-Beardmore diesels developed for the C-Canadian railway—"

Norway's stutter was irritating Burney. He kept rolling his eyes. "Railway engines?" he exclaimed, glaring at Norway.

"They weigh t-t-twelve hundred pounds each," Norway said.

"Forget them," Wallis said.

"What do *you* propose then?" Burney asked, turning on Wallis.

"We'll use Rolls-Royce Condors," Wallis said. "I've already made up my mind."

"Petrol?" Burney queried.

"We'll never get off the ground with diesel engines!" Wallis answered.

"Okay, Condors it is then. We'll get reconditioned ones. They'll be half the price and be as good as new," Burney said. "Any objections?" He glared at the group, daring them to oppose him.

"The government may not be happy with us using second-hand engines," Teed said. Wallis shook his head in disbelief.

"Doesn't say anywhere in our contract we can't use re-conditioned engines."

"We'd b-be breaking Lord Thomson's r-rules. He wouldn't be p-pleased. He wanted us to use d-d-diesels."

"To hell with Thomson and his rules. He's long gone—along with all his *comrades*."

Lou thought about the events leading to Thomson's departure last October. Since then, the communist editor and his henchmen had been tried and thrown in jail. "Poor Lord Thomson," he muttered.

Burney exploded. "That genius stole all *my* visionary ideas and took them for his own and then dreamed up this crackpot competition! The Conservative Government had agreed to my scheme long before that clown came on the scene and reneged on everything."

Lou choked into his fist.

Oh dear, now I've upset him.

"All for the sake of increasing the size of government and squashing private enterprise. It was for his own personal aggrandizement—to satisfy his wild ambitions! Not to mention he was trying to impress some bloody Romanian princess he's been after. Every inbred, royal, blue-blood European has been sniffing at that woman's drawers for years, like mongrels. She's like a bitch on heat. Now he's a lord, he thinks *he's* royalty. The woman's a siren. *She'll be the death of him!* No, he deserved to be kicked out. He's a bloody Marxist radical, a hypocritical bastard like the rest of those conmen—out for himself. Everything about those people is just one great big lie!"

Lou glanced at Wallis apologetically. No use; Wallis was seething.

Holy cow, that set him off! I wonder who this dame is. Must be quite some broad!

"Thomson might be back," Teed interjected lamely, but no one was listening.

"And where did *you* get all *your* great visionary ideas, *Mr.* Burney?" Wallis said glaring at Burney.

A painful pause ensued. Everyone waited for the next explosion.

"Now, you just wait a minute! You *did* work on the *R80*, a moderately successful airship and a few other small ones, but the building of six great airships was *my* idea!" Burney blustered.

"Fuelled by *me!*" Wallis answered.

"Okay, you kicked around the idea of building a bigger airship. Without *my* vision you wouldn't be sitting here, in your cocoon, working on a five-million-cubic-foot airship. It was *my* dream. It was *I* who conceived the building of six gigantic airships. It was *I* who made all this happen. Not *you!* Not even *Thomson!* You're forgetting your place, Wallis. Without *me,* you wouldn't have a job." Burney's bloodshot eyes swept around the table to Norway and Teed. "None of you would!"

Wallis pushed back his chair and stood up, buttoning his jacket. Burney looked up incredulously. "What are you doing? Where do you think *you're* going?" he shouted.

"I've heard enough." Wallis said as he walked out, closing the door quietly behind him. Lou stared after him with admiration.

That's class! Most guys would've slammed the door.

"Come back here at once!" Burney yelled.

Teed and Norway gave each other embarrassed looks.

Burney got up. "All right, gentlemen. We'll finish it there. I'll deal with Mr. Wallis later."

They trooped back to their own rooms in silence. Wallis had gone across the field to his bungalow. He wasn't seen for the rest of the day. Lou figured he must've quit.

Much to everyone's relief, Wallis appeared in his office next morning as usual. Nothing came of this altercation except that relations between the two men grew steadily worse. In coming months and years, things deteriorated to the point where they were working against each other, with Wallis looking for another, more peaceful, avenue to pursue and Burney publicly tearing down the design of both *R100* and *R101* in books and interviews. They were too small, he declared, and not the right shape—they needed to be flatter and oval shaped. His belief in the concept of airships hadn't waned.

18

'NERVOUS NICK'

Spring 1927.

During spring of 1927, the airship's frame steadily took shape with more workers being hired every day. One morning, a young man about twenty-five, came into the shed. He was very thin, roughly dressed and unshaven. Lou, Norway and the shop foreman stood talking at the foot of one of the fireman's ladders. He waited humbly by, until they'd finished speaking. At last, the foreman turned to him.

"What do *you* want?"

"Looking for work, sir."

"As what?"

"A rigger, sir."

"Done it before, 'ave yer?"

"Well, no sir, but I can learn."

"What's yer name?"

"Nick, sir, Nick Steele."

"Got nerves to match, 'ave yer?"

"Beggin' your pardon, sir?"

"Not nervous are yer?"

"No, sir. Not at all."

The foreman pointed to the ladder, which seemed to reach the roof.

"See this? It's 110 foot."

"Yes, sir."

"Any problem?"

"No problem at all, sir. Easy as pie!"

"Ever climbed one before?"

"Er, no, sir."

"Up you go then, lad. Show us what you're made of."

Nick walked boldly to the foot of the ladder, grabbed the rails and peered up the treads. The top was almost invisible. He set his jaw. Lou and Norway glanced at one another. This was going to be interesting. They'd been through this themselves. Nick set off suddenly at a vertical run, trying to overcome fears he didn't know he had until this moment. When he got about a third of the way up, he stopped, the ladder swaying wildly from side to side.

"Don't stop, lad. Keep going!" the foreman yelled. But it was useless. Nick reluctantly came down. "I'm sorry, gov'. I just couldn't go any further," he said, painfully out of breath and unable to hide his bitter disappointment.

It was lunchtime and Lou felt sorry for the man. "Hungry, Nick?"

"No, sir. I'm good, thanks."

Lou put his hand on the man's scrawny shoulder. "Come on, pal, we'll get you something to eat," he said.

Nick didn't protest and the four men trooped over to the nearby canteen, full of workmen in overalls eating bread rolls and drinking beer. Lou bought the despondent Nick a cheese sandwich and gave him a bottle of John Smith's ale. The others chose their eats and they sat at a wooden table, where Nick, between ravenous bites, told them he'd been unemployed for five months and things were desperate at home what with his wife and three kids and sick mother. After lunch they trooped back to the shed.

"Can I give it another go, sir?" Nick asked, looking at each of them in desperation. Please let me try it again."

"I used to be afraid w-when I f-first got here," Norway said. "Now I run around on the c-catwalks in the roof and climb the c-cat ladders without a second thought. Maybe you can get over your f-fear."

Once inside the shed, Nick made for the ladder again and went bounding up. He passed the point where he'd frozen the first time and kept going, but he slowed down with every step as the ladder swayed more the higher he got. He stopped three quarters of the way up. Norway and the foreman yelled up at him, "Go on! Go on! You can do it!"

"That was an improvement," Lou said.

Nick stood there for some moments, trying to find the courage and for the ladder to become still. He slowly started the descent and when he reached bottom, he burst into tears.

"What am I going to do?" he sobbed.

"Come on, buddy, I'll buy you another beer," Lou said, grabbing him by the arm and leading him away. "We'll be back shortly and he'll try again," Lou called over his shoulder.

Fifteen minutes later, Lou and Nick came back, Nick smiling. A crowd had gathered. Nick made for the ladder and without hesitation and with the crowd shouting "Go, go, go!" he made it to the top where he gave a triumphant yell and took a bow. Below, everyone cheered and gave him a big round of applause which filled the shed and echoed fifteen times.

"The trouble was, 'Nervous Nick' wasn't drunk enough!" Lou said. And from that day on, the name stuck—'Nervous Nick', the man who owed everything to John Smith (and Lou Remington, of course).

19

JESSUP

Summer 1927.

Jessup had become ingrained in their lives—someone they had to live with—like a third member in their marriage. He continued to follow Charlotte around and loitered near the hospital in plain view. Nothing had changed since Lou and Charlotte were married; in fact, things had become a whole lot worse. Lou went to the police station and filed a report. He was told Jessup had the right to stand wherever he liked in the street, as long as he didn't interfere physically with anyone, and, if he did, it'd be necessary to produce witnesses. It put a strain on Lou and Charlotte's relationship.

A couple of times after they'd gone to bed—once when making love and another after they'd fallen asleep—they were disturbed by sounds in the living room. Lou crept into the other room thinking they had a burglar. He found the bedroom door ajar—which they both swore had been closed—and the front door wide open. Lou heard the garden gate squeak, a cackling laugh, running footsteps, and moments later, a motorcycle kick-started. Lou knew the sound of a 490 cc Norton—the motorbike Jessup rode.

The situation continued to become more serious, perhaps even dangerous. Lou went to the police again, but after a polite interview and making a report, things went nowhere. Nothing had been stolen, no one had been hurt, no damage had been done, and Lou couldn't prove Jessup was the culprit.

Jessup filled Lou's thoughts incessantly. He worried about Charlotte, especially when he was away at Cardington. Powerless, he wondered how much their marriage could take. He didn't mention the problem to his colleagues at Howden. The whole business seemed too juvenile and embarrassing; the thought of bringing it up with them he found humiliating. Just when he thought things couldn't get worse, they did. He returned from Cardington to find Jessup in the shed, working alongside the riggers as a laborer with two of his yobos. Lou went to the foreman, trying his best to appear casual.

"New faces?"

"Took 'em on this morning," the foreman said.

"Who are they?"

"They're from Moortop over in Ackworth. Seem like decent lads. Very polite and they've been working pretty good."

"I see."

"They seemed desperate for work."

"Is that so?" Lou frowned.

"Do you have a problem with them?"

"Er, no."

"You sure?"

"Not at all."

Devastated, Lou stood glaring at Jessup who kept his eyes down. But Lou could see the smirk on his face as he worked. Lou knew his game: He'd lie low and not make trouble—the perfect employee—for the time being. Lou was in a quandary. He couldn't discuss the problem with anyone at the air station, but he'd have to tell Charlotte.

Lou went home after work and sat down heavily on the couch with a sigh of frustration.

"What's up, love?" Charlotte said, leaning over and kissing him. "Is everything all right?"

"No, it's not."

"What's the matter?"

"They've hired Jessup."

"What!"

"While I was down south yesterday."

"Oh no! What are you going to do?"

"That son of a bitch must've known I was in Cardington."

"You must tell them he's evil and should be sacked."

"I can't do that. They don't fire people for being evil. Perhaps they should, but they don't."

"You've got to go and explain what he's done to us."

"Charlotte, they'll tell me to go to the police and we've been all through that."

"You'll have to see him *every day*. You've got to talk to them."

"Charlotte, I'm not sure they'll believe us. The whole thing's bizarre. No question he's a mental case, but they might think it's you, I mean *we*, who have the problem."

"What do you mean? *I* don't have a problem!"

"Sorry, my darling. You don't, but you know how people are."

"Lou, do you remember the time I came home with a bruise on my arm?" Lou glared at Charlotte. Instinctively, he knew before she said any more.

"Yes, and you said an elderly lady grabbed you in the ward."

"Jessup did that to me. He said a lot of dirty things and laid his hands on me when I was walking to Ackworth Station."

"That must have been when the heel of your shoe broke off?"

"Yes."

"And you don't tell me until now!"

"I didn't want to upset you. I was afraid what you might do."

"But now you're not afraid?"

"I just want you to get him fired. That's all."

Lou was silent for a few moments. "Charlotte, I killed a man once."

Charlotte was dumbstruck.

"A German," he said quietly.

"What happened?"

"I'd shot a lot of Germans …" Charlotte was horrified. He'd not told her he'd even shot at anybody, although he had told her about the last day of the war. "But this was different. He was a POW who'd escaped. He came at me with a bayonet, terrified, babbling in German. He was just a kid …" Lou hung his head, "no more than sixteen."

"What did you do?"

"He had no chance. I snapped his neck in a second," Lou said, gesturing the action with his hands.

Charlotte turned her face away, sickened. "Oh, Lou, that's awful. My God!"

"It's hard to live with, Charlotte."

"You poor love. I understand," she said, turning back to him.

"I didn't need to kill him—not really. It was sadistic and it came natural. I regret it every day." Lou put his hands to his head, remorse tearing him up inside.

"I'm so sorry, Lou."

"When I was young, I was cocky and aggressive. I loved karate and the thought of meting out punishment to those I thought deserved it."

"That's natural, love."

"Sometimes when I look at Jessup, I see myself. I can't explain it."

"Oh no, Lou. That's silly."

"Charlotte, I can't describe to you the desolation I felt on eleven-eleven when I walked away from the battlefield leaving all my buddies lying dead in the mud. All I could think about was them …and that German boy. I wanted no part of violence after that. I vowed not to hurt anyone again."

He looked into Charlotte's eyes. Even though it was impossible, she had an uncanny way of understanding all he'd been through; another reason why he loved her so much, though they usually avoided the subject of war. It upset her too much.

"When I joined the Marines I was angry; when I left, all that was gone. I have an ugly side I'm not proud of, Charlotte, especially when someone close to me is threatened. In those days, I was always in a rage. My father told me over and over—I was a pussy and I'd never amount to anything."

"He must have caused it then. Perhaps he was jealous of you. Some fathers are."

"That's as maybe, but it's why I don't want to get into it with Jessup. It'd be too easy. I always remember what old Jeb tried to instill in me as a kid—respect for life. It took a while, but it finally took hold. Forgive and forget, he always said."

"Who's Jeb?"

"A great guy who stays on my Gran's farm. Known him all my life. I love the man."

"So, what are we going to do?"

"We'll wait. Things will be better when I get posted to Cardington."

The dirty secret hung over them—suffocating—like a filthy blanket. Lou didn't speak of it to Wallis or Norway, and Jessup and his friends kept their noses clean. To make matters worse, in the noisy turmoil in the shed where men shouted directions from the roof to the floor, while swinging around like stuntmen, Jessup's stature rose. He displayed extraordinary athletic ability and fearlessness as he climbed the massive webs of scaffolding. He dangled from the bosun's chair, raced up flimsy ladders and climbed ropes to great heights—as good as any high wire circus performer. All this was accompanied by annoying, shrill, two-finger whistles to his buddies signaling them to 'get up here' or bring something to him. It became one of his trademark mannerisms; part of his successful bid to dominate the shed. He became feared by all.

Wallis and Norway noticed him. He was a hard worker who got things done and could make the others jump to it. Bit by bit, he became brazen and smiled at Lou in his cocksure way. Now it was Lou's turn not to look at Jessup directly, feeling those wicked bug-eyes always on him. Jessup had got the upper hand. Over the coming months, Jessup became increasingly mouthy. He'd joined the union and been promoted to charge-hand foreman over his three buddies and three others. One day, a delivery of duralumin arrived on a truck and Lou went out to check it.

"Hey boys, here's the lieutenant." Jessup pronounced 'lieutenant' the American way – 'looootenant' instead of 'leftenant.'

"Where would you like to stick this, sir? Anywhere special? I can think of a place, if you can't!"

"Cut the crap, Jessup. Stack the stuff over there," Lou answered.

"Oooooh. Cut the crap, eh? You 'eard the lieutenant, boys. Put the stuff over there and cut the crap—we mustn't upset the brave lieutenant, must we."

Lou went to the driver and signed his delivery slip and returned to his office. This was the first time Jessup had stepped out of line on the job, and it caught him by surprise. Lou wasn't sure what to do and assumed the insults would escalate. A week later, a load of timber arrived for cribbage and shoring. The truck pulled into the shed and Lou went out to the driver. Jessup, his gang of apes in tow, surrounded Lou as the driver got down from the cab. The driver, a heavy-set man, had become friendly with Lou since the caravan incident. His brother, a rigger, had been aboard *R38* when it crashed, and Lou remembered him. He gave Lou a bright smile.

"Hello, governor. How are you today?"

"Not bad, Bill," Lou answered.

" 'Ere, you wanted a description of that peeping Tom trying look in your caravan that time. Remember?" the driver said, pointing his index finger in Jessup's face, whose bulbous eyes blazed in fury. "This is 'im right here!"

"Now you watch it, cock! Your health could take a nasty turn," Jessup yelled.

"Oh, yeah? Is that right, you pockmarked, grease ball? I'll cut yer dick off—if I can find it," the driver shouted back.

The foreman, hearing the commotion, came rushing over. "What's going on?" he demanded, glaring at the driver.

"It's not his fault," Lou said.

"What's all this about, then?"

"I saw this man here, peeking in the lieutenant's caravan window a while ago," the driver said. "Stinking little pervert."

"I'd come to find a job, that's all. But this bloke," Jessup pointed at Lou, "was inside with a woman. He must have bin havin' 'er away. The caravan was rockin' about an' she was screamin' like a wild woman. "

Jessup's crew laughed and sniggered. "Wo!" they yelled.

"That wasn't right. Not on *government* property," Jessup declared, puffing out his chest.

"All right, all right!" the foreman growled. "Bugger off, the lot of yer. Get to the other end of the shed. Report to the foreman down there."

"I'm going to report this to the shop steward," Jessup hissed.

"You can go and tell the Pope, for all I care," the foreman shouted.

After they were out of earshot, he turned to Lou. "Is any of this true, sir?"

"It was during the time of reconstruction. My wife had brought me my lunch …and she was giving me dancing lessons. We were doing the Charleston."

"And what was Jessup doing?"

"He was trying to look in the window," the driver said.

"Maybe he *was* looking for a job, like he said," the foreman said.

"You could be right," Lou said. "Let's forget about the whole thing."

The foreman shrugged and walked off to bring another crew to unload the truck.

"I'm sorry, sir. I didn't think …" the driver began.

"Don't worry. It wasn't your fault, Bill."

"I just wanted you to know, it was *him*. Dirty little wanker!"

"I knew exactly who it was," Lou said.

"Do you want me to do 'im for yer, sir?"

"No, please don't. I don't like violence."

"What are you going to do, guv?" the driver asked.

"I'm working on it."

A few weeks later, in the middle of summer, Jessup showed up uninvited to one of the Sunday afternoon picnics. He slunk around, trying to blend in. Charlotte spotted him and watched him sidle up to one of the wives who lived in a staff bungalow with her husband, a wispy-looking design engineer who was on the field playing cricket. Charlotte was on to them immediately. The woman was older than Jessup, obviously flattered by his attention. Charlotte nodded to Lou who quickly grasped the situation. He walked over to Jessup who, seeing him coming, moved toward Wallis and Molly and stood close to them.

"What are *you* doing here?" Lou asked.

"I'm sorry, sir. I thought this was a general thing for the workers on government property," Jessup said pleasantly.

"You're wrong and you know it, Jessup."

Wallis was listening.

"I'm awfully sorry, sir. I wouldn't have dreamt of coming—I was just tryin' to be sociable," Jessup said humbly, looking at Lou while shooting appealing sideways glances at Wallis.

"You need to leave, right now!" Lou barked.

"Wait. Don't be too hard on the man," Wallis said. "Let him stay today." Lou glared at Jessup, who stared meekly back at him with a hint of pleasure.

"Well, that's awfully kind of you, sir," Jessup said, smiling at Wallis. "I *will* stay a while. I think I'll try some of the ladies' English trifle. Looks awfully delicious." He looked at Lou, smiling sweetly, and then with a wink, "I'm awfully sorry, sir. I really had no idea—

honest!" Jessup snuck off and took up again with the woman he was trying to bed. Lou and Charlotte went home.

The following week, Jessup tipped the scales, putting his own health in serious jeopardy. As Lou walked to the other end of the shed searching for one of the foreman, Jessup came up behind him with his gang. "Look who's here, boys. It's our great American hero—hero my arse!"

"Get back to work, Jessup!"

"This is the man who deserted his shipmates, boys. They came up with a big story for the papers. He saved *this one* and he saved *that one*. He was hiding in the tail of his balloon wiv all them other gutless Yanks," Jessup yelled. "He ain't no bleedin' hero. He just got lucky! Then, what do they do? They give him a job here so he can knock off his old woman in a bloody government caravan—right here. Talk about benefits on the job!"

Lou went to Jessup and stood close. Jessup stared at Lou in surprise. Lou spoke quietly and the others gathered around trying to hear above the construction din. "Jessup, look at me. Look at me." They stood, their noses almost touching. Lou continued, while Jessup smirked. "Now listen. I'm going to ask you to knock it off, for your own good. I don't want anything bad to happen to you."

Jessup whooped. "Oh, listen to 'im, boys. He doesn't want anything bad to 'appen. And it's all for me own good!"

"Just don't say I didn't warn you. It'll be bad. D'you understand?" Lou said.

Jessup grinned. "Nothing's gonna change, Yank. I'm gonna keep on 'til you're gone from 'ere and you and yer wife are history."

"Okay, Jessup, this is how it's going to be."

Jessup put his hands on his hips. "Come on, tell me, Yankee boy."

"Old Hinkley's Farm."

"Yeah, what about Hinkley's Farm?"

"One hour. Be there. Bring *one* of these knuckleheads with you. You're gonna need help. But *only* one," Lou said, holding up one finger and glaring at the three stooges gathered around Jessup.

"Blimey. What d'yer know. I do believe he wants to fight. All right. One hour, then."

Jessup was thrilled. Lou turned away, making for his office.

"We got 'im now, boys. Damn! We got 'im now!" Jessup crowed.

20

OLD HINKLEY'S FARM

Summer 1927.

Lou put on his construction boots. In the bottom drawer of his desk he had an old black T-shirt and a pair of dungarees. He pulled them out and slipped them on. He left the shed and crossed the old railway line toward the perimeter of the field, walking briskly to loosen up. Lou trotted and walked alternately along the edge of the airfield toward the wood on the well-trodden path. Stepping along a fallen log, he crossed a small stream and disappeared into the forest, passing a bevy of deer.

Inside the tree line, the sound of birdsong increased. So did the drumming of rain drops from leaves overhead. He turned and retraced his steps after a mile or two and ran back past the animals. Feeling good, he jogged toward the aerodrome, re-crossing the spur railway line and onto the muddy field. His head and chest were clear, his blood pumping steadily, pushed by a strong heart. He took deep breaths of the damp, misty air drifting over the marshes from the river.

During his exercise, which was as much about psyching himself up to fight as anything, Lou planned his strategy. He must stay in control. Not lose his temper. Not kill anyone—although that might be difficult. He didn't want to be responsible for another man's death and go to jail, or worse. He had too much to live for: to be with Charlotte and take care of her. He hated this. He thought he'd left it all behind. He ran to the end of the air station and back across the field. It started to drizzle again. He entered his office in the shed and was putting on his motorcycle jacket when Norway appeared in the doorway.

"Lou, oh, are you leaving?"

"I'm gonna pop out for twenty minutes. Anything important?"

"No. I wanted to ask if you and Charlotte…"

"Nevil. I've got a meeting with someone. I don't want to keep him waiting. Can we go in your car? We can talk on the way. It'll save me getting wet on the bike." They headed for Norway's green three-wheeler parked outside the shed. Lou looked at it and smiled. Norway was so proud of this funny little car. They climbed in. It smelled of Balkan Sobrani.

This thing fits Nevil's personality perfectly and he's just so content.

Norway turned the key. After a few attempts, the engine sputtered to life. They chugged jerkily down the road, leaving a trail of blue smoke from the tail pipe. "She'll be all right in a minute," Norway said.

"Follow this road for two miles. So, what's up, Nev?"

"I wondered if I could take you and Charlotte to dinner this evening. They've just opened a new restaurant in Hull. I can take you in the car."

"What's the occasion?"

"I want to celebrate. My new novel's been accepted by the publisher."

"'Hey, Nev, that's great. Well done!"

"I also wanted to ask if you've read my new manuscript."

"As a matter of fact, we both have. We liked it. Sure, we can meet up for a chat. You know you should think about doing a story about building the two airships—you know, like rivals—a big adventure and all that."

"Hmm, maybe. We'll see how this saga turns out, but I expect it'd be dreadfully dull," Norway replied. They followed the road to the junction known as Old Hinkley's Farm.

"Here, Nev. Pull over on the grass, if you don't mind."

They were deafened by the roar of four motorcycles wildly revving up behind them. "W-what the heck is going on?" Norway said. "I b-believe they're t-trying to int-t-timidate us."

"Oh, don't worry. It's my guy. They're having a bit of fun that's all. He and I are going to have a little talk. Wait here. I won't be long." Norway peered uncertainly at the four hostile bikers. They kept looking over at the car and laughing as they pulled their motorbikes up onto their stands.

"Brought yer protection with yer then, Lieutenant?" Jessup said, grinning.

"Hey, Jessie, that's 'is armored car," one with rodent features shouted.

"It's right sporty!" said the tall one with no hair and snake eyes.

Lou saw Norway becoming increasingly unnerved. "I told you to bring *one* knucklehead, Jessup, not three," Lou growled.

"Yeah, well, they all wanted to come. They wanna see your guts splattered all over this field," Jessup said, pulling out a pack of Gold Flake. He lit one with a steel lighter and sauntered after Lou, the cigarette dangling from his mouth. Lou climbed over the five bar gate, pulled off his motorcycle jacket and carefully hung it on the gatepost. The gang of four followed Lou, who looked back at Norway leaning nervously on the gate. Lou spent the next seven minutes meting out punishment to Jessup and two of his gang. He allowed one to escape injury so he could render assistance to the others.

After Lou had done his worst, he ambled back to the gate. Norway looked sick.

"What's up, old buddy?" Lou asked.

"I heard that man's leg snap," Norway answered. "Lou, what the hell are you d-d-doing? Have you gone m-mad?"

Lou put on his jacket. "It's a long story, Nev. But you know, you really should think about doing a book about the airship business. Could be a best seller."

"Let's g-get away from here," Norway said, scurrying off to the car, "b-before you kill somebody." Once inside the car Lou did his best to calm Norway down.

"Look Nev, don't be alarmed. These low-down, dirty rats deserved what they got. That last one has been harassing and following Charlotte around for seven years and he's broken into our house at least twice—not to mention beating up and robbing Charlotte's cousin."

"Why didn't you go to the p-police?"

"I did. There was nothing they could do."

"Maybe I *will* write that b-book and *y-you'll* be in it," Norway muttered. He turned the key in the starter. The engine started after five or six tries.

"You know this is one hell of a car, Nev," Lou said.

"She'll be all right in a minute, when she's warmed up again."

"If your book's a success, maybe you'll be able to afford another wheel."

The car sputtered and took off merrily along the road to the Howden shed where Lou worked the rest of the day without further distraction, save for the sounds of ambulance bells ringing as they sped along the Selby Road toward Old Hinkley's Farm.

Jessup's recovery was slow. He spent six months in the hospital in Hull. Charlotte stopped by his ward every so often without him seeing her. He looked as though he'd been in a dreadful traffic accident. His jaw had been wired up and his head wrapped in bandages with only his eyes visible. His left leg was in plaster from the ankle to the hip and suspended from the ceiling. His arm was in a sling due to his broken collarbone and his right hand was wrapped in bandages, his fingers in splints. He complained of pains in his abdomen caused by a massive blow to the solar plexus. Jessup's bald friend was in the next bed for a week before being sent home on crutches. During his hospital stay, Jessup had a few visitors, including his sister Angela, as well as a few toughs from Moortop.

Most of the nurses knew of Charlotte's troubles with Jessup and kept her abreast of his progress and what he said to his visitors. For a month, he kept quiet, his jaw being wired up tightly. Jessup wasn't a happy man and took his fury out on the nurses. After that month, Charlotte was sent to work on Jessup's ward and when he caught sight of her, he became enraged.

"You see what he did to me, bitch? You see what he did! He's gonna pay for this. Just you wait. I'm gonna kill him!" Jessup hissed and spat through clenched teeth like an incoherent madman. Hearing the outburst, the matron came rushing down the ward.

"You listen to me, *Mr.* Jessup, one more peep out of you and I'll have you thrown out on the street! In the meantime, I'll inform the police of your threats," she said.

At that moment, Angela came into the ward to visit her brother and overheard the matron's bollocking. She glared at Charlotte with bitter hatred. Charlotte was sent to another ward. Later in the evening, she told Lou what Jessup had said. Lou shrugged and said he wasn't surprised—Jessup was a slow learner. A couple of weeks after the beatings, Jessup's friend with the rat-face, showed up for work at the shed with the unharmed member of their gang. He wore a dressing over his nose which covered most of his face. In comical nasal tones, he told the foreman he and his mates had been set upon by soldiers from the barracks in York. He said the other two were recovering.

Jessup returned to work with his bald friend nine months after their 'little talk' at Hinkley's Farm. He acted docile and the foreman let them work even though both limped badly. Lou learned Jessup was back and sought him out on the shop floor. When Jessup saw Lou coming, his face became mask of terror.

"Ah Jessie, I've been really worried about you, big guy," Lou said, taking his hand and giving him the smile of a caring friend. "I heard you got into a bit of a dust-up. Are you okay now?"

The shop foreman listened with interest.

"Yes, sir. I'm pretty good now," Jessup said, in a weird voice, his speech affected by his crooked jaw.

"They said you and your friends were set upon by a platoon of soldiers. Is that true?"

"No, sir, only six, not a platoon," Jessup answered.

"Well, that's mighty unfair. Anyway, keep me informed of your progress. I'm gonna be taking a close interest in your welfare from now on." Lou moved in close to Jessup and spoke in his ear. "Remember what I said, you little shit. You're on probation—you'll *always* be on probation."

"Yes, sir. I understand, sir."

"Now, the things you've been saying in the hospital about ...well, I don't need to repeat all of it, do I?"

"I'm so, so sorry. I was saying crazy things for a time. I was out of my head with the pain. You understand, sir. Please forgive me."

"All right, Jessup, we'll see how you shape up," Lou said.

21

A CHANGE IN ATTITUDE

Autumn 1928.

B y 1928, the skeletons of both ships had been fully framed. Shed No.1 at Cardington had been lengthened to provide more than adequate room, whereas at Howden they had only eighteen inches to spare each side. Lou realized the sheds had served as huge templates for the airships, growing like giant grubs inside their pods. The press continued to follow every detail during the construction of *Cardington R101*, which they considered the main story. *Howden R100* was second-rate in comparison and not paid nearly as much attention. George Hunter from the *Daily Express* however, didn't write the Howden ship off so quickly, remaining quiet on the subject. He visited Howden a couple of times a year where he usually met with Norway and Lou. He and Norway became friends. Wallis shunned the press.

In the autumn of '28, Lou made one of his monthly visits to Cardington. In Colmore and Scott's absence, he'd arranged to meet Richmond. Before doing so, he dropped in on Captain Carmichael Irwin in his site office in Shed No. 1. Scott had brought Irwin on board as the skipper of *Cardington R101* and, for the time being, he was familiarizing himself with the engineered drawings of the airship, its power and mechanical systems. Four years older than Lou, Irwin was unmistakably Irish, that is 'Black Irish', good-looking with jet-black hair and blue eyes, tall and somewhat shy. His nickname was 'Blackbird' or just 'Bird'. He was also known as 'the Crow', which would later become a *Cardington R101* call sign. They talked briefly about the war. Irwin had served with the Royal Naval Air Service as a commander of non-rigid airships in the Home Waters and East Mediterranean. Now, he was with the Royal Air Force with the rank of flight lieutenant. He was also a fine athlete, having represented Great Britain as a long distance runner in the 1920s Olympics in Belgium.

Lou found the soft-spoken captain to be a genuine and decent fellow. Knowing the Remingtons would be posted to Cardington early in the coming year, Irwin offered his help in finding them somewhere to live. Later in the year, he sent newspaper cuttings of homes for rent in the area with names of reputable estate agents.

After leaving Irwin, Lou met Richmond at his office in Cardington House. He found him slumped in his leather chair, shirt rumpled, sleeves rolled up, Air Force tie loose at the neck. His scoffing superiority seemed to have vanished."Oh, Remington, come in," he said wearily.

"Are you well, sir?" Lou asked.

"Rather tired, actually."

"Burning the midnight oil, are we?"

"That's about it. So much to be done," Richmond sighed.

"Always the way, sir."

"I shouldn't complain. I'm doing what I love most …I suppose. I can't seem to get any satisfaction out of it these days. I'm exhausted." Richmond leaned back in his chair, meeting Lou's eyes. "Just how are things at Howden? I want you to tell me *everything*. When we first met, you told me they were using 'geodetic' construction. Tell me more about that. I have my own ideas of course, but I'd like to hear *you* to explain it."

"For technical information you might want to speak with Mr. Wallis or Mr. Norway. You could pay them a visit. I'm sure they'd be more than glad to consult with you, sir."

"I doubt that very much," Richmond said, shaking his head.

"Perhaps you should try."

Richmond turned away, as though thinking about it. "We'll see. *You* tell me."

"The best way I can put it is—if one part of the ship fails, or is under stress, say like a girder or something, then other parts take up the load. They ride in to save the day, like the cavalry, so to speak." Lou put his fist to his mouth and made a bugle sound and grinned. "I'm sure Squadron Leader Rope's familiar with all that stuff."

Richmond puffed up his cheeks and blew out a long breath. "Fascinating. Tell me about their engines; I understand they're using petrol."

Lou had spoken to Wallis before coming down and asked if he should remain tight-lipped. Wallis's answer had surprised him. "Tell them whatever they want to know. Richmond's committed now. He can't change a thing—government won't allow it. They're overspent. And as far as my knowing what Cardington is doing—which is of no interest to me—I only have to read the papers. The Air Ministry puts out propaganda every day."

"Howden's using six Rolls-Royce Condors, two of which can reverse for maneuvering," Lou said.

Richmond's pain was obvious. *Cardington R101* had five engines, underpowered and overweight. One, a permanent reversing engine, was just dead weight ninety-nine percent of the time.

"I wish we could switch to petrol. We'd save tons. What about gas bags and harnesses?"

"As you know, the bags are coming from Germany. The harnesses are made and everybody's happy with them," Lou said.

"And the gas valves?"

"They should be in from Zeppelin any time."

"Well, ours are built. I hope they work." Richmond peered gloomily out the window.

"Oh, I'm sure they will, sir."

"What about servo assistance?" Richmond said, studying the wintry scene outside his window.

"They don't have any."

Richmond suddenly sat up and glared at Lou. "What! Why not?"

"Mr. Norway found it unnecessary."

"I can't believe *that!*"

Lou read his disappointment. "They've been through the numbers countless times."

"Rope said just the opposite. That damned gear weighs a ton!"

"If I may be so bold, sir, how is the weight coming out?" Lou asked innocently.

"Heavier than expected. I can't say anything now. We're working on it."

Underpowered and heavy. No wonder he's up at night. He's a pompous ass, but you can't help feeling sorry for the guy.

Lou remembered Wallis telling him and Norway the Cardington ship was bound to come out heavy. "They'll be depending on dynamic lift to stay airborne, you'll see," he'd said.

"How much did you say they'd spent so far?" Richmond asked.

"Actually, I didn't, but it's under two hundred and ninety thousand pounds."

Richmond was incredulous. "Under two ninety!" He put his hand to his brow, staring at his untidy desktop. "We've spent over two million pounds."

No wonder you look glum, pal.

Lou knew that at the end of the day, Vickers estimated they'd be at least a hundred thousand pounds over budget, but they knew that going in.

Richmond continued, "That's confidential. I shouldn't have told you."

"I shan't say anything, sir."

"How the hell does he do it?"

"How does who do what, sir?" Lou asked.

"Wallis. How does he do it?"

"It's all in his head, sir."

"Just like that?"

"Yep. He has a pretty amazing mind."

"Look, Remington, we've been talking openly. Keep all this to yourself. Don't divulge anything to Howden."

"Sir, I never do and they never ask. They're good like that."

"Quite."

"They have their own designs and ways of doing things."

"Yes, yes, I know. They're not going to steal our ideas."

"No chance of that."

"I just don't want information to get out, especially in the press."

"I understand perfectly, sir.

"Their confidence is astonishing," Richmond said.

"One thing I can tell you, sir. They're glad of oversight."

Richmond pondered this, puzzled. "You know, I'm a *chemist*," he said suddenly.

"Really, sir?"

"I expect they joke about me up there, don't they?"

Lou had heard them call him 'Dopey', but he couldn't remember who said it.

No point in upsetting the poor guy.

"I've heard nothing of the sort."

Richmond looked embarrassed for opening up the way he had.

"I depend on Bolton and Paul's engineers," he said.

"I guess they've got aeronautical design staff over there?"

"They're very experienced. They've done stout work here. I think highly of them and Rope oversees a lot of this stuff, of course—he's exceptional," Richmond said.

"The newspapers can't say enough about the guy," Lou agreed.

Richmond opened his bottom drawer and pulled out a sheaf of papers. He buzzed his secretary and asked her to bring in 'one of the special envelopes.' A young woman appeared moments later with a brown envelope. Richmond slid the papers inside and wound the string around its fasteners.

"I'd like you to give this to Mr. Wallis, with my compliments. It's a copy of our gas valve design. I'd be most interested to hear his opinion." Lou took the envelope wondering if this could be a new beginning; an era of cooperation.

In Howden the next morning, Lou handed Wallis the envelope, relaying Richmond's message. Wallis read the words 'TOP SECRET' on the front. He handed it back to Lou.

"Aren't you going to open it, sir?"

Wallis's answer was brief. "Send this back by special courier immediately. We don't have anywhere secure enough at Howden to store such valuable, high-level, top secret documents."

Lou was disappointed—this was Wallis's unforgiving, stubborn side.

"Don't look like that, Lou. These people are on the ropes. Do you think they'd afford us the same consideration if the situation were reversed? They've been kicking us around for the last four years and now they want to play nice. Don't be soft."

"Right you are, sir," Lou said.

22

GOODBYE LENNY

Autumn 1928.

L ate in summer of '28, afternoon tea was arranged at Candlestick Cottage. Wallis was present with Molly and their two children and Norway showed up with an unexpected guest —a new lady friend. Frances was a quietly spoken girl who worked as a medical practitioner in York. He'd met her at the flying club. John Bull dropped by with Mary and chatted with Charlotte's parents while Billy played darts with Lou and his dad in the garden. Lenny did his level best to play, squinting through his specs, a Woodbine in his mouth while he tried to suppress a chesty cough full of phlegm. But his darts kept falling short into the dirt. Charlotte stood inside at the window with Molly, each holding a baby. Fanny began to cry, her shoulders heaving. She held a handkerchief up to her eyes, her heart breaking.

"Fanny, love, what's the matter?"

"It's terrible," Fanny sobbed.

"What?"

"He's only got three months."

"Oh Fanny, what do you mean?" Molly gasped.

"He's got lung cancer. They said it's spreading—to his brain."

After that news, it became impossible to enjoy the afternoon. Fanny and her family soon left after tearful goodbyes. Everyone realized Lenny was a very sick man and when they were gone, Charlotte broke the news.

Lenny died two weeks later. Those present at the Sunday afternoon tea at the cottage attended the funeral at Western Cemetery, which brought back sad memories to Lou and Charlotte. They watched the autumn leaves fall on Lenny's coffin as it was lowered into the ground, while the distraught Fanny held on to her mother and Billy. After the service, the mourners returned to the cottage—everyone except Fanny and Billy, who went to Fanny's mother's in Selby.

Wallis told Lou that if the boy needed a job in order to help his mother financially, there'd be a place for him at Howden. Billy reported for work two weeks later. Lou took him to the shop foreman and told him to take good care of him. He earned twelve shillings a week—not bad for a boy of fifteen.

After a couple of months, Billy was shinning up and down the ladders and climbing the scaffolds and ropes with the best of them. Lou was glad he had a job; it'd keep his mind off his father's death. Fanny left their rented place near Hull and went with Billy to live in Selby. A position had been found for her at Goole Hospital.

23

LEAVING 'CANDLESTICK'

April 1929.

Lou hadn't slept at all. It was now 4:30 a.m. He rolled over and sat up on the side of the bed. The wind had strengthened and continued to howl through the trees and rattle the windows.

"What time is it?" Charlotte asked.

"Half past four."

"Suppose I might as well get up, too."

"Not much point in lying here."

"I'll make tea," Charlotte said.

Lou got up and dressed and went into the living room where boxes were piled high. He lit the fire in the grate. It was chilly. They sat around the fireplace drinking tea and eating toast, enjoying a couple more hours in this room they both loved. Charlotte held her cup to her lips, withdrew it, and stared into the fire.

"Oh, Lou, I don't want to leave Candlestick."

"Neither do I honey. I love this place as much as you. But once we get down there, we'll make new friends, you'll see. Remember, I already know lots of people."

"Yes, and you'll be off flying around the world in that bloody airship. And I'll be stuck at home on my own. … Oh Lou, …"

"Come on, Charlie. We'll give it a try and I promise if you're not happy, I'll quit."

"You promise?"

"I promise."

"I don't want to leave this place. I'd hate it if anything happened to you."

"Don't worry, nothing's gonna happen."

"What will John do with this place?"

"Perhaps he'll sell it."

At 8 o'clock, John arrived to take them to Hull Railway Station. They'd arranged with him to pick up their belongings and transport them down to Bedford at the weekend in his van. Lou had sold his motorbike and planned to buy a newer one in Bedford. He was looking forward to shopping around.

After putting two small suitcases in the boot of John's car, Charlotte and Lou went back inside the cottage for one last look and to make sure Fluffy was all right with plenty of food and milk. John would send her down with the furniture in her cage. He was going to look in on her in the meantime. Charlotte cried and Lou put his arms around her.

"Don't be sad, love," Lou pleaded.

Charlotte said nothing. She stared out the window at the rear garden and fond memories of their friends came back to her. Her snowdrops and shrubs were just starting to bloom and she wondered who'd care for them now. She remembered all the things they'd done in this house—their first real home together. It had always been full of friends and laughter. She could hear it now—so many happy memories, and some sad ones, too. She thought of Lenny, the baby that never came, and the box room where she hoped to put the crib—but which had gradually become full of junk. She was heartbroken, and for the first time in her life, bitter.

Charlotte walked to the car while Lou turned the key in the deadlock on the front door. Charlotte climbed into the back seat. John turned to her from the driver's seat and forced a smile.

"Come on, love, it won't be so bad. You're off on a new adventure."

Charlotte said nothing. She felt empty.

Lou climbed into the passenger front seat and handed the keys to John who slid them into his pocket with a final sad nod. They pulled away. Charlotte stared at the cottage until it disappeared from view. She believed she could never feel more miserable than this. But she was wrong.

PART FIVE

Cardington Shed No. 1.

CARDINGTON

24

THE IN-BETWEEN YEARS

1924 – 1929.

Whe the Labour Party had been kicked out of office, Thomson didn't sit around feeling sorry for himself. He visited MacDonald once or twice a year, traveling up by air with their good friend Capt. Hinchliffe, chief pilot with a Dutch airline. 'Hinch' sometimes rented a two or four-seater plane and flew Thomson and MacDonald to Lossiemouth on one of his days off. Thomson usually stayed for a week or two at The Hillocks, during which time they went for long walks, fished or played golf. They also visited local Highland beauty spots and dined at favorite hotels.

On their walks, Thomson and MacDonald strategized, devising new policies to get Britain on a permanent socialist footing once they regained power. MacDonald assured Thomson it would happen soon. Thomson believed him.

Thomson became 'a man in waiting'—a role he'd learned to live with for years. Besides Marthe, getting back in office was all he thought about. He yearned to be back behind his ornate desk at Gwydyr House.

Taking up residence in that mansion on Whitehall and setting up the New British Airship Program—his creation!—had been the greatest thrill of his professional life. He believed it to be his destiny. He loved his Air Ministry position and all it entailed—it remained key in his plan to win Marthe for good. She was the ultimate prize; his cabinet seat and elevation in stature were the means to that end and so obviously preordained—all he had to do was be patient.

For the first two years after leaving office, Thomson started his memoirs and got on with writing *Smaranda*, in part, a book about Marthe. During a visit to Bucharest, he presented it to her as soon as he alighted from the train with a note inscribed on the inside cover describing it as 'a testament of his devotion.'

Since his rise, Marthe had become more accessible—hard for him to admit, but true. She had her own life, a husband, and position— maybe even a lover or two. He tried not to dwell on that unbearable thought, reminding himself she had little or no interest in sex. As an acclaimed writer, possessing the gift of words, she'd won the highest honors and praise for her literary works in Paris. He'd been nothing but a soldier and a mere student of history, art and languages. A brigadier general wouldn't be considered lofty enough in her social circles. For her to have become 'Mrs. Thomson' would have been too embarrassing to even contemplate.

Now everything had changed, as he'd hoped and prayed it would. He'd become someone—a close friend and confidante of the British Prime Minister, a man who'd be in that position again soon enough. She asked after MacDonald constantly, which he noted. He was aware she adored powerful men.

Maybe one day, I myself might aspire ...

He met Marthe in Paris two or three times a year at her apartment on the fashionable Rue du Faubourg Saint-Honoré. He also visited her in Romania, where he stayed with her at Mogosoëa for ten blissful days. Thomson took pleasure in the beautiful gardens of the Romanian Renaissance palace with its magnificent courtyards, chapel, Venetian palace, ponds and lily pads, all set on the rolling banks of Mogosoëa Lake. They took romantic walks, picnicking beside the whispering waters, a perfect place to relax and prepare before re-entering the rough and tumble of British politics.

While in Bucharest, Thomson met Marthe's husband Prince George again. The last time they'd met was when they worked together in the war, destroying Romania's oil wells. George came by with his mistress and in the most civilized manner, the four had dinner together in the grand dining room. Although Thomson found it strange and offensive to his sensibilities, he accepted the situation—*she* was sitting beside *him*. That was all that mattered.

Thomson thought it ironic that he and Marthe's husband shared the same interest in aviation, although George was a highly skilled pilot. Thomson had no intention of ever being at the controls of an aircraft. After dinner, George, a little drunk, drove off in his Mercedes with his mistress to the house they shared, while Thomson and Marthe retired to their adjoining rooms.

Thomson served on several committees at the Royal Aero Club in London for a couple of years and was later voted chairman. This gave him stature and contact with the most influential people in aviation, keeping him in the eye of the top brass in the RAF and the Air Ministry. They regarded him as the next Minister of State for Air, assuming Labour regained power, which most thought inevitable.

During these years, Thomson traveled the United States and Canada from coast to coast, giving speeches on aviation and trade between the continents. These speaking engagements supplemented his income from the House of Lords, helping to finance his trips to Paris and Bucharest.

Marthe met him at the luxurious Willard Hotel on Pennsylvania Avenue in Washington, D.C. in December of 1928 where, as chairman of the Royal Aero Club of the United Kingdom, he headed a British delegation at the International Aviation Conference.

The circumstances were, once again, bizarre. As chairman of the Romanian Aviation Society, Marthe's husband had also been invited and had brought his mistress along. They too, stayed at the Willard, but in a luxurious suite. Thankfully, Thomson's and Marthe's adjoining rooms were on a different floor.

For Marthe, this trip had a dual purpose: to spend time with Thomson and to promote her latest book—already well received in the United States, Canada and Great Britain.

25

MOVING SOUTH

April 1929.

W hen Scott mentioned Lou had been posted to Cardington, Captain Irwin volunteered to put him and his wife up until they'd settled in. Lou had met him many times over the past year during his visits to Cardington. Lou and Charlotte had visited Bedford the previous month for Charlotte to inspect a property Lou had been offered for rent which, although expensive, looked promising. The house was on a terrace of homes on Kelsey Street close to Bedford, near the parade of shops Lou knew well. Bay windows ran up the front on three levels from the half buried basement to the third story bedrooms.

Concrete steps led from the parking area up to the entrance door at mid-level. On that level, the living room was at front, dining room at rear, overlooking a long narrow garden. The room below ground level at the front was protected by a retaining wall with a large railed open area, allowing light in the bay windows. That room was ideal for a workshop and storage.

The large main bedroom, situated on the third floor at the rear, had space for a wardrobe, dressing table and a chest of drawers. Two smaller bedrooms overlooked the street. Charlotte chose one she'd decorate as baby's room. The kitchen, located on the bottom floor had French doors opening onto the rear garden.

Charlotte thought the house had potential for entertaining and gardening. The drawbacks were the beige flowery wallpaper and green linoleum. At least the building had electricity and an inside bathroom on the top floor, unlike other places they'd viewed with gas lighting and no inside lavatory. For hot water, there was a gas geezer over the kitchen sink and bathtub. Although the amenities were better, the place wasn't as nice as Candlestick, but nothing ever could be. They took the house.

On arrival at Bedford Station, Lou and Charlotte took a cab to the Irwins' on Putroe Lane, a spacious, pebble-dashed bungalow with a slate roof. Being there was awkward for Charlotte in her unhappy state of mind. Olivia Irwin, tall, attractive, with blond hair and hazel eyes, and a bewitching Scottish accent, sensed Charlotte's discomfort and went out of her way to be kind. Soon, they were sharing confidences. Charlotte told her how she longed for a child and how she was on the verge of giving up. Olivia too, wanted a baby, but she and her husband had decided to wait just a little longer. She urged Charlotte not to be bitter and not to give up. Charlotte was relieved she had someone she could talk to now Fanny wasn't around.

Lou took a bus to Cardington and met the captain while Charlotte and Olivia were getting acquainted. Irwin explained he'd been reviewing blueprints and preparing flight manuals for *Cardington R101*. A wood-framed office had been built in the shed, which he and First Officer, Lieutenant Commander Noël Atherstone shared. Another office had also been set up for officers at the base of the tower for use when ships were moored there.

The three men went into the shed, where *Cardington R101* appeared to be at about the same stage as *Howden R100*. Both ships had been completely framed, with interior accommodations and finishings well underway. They climbed aboard via a stepladder, moved through the control car and went upstairs to the chartroom overlooking the control car. The layout was different from the Howden ship and the control car smaller. From there, they showed him the officer's cabins, crew berths and mess, dining room, lounge and promenade decks. Lou was impressed, but he remembered Wallis's words about things 'looking good in the shed.'

During the afternoon, Charlotte and Olivia took a bus to the house on Kelsey Street and Charlotte showed Olivia around. Mrs. Jones, a kindly neighbor, knocked on the door offering them tea. Close to the main street, the house was handy for shops and buses. Charlotte told Olivia she'd written for a job at Bedford hospital and was awaiting a reply. She didn't expect to start work immediately, as Lou would be spending time at Howden when they installed gasbags in *Howden R100*. Charlotte planned to accompany him and spend time with her parents during that time.

The Royal Airship Works folks at Cardington greeted Lou cordially, making him welcome. He bumped into Walter Potter and Joe Binks, now both gainfully employed on construction of *Cardington*

R101, thanks to Lou. They'd heard Lou and Charlotte were moving down and offered their services. Lou told them he'd be glad of their help.

The Remingtons stayed two days at the Irwin bungalow, with Lou and the captain at Cardington most of that time. Olivia and Charlotte spent time in Bedford buying furniture. They had two pleasant evenings at Putroe Lane when the conversation focused on airships and Lou's career in the airship service. Charlotte put on a brave face.

On the third day, a Saturday, Lou and Charlotte went to No. 58 Kelsey Street to wait for John Bull's van. Potter arrived at 10 o'clock with three other young men, anxious to help. Charlotte answered the door, delighted to find Potter on the front step, his face cracking into one of his familiar half-smiles, although she sensed he still bore the effects of *R38*.

"Walter, lovely to see you! Come in, all of you," Charlotte said.

Potter took Charlotte's hand and kissed her cheek. They trooped into the empty living room. Lou hung back while Charlotte was introduced.

"I've been looking forward to seeing you, Charlotte. It's been eight years!" Potter said. He cast his eye around the room. "Hey, this is nice."

"It will be when it's painted," Charlotte said.

"This is Joe Binks' cousin, Freddie. Joe's not here yet—he's always late." Potter pointed out Freddie who stepped forward and shook Charlotte's hand. Freddie looked pretty scruffy. Her mind went back to the pathetic souls she used to see leaving Macy's factory. His jumper was full of holes, shoes worn out and falling apart. She noticed him limp as he walked in. He probably had short leg syndrome, caused in the womb or during birth. She couldn't get over how much he reminded her of Robert, the young man she'd met during the war. He was much younger of course, but the resemblance was striking.

Such a sweet boy. What a lovely face! I'll take him under my wing.

"And I brought Arthur Disley along, our electrician," Potter said.

"Call me 'Dizzy'," Disley said, with a droll grin. Charlotte shook his hand. His grip was firm.

A 'cool customer'—not at all 'dizzy'—the reliable type.

"This is Cameron—one of the coxswains. His wife, Rosie, works in the gasbag factory."

Cameron smiled pleasantly.

The picture of innocence. An open, trusting face—he seems like a happy man indeed!

"We mustn't forget old 'Bad-Luck' Sammy Church, over there," Potter said, pointing at a tall, twenty-four-year-old dressed in a gray sports jacket, white shirt and red tie. His shoes were well shined. He was shy and soft-spoken, with strong features. He had a head of thick brown hair with that just-combed look. He nodded and smiled, not quite looking Charlotte in the eye.

He's proud of that hair. Loves his Brylcreem!

"Why *Bad-Luck?*" she asked.

"Just don't play cards with him. As he scoops up yer money he always says, 'Oh, bad luck, mate.'" Charlotte laughed. "And he'll show you a few card tricks, too," Potter said.

Church pulled out a new deck and held it up. "Glad to know you missus," he said.

Lou stepped into the middle and was shaking hands all round as a rat-a-tat-tat came at the front door.

"Our stuff should be here any minute. My old boss is trucking it down," Lou told them while Charlotte opened the door to a breathless Joe Binks.

"Sorry I'm a bit, late, missus," Binks said.

"Come on Joe, where you bin—lyin' in bed?" Potter chided.

"No, no, something came up," Binks stammered.

Charlotte greeted Binks. He'd made a hurried effort to dress and his hair was a mess. He appeared jittery, his right eye twitching, which made her smile.

This one wouldn't make a good fibber.

Ten minutes later, the van drew up and John Bull climbed out of the driver's seat. Surprised to see him, Lou and Charlotte rushed out to greet him at the curb.

"John, what happened? We thought one of the mechanics was driving down."

"I couldn't resist. I had to make sure you're all right, didn't I?" John said.

"You shouldn't have done that," Charlotte said. "But I'm so pleased you did!" Her eyes filled with tears.

John winked and put his arms around her. "I've got big surprises for both of you. Follow me." John led everyone to the back of the van. "Close your eyes, Lou," he said. While Lou closed his eyes, John opened the van doors, revealing an object covered with a sheet. John climbed up and untied it.

"Okay Lou, open your eyes." As Lou did so, John removed the sheet with a flourish. There stood a gleaming black motorcycle with two enormous chrome-plated tail pipes.

"What the devil's this?" Lou asked.

"A 1000cc *Brough Superior.* It came into my shop yesterday. Fella wanted me to sell it for him. Had your name written all over it didn't it?"

"It's gorgeous! And yes, I want it. How much does he want?"

"Nothing. It's a present from me to you."

Lou was dumbfounded. John pulled a plank down from the van and the six men carefully rolled the bike down. Lou climbed on.

"It's you all right, sir," Binks said.

"It's smashin'!" Freddie exclaimed.

"This is the motorbike Lawrence rides," John told them.

"Who's Lawrence?" Freddie asked.

"Lawrence of Arabia. You know the fella who rode around on a camel during the war. Well, he's traded in his camel and rides one of these now."

"Looks bloomin' powerful," Charlotte said. "You be careful, Lou Remington!"

"John, I don't know what to say," Lou said.

"Don't say anything, just take care, like Charlotte says," John replied. "And I have a little housewarming present for our Charlotte."

Further back in the van a larger object stood covered with another sheet, which John removed, revealing a brand new piano.

Charlotte's eyes lit up. "Oh, John! I don't believe it!"

"I took the other one back to your parents. Now you've one of your own," John said.

The six men carefully eased the piano down into the road. Charlotte lifted the lid and with one finger tinkled "Blue Skies".

"Grey skies—let's hope they've all gone," John sang.

"Do you play, Charlotte?" Freddie asked.

"Does she play!" John said.

John climbed back into the van and held up the cat in her cage. Fluffy let out a loud meow. "And last but not least, here's our Miss Fluffy!"

They spent the next couple of hours bringing in boxes and furniture and setting it up under Charlotte's direction. Finally, they sat down in the living room for tea and sandwiches brought in by Mrs. Jones from next door. Afterwards, Charlotte tried out her new piano which, after her mother's, sounded sweet indeed.

The house was beginning to look more like a home, Charlotte pleased to have her things around her. As for the piano—it took her breath away. Before everyone from Cardington left, Charlotte asked them round for Sunday afternoon tea with their wives and girlfriends. John stayed for a couple more hours chatting. Charlotte hugged him tightly and thanked him before he headed back up north. She thought things mightn't be so bad—she'd met some nice folks and they were finally free of Jessup.

The following weekend, Potter brought an army of fifteen men to the house and they painted the interior white from top to bottom. Charlotte plied them with tea and sandwiches while they worked and Lou provided paint, paintbrushes and beer. By Sunday evening, the house gleamed and smelled of fresh paint. Charlotte was delighted.

A week later, her upbeat mood was soured again. Lou learned that Jessup, at his own request, had been posted to Cardington for training, along with two greasy cohorts. They'd rented a place in Bedford. Lou didn't expect trouble and wasn't unduly worried. Charlotte was skeptical; the beating might have made him worse. She knew the people of Ackworth would be pleased to see the back of him.

26

VICEROY TO INDIA

June 1929.

T he mood in Britain during the early months of 1929 was bleak. With the General Strike not long over, unemployment and living standards worsening and the government's popularity plummeting, a general election became inevitable.

Labour won the most seats, with 287 against the Conservatives' 260, but still lacked a majority to form a government. The leader of the Liberal Party, Lloyd-George, whose party had won 59 seats, threw his lot in with MacDonald and Labour took over on June 5th. Just prior to taking office, Thomson was summoned to Lossiemouth. During their last few days of solitude, he and MacDonald made plans and chose cabinet members and staff for the new government. Thomson would be back at the Air Ministry.

MacDonald and Thomson also had the sad task of finding a new pilot to fly them back and forth to Lossiemouth. Captain Hinchliffe had gone off in a bid to fly the Atlantic from east to west, in an attempt to seize the record, as many others had previously tried (and failed) to do. Neither he nor his copilot had been heard from since—at least not in the flesh.

Thomson felt a little guilty, but he really *had* done all he could after receiving an urgent call from Hinchliffe, pleading for help. He and his heiress copilot were being evicted from Cranwell Aerodrome, their base of operations, due to strings being pulled by powerful people. Thomson had called his friend, the previous Air Minister, Sir Samuel Hoare, for assistance.

In an effort to save his daughter's life, the copilot's father had already spoken with Sir Samuel and got the eviction notice served. Sir Samuel told Thomson there was no way he'd intervene. Sadly, their eviction deadline, instead of causing the pioneer aviators to give up on their plan, pushed them into flying off prematurely into a horrendous storm.

At the beginning of June, Thomson moved back into Gwydyr House and MacDonald moved his staff and his furnishings into No.10 Downing Street, this time with the intention of a longer stay. To Thomson's delight, McDonald also took up residence at Chequers at weekends, as before.

During a visit to No.10, Thomson received a surprise. Thinking he'd been called in to discuss policy, he stood at the window overlooking the colorful rear gardens, while MacDonald sat musing behind his desk. Unlike Thomson's last visit to this room, it was orderly, with pictures of MacDonald's family and Highland landscapes adorning the walls—no unpacked boxes lying around. Thomson's head was full of thoughts concerning the airship program, but while he spoke, MacDonald's mind appeared to be elsewhere.

"How I love this room, Ramsay—it's the heart and soul of the Empire, you know."

MacDonald remained silent. Thomson continued. "I'm planning a trip to Cardington next week. I can't wait to see what progress they've made. We have to get those intercontinental voyages organized. There'll be lots to do in those far off lands to prepare for our mighty ships. The schedules have slipped badly—I need to get things back on track."

MacDonald remained silent. Thomson turned back to the window and studied the lush green lawns. Several minutes later, MacDonald spoke.

"The post of Viceroy to India will be vacant soon. I need to make a nomination to the King to fill that position."

"Do you have anyone in mind?"

"Yes"

"Who?"

"You!"

Thomson hadn't seen this coming. His mind went into a turmoil.

"Ramsay, that's impossible! The airship program will be in full swing. And if I'm gone, who will watch your back? Those jackals on the left will run amuck!"

"True, CB, but I'll manage. And my dear fellow, what could be more fitting than for you to return to the land of your birth as viceroy? Why, you'd be King of India and Marthe, your queen!"

This came like a hammer-blow. Thomson suddenly had a throbbing headache and put his hand to his temple. A spontaneous vision exploded in his mind.

He stood on a balcony dressed in a magnificent black tuxedo, vivid blue sash across his chest, Marthe at his side in a flowing silver gown, a diamond tiara upon her head. They waved to adoring crowds below, flanked by elephants and a sea of Indian soldiers in dazzling red uniforms under a dusty, orange sun ...

"Ramsay, I beg you not to say such things. That couldn't happen, at least, not as long as her husband's alive—and no doubt he'll outlive me."

Ramsay is like a brother who wants the best for me.

MacDonald's knowing blue eyes twinkled.

"My dear CB, as viceroy, you'll lay the crown at her feet. Nothing will be refused you. Rome would almost certainly grant an annulment."

"I seriously doubt *that,* after all these years. She was fifteen when she was married off and they have a child! It's true they aren't married in the real sense of the word ..."

"Well, there you are then!"

"You fill my head with things I dare not even dream about."

This wasn't true, of course. It was *all* he dreamed about.

"Marthe is a strict Catholic. She has a priest who's been her spiritual advisor since she was a girl in Paris," Thomson said. "He knows about me—in fact, I've met him. He always advises her against divorce."

"Then you will need to be more forceful, won't you. It's usual for a viceroy to be married. There'll be ceremonial duties for his wife to perform. Look, you're getting on in years. You deserve some real happiness. You'll have much to offer. This could be the chance of a lifetime, CB. Think about that."

Charlotte surprised herself, settling in rapidly. They had lots of Cardington folks around on Saturday and Sunday afternoons for tea. After the third week, they had a housewarming party with many of the crewmen and some officers and their wives or girlfriends, including

Potter, Binks, Freddie, Church, Disley, Cameron and Leech. Capt.
Irwin and Olivia and First Officer Atherstone and his wife showed up
and stayed for a couple of hours.

At these little soirées, Charlotte usually gave Freddie something to
wear, which she'd bought in Bedford—a pair of second-hand shoes or
a sweater, or something Lou didn't wear anymore—a shirt or a pair of
trousers (after she'd made alterations). Freddie was grateful and came
to adore Charlotte. His face would light up whenever she entered the
room.

Charlotte had been to the music shop in Bedford and picked up a
few songs in sheet music and practiced them when Lou was at work as
a surprise for him. He loved to hear her play the classics, which she
did rarely. Everyone fell for Charlotte, especially men; besides being
beautiful, she was a good listener and easy to talk to. After coaxing,
Charlotte played the piano, sometimes with Potter on the accordion
and Lou on guitar. Everyone gathered round and sang the latest hits.
As usual at these gatherings, Disley sat in a corner quietly playing
chess with challengers. Church dazzled the crowd by rolling pennies
over his knuckles, performing card tricks and cutting and shuffling like
a pro. Toward the end of the evening, he invariably managed to talk a
few into a bait-and-switch bet or a game of brag, during which time he
was heard to mutter, 'Oh, bad luck, mate,' as he pulled his winnings
across the table.

Binks, as it turned out, was an accomplished artist. He usually
brought a sketch pad and sat making pencil sketches and portraits of
anyone who cared to sit for him. Lou was surprised by his quiet talent.
Many, including Lou and Charlotte, had them framed.

He did one of Lou and two of Charlotte: Lou the flying ace in his
navy cap and leather greatcoat, collar up, an airship in the sky behind
him; Charlotte, a short-haired, ravishing twenties flapper, in a tight-
fitting, black, knee-length dress, a silver beaded necklace down to the
waist. She stood beside a grand piano, long cigarette holder in one
hand, champagne glass in the other. In a close-up, Binks showed
Charlotte again with short hair under a sequined, beaded skull cap,
huge eyes wide, her sensuous, full-lipped mouth and gorgeous smile,
stunning—a movie star! That portrait caused quite a stir.

During the week, Lou had homework in the evenings. He reviewed
drawings and new operating manuals for *Cardington R101*.
Sometimes, he worked on a navigation course under the tutelage of
Squadron Leader Ernest Johnston, who also attended their parties with
his wife. Johnston, the most highly experienced navigator in the

country, had made many landmark flights around the world and would serve as navigator for both ships. Lou got a kick out of Johnston—he was a hell of a wag.

Now he was based at Cardington, it became necessary for Lou to travel to Howden once a month. He was still responsible for ensuring documentation and as-built drawings for the Howden ship were updated and filed correctly. Lou would also be required to assist Wallis and Norway with not only the installation of the gasbags, but also with the engine trials in the shed—a subject he never dared discuss with Charlotte.

During the first week at Cardington, Lou sat down with Colmore and Scott a couple of times and once with Richmond. Richmond appeared to be in a more anxious state than when he'd last seen him. Lou couldn't understand why Cardington was so worried about the schedule. Richmond had said 'time was on their side.'

It became apparent that there were two factors pressuring Cardington. The first was the Germans: the Graf Zeppelin had made a successful maiden voyage to Lakehurst from Friedrichshafen in October and a round-the-world trip was scheduled in August via Russia, Tokyo and San Francisco. The second was Thomson: he was back at the Air Ministry and had let his displeasure over the slow progress of the airship program be known. He'd soon be here to assess the situation for himself. Cardington was filled with dread. In him, they began to sense a hard taskmaster who'd be on the warpath. They couldn't say this with certainty, since he'd been ousted in October 1924 before they'd built anything, but here they were in 1929, still fiddling around in the shed—at least, that's how they thought he'd perceive things. On the bright side though, Howden was no further along—or so it seemed.

On the day before Thomson's planned visit, Lou realized there was a third factor upsetting Cardington, more troubling than the other two. He went to Richmond's office to discuss matters concerning Shed No. 2 where *Howden R100* would be housed after her arrival later in the year. When he walked in, Richmond and Rope were huddled over Richmond's drawing board deep in conversation. Lou raised his hand and backed away, as if to leave.

Richmond looked up. "No, come in Lieutenant Remington. You're just as much a part of this team as anyone. We keep nothing from you."

This surprised Lou. "Okay, sir," he said and joined them.

"We're discussing her weight. We've done separate final calculations. After 20 tons for crew, ballast and stores, we only have 13 tons left for lift, d'you agree, Rope?"

"Yes, my figures agree," Rope said.

"Bugger! We should have built her another bay longer. We had plenty of room in the shed," Richmond exclaimed. He walked to the window scratching his head. "We've known for a long time she was coming out heavy."

I figured that's why you've become so stressed.

"Any suggestions, Remington?" Richmond asked.

"Lighten her, sir, and increase her lift," Lou replied.

"Quite. Quite." Richmond stuck his hands in his pockets, trying to look nonchalant. "Let's deal with the Air Minister's visit first. I won't dwell on the weight issue. I'll have to *touch* on the subject, of course. When he's gone, we'll give the subject our full attention. In the meantime, we'll keep it right here," Richmond said, looking from Lou to Rope.

"Absolutely, sir," Lou said, realizing why he'd been invited in.

"I'm sure these problems can be overcome," Rope said.

Lou glanced at Rope.

He looks confident enough.

27

THE FISHING PARTY

June 19, 1929.

The bedroom was dark, Charlotte sound asleep. Lou slid out of bed noiselessly and, taking his clothes with him, went down to the kitchen. He dressed while his coffee was brewing. After munching on a couple of slices of toast, Lou returned to the bedroom and opened the wardrobe door. His fishing rod was in the back corner for some silly reason. Wishing he'd retrieved it the night before, he leaned in and pulled it out. In the half-light, Charlotte raised her head from the pillow.

"Lou?"

"It's all right, love."

"What are you doing?"

"I'm meeting some of the guys. I promised I'd go fishing with them before going up to the shed," he whispered.

'What time will you be back?"

"About five."

"Five!"

"The Old Man's coming up from London. Everything's got to be perfect."

"Damn it, Lou, it's Saturday! I wanted us to spend the day together."

"We'll be together tomorrow, Charlie. I'm sorry; I can't help it."

Charlotte rolled onto her back, her hair spread across the pillow like a mane.

"Come back to bed for half an hour. I need you, love."

"I can't. The guys are waiting for me, honey."

"I suppose tomorrow you'll be studying, or fiddling with your damned motorbike."

"I mentioned in the week he was coming. You forgot."

Lou leaned over her to kiss her, but she rolled back on her side with a sigh, her hair cascading across her face. Lou went downstairs, put on his short black coat and went down to the motorbike. He strapped on his fishing rod, kick-started it and drove off sleepily toward the parade of shops where the 'boys' were waiting outside the corner store.

At St. Pancras Railway Station in London, Thomson marched down the platform, a walking stick hooked over his arm. This added accoutrement lent a certain gravitas. He was flanked by the two men closest to him at the Ministry. All three wore raincoats and hats. The air was chilly, but the morning sunshine streamed through the roof skylights, brightly lighting the station. The first man, Sefton Brancker, a staunch friend, had done much to help Thomson and further his career. It was *he* who, in those lean years of '21 and '22, had introduced him to people connected with aviation and was influential in him getting a seat on the Airships Advisory Panel. And during his time out of office, it'd been *Brancker* who'd arranged for Thomson to go on lecture tours throughout Canada and the United States, boosting Thomson's income. Thomson had been immensely grateful. He owed much to Brancker.

Brancker's looks were sometimes deceiving. In his early fifties and of average height, he appeared unkempt and ill-bred in rough tweed jackets—almost like a farm laborer. Though he seemed slack-jawed, his voice was rich and deep and he spoke the most beautiful King's English, as only the most well-bred could. To cover his baldness, he wore a toupée. He loved the ladies and they loved *him*—and his rakish mustache. They adored his vibrant personality and infectious enthusiasm, and the pains he took with them. He had an aura of self assurance and power. For Brancker's friends, nothing was ever too much trouble, especially if it enhanced the cause of aviation—his other great passion. Thomson liked having him around because he was such a positive force. At Gwydyr House, Brancker occupied the large office above his own.

Thomson's second companion was his personal secretary, Rupert Knoxwood, a tall, wiry fellow who had difficulty pronouncing his 'Rs', making him sound foppish when saying words like 'fwankly' or 'fwightfully', which he insisted on using. To Thomson, he was the consummate bureaucrat who understood him perfectly, anticipating his every need. As the three men strode down the station, Thomson spotted a uniformed railwayman heading in their direction. Thomson gazed at him, smiling like an old friend.

A potential voter!

The man, compelled to acknowledge Thomson, touched his cap. "Mornin', sir," he said.

"And a *very* good morning to *you*, my dear sir!" Thomson gushed.

"What carriage are you in, sir? Perhaps I can be of assistance." Knoxwood pulled out their tickets. "That's first class. Right this way, gentlemen," the railwayman said, leading them along the platform.

He stopped abruptly and opened their carriage door. They piled in while Knoxwood dropped a coin into the man's hand. They stashed their briefcases and raincoats in the overhead racks and got comfortable. Thomson gleefully rubbed his hands together like a schoolboy off to the seaside. A few minutes later, the doors slammed down the platform and the guard's whistle blew. The train jolted forward.

"Well, here we are again, Sefton. Back where it counts!"

"I can't tell you how pleased I am, CB," Brancker said.

"We'll need to visit Egypt. We must make sure everything's on schedule with the mooring mast and shed. Pity we lost our man, Hinchliffe. He'd have been ideal to fly us out there."

Brancker shook his head sadly. "Such a loss!"

"Perhaps you'll come back with another magic carpet," Knoxwood said, brightly. He knew one of Thomson's most prized possessions was a Persian rug presented to him in Iraq.

"Our magic carpet, Knoxwood, will be *Cardington R101* which will transport us first to Egypt and then on to India."

"Well put, CB," Brancker said.

"Perhaps the ship should be named *The Magic Carpet*," Knoxwood said, laughing.

"No, no. No fancy names," Thomson declared. He leaned his head on the headrest and relaxed. The train glided unhurriedly through grimy rows of terraced houses, wheels clacking rhythmically over the tracks. Thomson loved that sound. Train rides always put him in a good mood.

"Now, gentlemen, let's see what's what, shall we?" he said, delving into his red ministerial box. After reading his memoranda a few moments, he looked up suddenly, shooting a glance at Brancker, who was busy studying the form of a young woman pegging out the washing in her back yard.

"What happened to those trial flights to Egypt? We were going to use R33 and R36 for that purpose. What happened?"

Brancker turned back to Thomson. "Er, er, the trials got scrapped —budget cuts. Well er, ...not budget cuts exactly ...R36 and R33 needed a lot of money spending on them—especially after R33 got wrecked."

"Got wrecked! How?"

"Collided with her shed ..."

"Collided with her shed! Who was in command?"

"Scott, of course."

Thomson looked away in exasperation.

"Whatever is the matter with that man?"

Brancker raised his eyebrows but made no comment.

"Well, they should have rebuilt those ships," Thomson said.

"The funding just wasn't there CB," Brancker said.

"Budget cuts? Damn the Tories! Wish I'd been around. What else did they cut?"

"Nothing I can think of, but the emphasis is on heavier-than-air aircraft nowadays. Many in government don't like airships," Brancker replied.

"We'll see about *that!* I hope we don't live to regret cutting those test flights with the older ships. We could've learned a thing or two from a few trial runs to the Middle East. My main concern is the schedule. The Germans are getting way out in front. Our ships should've been in the air by now."

"Quite so, Minister," Knoxwood agreed.

The train rushed into a tunnel and they sat in the dark.'

Thomson continued. "So let's recap. Both ships are running three years late. We've taken twice as long to reach this stage. But on the brighter side, we've only spent half as much again. So, I suppose we can say we've given employment to more people, for a longer period of time. Fair assessment, Sefton?"

"I suppose you could put it like that, CB, yes."

Even in the dark, Thomson sensed Brancker was amused by his nutty logic. The train rushed out of the tunnel into sunshine, revealing lush green fields and blue skies. A happy omen.

"India by Christmas then!" Thomson exclaimed. Brancker and Knoxwood exchanged knowing glances.

28

THE BRIEFING

June 19, 1929.

O n the edge of Bedford, crewmen had gathered at Rowe's Tobacconists, the 'corner store,' adjacent to Munn's Dairy. Lou drew up at the curb and parked his motorbike alongside others. Potter was waiting with Disley, Church, Binks and Freddie. Cameron hadn't arrived. Lou noticed Capt. Irwin's Austin Seven approaching. The car stopped some distance away and Irwin climbed out. He cut a striking figure in his dark blue officer's uniform. This man had the keys to the city, admired and loved by all, especially his crewmen. Then Cameron appeared, his face tired and drawn.

"You all right, Doug?" Lou asked.

"No, but I don't wanna talk about it if you don't mind, sir."

Binks glanced across at Lou, shaking his head. He then turned to his cousin.

"Freddie, guess what? You know the lieutenant got me a job on the construction? Well, now I just got promoted," Binks said.

"To what?" Freddie asked.

"Engineer. I'll be in one of them engine cars."

"You liar!" Freddie exclaimed.

"God's honest truth. I'm set for life. Ain't that right, sir?"

Lou smiled. This week, he'd interviewed and recommended a few men from the construction team for jobs in the crew. Church, who'd finished a spell cutting and shuffling his cards and springing them from one hand to the other, was now busy combing his hair. "Yeah, and I'm gonna be a rigger. How about that!" he said.

Freddie gritted his teeth. "You lucky sods!"

Lou felt sorry for him.

"That's not all. Old Bad-Luck Sammy over there's doin' all right—ain'tcha, Sammy. Show 'em the picture of your new girl," Binks said.

Church stuck the comb between his teeth, pulled out his wallet and produced a photograph. He handed it to Freddie who scrutinized the well-endowed blond in a tight-fitting jumper with a pretty face. Everyone gathered round.

"What's her name then?" someone demanded.

"Irene," Church said proudly, stuffing the comb in his top pocket.

"Oooo, nice tits!" Freddie shrieked, holding the photo up close.

"Give it 'ere, you little sod!" Church yelled, grabbing Freddie's collar.

Freddie handed back the photograph. "Sorry, Sammy. No offense. I didn't realize it was serious." He peered up at Lou, meekly. "Lou, er sir, do you fink you could get me a job … please?"

"Give it a year or two, Freddie," Lou answered.

"Oh, come on, sir. He's me cousin, twice removed, and he's ever so old for 'is age," Binks pleaded.

Lou glanced away toward Irwin, closing on them. The group parted, respectfully for the captain.

"Good morning, men," Irwin said in his soft Irish brogue giving them all a smile.

"Mornin', sir," they said together.

Irwin proceeded to the shop doorway and went in, the bell inside jangling.

"Who was that?" Freddie asked innocently.

Leech, the foreman engineer, now joined them. "That, my son, is the captain of *Cardington R101*," he said.

It was Leech who'd given Lou a lift up to the main house from the guard gate on his first day. Lou was pleased to see him here with the younger crowd. He wouldn't miss a fishing party at the river, Leech had told them. Lou followed Irwin into the shop. The bell inside tinkled again as he stepped onto the well-worn floor boards. The sweet smell of confectionery, tobacco, and newsprint, reminded him of his days here with his *R38* crewmen. Irwin was at the counter.

"Ten Players, if you'd be kind enough, Mr. Rowe," Irwin said.

The shopkeeper reached for the cigarettes from the shelf behind him. "That'll be one and tuppence, sir."

"Oh, and a box of Swan and the *Daily Mirror*."

"Certainly, Captain." The shopkeeper reverently laid the cigarettes and the red-tipped matches on the counter. "They say it's gonna be a warm one today, sir," he said.

"Yes, indeed. Thank you," Irwin said.

Irwin gathered up his change and took a newspaper, glancing at Lou as some of the group came in. Lou realized the captain wanted to speak to him. He picked up the *Daily Mail* and a pack of Juicy Fruit, paid, and went into the street. Irwin walked to his car and climbed in, pausing to light a cigarette. Lou popped the Juicy Fruit in his mouth, watching Irwin's car move closer. Lou got to the curb as Irwin rolled down his window.

"You're going in later, right Lou?"

"Yes, sir. We're gonna fish for a couple of hours first."

"The Air Minister is scheduled to visit the shed at 2 o'clock."

"That'll give us plenty of time. We'll finish this morning and make sure everything's perfect."

"Wing Commander Colmore's anxious the Minister leaves with a good impression."

"You bet, sir."

They were disturbed by a noisy group across the street, yelling and attracting attention. Lou turned and saw Jessup and his cronies—three originals and two new faces. They hadn't spotted Lou, leaning down talking to Capt. Irwin.

"They're Howden crewmen. I see you've pitched in with the Cardington lads," Irwin said.

"Oh, no sir. They were all invited, but the Howden lot don't wanna mix."

"I've noticed that. I hope we're not going to have trouble with all these different groups—different ships—different construction crews."

"They *are* rivals, sir," said Lou.

"Yes, I suppose they are. Dumb really, isn't it!"

Jessup's crowd continued making a fuss—looking over and laughing. Jessup limped off, smirking while his gang laughed and whooped. They jeered at Cameron, who was on the verge of tears.

"Give it to 'er, Jessie," one of the gang shouted.

Jessup gave Cameron one of his two-finger whistles and pumped his fist in a crude gesture.

That son of a bitch is up to his tricks again, dammit!

"When they're not busy, they get into mischief, sir," Lou said.

"I don't like the looks of that one—could be a troublemaker. You know him?"

"I've had a few dealings with him."

"I'd better get moving, Lieutenant."

"Okay, Captain."

"It's good you're taking an interest in these men. They'll think the world of you for it."

"Thank you."

"Make sure you're in uniform this afternoon."

"Yes sir."

Irwin drove off. Lou went back to his group and they ambled to the river carrying rods and tackle. They spent two hours fishing. Freddie caught a couple of trout and Leech hooked a pike. After that, Lou left the river, arranging to meet Potter, Binks, Disley and Church at Shed No.1. Cameron didn't look up to it.

Thomson was still in high spirits when his train rolled into Bedford Station. The chauffeur-driven Airship Works Humber was waiting. He had fond memories of Cardington House and couldn't wait to see the place again. The driver touched his cap and opened the doors for the three men. Thomson settled down with a sigh of contentment beside Brancker.

"Ah yes, it's nice to be back in this city," Thomson said. "What's that wonderful smell in the air, Sefton, hm?"

"I don't smell anything, CB."

"I smell optimism, my dear fellow. That's what I smell— *optimism!*"

"Ah yes," Brancker said, smiling.

"Have the press been informed of my visit, Knoxwood?" Thomson asked.

"Absolutely, sir. I'm sure they're eagerly awaiting your awival."

"I'm getting hungry and we've been promised a bang-up lunch by all accounts," Thomson said.

The driver pulled out onto the high street. Twenty minutes later, they reached the Cardington gate, stopping at the guard house.

"Lord Thomson, we've been expecting you, sir," the gatekeeper gushed, grabbing the phone. The car glided smoothly up the winding driveway. Thomson savored every moment—like the returning warrior. They drew up outside the great house where Thomson leapt out and stood for a few moments surveying the building in its lush surroundings.

Ah yes, it's as beautiful as ever.

On seeing his team gathered with a dozen press people at the top of the steps, he handed his walking stick to Knoxwood. He bounded up two at a time like a man half his age, the photographers, catching the moment. What would they think of him? It'd been five years since they'd seen him. He looked fit and had put on weight, banishing the under-nourished look. He wondered how they'd fared under the strain. He made straight for Colmore, at center.

"My dear Colmore!" he said, taking his hand.

"We're so pleased to have you back, sir," Colmore lied.

"A few more grey hairs, I see. I'm sure you've earned them," Thomson said.

"Oh, yes, sir, we've had a few mountains to climb."

He turned to Cardington's head of design. "I hear you've been achieving great things, Richmond."

"We've been doing our best, sir," Richmond replied.

"Well, don't look so glum, man! The best is yet to come. All your hard work's about to pay off!"

Not so cock-sure by the looks of him. Must have all been tougher than he thought.

He held his hand out to Scott who appeared a little the worse for wear.

Looks like the drink's catching up with him!

"Scottie, my dear fellow! You're looking well. Wonderful to see you. You all know the Director of Civil Aviation, Sir Sefton Brancker, and my private secretary, Rupert Knoxwood." Everyone shook hands and made pleasantries and Colmore led the way into the grand, marble entrance hall. Thomson retrieved his walking stick from Knoxwood.

Their voices and footsteps echoed as though they were in a museum. Thomson paused, remembering that glorious day when he stood here between these great columns at the foot of the sweeping, stone stairs and announced his plans to the nation.

What a day that was! Well, there'll be plenty more days like that.

Thomson stopped and leaned on his walking stick peering at the ensign hanging forty feet up from the ornate, coffered ceiling, among gold leaf scrollwork and classical paintings of British battles on land and sea—a blaze of red, white and blue, cannons and muskets, blood, mud, fire and raging seas. Scott stepped forward and pointed to the ensign.

"We plan to fly that from the stern on her maiden voyage, Lord Thomson."

Sounds tipsy ...yes, I can smell it.

"What a splendid idea. It'll look superb fluttering in the wind from the world's mightiest airship. Bravo, Scott! I'm planning to be on that voyage, in case you've forgotten."

"None of us have forgotten your pledge," Colmore said.

"I'm looking forward to that," Thomson said. "You're coming, too, eh Sefton?"

"Oh yes, rather, CB. Wouldn't miss *that* show for the world!"

The group filed into the reception room for Earl Grey tea served in bone china cups with digestive biscuits and snacks, while the chief steward hovered. The engineering and design staff of the Royal Airship Works trooped in to shake hands with Thomson, who treated them like old friends. He remembered their faces and names from his visit in 1924 and the roles they played. This impressed them greatly. Naturally, he'd consulted a staff list he kept at the flat the night before.

After tea, and the opportunity to get re-acquainted, the group of forty-two moved to the conference room. The table seated thirty and the rest sat around the perimeter walls. Brancker and Knoxwood sat next to Thomson at the table. Anticipation was high: shades drawn, projector on, nerves on edge. Thomson had this effect on people, individually or en mass. It was time to crack the whip. They'd all had it too easy for too long—they'd fallen asleep at the switch. No excuse for that.

Richmond stood stiffly at the front, waiting for the room to settle down. People lit cigarettes and pipes. Soon the air was laden with smoke drifting across the projector's beam. For some, it became hard to breath.

"All right, Colonel Richmond, proceed. Perhaps you won't mind if occasionally I butt in with a question or two," Thomson said.

The lights were dimmed and a picture of *Cardington R101* appeared on a screen behind Richmond, who cleared his throat nervously.

"This is a side-view. Strength of the hull has been our first concern."

"Excellent!" Thomson said.

Richmond traced the outline of the ship with his pointer.

"*Cardington R101* is 734 feet long, 134 feet in diameter. You'll notice she's fatter than previous airships. This makes her more resilient and with a stainless steel skeleton, she'll be the strongest airship ever built."

"Good. Now tell me about progress."

The picture on the screen changed to one showing the gas bag harnesses hanging from the ship's interior.

"There have been some delays, but the features of this airship are, if I may say so, unique and innovative. We have designed a revolutionary new gasbag harnessing system—"

"What have you done to cut down the risk of fire?"

"We cannot eliminate the risk completely. Even static electricity can be deadly and is an *ever-present* threat—that's why it's necessary for groundcrewmen to *always* use rubber mats when picking up lines dropped from the ship. Static electricity can be deadly; it's a danger to the men and could cause fire. It's another reason we're using diesel engines in accordance with the original specification requirements, though they've turned out to be less powerful and heavier than expected."

"Is that so?" Thomson's tone was level.

I smell trouble. This man isn't telling me the full story.

"Of course, I expect you've already been informed Howden is using lighter petrol engines from Rolls-Royce which, by the way, I hear are second-hand."

"Second-hand petrol engines? No, I *didn't* know that," Thomson said flatly.

Thomson sensed Richmond's discomfort over the weight of the engines. Now he seemed to be alluding to the diesel versus petrol issue as a distraction. Thomson wondered if Wallis had got one over on the Air Ministry.

Damn Wallis! But at least he had sense enough to do some arithmetic first.

Thomson made an effort to hide his irritation, but his eyes narrowed. This was a dilemma. Richmond was a military man who'd followed the edict Thomson had laid down himself. He'd need to give the matter more thought later. Richmond continued, mentioning that the gasbags were manufactured by the workers of Cardington and ready to install—unlike Howden, who'd imported theirs from Germany. He talked about the new and complex design of the gas valves and servo assistance mechanism necessary for a craft of such immense proportions. Lastly, he explained the revolutionary approach to the process of doping the ship's outer cover, which he himself, had developed.

When the briefing was over, everyone was ushered into the dining room. Roast leg of lamb smothered in mint sauce, baked potatoes, and garden peas were served by immaculate stewards in white jackets and gloves under the watchful eye of the fussy chief steward. A Beaujolais was offered and Thomson and Colmore had a glass each; Scott drank more. Treacle tart followed the main course and then coffee, cheese, and biscuits. By the end of the meal, Thomson had mellowed somewhat. He turned to Colmore.

"How's the American doing? I expected him to be here."

"He's down in the shed supervising the finishing touches to the mock-ups for your inspection. He thought that was more important than lunch, sir."

"He's a conscientious chap."

"He's been a great asset and a fine liaison officer between the teams."

"So I've been given to understand," Thomson said, noting the chief steward perk up at the mention of *'the American.'*

"It's just before two. Perhaps we should make a move, sir," Colmore said.

"Yes, I can't wait!" Thomson said, jumping to his feet.

29

'SHOW ME YOUR SHIP, MY CAPTAIN.'

June 19, 1929.

The lunch party made its way to one of the huge green buildings in convoy, led by Thomson's Humber. He was always amazed by the size of this structure and how ridiculously tiny the staff entrance doors looked. He stepped inside, where silence was absolute. The reverent atmosphere surrounding the enormous space reminded him of a cathedral or even his favorite building—Westminster Hall.

Lou had been on board the airship with Potter, Binks, Disley and Church since 9:30 a.m. Using a layout issued by the drawing office, they'd placed furniture in the lounge, dining room, and smoking room, with setups of couches and easy chairs positioned around coffee tables and card tables. Deck chairs were arranged on the promenade decks with side tables. In the dining room, tables were laid with white linen, dinnerware and cutlery, shined to perfection. Two typical cabins were set up with bunks, chairs, linens and blankets. Once they'd finished, Lou sent the others home.

During the morning, while they worked, he'd asked them about Cameron. "What's up with Doug?"

"He's having trouble with Rosie," Potter said.

"What sort of trouble?" Lou asked.

"She's messing around with one of them Yorkshire blokes," Church answered.

"And he found out?"

"He did."

"Which one?"

"The ugly bastard with the pockmarks and eyes like lollypops," Binks replied.

Lou grimaced. This explained what he'd witnessed earlier.

"It's a bloody shame. They were really 'appy. Next we know she's gone overboard for that crazy lunatic," Potter said.

After they left, Lou made final adjustments to some of the lamps and cushions in the lounge. He thought about the change in Cameron. He and Rosie had been laughing and joking at the house-warming party. He'd need to keep an eye on that situation.

Damn Jessup!

Lou took a last look around the airship. Satisfied, he wearily sat down for a few moments in one of the comfortable easy chairs. He dozed off.

Thomson walked from the shed door toward the ship, mesmerized.

By Jove, what a sight!

Beaming with pleasure, he stared up at the massive skeleton. The structure was completely visible from bow to stern, her gas bags and cover, not yet installed. The stainless steel girders gleamed, giving the ship an aura of indestructibility.

We'll have no more structural problems like R38!

Thomson's gaze swept across the faces gathered around him.

"Where's our captain?"

Irwin, standing modestly four rows back in the crowd, raised his hand.

"Ah, there you are, my dear Captain Irwin. Show me over your ship, if you don't mind,"

Irwin edged forward in his unassuming way. "Not at all, sir. Please follow me."

Irwin led Thomson to a stepladder and they disappeared inside the control car. People in the entourage shuffled their feet and gave sideways glances, some slighted. Scott stood next to Richmond rattling loose change in his pocket, while Brancker stood beside Colmore and Knoxwood making polite conversation. Colmore showed no emotion —affable as always.

Lou came to, awakened by voices in the shed. He glanced at his watch and went to the promenade deck and peered down at the group gathered below. He'd planned to make his way down before Thomson arrived. Time had slipped away. He moved to the chartroom where he heard the voices of Irwin and Thomson. He stood and listened, unable to help himself.

This was the first time Thomson had been on an airship. He stared at one of the shiny ship's wheels in the control car. "For steering?"

Irwin pointed to the other wheel. "This one is, yes, sir. It controls the rudders. That one controls the elevators—the altitude." Irwin pointed to three valves attached from pipes from above. "And here, beside the height coxswain, are the valves for releasing water ballast."

"And these?" Thomson gestured to the telegraph equipment.

"These are telegraphs for sending instructions to the engine cars."

Thomson feasted his eyes on the hardwood wainscot, the floor and coxswain's consuls.

"It's like a ship, Captain, but the instrumentation reminds me of a submarine."

"It does, indeed, sir."

Thomson ran his fingers along the shiny hardwood windowsill.

"The workmanship is superb," he said, thoughts about weight and engines banished from his mind. Thomson looked out the windows wrapped around the control car.

"You'll have a pretty good view from here."

"Yes, sir. All five engine cars are visible and we'll be able to see where we're going."

"Always good to know!"

"Yes, sir."

"I look forward to standing here beside you, Captain, sailing the lofty skies."

"'Tis a nice thought, to be sure."

"I'm expecting great things from you, Irwin," Thomson said. "I know you're a man I can count on."

"I'll do my best, sir."

"Let's go up, shall we? Lead the way."

Irwin started up the mahogany steps. The spacious area above the control car doubled as control room and chartroom and was situated within the ship's envelope. A railing allowed officers and navigators to look down into the control car below. A high hardwood table had been built along the back wall for studying maps and charts with plenty of pigeonholes for storage. Irwin described the room's function.

"This is where the navigator will chart the ship's course and the officers will work on calculations and suchlike. You'll see it's convenient for keeping the officer on watch informed of their position and for him to call down new bearings."

"Very impressive, Captain. I can't wait to see the dining room and lounge."

"And don't forget the smoking room, sir," Irwin said with a smile.

Lou, having heard a good deal of their conversation, decided to stay put until he could slip out undetected. He stayed out of sight, but he caught a glimpse of Thomson, remembering the last time he'd seen him. He saw a big change. Thomson certainly looked healthier, and sounded self assured.

These last five years must have been good to him.

Irwin led Thomson to the lounge, which measured sixty feet by forty. Linoleum flooring, replicating hardwood, gleamed in the subdued lighting of table lamps and wall sconces, powered up by Disley and Lou earlier. Thomson admired the room and furniture.

"This is stunning! And tastefully done. Look at the size of it!"

He rushed to the middle of the floor and spun around, marveling at the fluted columns at the perimeter with their gold-leaf ornamental heads. "I'm delighted. It's better than I could have ever imagined. Why, they'll be able to dance all the way to India in this fabulous room!"

"I do believe you could be right, sir."

Thomson spotted the promenade deck and raced off to the polished wood guardrail in front of the huge plate glass windows and stared out into the shadows of the shed, oblivious to his entourage below. Irwin followed him.

"Oh, this is exceptional, Irwin. Can you imagine the view of the Mediterranean coast? The French Riviera! The Italian Riviera! My goodness, what a sight that'll be."

"Yes, it'll be grand, sir."

Thomson was deeply preoccupied with his vision of the future.

One day, I shall travel with Marthe in this beautiful airship. We'll arrive as husband and wife!

He turned and saw the captain patiently waiting.

"Do forgive me, Irwin. I was lost in thought. I look forward to returning in this airship to the land of my birth."

"India?"

"Yes, India. And confidentially, Irwin I hope to be taking a very special lady with me as my wife, one day."

"That'll be very nice, sir."

"It's fate, Irwin. Do you believe in fate?"

"I suppose I do."

"Yes, our fate is written."

"I'm sure you're right about that, sir."

Thomson grabbed Irwin's hand and clasped it, warmly in two hands.

"This ship will be the making of us, my dear Captain. *All* of us!"

30

THE OLD GASBAG

June 19, 1929.

After reviewing the dining room, cabins and smoking room—which everyone had made so much fuss about—Thomson posed for a few photographs before making for the gasbag factory. The fabric shop, another cavernous, corrugated iron building, stood among a group of utility buildings near the two main sheds. Within, eighty-seven excited women patiently waited, singing to relieve their boredom. On his arrival, Thomson was greeted by the sound of their voices drifting through the windows. He paused to listen. He'd heard the song a thousand times before.

> *Good-bye, Dolly, I must leave you, though it breaks my heart to go,*
> *Something tells me I am needed at the Front to fight the foe,*
> *See the boys in blue are marching and I can no longer stay,*
> *Hark I heard the bugle calling, good-bye, Dolly Gray.*

The haunting melody reminded him of France. Suddenly, he was back in Ypres listening to the soldiers. He heard the boom of guns, the whine of shells, explosions thundering in the distance. He became morbid—so much death. He shook it off and turned to Colmore and Brancker.

"Let's go in."

As they entered, the anticipation was palpable. The sun on the metal building made the interior oppressive, despite the open windows. A few electric fans placed in strategic locations did little to dispel the smell of rotting animals' intestines, dampness, body odor and glue. The women went silent, as if on cue from an invisible conductor, as Thomson's towering frame appeared in the doorway.

Members of his entourage silently eased their way in behind him, as though late for church. Lou, now in uniform, stood next to Scott. Photographers clutched their cameras, ready for a spread in tomorrow's papers. Seeing their eagerness, Thomson's face lit up, captivating the women. He stepped forward into the open space and took off his hat to survey the scene. Down one side, dozens sat on stools in rows, six deep, at tiny scraping boards working on wet, slimy substances with wooden-handled scrapers. Although dressed in protective smocks and unglamorous hats, he noticed they were wearing makeup.

Must be for me—how nice—I'm very flattered.

He unconsciously began to fan himself with his hat before he caught himself and stopped. On the floor, huge sheets of fabric were laid out with women on their knees joining the pieces together. It reminded him of parachutes being spread out for assembly, or the cutting and sewing of great yacht sails. Thomson raised his arms in a grand gesture and gave them one of his paralyzing smiles.

"Ladies! I beg you, please don't stop. I should enjoy to hear you sing. I love that you are so happy in your work, which I know is arduous—but so vital to this great undertaking."

A stocky, sergeant-major-like woman stepped forward and stood beside him. Thomson observed her closely. Even to him, she was intimidating. She wore a starched, sharply pressed, blue boiler suit, bright red headscarf tied in knots over her tightly cropped hair and shiny black boots. She placed her hands on her hips, ready for business.

"You 'eard the Lord, girls!" she bawled and then, pointing to one young woman in the middle, yelled, "Okay, sing, Millicent!"

Clearly struggling with her nerves, the one called Millicent took a few moments, but soon the great space was filled with the most beautiful operatic sound, continuing the song Thomson had heard outside. It took his breath away.

I have come to say good-bye, Dolly Gray,

It's no use to ask me why, Dolly Gray,

There's a murmur in the air, you can hear it everywhere,

It's time to do and dare, Dolly Gray.

So if you hear the sound of feet, Dolly Gray,

Sounding through the village street, Dolly Gray,

It's the tramp of soldiers true, in their uniforms so blue,

I must say good-bye to you, Dolly Gray.

At this point, all the women joined the chorus, producing a harmony enough to warm any choirmaster's heart; they sounded like a choir of heavenly angels.

Goodbye, Dolly, I must leave you though it breaks my heart to go,

Something tells me I am needed at the Front to fight the foe,

See the boys in blue are marching and I can no longer stay,

Hark I heard the bugle calling, goodbye, Dolly Gray.

It was Thomson's turn to be smitten. He almost choked up, not believing such a wonderful sound could come from this ragged-looking bunch of women. He stepped forward with his hand out to the forewoman.

"Welcome to the fabric shop, your Lordship," she bellowed.

"You're in charge?"

"I am indeed."

"And what's your name, if I may ask?"

My goodness, what a scary woman—must be a communist!

"Yes, you may. It's 'ilda, sir."

"'Ilda?" Thomson repeated.

The embarrassed women tried to hold back their laughter. He'd pronounced her name in Cockney. The forewoman corrected him.

"No, sir. 'Haych' as in H–ilda," she said, emphasizing the H with much heavy breathing.

"All right you lot, that's enough," she hollered.

"Oh, *Hilda*, of course! Do forgive me."

"Quite all right, me lord."

"Would you be kind enough to show me around and educate me on what these fine ladies are doing?"

"It would be my pleasure, sir. In this 'ere place, we make gasbags and canvas covers for the airships. First of all, what we call the 'goldbeater's skins' are shipped from Argentina and Chicago—that's in

America." Hilda led Thomson along the rows of women perched on stools, pointing at the skins on their scraping boards.

"What are they made of, these goldbeater's skins?"

"Cattles' bellies, sir."

Thomson already knew some of this, but wanted to give the woman her head. He wrinkled his nose, as though all this was completely new to him. "Cattle's bellies. Fascinating!"

Hilda picked up a sloppy, dripping skin and held it up, a respectable distance from Thomson, careful not to splash his face or his pinstriped suit.

"Then we take 'em and we stick 'em together on that there table over there. Then we glue 'em on them linen sheets on them slantin' boards what you see and then make 'em into big sheets on the floor," Hilda said, pointing at the women on their knees.

"Well, bless my soul. How many skins will you need for this airship, Hilda?"

"More than a million, actually."

"More than a million! Good Lord! You don't say."

Hilda flopped the skin down onto one of the women's boards, wiped her hands on a cloth, and threw it down. Thomson marched across to a petite, middle-aged woman perched on her stool. She had an impish face and big brown eyes.

"Now, please introduce me to this lovely lady."

"This 'ere is Nellie. She's bin 'ere longer than any of my girls. 'Eaven knows how many skins she's 'andled, this one!"

Giggling broke out across the factory floor; first among the women and then the entourage. Thomson's face showed no emotion, as if he didn't get the joke. But he did. Overcome by his intimidating presence, Nellie became painfully shy, blushing and perspiring like a sixteen-year-old. For Thomson, the experience of getting down to these people's level was exhilarating. He felt wholesome and good. He fawned over Nellie, knowing the effect he had on her. His interest was genuine and knew she completely understood that.

"Nellie, show me exactly what you're doing."

"She's wettin' 'er drawers is what she's doin'," a woman whispered behind him.

For the next few minutes, it was as if he and Nellie were the only two in that stifling shed. "I must tell you, it's good to see such wonderful work," he said.

"Oh, sir, it's ever such a pleasure, sir." Nellie was steeling herself to respond and squirming on her seat as he squatted down closely beside her, his voice soothing and seductive.

"Show me how you do it, Nellie."

Nellie became calm, reached into a barrel beside her and pulled out a skin dripping with fluid.

"What's that?"

"Oh, that's brine, what they come in," Nellie said.

"They're very slippery, aren't they?"

"Oh, yes, sir, they are!"

"As slippery as your willie, mate," someone said.

"Show me your technique," Thomson said.

"She'll show 'im 'er technique all right," another woman guffawed.

Nellie started working furiously and expertly with her tool, and in no time the skin was scraped as clean as a whistle. She held it proudly in the air for all to see. Thomson got up from his crouching position, applauding enthusiastically. Cameras flashed, the women cheered and clapped, while those in the entourage suppressed their laughter. Thomson spent the next fifteen minutes moving around the shed shaking hands, making eye contact and smiling at the workers like a campaigning politician.

"Now ladies, before I go, I want you to do one more thing. Will you sing for me again?"

Hilda was ready—as if she had control of the Moscow Women Workers' Choir.

"All right, *Millicent!*"

Millicent's haunting voice began the mournful intro to "What'll I Do"—an ode to, and chosen especially for, Thomson. He again became totally mesmerized.

At the chorus all the women on the floor joined in. Thomson stood enraptured until Knoxwood signaled it was time to leave. With a wave of his fine, long fingers and a gentlemanly bow, he put on his hat, turned toward the door and was gone. His people followed.

Before Scott left the building he leaned close to Lou and whispered in his ear. "This lot would have his trousers off in seconds flat, if we weren't here. Poor bugger wouldn't stand a chance." Lou smiled. He was the last to leave.

The women were staring at the empty space where Thomson had stood, as though it'd all been a dream—the spell now broken. They stopped singing and went wild with excitement, swarming around Nellie, the woman who'd handled so many skins. She was suffering the infatuation of a pubescent girl—beet red and sweating profusely.

"Oh my good Gawd, I ain't never talked to no lawd before! Oh my good Gawd," she kept mumbling over and over.   .

" 'Ee definitely fancied you, love," one shouted.

"You'd like to clean 'is skin for 'im, Nellie, eh!"

"Oh, 'ee was so lovely," Nellie swooned.

"Ah, look at the state of 'er, she's in love!"

Before he left, Lou noticed a girl waving to him and smiling. It took him a moment to figure out it was Rosie Cameron. He hadn't recognized her in her work clothes and protective hat.

I guess this is where Jessup met her.

31

SPEECHES & SURPRISES

June 19, 1929.

L ou left the gas bag factory laughing to himself—it'd been an education. He followed the rest of the party to Cardington House, where the press was being directed to the rear gardens. Afternoon tea was served by the men in white jackets in the reception hall—an assortment of sandwiches, followed by buttered scones with fresh cream and strawberry jam. The chief steward ensured cucumber sandwiches were on the table, remembering Thomson's favorable comments back in '24. He hovered around while Thomson munched and nodded his approval.

In the gardens below the open windows, the murmur of the assembling crowd drowned out the gentle splash of an ornate fountain —a romantic creation, peopled by stone cherubs clutching bows and arrows, presumably arrows of love. Toward the end of tea-time, Thomson gently tapped a silver spoon against his cup. The room fell silent.

"Last year, I had the honor, as chairman of the Royal Aero Club, to represent Great Britain at the International Conference on Aviation in Washington, D.C. Whilst there, I had the pleasure of meeting the Secretary of the United States Navy." Thomson's eyes fell on Lou, at whom he smiled benignly. "We spoke of many things concerning aviation and the Secretary takes quite an interest in their man over here —Lieutenant Louis Remington—who has diligently assisted in our endeavors over these past five years."

All eyes turned toward Lou. Thomson continued. "The Secretary asked me to personally convey his thanks to the lieutenant, along with his warmest personal regards. Captain Irwin, I would be grateful if you will do the honors."

On cue, Irwin walked to the top of the room and stood with Thomson who glanced at Lou. "Lieutenant, if you would kindly step forward," Thomson said. Surprised, Lou joined Thomson and Irwin. Thomson held something in his hand which he handed to Irwin who spoke next.

"Lieutenant Remington, it is my pleasure to inform you that your rank has been raised by the United States Navy to that of Lieutenant Commander."

Lou stood to attention while Irwin pinned the insignia to his collar. Irwin then stepped back and saluted. Lou returned the salute and everyone applauded. Lou glanced around the room at Colmore, Scott, Irwin and Atherstone—all in dress uniform.

Whaddya know, these guys all knew in advance!

"Thank you, sir," Lou said to Irwin, and then to Thomson as they shook hands, "I'm very grateful, sir."

Thomson smiled, pleased. He loved these occasions. The chief steward appeared to be swooning and nodding enthusiastically at Lou as he pointed to an iced cake on the front table.

"Now, if you will kindly move to the garden, I'd like to say a few words to you and the good people of Cardington and Bedford," Thomson said.

Thomson's entourage moved from the entrance hall down the stone steps into the garden, an area some two hundred feet square flanked by boxwood hedges and flowering trees. This had once been the previous philanthropic owner's outdoor theater, complete with a stage built of stone where Shakespearean tragedies were performed. Rough cut flagstone paving covered much of the area and two hundred steel folding chairs were occupied by a group of people similar to those who'd been present when Thomson made his announcement in '24: Royal Airship Works personnel, local bankers, businessmen, and solicitors. In addition, there were contractors, and general workers from the factories and sheds connected with the airship program with their families.

Crewmen and construction workers stood along the sides and at the rear of the gathering, leaving seats for VIPs and the elderly. The first four rows had been reserved for those emerging from the reception room. Journalists were seated in the front row with photographers positioned down each side in the aisles.

There were two in the audience of note, sitting at the front: Sir Arthur Conan Doyle and Mrs. Emily Hinchliffe, the wife of Thomson's pilot, dressed in black. A buzz went around the crowd as people noticed them. Lou had no idea who the portly, older gentleman was until someone told him he was the most popular author in the world. (He'd get a kick out of telling Norway about that!). Lou had met Mrs. Hinchliffe the previous year, during one of his monthly visits to Cardington.

A lectern had been set up on the stage with a microphone and six chairs. The crowd chattered excitedly. Thomson was pleased with the size of the gathering. They were all here out of self-interest. Times were tough and work was scarce. It was satisfying for Thomson to know he'd created jobs in two counties.

These people love me now, posh accent or not—they know on which side their bread's buttered!

Thomson sipped the last of his Earl Grey and replaced his bone china cup carefully on its saucer. He went out through the French doors, held open for him by the fawning chief steward and descended the steps like a conquering hero to enthusiastic applause. He walked stiffly down the center aisle to the stage where Colmore, Brancker, Knoxwood, Scott and Richmond sat. As he approached, they got to their feet, applauding and smiling. Thomson sat down. Colmore went to the lectern and waited for the applause to die down. All seats were occupied and the aisles down each side were filled with people standing between the chairs and hedges.

Lou stood at the rear of the garden with his crewmen, foremen, construction workers, and of course, Freddie. Chief Coxswain 'Sky' Hunt stood behind them. Lou had known Hunt for years and had great respect for him. He'd trained Lou for his job as chief petty officer aboard *R38*. He was gruff, but well-loved, known for a bark worse than his bite. Lou noticed Jessup standing with a group of six at the back on the other side. Jessup kept his eyes down. Murmuring in the crowd grew as tension increased. Binks found all the fuss amusing.

"Wonder what the old gasbag's got to say for 'imself," he said.

Sky Hunt turned to Binks. "Keep yer mouth shut, Mr. Binks," he growled.

Colmore cleared his throat and adjusted the microphone, causing a screeching whine from the speakers on each side of the podium.

"Good afternoon, ladies and gentlemen. It is my distinct pleasure to introduce the Minister of State for Air, Lord Thomson of Cardington, whom we all know and admire. He'd like to say a few words concerning our progress and the future of the British Airship

Program. Before I turn over the microphone, I'd like to say, all of us owe him a debt of gratitude, not only for revitalizing the airship program, but for making the Royal Airship Works central to his great vision." There was more enthusiastic applause.

Thomson got up from his chair and stepped up to the lectern. He adjusted the microphone up six inches, causing another earsplitting screech.

"Wing Commander Colmore is much too kind," Thomson said. "I'm just one man doing my small part. It is *you* who will make this program a success, not I. My job is to jolly things along. This great endeavor that you've worked upon with such selfless dedication—and I must say, I've seen it with my own eyes today—is one that will open the skies for the benefit of all mankind."

Binks was unable to resist. "Yeah, right, mate," he said under his breath. Lou frowned. Binks shut up.

"We've reached a critical stage in the development of the program. In some ways we're out in front—from the technology standpoint—but in other ways—on the practical front—we're falling behind. The Germans made their maiden flight last year, crossing the Atlantic in their Graf Zeppelin. They're preparing to make a round-the-world trip in August, and if we're not careful, we'll be in a position where we cannot keep pace."

Everyone now looked concerned. "With this in mind, I say to you: We must push hard to produce results as quickly as possible. We must show the world what we can do. It's been more than five years since I announced the start of the program and our ships are still in the sheds. I'll leave it there. I know you appreciate what I'm saying, and why."

Thomson was careful not to single anyone out with his icy stare, but could see the audience understood only too well. Richmond and Colmore had taken his words to heart. It was time to build them back up.

"Having said that, I'm certain we'll come out on top. When this ship emerges from her shed this year, she'll be the finest airship ever built—about that, I have no doubt." Thomson looked reassuringly at Richmond, but Richmond didn't exude confidence. Thomson went on.

"Now, we've embarked upon a great journey, you and I, and I look forward to the day when we fly together in this magnificent airship down the route of Marco Polo to India. And thereafter, we shall press forward with airship services linking our great empire around the globe and build bigger, more advanced airships that'll become technological marvels of the world."

Thomson stepped back and the crowd was on its feet, applauding. He'd rallied the troops. Everyone was smiling except Richmond. Success, or failure, rested with him. It was at this point that Mrs. Hinchliffe stood up and started saying something. Everyone turned in her direction. Lou couldn't hear what she was saying, but judging by the embarrassed looks, she must have been making some sort of protest. Thomson switched off the microphone and replied to her statements. This exchange lasted some minutes until Thomson, clearly irritated, descended from the platform and marched down the center aisle, followed by those on the stage.

They reached the throng of people at the top of the aisle, which parted like the Red Sea. Thomson climbed the steps, followed by the multitude. When he reached the top, he gave the crowd a jubilant wave. He swept through the reception room, out the main entrance and down the front steps to the Humber, where the driver held the doors open. They drove off slowly, the driver tooting his horn and Thomson waving his royal wave.

"Well, I think that went off all right, except for that damned Hinchliffe woman at the end. We'll need to keep an eye on her," Thomson said.

"Fwankly Minister, you were marvelous. I shouldn't worry about her," Knoxwood said.

"Top hole!" Brancker exclaimed.

Later, Lou jumped on his motorcycle and rode over to Shed No.1 to meet Irwin, who'd requested to see him. He waited beside the control car and soon heard the captain's approaching footsteps echoing across the shed.

"Ah, Lou. Let's go aboard," he said.

They climbed on board and Irwin led the way up to the lounge where they sat in the wicker easy chairs at one of the card tables. Lou wasn't sure why Irwin wanted to see him and worried perhaps he'd known Lou was on board earlier.

"You and the crew did a great job, Lou. The Old Man was thrilled."

"Thank you, sir," Lou said, relieved.

"Perhaps you should be an interior decorator!"

"No, all we did was set it up. He ought to be pleased; it's a beautiful ship."

"Looks can be deceiving," Irwin said. "We'll see what she's made of when we take her up." Irwin glanced down at the table for a moment, then back at Lou.

"Congratulations on your promotion today."

"Thank you, sir. That came as a big surprise."

"Everyone was pleased about it. You've done a great job at Howden. You're a natural diplomat and you've helped keep the peace."

"Thanks."

"How's Charlotte? Is she taking kindly to all this?"

"I think she'll be pleased with my promotion, and proud. She's settled down fairly well here now. She really didn't want to come south."

"Yes, I got that impression."

"She's been worried about safety, naturally, but everyone's assured her these new ships will be safe."

"Let's hope so," Irwin said.

"Charlotte's pleased I'm happy and doing what I like. I think once we've got a few trips under our belt, she'll be okay."

"She's a wonderful girl."

"What Charlotte needs is a child. In fact, she wants lots of children! But no luck so far. That's what makes her most unhappy," Lou said.

"We want a family one day—we've even chosen a name for our first," Irwin said.

"What is it, sir?"

Irwin looked away, concentrating on an image in his mind. "D'you know, when I close my eyes sometimes, I can see that child. His name will be Christian. I see his black hair and blue eyes."

"Just like his dad."

"It's all up to the good Lord," Irwin said.

"I guess so."

Irwin turned his eyes back on Lou, his expression now business-like.

"Lou, I'm going to propose you for another promotion—to third officer—if you want it. You'll be under my command aboard this ship and Captain Booth on *Howden R100*."

"Thank you. I don't know what to say, sir."

"You've got a good head on your shoulders and the crewmen look up to you."

"I suppose they do."

"You survived *R38* and that experience will make you careful."

"That was just luck."

"Nothing wrong with that. I need men with good luck on my ship."

"Kind of you to say, sir."

"If all the things the Old Man says come true, the sky's the limit. He'll be in need of captains for the fleet."

They got up and shook hands, went down to the shed floor and stood alongside the ship.

"Oh, one more thing, Lou. I like to see my officers and crew in church on Sundays." Irwin looked up at the ship, a hint of skepticism in his eyes. "We'll need all the help we can get," he said, before abruptly marching off toward the exit.

32

DINING ALONE

June 19, 1929.

T homson sat at the roll-top desk in the front lounge of his
Westminster flat. Though pleased with himself and his trip to
Cardington, he had a gnawing feeling something wasn't right
with that airship. Richmond had seemed gloomy. Thomson hoped
there were no major concerns, but supposed all would be revealed
when they launched her this year.

The Hinchliffe woman had put a damper on things. He tried to put
it out of his mind. He wondered about Barnes Wallis and his group.
They were a secretive bunch up there. He set these thoughts aside and
picked up his most recent letter from Marthe. He needed to inform her
of today's events—tell her about his triumphant return! She smiled
down from a silver picture frame on top of the desk.

The long, austere room had ornate ceilings and cornice work with
cream-painted walls and moldings similar to the rest of the flat.
Although comfortable, the place lacked a woman's touch. The tall,
Georgian windows overlooked the street where Saturday night traffic
passed to and fro with a gentle hum. The furniture, various shades of
browns and beiges, was second-hand, but passable. A brown, woven-
wool couch faced the fireplace, complemented by a mahogany coffee
table with a black leather top. He liked it when he found it in the
furniture shop in Stockwell and the dealer threw it in for an extra ten
bob.

A huge oil painting of the Taj Mahal in a chipped gilt frame had
also caught his eye, and when the dealer offered to splash a coat of
gold paint on the frame for an extra half crown, Thomson jumped at it.
He thought it must be a sign. The picture now hung over the living
room fireplace in all its glory. He decided he'd have Buck install it in
his office at Gwydyr House the following week. The whole lot had

cost twelve pounds fifteen shillings, including the slightly worn, blue silk chaise longue and delivery by a man with a horse and cart.

He paused looking at the Taj with satisfaction—he suddenly had a great idea. He'd speak to Winston Churchill about it when he next saw him—he'd heard he was something of an artist. Meanwhile, he must write to Marthe. He picked up his fountain pen and began in his bold, beautiful script.

My Dearest Smaranda,

Just home from Cardington. It was a great day and wonderful to be back up there. What an enthusiastic crowd they are—dedicated and determined to make R101 all that she can be. Airships! They are my pride and joy—my phoenix twins, rising from the ashes—I am so passionate about them. There is of course only one precious thing I am more passionate about. No need to remind you of that!

His thoughts were interrupted by a gentle knock on the door. Gwen, his housekeeper, popped her head in; mid-fifties and well rounded, she wore a white apron and matching headscarf.

"Lord Thomson, dinner's ready to be served, if convenient, sir," she said in her R-rolling Devonshire accent. Thomson slipped his unfinished letter into the top drawer.

"Very well, Gwen, I'll come now."

He'd burned a lot of energy today and felt hungry again. Later, after dinner, Thomson sat alone with his thoughts. Gwen's chop had been delicious, even though he'd already had lamb for lunch. He didn't tell her of course. She reappeared as he was finishing his apple pie and custard.

"Will there be anything else, Lord Thomson? Would you like coffee?"

"You know what? I think I'd like a glass of port, if you don't mind."

Gwen beetled off and brought back a bottle of port and a wine glass on a tray and placed them on the table in front of him. She poured out a decent measure.

"Thank you, Gwen. That will be all for tonight."

"Are you sure, sir?"

"Oh yes, I'll be fine."

"Good night, Lord Thomson."

"Good night, Gwen."

Thomson put on his red and black silk smoking jacket and moved back into the front lounge. He put some music on the gramophone, enjoying his favorite pieces while sipping the delicious port. Hearing the music, Sammie, Thomson's huge black cat, strode into the room with a big meow, jumped onto one of the soft arm chairs and settled down, purring like a tractor.

"That's what I like—a cat who appreciates opera," Thomson said.

The cat rolled on its side, understanding perfectly. Thomson took another sip and placed the glass on the coffee table. He put on his favorite recording—V*esti la giubba*—sung by the great Enrico Caruso. He turned up the volume and sat down on the chaise, where he rummaged through his dispatch box. Beside him, on a side table, stood another picture frame from which Marthe peered at him from the steps of Mogosoëa. Thomson looked up from his documents and rested his eyes on her and laid his head back on the chaise, allowing his mind to wander. Marthe would be in London in a couple of weeks.

Dear God, how I long to see her!

He remembered how he'd comforted her in her boudoir in Mogosoëa, in 1915. It was a bitter sweet memory. Within seconds, while Pagliacci's heart was breaking, Thomson fell asleep.

He found himself drinking coffee at his usual table by the window of a popular café on Rue de Rivoli—one of the most fashionable streets in Paris. In British Army uniform with the rank of lieutenant, he gazed at the beautiful girl sitting in an open-top carriage under a white parasol, shading her unblemished, white skin from the blazing sun. She fanned herself with a cream and white rice-paper fan. A matching wide-brimmed hat partially obscured her face and her shoulder-length, dark brown hair. She sat with aristocratic grace, her black eyes—or dark green?—revealed intelligence and innocence.

Much of what he took in was not only by sight, but by clairvoyance. He seemed to know so much about her—as if they were close. Perhaps he'd known her in some previous lifetime. But to her, *he* was always invisible.

Thomson realized he had to seize the moment—she'd soon be gone and an encounter might never come again. There was always this kind of desperation. He jumped from his seat, almost tipping over his chair and ran out the glazed wood doors into the street, just in time to see the driver snap the reins and loudly click his tongue, signaling the two magnificent white horses to pull out and move in slow motion toward him.

Thomson stood poised at the curb, hoping for some communication or acknowledgment, but the girl remained oblivious to his existence, staring straight ahead, so close, he could have reached out and touched her—and he had a burning desire to do so. As he dreamed (and he realized this was a dream), he knew he'd seen her many times before in other dreams such as this on Rue de Rivoli. As the carriage drew level, the driver looked down at Thomson with evil, piggy eyes and smiled his cruel smile. Thomson remembered him also —only too well.

You always smile at me with devilish intent. Damn you! You do it to torment me, injure me, torture me, aggravate me, toy with me, tantalize me—yes, all of those things!

Overcome by blinding love, his heart sinking, Thomson watched helplessly as the carriage slowly moved away between white, cloistered buildings, its grinding wheels and thumping hooves churning the gritty dirt. When at last it disappeared, the previously immaculate dress uniform in which he stood was now completely covered in white dust from head to toe. He looked and felt like Caruso's pathetic clown, Pagliacci, the all-too-familiar pain of longing burning like a knife in his gut.

Thomson woke with a snort, coughing and spluttering, tasting the grit in his mouth. The gramophone turntable revolved like the wheels on her carriage, the needle swinging back and forth in the grooves beside the label, making a dreadful scratching sound. Thomson reluctantly opened his eyes, his gold pinz-nez spectacles at the end of his nose, barely hanging on.

He came round in the awful moment of realization: this wasn't Paris, not the year 1902, but 1929. He was in London as the Secretary of State for Air. He shook off the nostalgia and his Cardington visit flooded back into his mind like water bursting from a dam. He glanced down. Sammie sat on his lap among his ministerial papers guiltily staring up at him, purring as softly as he dare. Thomson reached down, pulled the cat up to his face and nuzzled him affectionately.

"Oh, Sammie, you're such a naughty boy. But I know I can always count on *you* to tell me the truth, can't I!"

The cat meowed a loud response, sounding human—uncannily so.

After meeting Irwin, Lou went home with the chief steward's iced cake. Before he could even put the key in the front door, Charlotte opened it with a flourish. He stepped inside and she threw her arms around him, kissing him feverishly.

"Oh, Remy, my darling. I love you so much. I'm sorry I was so mean to you this morning. You will forgive me, won't you?"

Lou was surprised, but relieved.

"Of course, Charlie. You must've been tired. I'm sorry I had to be out all day."

"I want to talk to you tonight about things," Charlotte said.

"What about?"

"Well, about '*us—and things*'."

They went downstairs to the lower level to the breakfast table looking out into the garden. It was still sunny and a few of Charlotte's flowers were in bloom. Lou unwrapped and placed the chief steward's cake on the table.

"What's that?" Charlotte asked, reading the icing. "'Congratulations!' What for?"

"I'll tell you in a minute. It's a present from the chief steward," Lou said, trying his best to remain expressionless.

"Oh, I see. What's his name?"

"Er, I don't know."

Charlotte batted her eyes and pursed her lips, taunting.

"Oooh, should I be jealous?"

Lou chuckled, not biting. She opened a bottle of white wine and poured two glasses. She held one out to him. The kitchen was warm. He breathed in the dinner cooking in the oven.

"Smells good," he said.

"Roast beef and Yorkshire pudding—your favorite."

"Mmm, lovely."

"Well, how did it go today?"

Lou's face lit up. "So much to tell!"

She was intrigued. "Why? What happened? Tell me!"

"We fished for a while, and before that, the captain came by and spoke to us at the corner store." He didn't mention Jessup or Cameron. "We went to the ship and finished setting up the furniture and I must say, it looked pretty damned good! Then the Old Man arrived. I was stuck on board while Irwin showed him over the ship. I stayed out of sight—I couldn't very well announce my presence. I heard everything they said. It was pretty damned embarrassing."

"What did they say?"

"Well, Lord Thomson got a bit flowery about the ship and the future and how he was depending on the captain—and a lot of stuff I should never have heard."

"What sort of stuff?"

"He talked about a woman he hopes to marry one day."

"Goodness! Did the captain know you were there?"

"Nobody knew and I won't say anything. Anyway, they all went off to the gasbag factory. I put on my uniform and joined them. The Old Man had them old gals eatin' out of his hand. Funny as hell."

"What did he say?"

"Oh, he told them they were special and doing important work and all that *old jaboni*. He gave them all a boost. They were tickled to death."

"That's good. He must be a very nice man," Charlotte said.

"Yeah, he's all right, I guess. Anyway we all went to the big house for afternoon tea and sandwiches. And then, you can't imagine what happened!"

Charlotte couldn't contain herself, "Well, tell me then!"

"The Old Man got up and gave a short speech."

"What about?"

"*Me!*" Lou said, cracking up.

"*What!*"

"He said he'd been speaking to the Secretary of the Navy in Washington and he'd asked about me and how I was doing over here."

Her eyes had become saucers. "Oh go on! … Really?"

"Yes, and then everyone stood up and Captain Irwin did the honors and I got promoted! I'm now Lieutenant Commander Louis Remington! Ta da!" Lou stood to attention, saluted and then bowed with a flourish, as though to the Queen.

"Oh, Lou, I don't believe it! So what is a lieutenant commander?"

"It's the same rank as a major in the army."

"That's amazing!"

"But that's not all. The captain talked to me afterwards."

"What did he say?"

"He said I'd done a great job not only with the furniture and how the Old Man was pleased, which of course I already knew because I'd heard him with my own ears—but he said I'd done a good job at Howden and with the liaison work between them and Cardington."

"Well, it's true. You've done a bloody good job!"

"Anyway, he's nominating me for promotion to Third Officer."

"Two promotions in one day! Lou, I'm so, so proud of you."

Lou finished his wine and put the glass down on the table.

"You said you wanted to talk about '*us and things*'," Lou said.

"Oh, it doesn't matter. It was nothing important."

He looked at her, puzzled. She wrapped her arms around him and put her luscious, wet lips over his mouth, kissing him gently—at first. Then things rapidly got out of hand.

"I think we'd better turn the oven down low—we'll eat later," Lou said, and then taking her hand, he led her up the stairs to the bedroom.

END OF VOLUME ONE

To be continued ...

Airship R38/ZR-2

R38/ZR-2 under construction at Cardington, 1920.

Commander Lewis H. Maxfield, US Navy, Captain of R38/ZR-2.

Commodore Edward Maitland (in white) and Major George Herbert Scott after landing in America aboard *Airship R34*, July 6th, 1919.

Captain Archibald Wann, survivor of the *R38/ZR*-2 disaster.

Harry Bateman of the National Physical Laboratory.

Assistant Coxswain Flt. Sergeant Walter Potter.

Stern cockpit on a British airship similar to the one on *R38/ZR-2*.

Promenade Deck on Victoria Pier, Hull.

At 5:28 pm August 24, 1921, *R38/ZR-2* breaks in two over the River Humber.

Hull Docks from the air.

Front half
came to rest
here

KINGSTON UPON HULL

Track of R38/ZR-2

Airship breaks
in two

R I V E R   H U M B E R

R38/ZR-2 flight path over the River Humber.

Searching for bodies in the wreckage of *R38/ZR-2* in the River Humber.

Sad, gruesome scenes greet rescuers.

A mass of tangled metal in the Humber Estuary.

Men search for survivors aboard the wreck of *R38/ZR-2*.

Wreckage of *R38/ZR-2* is brought ashore.

Funeral procession for British victims proceeds toward Western Cemetery.

Funeral for the British victims of the *R38/ZR-2* proceeds through Hull.

R38/ZR-2 Memorial in Western Cemetery, Hull, Yorkshire.

His Majesty's Government

Christopher Birdwood Thomson.

Cotroceni Palace, Bucharest, Romania, where Major Thomson first met
Princess Marthe Bibesco.

Mogosoëa Palace: Princess Marthe's home in Bucharest, Romania.

Rue de Rivoli, Paris, around 1899, where the young Major Thomson first set eyes on the girl in the white carriage. She became the love of his life, at least in his dreams.

The footbridge over the River Lossie, leading to the seashore of East Beach, Lossiemouth, Scotland.

Prime Minister Ramsay MacDonald, 1923.

Air Vice Marshall Sir Sefton Brancker, Director of Civil Aviation.

Chequers.

Chequers, constructed in 1565, was acquired in 1912 by Lord and Lady Lee of Fareham who donated the property to the government in 1921.

A stained glass window in the Long Gallery bears the inscription:

'This house of peace and ancient memories was given to England as a thank-offering for her deliverance in the great war of 1914-1918 as a place of rest and relaxation for her Prime Ministers for ever.'

Besides being used by Prime Ministers for the purpose specified, the house is used for entertaining visiting foreign dignitaries.

Howden Airship R100

Dennistoun Burney, head of the Airship the Guarantee Company, a subsidiary of Vickers, builders of the *Howden R100*.

Barnes Wallis, Chief Designer for *Howden R100*.

Nevil Shute Norway, Chief Calculator for *Howden R100*.

A *Howden R100* curved girder is completed.

Howden R100's installation of girders begins.

Howden R100's hull takes shape (note the men on top girders).

Howden R100 nears completion.

Howden R100: almost ready to launch, Autumn 1929.

Cardington Airship R101

Wing Commander Reginald Colmore, Deputy Head of the Royal Airship
Works, Cardington.

Flt. Lt. Carmichael Irwin (captain), Lt. Colonel Vincent Richmond (designer) and Major Herbert Scott (in charge of flying).

Sqdn. Ldr. Rope, Asst. Head of Airship Design & Dev., *Cardington R101*.

Cardington R101: construction rings fabricated.

Cardington R101: construction framing.

Cardington R101: floor framing.

Cardington R101: workmen frame the interior.

Cardington R101: control car framing.

Cardington R101: workers on the girders.

Cardington R101: a starter motor inside an engine car.

Cardington R101: R.A.W. discussions on the shop floor.

Cardington R101: dining room interior construction.

Cardington R101: a construction worker finishes corridor walls.

Cardington women scraping goldbeater skins.

Gas bag fabric is marked out.

Women fabricating gasbags.

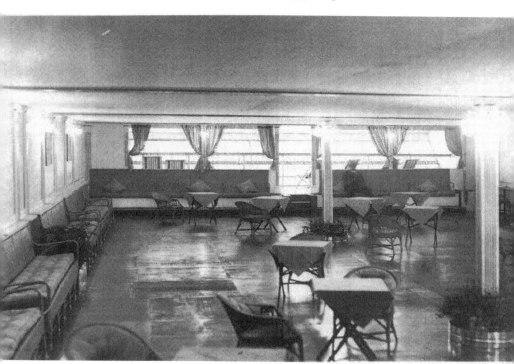

Cardington R101: lounge.

AUTHOR'S NOTES

This is a work of fiction—pure fantasy, if you like—based on actual events. It is not a historical nonfiction documentary written to 'set the record straight'. It is my hope that this novel piques the reader's interest in this dramatic era of aviation history. Some characters are based on real people, others are fictional. Some events in the novel took place, others did not. After some years of research, I took what I thought was the essence of the characters involved and built on those qualities for dramatic effect, with fictional characters woven into the story to take part and to witness events. In the end, Lou Remington and Charlotte Hamilton became as real to me as Brigadier General Christopher Birdwood Thomson and Princess Marthe Bibesco.

I did not see any real villains in this story and did not set out to portray anyone as such. But I did see all the characters as suffering with that one trying malady—being human. The myriad symptoms of this disorder include: unconditional love, passion, ruthless ambition, pride, megalomania, greed, spinelessness, jealousy, deviousness, murderous intent, loyalty, duty, trust, obedience, honor, patriotism and selflessness.

I took liberties for dramatic effect: Scott and McWade were *not* on Victoria Dock in Hull when the *R38* went down, as far as I know. Hull Infirmary is not on the waterfront. The scenes aboard *R38/ZR-2, Howden R100* and *Cardington R101* during their flights and crashes are painted mostly from my imagination with information drawn from many books (see bibliography). Actual events on board those ships, as well as the dialogue throughout the novel is, of course, conjecture. And no, as far as I know, Cardington R101 did not deviate from her route to India in order to show herself over the West End of London on that fateful night.

There is a great deal of truth in what I have written as a fictional account, but like the extraordinary Princess Marthe, the truth is elusive. Much I have taken from reading between the lines, exaggerating or emphasizing for dramatic effect. Some is pure speculation. The grand events are true, save for those actions carried out by fictional characters.

Lord Scunthorpe, the Tyson family and Tyson's Lumber & General Hardware Co. are fictitious entities, not based on any persons living or dead, any organization or corporation.

In order to help differentiate between airships *R100* and *R101*, I took the liberty of adding the prefix of the place of their birth, calling them *Howden R100* and *Cardington R101*.

ACKNOWLEDGMENTS

I have been blessed with a tremendous amount of help from many amazing people while researching and writing this book. Very special thanks are due to my consulting editor at LCD Editing (lcdediting.com) who has put many years into this project and kept me focused and on the straight and narrow. Thanks also to Steven Bauer at Hollow Tree Literary Services for his expert guidance and editing. Grateful thanks must go to Edith Schorah for additional editing and proofreading. My appreciation also goes to Kathryn Johnston and Jon Eig at the Writer's Center, Bethesda, Maryland for their patient and professional coaching during workshop sessions.

I am indebted to John Taylor, lighter-than-air flight test engineer and consultant and writer of *Principles of Aerostatics: The Theory of LTA Flight*, who conducted a technical review and spent many hours reading and critiquing this manuscript and offering a wealth of advice, not only regarding airships, but also on formatting and preparing these books for publication.

Special thanks to Eddie Ankers who worked tirelessly on book design and artwork, producing the cover for Volume One - *From Ashes*. Thanks also to Bari Parrott who created cover art for *The Airshipmen* and *Volumes 2 & 3*.

Deep gratitude is due to Katie Dennington who did a wonderful job of designing and setting up the website http://www.daviddennington.com (although she is not accountable for its content). Katie was also responsible for helping me get started in the realm of novel writing. Throughout this five year process, she gave me the spiritual fortitude and encouragement to see it through.

I am also very grateful to Frank Dene at Act of Light Photography who produced the website video and assisted Katie.

I owe a debt of thanks to the people at Cardington Heritage Trust Foundation for their kind help over the years, especially Dene Burchmore and Sky Hunt's son, Albert, who showed me around Shed No. 1. Special thanks to Alastair Lawson, Chairman of the Airship Heritage Trust, for providing extra images for this trilogy. Thanks also to Alastair Reid, C.P. Hall and to Dr. Giles Camplin, editor of *Dirigible Magazine, Journal of the Airship Heritage Trust*, who kindly assisted with contacts in the airship community and photographs for these books and for my website. Many thanks to Paul Adams of the British Airship Museum and Jane Harvey of Shortstown Heritage Trust, Christine Conboy of Bedfordshire Libraries, Paul Gazis of The Flying Cloud, Trevor Monk creator of Facebook pages relative to the sheds and airships, and John Anderson of the Nevil Shute Foundation, all of whom advised on or shared photographic information.

I would like to thank the following for their help and encouragement: my dear wife, Jenny (my own special Yorkshire lass), Lauren Dennington and Lee Knowles, Richard and Katie Dennington, Dawn and Nick Steele, Alan and Violet Rowe, John and Sandy Ball, Katya and Michael Reynier, Edith and Michael Schorah, Cliff and Pat Dean, Ray Luby, Chris and Jan Burgess, John and Sally Slee, Richard Lovell, Julie and Marty Boyd, Aaron Kreinbrook, Derek Rowe, David and Susan Adams, Commander Jason Wood, Graham Watt, brothers Karl and Charles Ebert, Ruta Sevo, Harry Johnson, Alan Wesencraft of the Harry Price Library at the University of London, and Mitchell Yockelson at the U.S. National Archives. I am grateful to Isabelle Jelinski for consultation regarding French translation (any errors are mine).

And lastly, my sincere appreciation goes to the marine who helped distill into words what I thought it must be like to search for a reason to go on after surviving horrific events and having experienced your friends and brothers-in-arms dying all around you. He confirmed that 'survivor's guilt' is all too real. He told me how once home from the war in Vietnam, he was unable to speak of it to anyone, even to the woman he married after coming out of the VA hospital. He allowed his wife to believe for years that his wounds were the result of a traffic accident. This veteran's experiences and his reactions to them are, seemingly, not uncommon.

BIBLIOGRAPHY AND SOURCES

Inspiration, information and facts were drawn from an array of wonderful books, as well as newspapers, magazines and documents of the period, including:

Report of the R101 Inquiry. Presented by the Secretary of State for Air to   Parliament, March 1931.

Eleventh Month Eleventh Day Eleventh Hour. Joseph E. Persico. Random House, New York.

American Heritage History of WW1. Narrated by S.L.A. Marshall, Brig. Gen. USAR (ret). Dist. Simon & Schuster.

Icarus Over the Humber. T.W. Jamison. Lampada Press.

To Ride the Storm. Sir Peter Masefield. William Kimber, London.

Lord Thomson of Cardington: A Memoir and Some Letters. Princess Marthe Bibesco. Jonathan Cape Ltd., London.

Enchantress. Christine Sutherland. Farrar, Straus & Giroux. Harper Collins Canada Ltd.

Barnes Wallis. J. Morpurgo. Penguin Books, England. Richard Clay (The Chaucer Press) Ltd., England.

Howden Airship Station. Tom Asquith & Kenneth Deacon. Langrick Publications, Howden UK.

The Men & Women Who Built and Flew R100. Kenneth Deacon. Langrick Publications, Howden UK.

Millionth Chance. James Lessor. House of Stratus, Stratus Books Ltd., England.

Sefton Brancker. Norman Macmillan. William Heinemann Ltd., London.

The Tragedy of R101. E. F. Spanner. The Crypt House Press Ltd., London.

Hindenburg: An Illustrated History. Rich Archbold & Ken Marschall. Warner Bros. Books Inc.

My Airship Flights. Capt. George Meager. William Kimber & Co. Ltd., London.

Slide Rule. Nevil Shute. Vintage Books/Random House. William Heinemann, GB.

Chequers. Norma Major. Cross River Press. Abberville Publishing Group.

The Airmen Who Would Not Die. John Fuller. G.P. Putnam's Sons, New York.

R101 - A Pictorial History. Nick Le Neve Walmsley. Sutton Publishing, UK. History Press, UK.

Airship on a Shoestring: The Story of R100 John Anderson. A Bright Pen Book. Authors OnLine Ltd.

Airships Cardington. Geoffrey Chamberlain. Terence Dalton.

Dirigible Magazine: Journal of the Airship Heritage Trust, Cardington UK.

Aeroplane Magazine.

Daily Express, October 4, 1930 newspaper articles.

Daily Mirror, October 4, 1930 newspaper articles.

Daily Mail, October 4, 1930 newspaper articles.

Journal of Aeronautical History.

Stern Cockpit on a British airship similar to the one on R38/ZR-2: Icarus over the Humber by T.W. Jamison, Lampada Press.

Promenade Deck on Victoria Pier, Hull: Postcards of the Past website.

At 5.28 pm August 24, 1921, R38/ZR-2 breaks in two over the River Humber: from Sky Sailor by Kenneth Deacon.

Hull Docks from the air: Icarus over the Humber by T.W. Jamison, Lampada Press.

R38/ZR-2 flight path over the River Humber: Base map courtesy of Old Yorkshire Maps, UK.

Searching for bodies in the wreck of R38/ZR-2 Icarus over the Humber by T.W. Jamison, Lampada Press.

Sad, gruesome scenes greet rescuers. Naval History & Historical Command.

A mass of tangled metal in the Humber Estuary: Naval History & Historical Command.

Men search for survivors aboard the wreck. Naval History & Historical Command.

Wreckage of R38/ZR-2 is brought ashore: From Historical Howden, courtesy of Kenneth Deacon.

Funeral procession for British victims proceeds toward Western Cemetery: Hull City Council Archive.

R38/ZR-2 Funeral in Hull for British victims of R38/ZR-2 disaster: From Historical Howden posted by Kenneth Deacon.

R38/ZR-2 Funeral in Hull for British victims of R38/ZR-2 disaster: From Historical Howden courtesy of Kenneth Deacon.

R38/ZR-2 Memorial: Naval History & Historical Command.

THE GOVERNMENT

Lord Thomson of Cardington: Public Domain.

Cotroceni Palace, Bucharest, Romania: Photographer Alexandru Antoniu. Public Domain.

Mogosoaia Palace: Princess Marthe's home in Bucharest, Romania. Public Domain.

Rue de Rivoli, Paris: Photographer unknown, Wiki Media Commons. Public Domain.

Footbridge over the River Lossie: Attribution-Share Alike CC BY-SA 2.5.

Ramsay MacDonald 1923: Wikimedia commons. Public Domain.

Sir Sefton Brancker, Director of Civil Aviation: Wikimedia commons. Public Domain.

Chequers, official country home of the British Prime Minister: Wikipedia. Public Domain.

AIRSHIP HOWDEN R100

Commander Sir Dennistoun Burney: From The Men and Women Who Built and Flew the R100 by Kenneth Deacon.

Barnes Wallis, Chief Designer of Howden R100: Courtesy of the Barnes Wallis Foundation.

Nevil Shute Norway, Chief Calculator for Howden R100: From The Men and Women Who Built and Flew the R100 by Kenneth Deacon.

A Howden R100 curved girder is completed: Courtesy of the Airship Heritage Trust.

Howden R100's installation of girders begins: Courtesy of the Airship Heritage Trust.

Howden R100's hull takes shape: Courtesy of the Airship Heritage Trust.

Howden R100 nearing completion: Courtesy of the Airship Heritage Trust.

Howden R100 almost ready to launch, Autumn 1929: Courtesy of the Airship Heritage Trust.

ABOUT THE AUTHOR

As a teenager, I read all Nevil Shute's books, including *Slide Rule,* which tells of his days as an aeronautical engineer on the great behemoth *R100* at Howden and of his nights as an aspiring novelist. I was fascinated by both these aspects of his life. He inspired me to write and to fly (ignorance is bliss!). The writing was put on hold while I went off around the world assisting in the management various construction projects and raising a family. I picked up flying in the Bahamas, scaring myself silly, and sailing in Bermuda. This was all good experience for writing about battling the elements, navigation and building large structures.

Many years later, I read John G. Fuller's *The Airmen Who Would Not Die* and my interest in airships was rekindled. It was time to pursue my dream— writing. My daughter was in Los Angeles, trying to get into films. I thought, stupidly, I could help her by writing a screenplay.

I had done extensive research on the Imperial British Airship Program and attended many screenplay writing workshops at Bethesda Writer's Center. I wound up writing two screenplays which had a modicum of success. The experts in the business told me the stories were good and that I just *had* to write them as novels. So, back to the Writer's Center I went to learn the craft of novel writing. Five years later, with my daughter working as my editor and muse, *The Airshipmen* was finished and later turned into this trilogy.

CAST OF CHARACTERS FOR THE TRILOGY
(*Fictional)

A

*Alice—Jeb's Wife.

Atherstone, Lt. Cmdr. Noël G.—1st. Officer, *Cardington R101*.

B

Bateman, Henry—British Design Monitor, *R38/ZR-2*, National Physics Laboratory.

Bell, Arthur, ('Ginger')—Engineer, *Cardington R101*.

Bibesco, Marthe, ('Smaranda')—Romanian Princess.

Bibesco, Prince George Valentine—Princess Marthe's Husband.

Binks, Joe —Engineer, *Cardington R101*.

Booth, Lt. Cmdr. Ralph—Captain of *Howden R100*.

Brancker, Air Vice Marshall, Sir Sefton, ('Branks')—Director of Civil Aviation.

*Brewer, Tom—*Daily Telegraph* Reporter.

Buck, Joe —Thomson's Valet.

*Bull, John—Lou's Employer and Close Friend.

*Bull, Mary—John Bull's Wife.

*Bunyan, Fanny—Nurse at Hull Royal Infirmary and Charlotte's Best Friend.

*Bunyan, Lenny—Fanny's Husband.

*Bunyan, Billy—Fanny and Lenny's Son.

Burney, Dennistoun—Managing Director, Airship Guarantee (*Howden R100*).

*Brown, Minnie—Nurse at Hull Royal Infirmary.

C

*Cameron, Doug—Height Coxswain, *Howden R100 & Cardington R101*.

*Cameron, Rosie—Doug Cameron's Wife.

*Cathcart, Lady—A Friend of Brancker.

Church, Sam, ('Sammy')—Rigger, *Cardington R101*.

Churchill, Winston—Member of Parliament.

Colmore, Wing Cmdr. Reginald—Director of Airship Development (R.A.W.).

Colmore, Mrs.—Wing Cmdr. Reginald Colmore's Wife.

D

*Daisy—Thomson's Parlor Maid.

Disley, Arthur, ('Dizzy')—Electrician/Wireless, *Howden R100 & Cardington R101.*

Dowding, Hugh—Air Member of Supply & Research (AMSR), Air Ministry.

F

*Faulkner, Henry—WWI Veteran—Lou's Wartime Friend.

G

Giblett, M.A.—Chief Meteorologist at Royal Airship Works Met. Office.

*Gwen—Thomson's Housekeeper.

H

*Hagan, Bill—*Daily Mail* Reporter.

*Hamilton, Charlotte, ('Charlie')—Nurse at Hull Royal Infirmary.

*Hamilton, Geoff—Charlotte's Cousin.

*Hamilton, Harry—Charlotte's Father.

*Hamilton, Lena—Charlotte's Mother.

*Harandah, Madam—Gypsy Fortune Teller at Cardington Fair.

Heaton, Francis—Norway's Girl.

*Higginbottom, Peter, 'Pierre', Chief Steward, *Cardington R100 & Howden R101.*

*Hilda—Forewoman at the Gas Factory, Royal Airship Works, Cardington.

Hinchliffe, Emily—Wife of Captain Hinchliffe, MacDonald and Thomson's Pilot.

*Honeysuckle, Miss—Brancker's Pilot.

Hunt, George W. ('Sky Hunt')—Chief Coxswain, *Cardington R101.*

*Hunter, George—*Daily Express* Reporter.

I

Irene—Sam Church's Girl.

Irwin, Flt. Lt. H. Carmichael, ('Blackbird')—Captain of *Cardington R101.*

Irwin, Olivia—Captain Irwin's Wife.

Isadora—Princess Marthe's Maidservant

J

*Jacobs, John—*Aeroplane Magazine* Reporter.

*Jeb—Tenant and Friend Living at Remington's Farm.

*Jenco, Bobby—American Trainee Rigger, *R38/ZR-2,* Elsie's Boyfriend.

*Jessup, William, ('Jessie')—Charlotte's Ex Boyfriend.

*Jessup, Angela—William Jessup's Sister.

Johnston, Sqdn. Ldr. E.L. ('Johnny')—Navigator for *Howden R100 & Cardington R101.*

*Jones, Edmund—*Daily Mirror* Reporter.

K

*Knoxwood, Rupert—Thomson's Personal Secretary, Air Ministry.

L

Landsdowne, Lt. Cmdr. Zachary USN—Commander of *Shenandoah.*

Leech, Harry—Foreman Engineer (R.A.W.), *Cardington R101.*

*Luby, Gen. Raymond—U.S. Army Chief of Staff, Fort Myer, Arlington.

M

MacDonald, Ishbel—Daughter of Ramsay MacDonald.

MacDonald, Ramsay—British Prime Minister.

Mann, Herbert—Cardington Tower Elevator Operator.

*Marsh, Freddie—Cardington Groundcrewman, Joe Binks' Second Cousin.

McWade, Frederick—Resident R.A.W. Inspector, Airship Inspection Dept. (A.I.D.).

Maitland, Air Commodore Edward—British Commodore, *R38/ZR-2.*

*Matron No. 1—Matron at Hull Royal Infirmary.

*Matron No. 2—Matron at Bedford Hospital.

Maxfield, Cmdr. Louis H. USN—American Captain of *R38/ZR-2.*

Meager, Capt. George—1st Officer, *Howden R100.*

Mugnier, Abbé—Princess Marthe's Priest and Spiritual Advisor.

N

*Nellie—Worker at the Gasbag Factory, Royal Airship Works, Cardington

*'New York Johnny'—American Trainee Engineer, *R38/ZR-2.*

Norway, Nevil Shute, ('Nev')—Chief Calculator.

O

O'Neill, Sqdn. Ldr. William H.L. Deputy Director of Civil Aviation, Delhi.

P

Palstra, Sqdn. Ldr. MC, William, Royal Australian Airforce, Liaison Officer to the Air Ministry—representing the Australian Government.

*Postlethwaite, Elsie—Nurse at Hull Royal Infirmary, Bobby Jenco's Girl.

Potter, Walter—British Coxswain, Mentor of American Crewmen, *R38/ZR-2.*

R

Rabouille, Eugène—Rabbit Poacher, French eyewitness.

*Remington, Anna—Lou's Sister.

*Remington, Charlotte—Lou's Grandmother.

*Remington, Cliff—Lou's Father.

*Remington, Violet—Lou's Mother.

*Remington, Louis, ('Remy')–American Chief Petty Officer. *R38/ZR-2*.

*Remington, Tom—Lou's Brother.

Richmond, Lt. Col. Vincent—Head of Airship Design and Development (R.A.W.).

Richmond, Mrs. Florence, ('Florry')—Richmond's Wife.

*Robards—Ramsay MacDonald's Bodyguard.

*Robert—Charlotte's first love.

Robertson, Major—*Flight Magazine* Reporter.

*Ronnie—Works Foreman, Cardington Shed No. 1.

Rope, Sqdn. Ldr. F.M.—Asst. Head of Airship Design and Development (R.A.W.).

S

*Steel, Nick, ('Nervous Nick')—Rigger, *Howden R100*.

Scott, Maj. Herbert G. ('Scottie')—Asst. Director of Airship Development (R.A.W.).

*Scunthorpe, Lord—Member of the House of Lords, Opponent of LTA.

*Smothers, Helen—*Washington Post* Reporter.

Steff, F/O Maurice—2nd Officer, *Cardington R101 & Howden R100*.

*Stone, Josh—American Trainee Rigger, *R38/ZR-2 & Shenandoah*.

T

Thomson, Christopher Birdwood, ('Kit' or 'CB')—Brigadier General/Politician.

Teed, Philip—Chemist in Charge of Manufacture of Hydrogen, Howden.

*Tilly, Mrs. Queenie—Patient at Hull Royal Infirmary.

*Tyson, Julia—Lou Remington's first love.

*Tyson, Rory—Julia's Uncle, Proprietor, Tyson's Lumber and General Hardware Co.

*Tyson, Israel—Rory Tyson's Son.

W

Wallis, Barnes—Designer-in-Chief, *Howden R100.*

Wallis, Molly—Barnes Wallis' Wife.

Wann, Flt. Lt. Archibald —British Captain of *R38/ZR-2.*

*Washington, Ezekiah, II—Train Steward aboard *The Washingtonian.*

*Wigglesbottom, 'Moggy'—Owner of a 15th Century Cottage, Bendish Hamlet.

Y

*Yates, Capt. USN—Washington Navy Yard, Washington, D.C.

THE GHOST OF CAPTAIN HINCHLIFFE

Some characters in *The Airshipmen* also appear in *The Ghost of Captain Hinchliffe*. Available online at Amazon worldwide and at retail booksellers.

Millie Hinchliffe lives a near perfect existence, tucked away with her loving fighter-pilot husband in their picture-postcard cottage in the glorious English countryside. As a mother, artist, classical pianist and avid gardener, Millie has it all. But when 'Hinch' goes missing with a beautiful heiress over the Atlantic in a bid to set a flying record, her world is shaken to the core. Heartbroken and facing ruin, she questions the validity of messages she receives from 'the other side'—messages that her husband is desperate to help her. In this suspenseful tale of unconditional love, desperate loss and wild adventure, Hinch charges Millie with an extraordinary mission: *Put a stop to the British Airship Program and prevent another national tragedy.*

PRAISE FOR *THE GHOST OF CAPTAIN HINCHLIFFE*

Another riveting tale from David Dennington, author of The Airshipmen. This time, he cleverly weaves together a couple's amazing love and the temptation it faces with the drama of a transatlantic flying record attempt and spine-tingling psychic connection from beyond the grave that becomes the only hope of preventing a horrific aviation disaster. It's an intriguing recipe that makes it hard to put down *The Ghost of Captain Hinchliffe.*

David Wright, Daily Mirror Journalist.

YouTube promo: The Ghost of Captain Hinchliffe

Available worldwide in paperback or Kindle from Amazon

Author's website: http://www.daviddennington.com

Printed in Great Britain
by Amazon